NEMESIS

Carolyne
Readedigest

Allen.

By

Allan Williams

Cover photo and design:
Carlos Mestanza and Enzo Pranzini

Shield Crest

© Copyright 2021 Allan Williams

All rights reserved.

ISBN: 978-1-913839-12-3

MMXXI

A CIP catalogue record for this book
is available from the British Library.

Published by
ShieldCrest Publishing Ltd.,
Aylesbury, Buckinghamshire,
HP18 0TF England
Tel: +44 (0) 333 8000 890
www.shieldcrest.co.uk

To the

AAA CLUB

(true beach lovers)

Natural emeralds   **Cut emerald**
(USGS, Unisplash)   (engin akyurt, Unisplash)

'Life's but a walking shadow, a poor player

That struts and frets his hour upon the stage

And then is heard no more: it is a tale

Told by an idiot, full of sound and fury

Signifying nothing.'

William Shakespeare, Macbeth, Scene V.

Nemesis: a means of retribution or vengeance.

Collins English Dictionary.

SOME VIEWS

'History can have thousands of versions, as many as people tell it. Allan Williams is bringing us a version of Colombia's recent history never before told, turning readers on to a first-hand witness of the Cartels and Guerrilla's evolution during the 1980s in this turbulent tropical country. The author's knowledge and understanding of Colombia's geography and recent history is impressive and captured in this book.'

Magdalena Buitrago-Zuluaga, Historian, Colombia.

'A very detailed, accurate and exceptional account of the fight scenes which adds superb credence to the story.'

Gary Southall, 4th Dan, WBH karate UK.

'This book races along like a runaway jet plane. Detailed backgrounds not only of countries, but drug chemistry, art, emerald prospecting, gastronomy, etc. enhance the superb story line where the distinction between fact and fiction becomes increasingly blurred. A great read and the ending is absolutely outstanding.'

Professor E. Ozhan, President of Medcoast, Turkey

'A truly riveting and intriguing storyline. This thrilling novel immerses the reader into a vivid world, expertly described, of geology, art, food, culture and drugs. The book is extremely well researched, the details exemplary and the story is a real page-turner. It is fast paced, leading to a dramatic ending. On finishing, I immediately had to read it again to find the subtle clues'.

Dr. Cliff Nelson, Managing Director, Atlantic Crest, UK.

i

SOME BOOKS by the author.

NON FICTION

Williams, A.T., N.E., Caldwell, and P. Davies. 1981. *Landforms of the Glamorgan Heritage Coast,* Mid Glamorgan Joint Management Committee, 64 pp.

Jones, P., Healy, M.J., and A. T. Williams. 1996. (Editors): *Studies in European Coastal Management,* 299 pp, Samara Publishing, Cardigan, UK, 292 pp.

Earll, R., Everard, M., Lowe, N., Pattinson, C., and A.T. Williams. 1996. Editors: *Measuring and managing litter in rivers, estuaries and coastal waters: A guide to methods,* CMS, Kempley, Gloc. UK, 87 pp.

Williams, A.T., Davies, P., and N. E. Caldwell, 1997. *Coastal Landforms and Processes - the Glamorgan Heritage Coast,* Bridgend County Borough Council, UK. 90 pp.

Allan Williams and Anton Micallef. 2009. *Beach Management: Principles and Practices,* Earthscan, London, 445 pp.

Markovicic, M., Micallef, A., Povh, D., and A.T. Williams, 2011, *Smjernice I prioritetne Akcije (Guidelines for integrated Coastal Management),* PAPRAC, UNDP, Split, Croatia, 218 pp.

Enzo Pranzini and Allan Williams, 2013, (Editors), *Coastal Erosion and Protection in Europe,* Routledge/Earthscan publishers, London, 454 pp.

Allan Thomas Williams. 2017. *Beach changes at some selected Hong Kong bays,* Open University Press, DOI. 10.5353/th_3122910, 365 pp.

FICTION

A T. Williams, 1992. *Hong Kong Nemesis,* Book Guild, Lewes, 182 pp.

A T. Williams, 2003. *Ireland Nemesis,* Upfront publishers, Leicester, 313 pp.

CHILDREN'S BOOKS

A T Williams and I. Ozman, 2006. *A day at the beach with Jack, Jill, Sammy and friends*. The Council of Europe, EUR-OPA Major Hazards agreement, (Translated into 5 languages), 19 pp.

A T Williams and I. Ozman, 2007. *A day at the beach with Jack, Jill, Peter and friends*, The Council of Europe, EUR-OPA Major Hazards agreement, (Translated into 5 languages), 23 pp.

SHORT STORIES

A T Williams, 1991. Oscar's Tale. (In), *Journal of the Dachshund Club of Wales*, 25-27.

A T Williams, 2001. Continuance. (In), *Tales from Futures Past, A collection of short stories*, (ed.), H Killingray, New Fiction, 64-67.

A T Williams, 2004. My Hero, (In), *All in Time*, (ed.), Sarah Marshall, New Fiction, 41-44.

A T Williams, 2018. A rose by any other name, (In), *A Write Crew*, (ed.), M Humphries, J Brookes and J Mathews, University of the Third Age, Porthcawl, UK, 67-71.

A T Williams, 2020. Beach people, (In), *Stories from the Field: 50 years of coastal field work (1970 - 2020)*, Journal of Coastal Research, Special Issue, (ed.) A. Short and R Brander, vol. 102, 25-29.

A T Williams, 2020. Organisms and octopuses. (In), *Stories from the Field: 50 years of coastal field work (1970 - 2020)*, Journal of Coastal Research, Special Issue, (ed.) A. Short and R Brander, vol. 102, 206-209.

List of main characters.

Adam Lathey, the story narrator. A geologist who worked extensively in Colombia.

Anton Mikullovci Copje, London based Albanian criminal who travels to Colombia to set up a drug deal with Pablo Escobar.

Col. Drew Ortsh, Russian-Australian-Cuban parentage who leads a vicious army of rebels in the Colombian Pacific coast jungle.

Daler Hanoz, a charismatic Turkish citizen, previously a mercenary in the Congo and now a freelance hitman. Lover of art and music.

Pablo Escobar, 'The drug King' of the Medellin cartel, Colombia. Estimated wealth of over £5bn.

Paddy Mahoney, Irish roustabout, freelance mineral prospector and trouble maker especially when drunk. Found the original deposits for La Libertad goldmine, Nicaragua.

Sir George Fusano, chemistry Nobel Laureate, ex diplomat and in Colombia ostensibly to give a series of lectures.

Sonnel Gelran, a friend of Lathey's, also a geologist based in Colombia.

Zafar El Arab, Italian biochemist named Vittorio Alebar who has taken up Arab identity and became friendly with Paddy Mahoney.

Names of the people involved in the global drug trade and Colombian politics are factual, as are the places mentioned in the book (buildings, FARC camps, oil fields, tourist sites, geological descriptions, etc.) and many of the incidents described in the novel were experienced by the author. The paintings, 'The Nativity with Saint Francis and Saint Lawrence,' by Caravaggio, and Rembrandts, 'Christ in a Storm in the Sea of Galilee,' are still missing. The others are all in the museums mentioned.

Publishers Note

This story written over 30 years ago was found stored in an old filing cabinet in our basement whilst we were undergoing renovations. A lot of the novel is factual, for example, descriptions of the various drug cartels, associated personnel and smuggling techniques, gang turf wars, emerald prospecting, cocaine chemistry and production, FARC, museums and Art, Operation Condor, Operation Orion, the Congo and Angolan wars. In the 21st century the Italian Ndrangheta and UK Albanian Mafia cartels mentioned have consolidated their hold on the UK cocaine trade. With respect to the latter, a big surge occurred as a result of the 1998-99 Kosovo conflict when Albanians fought Serbs in the then government of Yugoslavia. Asylum in Europe was given to many Albanians from the ethnic cleansing that followed. In the UK, the Brighton area alone took in over 2,000. Most were hardworking people, but they did include a sprinkling of criminals.

The reality now is that the market for cocaine seems to continue increasing at an exponential rate. The UK is the prime destination for exports from Latin America and the illicit drug market is worth at least £5 bn with 23 kg consumed daily in London alone. This is more than the next three European cities combined. Cocaine is not only used for recreational, purposes, it has even been found in racehorses. Walk in the Sun, a 5:4 favourite in a novice stakes meeting at Kempton Park, UK on 26.01.2018, was disqualified after returning a post-race positive for cocaine.

Little impact has been seen on stopping the drug flow even though more than £1.6 bn has been spent on drug enforcement. The number of UK drug seizures are now over 100,000 (181 tonnes), suggesting an 'unprecedented level of availability,' (Alexis Goosdeel, Director of the European Monitoring Centre for Drugs and Drug Addiction). Consumers and dealers have now turned to trading online in 'dark net markets' and the COVID pandemic has seen a huge rise in cashless drug purchases. Cocaine is brought into the UK by planes, the postal service, ships, shipping containers and even by submarine. In November 2019, a submarine with 3,000 kg of cocaine was intercepted off the coast of Spain; in 2018, a ship registered in the Netherlands was intercepted off Cornwall and 2,100 kg of cocaine seized. On the 6th October, 2020, at São Sebastião, Brasil, police discovered 1.5 tonnes of cocaine in 15 sacks on a ship - the Unispirit - loaded with corn bound for Spain. On 20th October, 50 nautical miles off the island of Gran Canaría, Spanish police reacting to a tip off, boarded the same vessel and on berthing at Las Palmas, found another 1.2 tonnes of cocaine hidden amongst sacks containing 3,500 tonnes of corn. However, things can occasionally go wrong for smugglers, for example, in 2016, 1.5 tonnes of cocaine washed up on a west coast beach in Cork.

In 2020, the UK National Crime Agency, National Firearms Threat Centre, showed that intelligence from EncroChat, an encrypted phone and chat service, indicated that outside of London, Liverpool is now the centre of both gun and cocaine imports. There is a historic credibility of Liverpool's organised crime. For example, Curtis Warren from Toxteth, Liverpool, was once Interpol's Target One and thought to have made £330m from drug smuggling alone in the 1990s. His climb to the top started with the Toxteth Uprising in 1991.

We would add the closing couplet of Shakespeare's play, The Tempest. 'Without lovers of books, I would have no business.' Consequently, we intend to publish this book and royalties will go to a cancer charity.

Prologue

South Africa

The raptor glided serenely on the warm thermal current that supported its large wingspan, courtesy of the heat from the broiling sun that rebounded from the scorched brown ground below. The habitat beneath its wings was one it favoured, semi-desert, savanna plains. The prominent ridge above its eyes shaded the sun's rays and it could easily see the extensive harsh *veldt* beneath.

It had looked and easily eliminated the sight of two Land Rover Safari vehicles parked beside a *kopje* far below and the six men who were milling around with beer bottles in their hands. If it had any notion of time, it could have read it from the Rolex wristwatches worn by two of the men.

The eyes had also easily picked out another vehicle and lone man that was parked some four km away. The bird coasted away, still on the thermal, saving its energy for a kill later in the day. The lone man was doing exactly the same, saving his energy for a kill later in the day.

The raptor had no conception that its name came from the Latin word *rapere,* meaning plunderer that is synonymous with birds having hooked bills and sharply hooked talons; or that possessed in its retina were rods, double cones and four spectral types of single cones. Its number of visual cells /square millimetre dwarfed those of the human eye, (1 million to 200,000 respectively). Each eye looked outward and its visual field (the overlap of both eyes called the binocular region) was small, some 20-30°, as compared to the 120° of the human eye, but its keenness of vision and ability to focus was extraordinary, all due to these large eyes and retinal images. Added to these, extra neck bones enabled its head to move sideways, as eye movements were limited to its bony socket. Its head was moving now as it was hunting to feed its two chicks located in a stick nest on a tree some five km away. It glided serenely onwards.

The six men lay sprawled out on the rocky ground. They had unloaded the vehicles, three tents had been set up and a fire prepared for the evening's *braai*. Joseph Kimbala, sitting in one of the collapsible chairs, beer bottle clutched in one hand looked around and was unhappy. The two days drive out from Johannesburg had meant a lot of hard driving, but now out in the open *veldt* and away from human society, he felt…. what? Uneasy was the thought that came into his mind. His life had been spent in urban areas, but ever since he was little, he'd always had a dream of going on safari into the African bush. Now he was doing it, he felt, dare he admit it … afraid.

He had come up from Cape Town to Johannesburg for a meeting of the Black Mamba crime syndicate. It had been very successful and one of the members, merry with drink, had suggested that they celebrate with an impromptu safari holiday. This had been quickly agreed. A telephone call had been made and the next day, Joseph found himself en route out of the city along with five other members. After one night in the *veldt* his head was hurting from a severe hangover and last night he had not slept well in his cot in one of the three tents. His tent partner had snored throughout the night and the thought of several more nights in the wilds made his headache even worse.

'Hey Joseph,' the voice came from the bull-like figure of Marcus Tshombe, head of the Black Mamba criminal gang.

'I like it here. We'll stay for a few nights. It's nice and peaceful and that's what we all need right now. Make yourself comfortable. I wish now we'd brought along a few of the gals. Whoever thought of this male bonding stuff? I shouldn't have listened. You awake or asleep?'

'Awake and happy to stay here, as bumping jarred my spine.'

'And there aren't no chiro practitioner anywhere near. In fact, there's nothing anywhere near us, but snakes and lions.'

Squinting up to the sky, he added, 'and bloody big birds.'

The raptor flew on eventually disappearing from sight.

Tshombe was wrong. At the other camp the lone man was sitting beside a small pup tent. Spread out on a blanket in front of him, were the well-oiled parts of an Y2 MGL (Multiple Grenade Launcher). The weapon developed and manufactured in South Africa by Milkor (Pty) Ltd, is a lightweight (5 kg), low-velocity shoulder-fired grenade launcher, with a progressively rifled steel barrel length of 30 cm and muzzle velocity of 75 m/second. He liked it because it was a simple weapon, rugged and reliable, capable of firing six high explosive rounds at three rounds a second on rapid fire, as fast as one could pull the trigger. As a bonus, it could not be discharged accidentally if dropped. He had added the Armson OEG collimator sight in the quadrant, designed for range estimation but it really was not needed for his present purpose. The spring-actuated revolving cylinder magazine automatically rotated on firing, but needed to be wound back after every reloading. According to the manufacturers, the effective distance of fire was 400 metres but at dusk he intended to be much closer than that; less than 100 metres in fact.

He made himself some tea and reflected on the past two days. He had been tracking the activities of Tshombe for the past week. Rather it had been personnel from the South African Security and Intelligence Services, who had been doing the following and from information obtained courtesy of tapped telephones, had been able to plant a location tracker devise on one of the Land Rovers booked for their safari. It was not much of safari, as no guides had been booked, simply six key members of the Black Mamba gang going into the *veldt*. They had been causing huge problems to the Apartheid government and he had been contracted to do a job.

The consensus at a late-night meeting of a small group of Security and Intelligence personnel had been that the Mamba group were aiming to have a good time and would be drunk for most of it. His mission started when the group left Johannesburg. He followed their trail at a distance that varied from 5 to 10 km and he felt as a leopard must feel on following an impala's spoor. His body had glowed with the thought of action once again.

After a drink of tea, he re-assembled the weapon with loving care, giving it a last oiling. Glancing at his watch he saw that he had about three hours before sundown, so stretched out in the shade of his tent he slept for two hours. Awaking, he packed his tent and basic equipment into the Toyota Land Cruiser, picked up the launcher and his ubiquitous belt pack and made his way northwards to the Black Mamba campsite. He walked slowly, as he did not want any bird disturbance to indicate movement. He saw the fire smoke and heard the camp noise from well over a 1 km away. He crouched and his camouflaged figure melted into the ground. He debated whether to leopard crawl the remainder of the distance; but decided against it.

He stealthily approached the camp, dropping to the ground when some 800 metres away. By now the light was failing fast. Flat on the ground he crawled forward, every movement being slow and deliberate. His eyes had spotted a small bunch of rocks sited about 70 metres from the camp and he made his way towards these. Dusk had now fallen and the six men were huddled close to the fire. With the sun's warmth no longer available, the night chill on the high *veldt* was noticeable and four of the men had put on sweaters.

The man smiled. The grouping around the fire made it much easier for the kill. He could even hear the conversation of the men, although he did not understand the language. Settling his back against a large rock, he jammed the stock into his right shoulder and levelled the launcher. Controlling his breathing and with both eyes open, he looked along the sights to the group. The trigger was caressed and gently pressed, causing a double-action to take place; the firing pin cocked and then released to fire the grenades. Six rounds of high explosives smashed into the midst of the six men. Acting purely on instinct he reloaded by releasing the cylinder axis pin and swinging the frame away; the cylinder rear unlatched and by pivoting it counter-clockwise the chambers were exposed. Inserting fingers into the empty chambers and rotating the cylinder, he wound it back against the driving spring inserting new grenades one by one. He walked forward and saw that another shot was not needed. The men had been obliterated.

He left and walked back to his Toyota Land Cruiser, started it and set off on the long drive to Johannesburg. Job well done and a hefty increase in his Swiss bank account would soon accrue. His name was Hanoz.

1.

Colombia, Italy and London.

I had always dreamt of being a Somerset Maugham type of writer, one who travelled extensively, was a habitué of many Colonial type clubs and hotels and based himself in a corner listening like a volunteer for the Samaritan Movement. I only did part of the first bit. In this story, I am not only the character with a tale to tell but also the writer, a significant difference. I always loved Maugham's short stories and he must be amongst the No. 1 writers of this genre, besides authors such as Melville, Conrad, de Maupassant, Chekhov and Alice Munro. Who can ever forget the characters in Maugham's many short stories such as 'Red,' or 'The Verger' in the stories of the same name? Names of these individuals and places can roll off the tip of my tongue. I can visualise white South Pacific beaches, deep blue water with white surf breaks, scudding white clouds blowing across sun-kissed blue skies, like kittenish ponies of old, let out for two weeks from deep underground coal mines. Boy, do I wish I was there amongst those coal tips, anywhere but here……. make that cubed? I wonder what Maugham would have made of this story.

Aldous Huxley in his classic book, Brave New World, remarked that to 'begin at the beginning' was good advice, so I shall try to put my thoughts down in an orderly manner, although when I look around this is difficult. Nietzsche wrote: 'Memory says, I did that. Pride replies, I could not have done that. Eventually, memory yields.' What follows is an accurate account, as far as I could judge, as pride has taken a very back seat. To make some semblance of sense to these notes and to help the reader understand the narrative, I have added pieces that I was told about and to make it more interesting, have woven them into the story as I see fit.

So where do I begin – that sounds like a love song sung by a mid-20th century crooner. I guess the story starts when I was a geologist working in Colombia looking for gold along with my mate Sonnel Gelran when we were both friendly with FARC personnel belonging to a guerrilla army fighting the Colombian government.

* * * *

The rain drummed down, no slammed down onto the galvanised sheeting that was supposedly a semblance of a roof. The noise permeated into my skull as if a navvy had been ramming a Jackhammer into a tar-macadam road. A slight shake of the head amplified that noise even more and it seemed as if my head was now encased in a Ned Kelly type of bucket on which several hammers were being bashed. I have never had my head jammed in a vice, but now believe I know what it would feel like. I tentatively tried to open one crust rimmed eye, but it was too much for me, so with a groan I decided to stay as still as possible. What the hell had happened to me last night? Who was I? I could not even think of my name. Time passed as I lay there and eventually, the noise diminished before I tried opening an eye once again. This time I succeeded.

I was lying on a rickety old cot outside some type of building where the roof was held up by some rackety old posts that were well past their sell-by date. A bale of what looked like hay stood in one corner under which a scrawny cat crouched crunching a mouse. A roll of barbed wire was stored in the other and a few rusted tin sheets were stored against one wall. A few similarly rusted tin cans caught some of the rain streaming through gaps in the galvanised roof. The floor was initially baked mud, but now was no more than a sheen of water over which little rivulets were forming. The rain eventually went into a steady tick-tock against the roof, so I guessed it was slackening in its intensity.

Where was I and why was I feeling like a punch-drunk old pug? I slowly rose into a sitting position before my head once again exploded. I stayed in this yoga-like pose for some minutes before deciding that if I went a few paces I could stand in the rain and this might help. The temperature was warm and the morning haze started enveloping me like a shroud, but I knew that soon the humidity would begin to rise. Humidity hurt me because occasionally it brought out what we used to call in Ghana, West Africa the 'dhobi itch.' Not recommended, as it made one walk like John Wayne the movie cowboy, i.e. with bowed legs, the space between representing where the horse went. I hated it. My nose started itching as it smelt wood smoke. Someone upwind had just started a fire, no doubt lunch was being prepared and the aroma of roast chicken would soon accompany the smoke.

At least I knew I was in a tropical country, but which one? Colombia that was it. My brain neurons, synapses and telomeres must have been all killed, shrunk or collapsed, as not much help came from that organ. I tried to stand up but quickly fell back down. As I did the thought came into my mind that I had been drinking Tequila Sunrises (TS) the previous night. I remembered that I had three, but after that it was all a blur, a black hole in the cold inhabitable desolate vastness of space that was my brain. TS is a drink customarily served in a cocktail glass; in this country, it comes in bloody pint glasses.

I recalled being with my fellow geologist Sonnel Gelran and that was it; where was he anyway? I had known him from university days and it was due to his insistence that I was now in this hot, humid country getting eaten alive by ravenous mosquitoes that seemingly dive-bombed me every night hour. He used to tell one and all that his father was in the chalk industry. Chalk my eye; that was hogwash. I found out long afterwards that it was merely another name for cocaine. My mind was a complete blank regarding the current situation. It must have been one goddam hell of a blast.

Macho me. I had tried to emulate him in drinking TS and this was the result. I slowly got up again and this time made it into the rain, at least it was warm and greedily I sucked moisture into my mouth, gulping it down, as I was as dehydrated as a sun-bleached dingo dog's backside. I suddenly realised that it seemed as if I was wearing the weather on my shoulders like a sodden bath towel. I struggled out of all clothes apart from my shoes and walking out some metres, let water drizzle over my body. It felt good, really good. I glanced around. Unfortunately, the view that greeted my eyes was not very attractive. The place looked unfinished, lumpen even, as if the building, if that was the right word for this ramshackle place, had been designed as a film set for the aftereffects shown in a World War III movie. This was home sweet home. I tried shaking my head, but it hurt. So, I stopped.

I stood there for at least 15 minutes before staggering back to my cot and things became a bit clearer. I now knew that I was in Colombia and last night had gone out on the razzle ending up at this no-name village near Medellin, the second-largest Colombian city and the cocaine capital of the world. It is 1500 m above sea level, which initially made any exercise hard due to a lack of oxygen, but I loved the idea of generating more red blood corpuscles. In the late 70s - early 80s when I was there it was probably the world's murder capital due to the drug trade with which the infamous name Pablo Escobar is forever ensconced - more of him later. I had a permanent room at the Dann Carlton Medellin hotel, but that was lord knows how many kilometres away from where I was right now. Anyway, where was I?

The drinking was to celebrate the end of a contract I had with one of the many gold/silver mining companies, Frontino gold mines to be exact. The company had asked me to extend the contract into an area controlled by the Los Pachelly, a leading Bello municipality drug cartel. They were part of several Colombian crime syndicates and I did not like them one bit. I had crossed swords with a few of their members and these people kept long grudges.

Having experienced and got over my gold fever life phase with the Frontino Company, I was now going to realise my childhood dream of looking for the delicious almost translucent green colour of that most lovely of all precious minerals - emeralds! I had loved them ever since as a young teenager living in a small South Wales village, I had almost lived in the village library voraciously reading about them. I even dreamed of them. I devoured the tales of Col.

Percy Fawcett and his search in Amazonia for the lost city of gold together with the jungle novels of Peter Fleming. A 6th form school field trip to Cornwall had included a Wheal Gorland mine visit and I came back with a crystal of kernowite, an emerald green coloured mineral. I was enchanted and trapped. Now I was certainly in the right place. Because of hot water mineralisation, emeralds have been readily found in Colombia's emerald belt in what is called the Rosablanca, Paja, Muso and the Furatena Formations. The later formation is the best and Colombia stands head and shoulders above any other country in the world for emerald production.

Emeralds had fascinated me ever since I had read in that library about the famous Colombian legend of Queen Fura and her husband who ruled over Muzo (now central Boyacá and six hours drive north from Bogotá). Today, this branch of the Andean branch, known as the Cordillera Orienta, boasts many small mining towns, e.g., Muzo, Chivor, Coscuez, where deep mines are used to extract emeralds. In Queen Fura's day, a no good, blond, blue-eyed cad of a man called Chisgo turned up. I think he must have been a Brit called Chris whose name had mutated into Chisgo. She fell in love with him and the appalled gods turned her into stone. Her distraught husband, still madly in love with her also pleaded to be turned into stone and the gods obliged. Seeing this, Fura stricken with grief cried and her tears had trickled down her stone body turning it deep green. I loved the story and to my young self, I wanted it to be the origin of La Fura, the largest emerald in the world, a 15,000 carat, deep green emerald weighing some 2 kg that has never been divided. Being the romantic idiot that I was, I fell in love with emeralds so much that I tried to read all that had been written about them. I started with the 13th-century Persian cosmologist and geographer Al-Qazwini, who in line with readings of the Qur'an, searched for Mount Qaf where knowledge about oneself and the world around could be found. He thought that mountains encircled the world as a whole while its green emeralds gave the sky its blue colour. I loved it.

Walking back to the cot, I squeezed water out of my clothes and put them on a wire bail in the hope that they would dry a bit, although I knew that this would be very unlikely. July here is too damn hot and has far too much rain. The weather also was as dramatic as a troubled grounded teenager in the west. Peering out of one eye I could see curved mountain tops that appeared to be like rounded whales surfacing from an ocean of clouds. The air rippled with thick black cumulus clouds, but at least they were not the alabaster cumulonimbus ones. I listened to the rolls of thunder that pealed through the sky above.

For modesty's sake, I pulled on my pants and sat down again. More significant discharges of rain followed, enhanced by forked lightning then the thunder roll and the word petrichor flashed into my mind, the smell of rain after a prolonged dry period. I do not know why this happened, as here it rains incessantly during this time of the year, but the brain is a queer place. I guess I had a longing for my childhood home my nose twitching, as though the smell of new-mown hay was wafting over its membranes.

More rain splattering over me reminding me of those childhood days and I grimaced at this thought, as those carefree days had been very happy ones. I had an uneventful early life, being born in a small South Wales town, which was more like a village, built around steel and its ancillary industries. The town had one main road and rows of neat grey stone houses at right angles to it. However, it supported some 50 chapels/churches and about the same number of public houses. I grew up in one of the latter, the classiest pub in town of course. We served an eclectic array of oddball characters who supped at the pub: Dai Bread (baker), Howell the Milk (milkman), Doug the Harp landlord of my home the Harp Hotel and my father, Joe Belgium born in Belgium, Ivor One Arm who could charm away warts by rubbing his stump against the wart, Tommy Ten to Two as his feet were always in that position and Will the Wac – I still had no idea as to what this reference meant. The primary school I attended could boast a catholic array of alumnae ranging from several who had enjoyed the hospitality of HM prisons to a Member of Parliament. It was probably the happiest period of my life, as I loved the school and started friendships there that have lasted to this day.

The village had a delightful park behind which rose a forest-clad hill that extended far away to north Wales. My non-school hours were happily spent in climbing trees, building dens amongst the many rhododendron bushes and swimming in the cold waters of the local reservoir. This was a daring adventure, as stories abounded that dangerous currents, the undertow, existed that could drag you under and drown you. All rubbish of course, but it took some bravado to swim there, but all of us did. Young macho pride dictated that one had to follow the alpha male, namely 'Buster' Morgan. At primary school, he used to make us climb a ladder and jump off the school wall, which was at least twice our height. If we didn't, he'd thump us. One boy, Neal Caldwell broke an arm, John Howden a leg and both received a thump from Buster for not going back up the ladder. I loved it when rain hammered down on that reservoir making magic circular patterns on the surface that shimmered and glistened in a silvery fashion before being destroyed, as the circles bumped into each other. To us, it was a mirror to the underworld and all that was missing was Charon.

I switched off the fuzzy memory banks, as I was now another person, but for the life of me my brain was refusing to work. I forced myself to think. I had left the UK in the 70s after doing a geology degree and M.Sc. in Mineral Exploration at Imperial College, London. I had taken a five year contract looking for potential diamond sites in Ghana and did pretty well in that time. I accumulated a fair stack of money as diamond prospecting was a very profitable occupation, but where had it all gone? Charles de Gaulle, once President of France recognised that there were three ways to make a man destitute – gambling, liquor and women and of the three the latter was the most pleasurable. Take your pick, old man.

At the end of the contract, I had decided to try my luck elsewhere and reap the total benefit of finding a lucrative metal/mineral site, hopefully emeralds, rather than letting my employers take most of the money. It did not quite happen. Sonnel called and I ended up here working again for a big mining company, this time gold though, but in the country of my boyhood dream – emeralds. In all my time here I had yet to really prospect the Furatena formation although I had explored the fringes. Little did I know that soon I would be doing just that, but not in the manner envisaged. I would be in harsh, humid jungle conditions with a motley gang of people that included an unstable Irishman, a Turk who was cerebral, but with a penchant for violence and an Italian who thought he was an Arab. Oh, and before I forget, all financed by a mega drug dealer. Bizarre is not the word for it.

I shook my head and sank back onto the cot and slept.

'¿Adam, como está usted?' ('Adam, how are you?') This was accompanied by much shaking of my body.

I opened an eye and was immediately blinded by the sun's rays. The rain had stopped and squinting, I made out the shape and rugged features of Rod. He was one of several lieutenants of the Fuerzas Armados Revolucíonarías de Colombia (FARC, Revolutionary Armed Forces of Colombia) that mainly controlled the Colombian Pacific region and made it safe for *gringoes* like me to be able to work there. FARC had divided up areas of the Colombian Pacific coastline and elsewhere into large fighting groups called blocs, made up of smaller guerrilla groups.

Rod was not a Paisa, a Medellin native, but from Calarca in the Quindio region. I think he was the deputy head of the Magdalena Media bloc and travelled around a lot as a kind of liaison officer to the various blocs. At this moment he was some 450 km from his home base. The whole FARC organisation is run by about a dozen commanders who form the Secretariat and they dictate policy and strategy for some 20,000 people, both male and female who make up the Army. They are a ferocious and disciplined legion.

'Maldita sea, la cabeza me va a estrellar.' ('My head is going to explode,') was my reply. A laughing Rod grinned and picked up a rusty can full of water. The next thing I felt was a sheet of water cascading over my head. It made little difference.

'¿Por qué se ríe, es mala mi pronunciación?' ('Why are you laughing, is my pronunciation that bad?') I mumbled the words.

'It's lousy. You never even mastered the basics of my language. You're a typical god damn monoglot Brit. So come on, get up and let's go.' His English was flawless, as was his Russian.

I stood up splaying water everywhere and gently shook my head. As I did so, sunlight glinted on slivers of glass in a broken wooden mirror frame. I felt like saying, 'Mirror, mirror on the wall who is the ugliest of them all,' but the answer was obvious.

'Where's Sonnel?' I croaked the question.

'He was last seen cavorting with two very nice ladies at that bar where you passed out,' was the reply. 'When I turned up, you had taken off to the toilet, never to be seen again. We thought you had gone to your room and it was only this morning we discovered your bed hadn't been slept in. Hence search parties, i.e. me, were sent out to look for you. I believe that Sonnel is waiting at the hotel in case you stagger in.'

I shook my head and gazed around at the semi-ruined shed that had been my lodgings for the night. I stared at the pools of congealing vomit and shuddered. I must have been responsible for this mess.

'By the way, I have to thank you, as one of the ladies was extremely kind.' He winked, 'also, I'd have thought you'd be well aware by now of how powerful the local TS is.'

I hesitantly put one foot forward and stayed upright. So I tried it again and the same thing happened.

'I can walk,' squawked out of my clenched jaw.

'Come on then, let's walk slowly back to the hotel and see if we can find your mate.'

*　　*　　*　　*

Daler Hanoz was smiling as he thought of his bank balance. He had just arrived in Verona from Cape Town via London and Malta where a successful 'disposal' had been carried out of six members of the Black Mamba gang. I later found out from him that this had been a secondary job, as he first went to Mozambique as part of Operation Long Reach, a top-secret project geared to eliminate opponents of the South African Apartheid government; in this instance the anti-apartheid activist Ruth First. He was paid by the South African Security and Intelligence Services, arranged via his contact with Bertil Wedin, a Swedish mercenary and friend that he had served with in the Belgian Congo. Now he was delighted to be an ex- Congo mercenary who had served time with 'Mad' Major Mike Hoare and currently was what is termed a hitman. In this line of work there was less chance of being shot and what was even worse captured.

I recently read in a discarded newspaper about the murder of Olof Palme, the Swedish Prime Minister. The four main suspects were: the South African Apartheid Intelligence Services, motivated by Palme's support for the African National Congress together with his attempts to close down arms and smuggling rings; the Turkish separatist movement of the PKK; the CIA, due to its support not only for the war in Vietnam, but also the communist governments in Cuba and Nicaragua; Swedish police with far-right sympathies and lastly a lone assassin, Stig Engström, who for ideological reasons hated the Social Democrat leader. To me, it had all the Daler Hanoz hallmarks of a successful kill and I am convinced it was him. If so who paid him? Palme was strolling home on Sveävagen Street, Stockholm from a cinema visit with his wife Lisbet at 11.21 pm, 28th February, just two people amongst many. A hand on the shoulder, one bullet from a Smith and Wesson magnum .357 fired into the back severing the spinal cord, another bullet injuring his wife, then an exit via 89 steps to a parallel street above before disappearing. To me, that was pure Hanoz and he had previous with Operation Long Reach.

His London stopover had been because he wanted to see yet again Caravaggio's 'Supper at Emmaus' at the National Gallery. He was mesmerised by the artist. The flowing gestures when the disciples recognise that it is Christ who sits with them, the Pecten nobilis shell emblem, the ripped jacket elbow, a misjudged extended hand, the table edge that seems 3 D style to almost jut out of the picture and strangely the roast chicken feet, which are usually removed from any carcass. The whole never ceased to amaze him.

The next stop had been a flight to Italy via Malta to stay with a friend on Gozo, the novelist A J Quinnell and a visit to Valletta cathedral to see yet again, 'The Beheading of the Baptist,' the largest painting produced by Caravaggio and the only one signed by the painter with his blood. The setting is extraordinary with its severe prison wall backdrop. Through a wall window two figures peer at the butchery being carried out below. The lighting is concentrated upon the executioner and the red robe of John the Baptist. Around John are some well-known characters from Caravaggio's other paintings. One is drawn into the scene as if by hypnosis. It is an extraordinary, exemplary painting of harsh realism.

After Malta, he treated himself to a visit to Italy; a country he'd visited many times, as he loved its ambience, especially the wine and the women. He had arrived in the Aeolian Islands where he fulfilled a long-held dream of walking with a guide to the top of Stromboli's active volcano. The boat ride back to Lipari had been via Strombolicchio, an offshoot of the old central volcano that rose pinnacle like from the sea. He had been watching a beautiful, flaxen-haired woman who had been leaning on the boat-rail looking at the imposing sheer rock face while casually brushing a wisp of hair from her face. The movement dislodged her sunglasses that had tumbled into the cobalt water.

'Damn it,' was the forceful comment.

'If I was Tarzan I'd now shout, 'Arghh arghh arghh ah,' and swallow dive into the ocean to rescue them. Alas I'm not, but if you'd like a pair of sunglasses you may borrow my Ray-Bans?'

She turned and looked at Hanoz. His long, dark, curly hair was rippling in the breeze, white teeth gleamed from a tanned, lean face and the casual stance of his honed body betrayed natural confidence and charisma. He held out the sunglasses in his left hand.

She smiled. 'OK. Thanks. I'm KK,' then laughed. 'It's Kate Kingdom originally from Cardiff by the Sea, California and I'd be grateful for the glasses. This is only my second day here and strong sunlight does hurt my eyes.'

Pleasant chat followed and he was told that she was an executive with Goldman–Sachs based in Los Angeles and had been with them ever since graduating from Yale University with an undergraduate degree in mathematics and archaeology, which was followed by a Master's in mathematics. His reply was that he was in the import-export business. I liked the exporting business, as in his case it invariably meant exporting souls to the next world.

The next day she cancelled her reservation and moved out of her hotel and into his room at the AKTEA hotel. They took bus rides to destinations picked at random to see the east and west coasts, Quattropane and Aquacalde respectively. At the latter, they stopped for lunch. At the table and looking at the smoking Stromboli volcano, Hanoz raised his glass at the sight saying, 'Here's to Stromboli, as it was there that I met my goddess.' They had gazed into each other's eyes and gently kissed. The romance was really taking off.

One day was spent visiting the excellent Archaeological Museum. Hanoz had an abiding interest in classical music and art, but his knowledge of ancient civilisations was very sketchy. At the Lipari house section, he was more taken with a large lump of volcanic obsidian rock. It was there that he said, 'This would look very nice in our house,' the first time that he had shown the growing depth of feeling he had for her. She had looked quizzically at him and gently squeezed his hand. Kate, having done many courses in archaeology, took much delight in pointing out and sketching in the various periods that had existed in the islands. They did have some difficulty though in finding the necropolis of Diane tucked away some 100m along via Guelielmo Marconi, a street at right angles to the main road and both were slightly disappointed with the site.

However, most of the time in that first week was spent in swimming either at Canneto's pebble-strewn beach or more frequently in the magnificent hotel pool, followed by sunbathing and an afternoon siesta in bed, which usually did not involve much sleeping. Evenings had been a wander along the main street to the commercial harbour and finding a convenient eating place such as Gilberto and Vera's Eco Paninitech bar. At the La Cambusa restaurant, via Garibaldi, he had enjoyed comparing her to Audrey Hepburn whose smiling face framed by a large sun hat, delicately chewing on the tip of the arm of her sunglasses adorned a wall of the restaurant. Whenever they saw it he reminded her that she still had his Ray-Ban glasses, but that they looked better on her than him.

His original plan had been to go to see old friends first in Naples, then Palermo in Sicily, but following Clausewitz's, third rule of war (when war breaks out, rip up all your plans, as the attack was not going to come from the direction envisaged), he changed his itinerary to coincide with hers, as she had planned to see Florence and Siena.

'Let's not stay in an expensive hotel,' she had snuggled up to him, 'but somewhere small and bijou.'

They caught the early morning Liberty Lines catamaran to Milazzo, a bus to Catania and flew to Pisa. The airport bus dropped them off at the Firenze station of Santa María Novella where after walking some 100 metres and looking down the first turning to the left they saw the sign, Hotel Lombardy. Entering they were given the Botticelli room by their host Vincente. They had struck pure gold in terms of a hotel and became firm friends with him and his sister Valeria. Vincente proved an invaluable ally in that he knew a man who knew a man etc. who would rent a balcony for the forthcoming *Il Palio* the famous horse race around the Campo in Siena, which by chance was occurring the next day.

After several calls by Vincente, Hanoz negotiated with the flat owner by doubling his asking price on condition that Kate could sit in one of the balcony front seats. He was content, as he had heard about the race but thought nothing of it. After all the travelling they had an early night and in bed Kate had called him a rhinoceros. He was unsure if this was a compliment or insult, but she soon reassured him. Taking the bus to Siena the next morning, he excused himself for a short time before returning and presenting her with a rhinoceros bracelet, the symbol of one of the 19 birth districts in Siena. Kate laughed and embraced him.

'I'll wear it only on special occasions,' she said as she kissed him, 'as you are an extraordinary man.' The reply spoken with a sincerity he did not know he possessed, was a quote from a poem called 'Dew drop and Diamond,' by Robert Graves, 'She like a diamond shone, but you; shine like an early drop of dew.' He was smitten.

When at the end of her stay the time came to return to the US, tears shed from her eyes when at Pisa airport she said goodbye. Hanoz badly wanted her to stay insisting that together they could amble around Italy, but work constraints, a strict two and a half weeks' vacation, meant she had to depart. She had fallen for the debonair Turk. He had fantastic charisma and charm described by Albert Camus, 'as the ability of a man to get any woman to say, yes, without even asking the question.' Hanoz later told me that by this time, he had also become very attached to Kate, but had decided that long term romantic arrangements were not for the life he led. It all came out later when we were in dire straits in the jungle, followed by rest and recuperation in Sicily.

Some four hours later he flew to Verona to attend the opera Aida in the Coliseum and also to see the Casa di Giulietta, Juliet's house. The romantic in him wanted to believe the story associated with the balcony even though he knew it was an urban myth. It had been renovated at least four times in the past two centuries. He booked into a small hotel close to the Gavi Arch near Castelvecchio and after a walk sat at an outside table of a cafe next to the church of San Fermo Maggiore on the banks of the Fiume Adige and ordered a spritzer. It was a short stroll along the Via Leoni to the Ponte Aleardi Bridge and then to the Casa di Giulietta.

His thoughts drifted over how life had turned out since he had grown up in Kisla, a small village near Dalyan in Turkey where he had been very good at all sports, especially gymnastics. Called up for national service his basic training had been carried out at Bolu and advanced training for the Parachute battalion at Kayseri, using both T-10 and T-16 parachutes. He had stayed in the military and had risen to the rank of Bascavusas (sergeant).

Reaching that rank, he left the Army and went to the Belgian Congo to fight as a mercenary. After three years of fighting, he had returned to Turkey with a healthy bank balance, but severely disillusioned by the insane combat he had experienced. He could never understand the belief that natives had on being told that a special magic ingredient protected them from death. This was called *dawa* and when mixed with water and ritually applied by a medicine man would make fighters impervious to any bullets that hit them. He had mown down more men than he could think of, as they charged at him some just waved spears and clubs. His latter comment to me was that they just kept coming and were slaughtered. It was blood, blood and more blood and sickening to behold.

Back in Turkey, he re-enlisted in the Army and again found himself involved in war. In the early seventies, EOKA, the extreme Greek Nationalist organisation backed by the Greek junta called for Enosis, Union with greater Greece and Cyprus and bloody skirmishes took place on Cyprus soil. When President Archbishop Makarios 111 was deposed, the Turkish Defence Organisation called for *Taksim,* a partition of Cyprus that resulted in Turkish troops landing on Cypriot soil on the 20th July 1974. He had been one of the first 'stick' out of his plane. The result of this 'liberation' as he saw it was established on the 16th August. The180 km line still divides the island.

In Cyprus and much to his surprise, he was ordered to the Kara Kuvvetleri Komutangligi (KKK), the Turkish Army headquarters on Ismet Inonu Bulvari, Ankara. He was told that he had been selected for secondment to the Directorate for Intelligence, in the Mille Istihbarat Teskilati (MIT), the National Intelligence Agency on Cem Ersever Caddesi, Ankara, headed by Senay Giner. There he learned many of the devious tricks involved in covert operations, especially Black Ops and first made contact with the criminal underworld. He loved it and soon saw the money that could easily be made… and he loved money. It was this background that had made him what he was today – a professional killer and it was all due to being in the right place at the right time. He was a great believer in the dictum that life was a series of points and these nexus points were the key to one's journey through it.

As a result of his training, he idly scanned the surroundings and nearby people. This was now second nature to him; it was as if he had an in-built survival gene that had been honed by MIT. He termed this as being on amber alert. His antennae had noticed that some 50 metres away was parked a black, sedan car with its engine idling. In the car were three men, all smoking heavily, as smoke billowed out of the windows; a few elderly couples were slowly walking towards him; two teenagers had just come out of the church, as well as two attractive females and the latter were in the process of sitting at the next table to him. One smiled demurely at him. He reciprocated.

He saw the black car move and watched it slowly creep towards the café. It was this slow speed that made him sit up and observe more closely. The elderly couples walking towards the church had now entered; the teenagers had left in the opposite direction. The car suddenly accelerated before braking to a stop at the tables and two men jumped out. They had swarthy complexions and were dressed in black jeans, brown loafers and white polo shirts that showed off their bulging arm muscles. Both had shaven bullet heads that glistened like polished white billiard balls.

There was no hesitation. One ran and grabbed one of the seated women by both arms and started dragging her to the car. Her screams rang loud and shrill. The other assailant grabbed her friend's shoulders. She fell from the chair, the table was overturned and she was also hauled towards the car.

Hanoz also did not hesitate. He launched himself from his chair and a *Shuto* blow (a rock hard palm edge) slashed across the first man's neck and his knee hit the man's groin. The clean-cut movement ended with a pivot that swept the assailant's legs away. He kicked the close-cropped head hard onto the floor and kicked it again with a force that would have made any football centre forward happy. Turning, he swerved from an attempted blow made by the other man before grabbing his wrist with one hand and with the other launched a *Yokomen,* another head hit. He twisted the arm viciously and his other hand made a fist and smashed a blow to the elbow joint hearing the characteristic crack when it shattered.

From the corner of his eye, he saw the driver coming at him and received the full force of a blow to the face. He staggered, crumpled to the ground and rolled to one side as best he could. He received two viscous kicks in the ribs and sensed rather than saw people running out of the church, as the driver dragged and pushed the two men into the car. It accelerated rapidly and screeched off, but without the women.

Slowly he staggered to his feet. There were three people around the two females while two others helped him to his feet.

'Are you ok?' This came from an American voice and Hanoz saw that it emanated from a slim T shirted youth wearing very long Bermuda shorts whose arms were held out to help him.

'My buddy and I raced out of the church when we heard screaming. I must say that you were bloody brave to face those people. There's no way I'd have tackled them as you did. They would have taken those females, there's no doubt about it.'

The two ladies in question came over, kissed his cheek and hugged him.

'Gracias, gracias,' was all he could hear. This was repeated many times.

Eventually, things quietened down and one said in English.

'How can we ever thank you? My name is Adriana and this is my sister Anna María.'

María grasped Hanoz's hand in both hers and squeezed tightly. She appeared to be very composed after such an incident but said nothing.

'We are staying at the Mastino hotel just across the Piazza from the Arena. Please come there with us. I invite you to be my guest and do let's have dinner together. You've no idea as to what you stopped and we would like to talk and thank you properly.'

'It would be my pleasure.'

Hanoz hailed a passing taxi and they bundled into it. Exiting at the Mastino, Adriana walked to some rattan chairs in the corner of the hotel and gestured for Hanoz and María to sit down. María kept clinging to his arm and gazing at him with moonstruck eyes.

Adriana excused herself, saying that she had to make an immediate phone call. On her return, she ordered drinks from a passing waiter.

'Two large gin and tonics,' she looked at Hanoz; who nodded, 'and you'd better make them very large ones, plus an orange juice.'

She settled back in the chair.

'I had to call home about this, but couldn't get the person I wanted so left a message. Incidentally, María does not speak English, but she wanted me to tell you how grateful she is for what you did. She cannot thank you enough.'

María smiled at Hanoz and again reaching for his hand squeezed it tightly.

'We're from Medellin, Colombia and have been travelling around Europe to see its lovely sights. It is a pre-wedding present given by our brother, Don Pablo Escobar. Another brother is getting married in three months and we are looking at possible bridal outfits.'

The nearby hotel phone rang.

*   *   *   *

Pablo Emilio Escobar Gaviria walking through the garden of his home, the Hacienda Nápoles at Envigado, 100 km east of Medellin, was in a very happy mood. Yesterday he'd had in-depth talks with his close friends José Gonzalo Rodríguez Gacha, alias 'El Méjicano,' Alvaro Prieto and Oscar Benel Aguirre. The gist was that conclusion of a huge drug deal was imminent, as his cartel co-founder Carlos Lehder had been able to buy Norman's cay a Bahaman island, which was an ideal site for any person involved in drug activities and the US market.

The island, he had explained to his friends, was some 300 km from the US coastline and made an ideal point for smuggling cocaine into the USA. It had an airstrip, harbour and many storage buildings and houses. This meant that a potential 70 tonnes of cocaine could be sent each month to the US; 10 tonnes per flight in a jet and up to 160 tonnes in a boat or submarine, of which he already possessed two. Additionally, he had arranged a meeting with Roberto Suarez Gomes to discuss a recent proposal of going further into the European market, one which was ripe for exploitation and a meeting had just been arranged with London personnel.

Arriving at the palatial wooden framed central doorway, Pablo Escobar stood for a moment and admired the view. He loved mornings. The air was clearer and the sun had not yet sucked up abundant moisture to form large clouds that later in the day seemed to be painted in the sky; but clouds that would return the moisture as rain. Each morning, he usually walked around parts of the spacious ground and invariably this entailed a visit to the four hippopotami cavorting in the stream and ponds provided for them.

Earlier that morning, an hour had been spent on the phone talking to New York-born Ed Zacharias now based in Los Angeles; another was spent talking with Jack and Tony Moreno who controlled the central California drug trade and the final 20 minutes, a clandestine social call only, was with New York's Harlem 'Robin Hood' drug lord, Nicky Barnes, who had earned the nickname by giving out free Thanksgiving turkeys to Harlem residents. Amazingly, convicted in 1977, he ran his drug empire from prison, where incensed at the way his former associates were ruining his drug domain he decided to testify against them and entered a witness protection programme. He had even made the New York Times Magazine cover as 'Mr Untouchable.' All belonged to various US Mafia groupings. Escobar had a particular fondness for Moreno's chief hitman, one Max Green, who based himself in Las Vegas. Both men were vicious killers who loved the brutality associated with the taking of a life.

The discussion with Tony Moreno had been about Juan Bautista, one of Escobar's men currently in the US who was suspected of doing a little drug dealing of his own. This was utterly forbidden and the decision was made that he had to be 'disposed' of, as soon as possible. Escobar's usual strategy followed the dictum of bribery (*plata* or silver), which if refused, ended up in the death (*plomo* or lead) of the person concerned. No bribery was on offer in this case. Moreno promised to send him back to Colombia within the week on some pretext or other. This brought a smile to Escobar's face as occasionally he enjoyed being involved in such matters; he loved the idea of *schadenfreude*. Mentally caressing the baseball bat he was fond of using on these occasions, he dismissed the thought. It could wait until tomorrow. Violence, blood and fear were very effective tools and anticipation of future violence was sometimes better than the actual killing.

Another hour and a half had been spent talking to his Argentine connections. There, the drug trade was again run by many family clans and they had been happy to use tactics first brought out by Machiavelli in Italy, i.e. divide and perhaps not entirely rule. His primary contact in Rosario was with the Cantero family who ran the Monos cartel; their main opposition being the Bassi, Funes and Camino families. In Buenos Aires, the Torres and Loza clans controlled the cocaine trade and it was in these discussions that the idea of penetrating the Far Eastern market including Australia and New Zealand had been brought up. They could use the many Pacific islands such as Fiji as staging posts. He liked the idea and filed it away for future reference. There were many other smaller families that he did not bother with, deeming them too insignificant to be even considered, e.g., the three who controlled Itatí on the River Parana. He had tried making contact with the Mexican cartels, especially the very large, powerful Sinola one, but had been rebuffed.

He smiled and the thought that came into his mind of his six siblings and his father Jesús Dari Escobar Echeverri and mother Hemilda de Los Dolores Gaviria Berrío. Thinking back to his childhood, he murmured:

'You've certainly come a long way since being born on December 1, 1949, in Rio Negro.'

After dropping out of the Universidad Autónoma Latinoamericana of Medellín, he had risen rapidly above the many drug dealers in Medellin and had never looked back after arranging for a major dealer Fabio Restrepo to be killed in 1975. Once when arrested he had even ruthlessly issued an order to kill all police involved in the arrest. The case was somehow dropped.

He missed his sisters travelling in Europe and his family who were away in Florida, but currently, Helena Tippetto kept him occupied in the nights. As he thought of her, his pulse quickened, as he knew she was somewhere in the Hacienda.

Escobar made his way into the hallway, past the large Caravaggio painting, 'The Nativity with Saint Francis and Saint Lawrence.' This had been stolen on the 18th October 1969, and razor blades used to slice the picture away from its frame in the Oratorio di San Lorenzo church, Palermo, Sicily, where it had hung for more than 300 years. It was one of the most sought-after artworks in the world with the American FBI terming it the Holy Grail of stolen artwork with a worth of $20-$30 million. To someone whose wealth was at least over $25bn this meant little. It had been given him as an afterthought for part of a drug deal done with the Sicilian Mafia boss Gaetano Badalamenti.

He had several such stolen paintings scattered around the house including Rembrandt's only known seascape, 'Christ in a Storm in the Sea of Galilee,' stolen from the beautiful terracotta cobbled floor and green silk wall-papered Dutch room of the Isabella and Stewart Gardiner Museum, Boston. This had been given by James 'Whitey' Bulgar, head of the Winter Hill gang, based in Boston, USA. Bulgar was a well-known IRA sympathiser involved in many arms/drug deals to the Irish Republic. He was a customer that Escobar loved to liaise with even though Boston was part of the territory run by a rival Colombian clan, the Orejuela brothers. Escobar wanted more of the US trade.

Barely glancing at the painting, he was met in the spacious hallway by Lucky, his virtually permanent house guest. As usual, he was amazed at the change in the man's appearance from their first meeting in Buenos Aires in the mid-late 1970s. There he had been working for Alexis Camino. During that time he had been a good looking well-groomed lean Englishman with a neat left-side parting to his glossy, black, brushed hair and a thin 1940s style moustache of which he was most proud. He was the textbook matinee Englishmen. Alexis Camino had been fascinated by him, not least because he was a wanted man in the UK and Camino liked having people around him over whom he had some kind of control. Unfortunately, Camino had been jailed and other family members had been suspicious of the languid Englishman who had quickly turned his undoubted charm on Escobar and eventually received an invite to Colombia.

Now his head was regularly shaved and a full beard covered his face. Living in the sun for so long meant that his still lean body and skull were the colour of brown mahogany. He was favoured by the drug baron, not least because he could teach English to members of the cartel and his family, but more importantly, he was a useful front man for the US market and anyway Escobar simply liked having him around.

Lucky held a phone in his hand and was about to speak when Escobar said.

'Lucky is Helena around?'

'*El mágico,* I last saw her in the rear garden,' was the reply. 'She'd just come out of the pool and was mixing a drink. I was coming to look for you, as there have been several phone calls asking for you. There is one from your brother Nelson who wanted to speak to you and your sister asked you to call her immediately. She said she needed to speak to you very urgently.'

Escobar took the phone and dialled the number written on a note pad.

'Hola Adriana, lovely to hear from you. What have you two have been doing in Italy?'

'What?'

*   *   *   *

Outside the tower block of Crispe house built in the 1960s in east London's Gascoigne estate, Anton Mikullovci Copje leaned against the wall whilst smoking a new Marlborough cigarette. He was fascinated by the picture of the rugged cowboy who smoked Marlborough cigarettes in movie and newspaper adverts and was feeling very satisfied with life. His gaze took in the distant River Thames together with the A13 and North circular road to the south and west. To the east were massive container ports where amongst other goods, multi kilogrammes of cocaine were offloaded. A light rain started to fall, but he was immune to it.

His mind flicked over recent events featuring Delroy 'King' Lewis, the head of the Jamaican gang - or rather the ex-Jamaican gang, that was selling cocaine and heroin on the estate. The fighting had been vicious and he, Loscar Vilas and Viktor 'Clode' Bashkin had been at the forefront of the fracas in which three people had died and many more injured. Violence was now very much enjoyed and his muscles tensed as his thoughts roamed over the fight that had ended the Jamaican's rule of the estate. He was hoping for more of the same with the nearby Newham Beckton Black Squad. He had come a long way from being a youth in the small village of Butrint, south of Saranda town, Albania. A backstreet layabout and occasional waiter at the Mussel House restaurant who had managed to obtain a university place to study law.

He had not been back for some eight years and still hankered after the *xhiro* – the slow meandering along café lined boulevards a la the French *flaneur*, the Italian *passeggiata*, or the Spanish *paseo*. He solely missed the rough track drive up to Berat the city of a thousand windows via the 2,500 year-old Illyrian city of Bryllis, especially in winter when it was surrounded by snow-clad mountains. The city straddled the Osuni River and was a place where he had set his heart on marrying his fiancée Sally with the reception afterwards being held in the Antipatria restaurant. Now it was never going to happen, as she had been murdered. Reflections on the *byrek me spinak* (flaky pastry spinach pie) and *tave kosi* (sour lamb baked in yoghurt), made his mouth water.

It was not just the contemplation of food that made him smile though, but the result of a recent deal he had been instrumental in setting up meant he had been promoted to the top level within the Hellbanianz, the cocaine retail and vicious enforcer arm of the UK Mafia Shqiptare Albanian crime syndicate. The deal had been the formation of an alliance with the Ndrangheta, the syndicate that was probably the richest and most powerful of all Italian mafias, one that had a truly global reach. The result was a ditching of the old drug business model of importers working separately from wholesalers, which often resulted in differing pricing structures and drug purity.

Standing at the corner waiting, his mind recalled what had happened just over three weeks ago.

He had personally been invited to Italy by Girolamo Piromalli, erstwhile head of the Ndrangheta. After clearing it with Ferdi his boss, in Naples he was met by Piromalli who introduced him to Paulo Di Laura, ('Ciruzzo o milionario') the Camorra clan boss and Salvatore Rina, the Cosa Nostra boss. These three powerful syndicates ruled the Italian drug trade, all being amorphous groupings of various clans and families: Rina, the Cosa Nostra head, was nicknamed 'The Beast' because of his cruel lust, a man who not only assassinated criminal rivals but judges, journalists and anyone who he thought was in his way; the Ndrangheta originally from the southern Calabria region controlled some 80% of the cocaine trade; the Camorra hailing from the Compania region of Naples had political links especially with the Christian Democratic Party. Loose alliances existed, but flare-ups were frequent amongst the groupings.

The choice of Naples, as a meeting place, a city sitting on a fault line and in the shadow of a volcano had been deliberate. It showed Piromalli's power in Camorra territory. A long luncheon held at the Airone piano bar had ended on a high note when all raised their wine glasses and toasted 'the future.' This was followed by a visit to Enzo Cosenza's Bollicine (Bubbles) bar behind Piazza Leopardi station in the Fuorigrotta quarter. Cosenza took them to the famous Curve B end of the Studio San Paolo football stadium, where each weekend the chants of 20,000 *ultras,* usually conducted by Gennaro Montuori ritually filled the stadium. Typically the chant was, '*Napoli non è Italia.*' Montuori was waiting for them and produced a white and sky blue coloured scarf, Benito Mussolini colours, taken from a Lazio *ultra*-supporter the previous week who, Copje was told, was a member of the *Eagles.* The street fighting had been pretty weak, as the *Eagles* were having problems with a rival *ultra*-gang called the *Irriducibilli.* The new gang had as a symbol a bowler hatted character named Mr Enrich and his leg was shown as giving a kick and the recipient was not a football. Apparently the donor had objected to the scarf removal and duly received a thorough kicking.

Next, he was taken to Le Vele, a sprawling downbeat estate in the suburbs of Naples. Le Vele was where sewage spilled out of broken pipes, syringes were scattered around the canyon-like streets; windowpanes were shards of glass and the people cowed. The estate was built by a Neapolitan architect Franz di Salvo and meant to replace the slums of the city centre. Di Salvo was an admirer of Corbusier and a believer in, *le case per tutti*, houses for everyone. He built seven blocks to house between 210-240 families that were to fulfil the traditional neighbourhood lifestyle of *vicoletti Napolitani*, the old centre's backstreets. Corruption meant that funds were siphoned off and the end result was a housing mess. A vicious territorial war had been fought for control of the Camorra drug trade between Paulo Di Lauro's syndicate and the Secessionists, a breakaway movement led by Raffaele Amato and Cesare Pagano that resulted in well over 400 killings. The streets still bore the scars. The Secessionists lost and a brutal revenge enacted.

The Scampia and Secondigliano areas were also included in the visit, as they were strongholds of the Camorra clan. This was showing Piromalli's power in its crudest form not only to Copje but also to Di Lauro. Di Lauro appeared to be a gentleman, but Copje was aware that he had personally killed the clan head, Aniello La Monica and taken control of the whole business empire. Nothing as crass as cocaine was offered to Copje and he turned down the offer of the services of call girls from the top end of the profession.

The business principle was simple. Profits were vast, so why not undercut any rivals by reducing price and increasing purity? The fact that the latter might cause earlier deaths amongst customers was unimportant. Cocaine bought from the Colombian cartels was one-fifth of the price charged by buying from Dutch wholesalers. As a result, more cocaine could be shipped, for example, to the UK. For the business model to work, strong control of several European ports was needed. Enter the Ndrangheta, who had some 200,000 people working for them in places such as Rotterdam, Antwerp, Tilbury, Liverpool, Harwich and Hull ports. These were all key focal points from which cargo could be dispersed in the UK to the main distribution centres of London and the satellite cities of Birmingham, Newcastle, Liverpool and Glasgow.

A sustainable price together with good quality was the key. Do not be too greedy and follow the Albanian code of 'keep the promise,' i.e. always deliver with no questions asked. It related to the Albanian ancestral code of *kanun* laws, as well as a social code of honour (blood feuds) called *hakmarraja*, which made the syndicate ruthless enemies. This was all about revenge albeit for a slur on honour or humiliation. *Besa* a word that signified honour and trust was the key. If this was given it meant much more than a signed paper or handshake.

He heard that contact had been made with the Colombian cartels, so shipments could be made directly from Colombia, all done in house for a £4 bn. cocaine market. Finance and psychology played a huge part in growing the coca crop in Colombia. The government paid $2 an acre for corn, the cartels $7 an acre for coca. They also threw in schooling, sporting facilities, health cover etc. The fact that it was going overseas to satisfy a huge *gringo* demand was immaterial. Who cared if some far away idiots were going to frazzle their minds? No contest.

He was aware that like Italy, Colombia had many cartels of which the Cali run by the Orejuela brothers and Pablo Escobar the so-called 'King of Medellin,' were the major players. What was new to him was that the Orejuela brothers ran the cocaine trade in New York and the US northeast area, whilst Escobar controlled the Miami hinterland; but was extremely ambitious and wanted more. Copje had not visited Colombia. Ferdi, the head of the London Albanian Mafia had recently done that and had kept his close lieutenants informed. Copje was aware that FARC, a guerrilla army, dealt with both Cali and Medellin cartels and knew that more than pilot talks had been initiated between Ferdi and Gilberto Rodriguez Orejuela, the more amenable of the brothers, one who if possible preferred doing business rather than violence. Apparently Pablo Escobar preferred to do things in his own particularly brutal fashion, one which even involved very heavy fighting against the Colombian government.

No love was lost between the Orejuela brothers and Escobar. The brothers had even hired hitmen to kill Escobar (they failed) and now an uneasy peace was the order of the day. Both wanted a stable market, as they strived to consolidate further territory in the US. Seeking control of the US markets meant ferocious wars unlike the European markets, which were not quite as volatile. The latter was how Copje preferred to do business.

Copje now heard about a future whereby the land given over in Columbia to cocaine production would be some 170,000 hectares. There was an estimated European market of 17 million users in Europe, I million in the UK, let alone the US market. The sheer scale of the trade would reduce street prices so hopefully increasing demand. As well as being the drug of choice for hard-core drug users, it would be the dream recreation drug for upper and middle classes. He wanted to embrace this future.

What intrigued Copje was that he was party to a cadre of people involved in wide-ranging discussions of further ways of generating revenues. One cunning Italian strategy was a move into agriculture, which helped legitimise the business. This started in 1979 where two lorry drivers were shot at Rizziconi en route to pick up oranges to be bought at a fair price in Verona. The Ndrangheta wanted to be the sole buyer so eradicated competitors, as they wanted to be the supreme protagonist for the entire commercial chain, i.e. in charge of ALL matters, from picking, packaging to delivery. Land itself could also be bought to launder profits via EC subsidies in the 1980s under the Common Agricultural Programme. By taking over farmer's co-operatives, the EC could be invoiced, for example, for billions for oranges that existed only on paper; the same lorry load could be weighed six times. When garbage collection was privatised, they used the opportunity to dump refuse, including toxic waste, e.g., dioxin, particularly in the Naples area. Piromalli had even boasted how he had taken over the Milan fruit and vegetable trade from the Morabitos clan.

He was aware that further deals with the Mexican and Brasilian cartels were also being explored by Ferdi, the Italians and Colombians. In fact, he was due to visit Mexico soon and had provisional meetings arranged with the Sinola or Guzmán-Loera Organisation cartel headed by 'El Chapo' Joaquin Guzmán; the Gulf cartel headed by Juan Nepomuceno and Juan Garcia Abrego; and the Juarez syndicate headed by Pablo Acosta Villarrea and Paco Asensio-Montesinos. He was looking forward to meeting up with the drug Queen, Sandra Avila Beltran, one of the very few women who had risen to the top of a cartel. He was going to earn a lot of air miles, currently he had very few.

He switched from thinking of the past back to the present. Flicking the cigarette to the dusty unkempt pavement, with his right foot he stubbed it out for coming around the corner of the building appeared the large, shambling figure of a Portuguese man who was his brother-in-law Loscar Vilas and therefore an honorary Albanian. As Copje watched Vilas slowly walk towards Crispe house, his thoughts once again wavered over the state of Vasil's marriage. As far as he knew it was a good one, but he could not help thinking about what would happen if it floundered. He could just about accept an amicable split but a messy one would necessitate some drastic action, and this troubled him.

Into his mind again came the thought of Sally Rivett, the girl some five years previously with whom he was engaged to be married. When she died, that fateful night changed him entirely from a bright young law student at University College, London, one who loved amateur boxing, into this new, altered version. He had given up his studies, temporally he kept telling himself and had slowly slid into the Albanian underworld. Copje recognised that he was now a very hard man, but if he ever became involved in a fight with Vilas, he would be unsure as to the result. Deep down, he knew that both would be beaten to a pulp and one, or both, would end up dead, but if any dishonour to his sister occurred, *kanun* had to be respected.

From witnessing some of Vasil's fights, he was aware that when, as it was colloquially called, the red mist assailed Vasil, he did not know when to stop. He had personally seen over a dozen badly beaten men curl up in a foetal position on the ground, kicked by Vasil to a coma and disfigured for life, before the gang pulled him away from his opponent. Four men had died as a result of the savage head kicking by Vasil's steel toe capped boots. Not for nothing was Vilas the syndicate's primary enforcer.

In a warehouse knife fight in Lisbon, a lucky knife lunge from his opponent, another Albanian called Pajtim, had produced a facial scar that ran from the corner of Vilas' mouth, four centimetres to the right eyelid. Over two hours, Vilas had brutally and slowly sliced Pajtim to pieces pre killing him. Fingers had been snipped off and then both arms and legs broken with an iron bar. Whenever Pajtim passed out, a bucket of water was splashed over his face. His genitals had been sliced off and stuffed into his mouth and the jaw rammed shut several times. All the while Villas' blood clotted face had been impassive, as he mechanically did the job. The only time a semblance of a grin had appeared was when he rammed an iron bar some five cm into the right eye socket and watched blood and eyeball spurt forth. He had watched the tortured man and played with him like a cat with a mouse before eventually tiring of it all and slitting Pajtim's throat. As Vasil came near, Copje glided lithely out to the pavement.

'Miremengjes. Gjëra të mira?' ('Good morning. Things OK?')?

'Let's go,' was said in English, as Vilas' Albanian was not very good. They moved off down the street. They had a job to do.

2.

Colombia.

We slowly made our way back with me clutching Rod's shoulder. As I walked my head started to become a little clearer and the morning haze helped, as it cooled my body and I found that I could think and string words together. Boy was I improving. Rod did not say much, so I was able to gabble on about anything that came into my mind. Funnily, Edmund Lear's nonsense verses seemed to bubble through my sub-conscious.

En route back we passed the infamous bar where I had passed out and who should we see sitting in a lounge chair drinking tea was Sonnel. Laid out on a neat table in front of him was a pale blue crockery set that had pink flowers entwined in the cup, saucer and two pots. A Colombian who loved tea, a habit picked up when he was a student in London along with me. The whole incongruous scene was bizarre, to say the least. He was freshly scrubbed and shaved, wearing black jeans and a hideous coloured tie-dyed shirt. As was his usual practice in civilised surroundings, although I would not call where we were by that term, he was barefoot.

A languid arm wave greeted us. Sonnel put down the cup and a huge grin spread across his face.

'Hola amigo. I thought we'd lost you, or you'd been kidnapped by the Cali cartel.'

'Get lost,' was my not entirely apt reply.

We pulled up chairs and Sonnel called for two more cups that arrived within seconds. He made to pour out the tea.

'No, not for me,' I cried. 'I want real coffee, hot and black.'

Rod nodded and added, 'I was once a coffee plantation worker and now cherish and love my coffee.'

I chipped in, 'Any Colombian, even half a one as you are,' I knew that Sonnel's father was Norwegian, mother Colombian, 'would know that tea is the English man's drink. I'm from Wales so bring coffee to me in a bucket alongside another bucket, this time with water, as I'm dehydrated.'

'Are you sure you'd not want another bucket as well,' grinned Rod, 'you certainly made quite a mess back at your sleeping place?'

Nothing more was said until the steaming hot, rich, black coffee materialised. I gulped a mouthful followed by a giant slug of water. It hit my insides and its good deeds started to operate. I felt a bit more human. At that moment a truck plus trailer followed by a long wheelbase Land Rover Safari pulled up outside the hotel. Two men in military fatigues jumped out and immediately Rod got up and with a quick movement of his head gestured them to go inside. He excused himself to us and followed them into the hotel returning some 15 minutes later with a suitcase in his hand.

Sonnel and I looked at each other and he grimaced.

Rod clapped his hands to get our attention. 'I have news for you amigos. I have to leave immediately to go to Ocaña and La Playa de Belén in western Catatumbo. Unfortunately, we are not the only guerrilla movement in Colombia. For example, the National Liberation Army (Ejército de Liberación Nacional - ELN), also a Marxist group that like our movement is based upon our peasant population; the M-19 (Movimiento, 19 de Abril) group is mainly a student based urban movement, one that I believe is surreptitiously funded by Pablo Escobar. There exists an uneasy pact between movements that tends to make minor rather than major disturbances between us. A fracas has occurred and I have to go. I don't like it.'

He stopped and looked expectantly at us. Nothing was said.

'There is a matter I want to talk to you about. You two have always wanted to know more about FARC. I had arranged to take both of you to meet a colleague of mine Carlos Antonio Lozada. He is the commander of our southern bloc and was coming to meet me at Camp Diamante. We were meeting to discuss what to do about our hard-line Colombian President who has just formulated a 'Plan Colombia.'

He winked at me as he said this, the thumb of his outstretched hand pointed downwards.

'I should tell you that Camp Diamante is the nerve centre of the FARC Eastern block and is situated deep in the interior of the Yari river basin. The camp lies between Caquitá, Mata and Guaviare. To the north exist the plains where coca is grown extensively, while to the south-east is the Amazon region, where Camp Diamante is located.'

Sonnel and I looked and smiled at each other across the table and I realised that I had sobered up very quickly.

I spoke. 'Sorry, but this is a bit much for me at least to understand. As I have finished my contract with Frontino it's no problem to go there. I'd love it. It's a kind of bonus. I have with me my wallet and passport, although the latter will be pretty useless.' In light of what happened subsequently, I was very glad that Colombian law made it mandatory to produce a passport at any hotel. I surreptitiously touched my pocket as I said those words. They were there. 'What more do I need? Count me in and thank you.'

I turned to look at Sonnel. He spoke.

'I have a job still and cannot take off at a moment's notice.'

Reaching over, I poured out more coffee from the jug, gulping it down. There was enough for all, as the two men with Rod had brought full cups to the table. We sat silently for a minute or two to let all he had said sink into our heads. Sonnel broke the silence by addressing Rod.

'Adam and I have known you for some years and we've had some super times together.' As he said this my mind went back to when we had met this remarkable, intelligent man, but that is another story.

Sonnel continued. 'Adam is a freelancer now, but I still have my job and am expected to turn up tomorrow, so I can't just go off with you at a moment's notice?'

'Think about my offer, you have until lunchtime to decide. Sonnel, it's no problem getting you time off. After all, if FARC requests something in this territory… well, you know the answer.' He gave a sardonic smile as he said this.

'Let me introduce you to my comrades, José Marquez and Camilo Terobo. José is a young man who will go far in the movement. He and I are on the same wavelength and one day we hope to unite this great country of ours and eliminate corruption. It might surprise you that we also wish to eliminate the drug trade.'

He grabbed a cup and filled it with coffee. 'Now, unfortunately, I have to leave immediately with Camilo, but José will take you there and we will meet up soon.'

He rose, shook hands and walking out jumped into the Land Rover. His case had already been put on board by Camilo who drove off in a swirl of dust.

Unfortunately, we never saw him again.

*   *   *   *

Sir George Fusano, (Eton, Army, Balliol College, Oxford) Nobel Laureate in chemistry, ex part time diplomat, now Master of St John's College, Cambridge, UK, mopped his brow with a large floral handkerchief and gratefully slid into a large armchair. He fumbled in an inside pocket and withdrew a Corona cigar that was lighted with evident love and care. Sinking back into the chair, he inhaled deeply the blessed smoke and once again patted his brow. He had forgotten about the high temperatures and humidity that was normal in the country. All previous visits had been in the 'dry' season.

He was wearing a charcoal grey, pinstriped suit, black leather shoes and white shirt with the Brigade of Guards navy and maroon striped tie. His once highly polished black shoes were now streaked with mud from the walk to these rooms from the lecture theatre. The man opposite him, the Provost of Barranquilla University, was wisely dressed in slacks and open-necked shirt and knew from experience that Sir George would rather face the death of a thousand cuts than not wear a suit at a formal occasion. He was quite different and very pragmatic in his needs and had dressed sensibly, well aware of the high evening temperature and humidly, particularly as the air conditioning in the large lecture theatre had failed. It often did. It was he who quietly turned up the room air conditioning, which surprisingly worked.

Sir George was a frequent visitor to the university and this time was on a British Council sponsored tour of Colombian Universities. His lecture on, 'Is God Left-Handed?' had been rapturously applauded but one hour previously.

'May I have a jug of water, please,' said Sir George, 'and you had better make it a large jug.' He smiled, 'and I wouldn't mind an even larger single malt scotch.'

The Provost also smiled, nodded and called out through the open door. A smiling attendant brought in a large jug complete with ice cubes together with some canapés and a bottle of Talisker.

'I should have stayed on whisky earlier on when you took me to the Cafe del Mar for a pre-dinner drink and then to the Cafe Santo Domingo restaurant that Gabriel Garcia Márquez used to frequent instead of having a small glass of Tequila Sunrise. Small,' he shuddered. 'I left half of it otherwise I'd have been in no fit state to give a lecture.'

The Provost nodded. 'I know. I finished it off.'

They both laughed.

'I should have given that lecture naked and with a hosepipe playing on me,' was the next comment. 'Although if that had happened, I doubt if the lecture would have been heard due to laughter at a middle-aged pot-bellied Brit. with Italian ancestry. Halfway through, I wanted to jump into that Olympic sized pool that you have in the Aquatic area. Anyway, the next few days are rest and fun days, so I hope I can just wear shorts and a Polo shirt. Where are we going?'

The Provost smiled a shy smile. 'It's a mystery trip for you, George and I cannot tell you much, as I simply do not know. You will have to wait and see. My original idea was to take you from Barranquilla along the Magdalena River to the Honda rapids, which is all navigable. In the old days we had about 70 Mississippi type three-story paddle steamers called *vapores* travelling the river, now zero. Unfortunately they used wood for fuel; the basic unit being the *burro de leña,* a donkey load of approximately 100 1 metre length logs. Furnaces that powered these large steamers would burn 100 *burros* a day, which resulted in destruction of the fringing forests. As well as this, the river provided the pathway for hunting parties to decimate the wildlife. You should read the memoir of Gabriel García Márquez. Tragic. Back to the present, even if we found a boat the journey would take far too long.'

'What a lovely trip that could have been,' interjected Sir George.

'I agree and I'd accompany you if this could be arranged. I'm amazed that some Company has not thought to reintroduce this idea for tourist purposes. A 700 km trip along this river, one that starts some 4,000 m in the Andean *páramo* would be magic. We'd pass through gorges fringed with clouds; see the mysterious megaliths at San Augustín. Drat, it'd be marvellous particularly with one or two gin and tonics in our hands.'

He sighed.

'I'm a historian and the 1500 km Magdalena is the commerce corridor of Colombia. It represents the history of the country, ranging from the genocide caused by the Conquista, a graveyard for the thousands slaughtered by the civil wars of the 50s, the current cocaine wars and FARC. One day I'll write the story.'

'I can't wait to buy the book,' quipped Sir George.

The Rector gave a wry grin.

'However, to come back to the present, I know that you are going to Cartagena and then Bucaramanga where there is an interesting archaeological dig, but that's all. Prof Juan Gallego, Head of Archaeology, will accompany us for the trip, but I can only go as far as Cartagena as I have to return to the university. You'll certainly see the jungle and can wear a loincloth a la Tarzan if you like.'

Sir George burst out laughing.

'That would be a sight for sore eyes I can tell you. But Bucaramanga, correct me if I'm wrong, but isn't that FARC territory?'

'No, it's some 400 km away from their borders and they tend to obey the unofficial war rules. You'll be quite safe. Changing the topic, I must say that I found your lecture fascinating. I particularly enjoyed your comments on right and left-handedness. The examples you gave of our right/left hands although perfect images of each other are not identical, as you cannot put a right hand in a left-hand glove; the ability of taste buds to distinguish between sweet and sour food, all were easy to follow. The statistical analysis of protein building blocks, which should be represented by an equal number of both right and left-handed components, but are not because all of them are left-handed was magnificent. That was much harder for me to follow, being a mere arts graduate. Your conclusion of handiness was superb, one hand being favourable, the other poisonous and the examples given regarding the pharmaceutical industry. Whaw.'

'Thank you. I have four lectures with me on this trip, but the one I like best is on how to predict three-dimensional protein structures from their amino acids.' The Rector's face blanched. 'These biomolecules are fundamental for all animal life and assemble themselves into structures of astonishing complexities. To understand this 'folding' process is a key challenge in biochemistry as proteins are necessary for every single body cell. This is a gigantic task and one that Cyrus Leventhal in 1969 formulated as a famous paradox. Proteins can fold in an astronomical number of ways. It'd take longer than the universe has existed to test every configuration yet they fold in milliseconds, as atoms are moved at the nano scale. How is this done?' He shook his head. 'It's unbelievable.'

Glancing at the Rector, he noticed the glazed look in his eyes and the comment.

'Ok George, you've lost me. That was much too complicated for my pea brain. If you had given that talk, the hall would have emptied. Keep it for a more scientific audience.'

'I'm sorry. I apologise as this is a hobby horse of mine.'

'You've no need to George. The audience lapped it up. Incidentally, the last British Council lecturer we had was by a Dr Evan Sams. 'Exoticism in Salammbo: The languages of Myth, Religion and War,' was the topic. Apparently it was a challenge to Flaubert's famed Salammbo book. His argument was about the dialectical oppositions between male/female, sun/moon etc. No one understood a word. It was terrible and the hall emptied albeit slowly.'

Sir George nodded and rose slowly. 'I see it's now 11 o' clock and think it's time for bed. May I again thank you for that lovely meal we had earlier on and for a greatly appreciative university audience?'

They rose; shook hands and Sir George left the room, en route casually picking up the whisky bottle. The Rector looked quizzically at him.

'Henry Miller once wrote that life is insomnia.' He flashed a grin. 'This helps me sleep.' He nodded to the Rector and made his way down the stairs to the university guest suite. Entering, he turned the air conditioner up to its maximum; it was working. Cooling the auditorium might have been too big a task for the antiquated larger system, but it was fine for smaller rooms.

Slipping out of his clothes, he had a shower before putting on convict striped pyjamas given him as a Christmas present by his late wife. Creeping gratefully into the large bed his head hit the pillow and his thoughts drifted to the jungle. It brought back hidden memories, some good, some not so good.

After Eton, he had been called up for National Service. His father, being a retired General had persuaded him to reluctantly sign on for more than the required two years and had arranged for him to be assigned to his old Regiment. After officer training, his first posting was to join his Regiment on guard duty at Buckingham Palace. This was not what an adventurous young officer needed and in the Officers Mess he heard about Brigadier 'Mad' Mike Calvert, who in the European theatre of WWII had commanded an SAS Brigade. This excited him so much that he applied for a transfer to the SAS. He passed the endurance training in the Brecon Beacons with ease and the Selection course based at the Parachute Regiment's depot at Aldershot.

Within weeks he was on a RAF plane bound for Malaya towards the tail end, it lasted for 11 years, of what was termed the Malayan Emergency. From the air in the bright sunshine, there appeared to be one vast canopy of green trees through which drifted wisps of mist. It was ethereal. The moment he landed changed his mind, as that canopy blocked out sunlight and the heat and humidity were horrendous, as were the midges. Insects chirped, monkeys squawked and other odd screams permeated the air. That was nothing compared with the nights and incessant bombardment by mosquitoes.

In Malaya, British forces were deployed in fighting insurgents who originally had formed the mainly Chinese Malayan People's Anti-Japanese Army, allies of the British in WWII. Their leader Chin Peng, secretary-general of the Malayan Communist Party had even been given an OBE in the Victory honours list. The British government's plans for Malaya's future did not include Communists, so Chin Peng took 3,000 troops and over 6,000 clandestine supporters, the Min Yuen, back into the jungle to fight for an independent Malaya.

Arriving at Kota Tinggi near Johore he was assigned to 'B' Squadron, the Chelsea Chindits, rather than the traditional 'G' the

Guards Squadron and his first task was an introduction to jungle (*ulu*) fighting. A march through the green tall primary jungle trees to a camp made sweat stream like rivulets down his back. There the first lecture had been given by Captain John David. Always have your belt kit, *golock* (machete, the top of the weapon was heavier than the rest so made cutting things easier) and weapon at hand and never venture into the jungle alone - always be in pairs. At all times have a dry (for sleeping) and wet (the ones you wore daily) set of clothes. With regards to safety, always look where you were going and if a snake bit you, make sure that it was killed and brought back to camp for appropriate antidote treatment.

These had been followed by instructions, for example, navigation where all one needed was a map, compass, pacing and following ground contours, or cross graining where one went up and down the terrain; live firing along jungle lanes with the butt cradled in your shoulder, sights up; long range Morse signalling; stalking each other with high powered air rifles, faces covered with fencing masks; fishing with hand grenades; two/four-man patrols and contact drills; CTRs (Close target recce) bringing the troop together ready for infiltration to previously stored ammunition, explosives and food caches; increasing a mortar's range by squirting petrol down the barrel; building A-frame structures that supported your hammock. These stopped some of the multitudes of insects that festooned the jungle floor from wandering over one at night. Leaches were everywhere. They squirmed through clothing seeking out the softest body parts. At the night stop, a body hunt was mandatory. He was invariably amazed that the Dyak and Iban trackers imported from Sarawak who formed a ranger unit to work with the SAS were seemingly immune to such things.

Above the hammock and mosquito net, the tautly stretched poncho or *basha* sheet bungeed into the nearest trees kept rain away that fell with monotonous regularity. Another essential skill was blasting trees with PE4, to form a secure landing site for Sycamore helicopters both for insertion purposes and also in case injured personnel needed to be casevaced. These fundamental truths had been hammered home, especially the need for splashing on plenty of mosquito cream and taking Paludrin anti-malarial tablets. There are no seasons in the jungle. It is simply hot and wet. He did learn to enjoy the quiet at dusk when bone tired and stretched out on his hammock the only sound to be heard was the hissing of raindrops on the leaves of trees and his poncho.

Training was immediately followed by three month jungle patrols, provisions and ammunition being parachuted in at monthly intervals. A three-week respite was given at the end of a tour and then it was back to the jungle. He grimaced as he recalled the six kg in weight he had lost in one month alone. He helped in moving villagers via the Briggs Plan, from their *kampongs* into fortified villages protected by the Army. By this means food supplies to insurgents were cut off at source and they had to retreat into the jungle where they either grew their own or obtained it from scattered aboriginal tribes. When they withdrew into the jungle, he had to follow.

His last patrol had been in the swamps of Telok Anson, Selangor, where along with his fellow officers Doug 'Taffy' Jones and Ant Bennett they were part of a 37-man troop led by Harry Thompson tracking several guerrilla groups. One group chased was a very special one led by Ah Hoi, nicknamed the 'Baby Killer,' as a result of a pregnant woman's public execution that he had carried out. Armed with sawn off shotguns, rifles and Patchet submachine-guns, he personally preferred the Owen submachine-gun, the troop obtained the surrender of the counter terrorist groups. After having all the adventure he'd craved, a return to the UK to read chemistry at Oxford meant a tumultuous change in the direction his career would subsequently take.

His thought patterns suddenly switched to the present and he wondered what the next few weeks would bring? He was reassured by feeling the hard outline of the 9 mm Browning automatic pistol pressing through the soft pillow down. It had personally been given him by John Davidson, Military Attaché at the British Embassy in Bogotá.

The first part of his mission had been accomplished, albeit the easiest.

3.

Nicaragua, Colombia.

eanwhile in Nicaragua up coast from Colombia, Zoen Zinnrapi Mahoney, almost from birth called Paddy, had gone looking for gold and found it. The geology in his exploratory area was very favourable for high grade economically viable deposits. Three gold areas currently exist, namely Limon, Bonanza and La Libertad and he was the original discoverer of the open cast La Libertad gold mine, which produces some 140,000 oz. of gold per year. As usual, it was the La Libertad Company who employed him that took the spoils, all Paddy received was a significant bonus that was spent at many places including the bar of Flannery's Hotel, Galway city. Ireland. He soon blew the money away and never had such luck again.

On occasional visits back to Ireland, he had often gone gold prospecting in the Sperrin Mountains of County Tyrone. He was convinced there was gold to be found in what is called the Dalradian Supergroup suite of rocks that run some 700 km from Ireland to Scotland. He never found any. Gold is seven times denser than quartz, the most common mineral on earth and accordingly is moved in water alongside much larger sized grains composed of lighter materials, for example, river pebbles and it was these riverbeds that he had conscientiously sampled. To date, his Ireland preliminary panning work had found only the odd speck of gold in a few river gravel beds.

He was originally from Galway and according to him descended from royalty via his paternal lineage. His mother, Rita Zinnrapi, was an Italian who had run an ice cream parlour in Loughrea, the town of the grey speckled lake. After a marriage that lasted a bare eleven months, for unknown reasons she had secretly sold the business and was never seen or heard of again, leaving baby Zoen behind.

Father, child and paternal grandparents went to live in Tynagh a small village some 25 km from Loughrea where Paddy eventually commenced work for Base Metals, Tynagh Ltd. This was mainly related to mining lead and zinc and was a significant employer in the region. It was here that he obtained his taste for geology and love of oddball words. It was the latter that had helped him make the La Libertad gold discovery in Nicaragua, as gold was found in the vuggy, drusy and banded quartz veins of the bedrock. He loved those daft names.

He had little use for academic geologists learning his craft the hard way, working on oil rigs as a roustabout and joining mineral firms as an assistant who was prepared to do anything and go anywhere.

He was very fond of his father and grandparents. The former was killed in a car accident a few weeks after he had reported his gold findings to the La Libertad Company; his grandparents died four years later. At hotel bars around the world, he would often snarl between clenched teeth the words written on the Galway Coat of Arms, *Ceart agus Cóir* (Righteousness and Justice) before hurling his glass to the floor. He would then launch forth into a tirade about the absence of justice in the world, stating that the Coat of Arms should read Lawlessness and Injustice. These were frequently called out in Irish. He was a native Irish speaker having been brought up in the Gaeltacht Irish-speaking region.

Paddy, a huge, unruly, frequently bearded, sometimes with only a moustache, never bare cheeked, was an especially foul-mouthed man when under the influence of drink; but was also a charismatic, smooth-tongued, rascal if ever there was one. He had brawled around the North Sea coastline, S.E. Asia and Latin America for many decades, brawls never started by him of course. There were rumours of a marriage to a Malaysian and a son Tin or Tim, but as far as I was concerned, they were simply rumours, as I could not envisage Paddy ever getting hitched. He had a habit of launching into Irish songs at the drop of the proverbial hat. If I ever again hear, 'If you ever go across the sea to Ireland......and watch the sun go down on Galway Bay,' I'll, I'll, … I don't know what I'd do, but there's fat chance of that now.

The late 70s was not a good time to be in Nicaragua. A civil war had broken out and Marxist (Sandinista de Liberación Nacional; FSLN) guerrillas of Daniel Ortega Saavedra in 1979 overthrew the National Guard of the Anastasio Somoza Garcia family who had ruled the country for some 40 years and treated it as their personal fiefdom. The FLSN formed in 1962 as a socialist group was dedicated to the overthrow of the Samoza family and they united other political parties to form one cohesive group of about 5,000 fighters. It was a similar story to that of FARC in Colombia. However, fears were rife in Nicaragua that the US would soon be backing anti-Sandinista contra guerrillas along the Honduras border and the situation was extremely fluid. To add to the confusion, the capital Managua had suffered a massive earthquake in 1972 that killed more than 10,000 people and the town still looked like a disaster area over 10 years later. This situation was unfortunately all too common in Latin American countries, where ideological loyalties can be bafflingly fractured.

This was where Paddy now found himself after returning to the country years after his initial claim to fame. He soon moved out of the capital, ending up on the English speaking east coast, drinking heavily in a Bluefields bar after a frustrating four-week reconnaissance of some exposed strata in the barren hills of central Nicaragua. He had been turned down for positions in the Bonanza and Libertad gold mines because of his unstable behaviour, had gone prospecting on his own and found nothing. On his return, he was in a surly state of mind, as well as being short of money. That mean disposition of his together with alcoholic drink and he had drunk many of the local Flor de Cana, made a bar room affray inevitable.

The inevitable did happen and bruised, bloodied and battered he ended up in jail. He was thrown into a cell filled mainly by locals, all of whom were the worse for wear. When he came round, it was there that he encountered Zafar El Arab, an Italian originally called

Rio Alebar, who in London had decided to renounce the western way of life and become an Arab. Paddy, cheek by jowl with him and after emitting a groan and an oath, was surprised to hear an English voice asking how he was feeling.

'Bloody lousy,' came the reply and a friendship of a sort started, even though he had an inbuilt dislike of Italians as a result of his mother's disappearance.

*   *   *   *

José was a short, wiry man, olive-skinned with a thin moustache who wore tinted rimless glasses. He spoke excellent English and I wondered what his background was. He must have read my thoughts.

'Hola Adam. El Comandante has told me all about you. Sonnel, you and I all seem to have a common UK university background. I studied medicine at Oxford University, although that was some time ago. I think that this might be a big surprise for you.'

With that he rolled up his sleeve and we saw the twin serpent caduceus of Hermes tattooed on a surprisingly muscular forearm. He allowed himself a grin.

'Getting this symbol was more expensive than the single snake associated with Asclepius, but was worth it. I did consider having a barber's pole as well, but it didn't go well with the snakes. From saving the lives of people to taking them is a rather large change, but one that is necessary under today's conditions.'

'When does the surgeon's scalpel become the butcher's knife?' was my comment.

'The end justifies the means,' was the instant reply.

I shook his hand and again the thought that went through my mind was how educated people could have the mental and physical stamina to become guerrilla fighters for many years in the

Colombian jungle's steamy heat and humidity that regularly brought rashes out on my groin.

José turned to us.

'I have been ordered to accompany you to one of our main camps and to show you how FARC is run. Do you have any idea as to what we are and what we do?'

Sonnel and I were well aware that FARC, unofficially formed in May 1964 in the Marquetalia municipality, initially took their lead from Cuba and that Hugo Chavez from Venezuela had given them a lot of help.

Sonnel nodded.

'We know a bit about FARC, who couldn't if you lived in Colombia? Everyone knows about your early history. We know that originally it was based as a small peasant agricultural commune distinct from the massive amounts of land owned by elite landowners. The latter took offence to this commune and its short-lived existence was brutally suppressed because their communist views espousing the ideology of Marx and Lenin were deemed a threat to the landed gentry. The army was sent in to sort out matters and as they say, the rest is history. As a result, FARC, consisting of less than 50 fighters, was officially formed in 1966 and considered themselves to be the military unit of the Colombian Communist Party.'

José listened quietly to Sonnel.

'Ok, a very good synopsis now let me tell you something about our current movement. We exist as a surrogate family with a collective spirit and have grown, believe you me and now are all-powerful in huge areas of the Pacific coast and Amazon region of my country.'

I nodded agreement at this point. All mining companies pay money to FARC. Without their support, Frontino would never have ventured into this region, as it was far too dangerous. I was under 100% FARC protection and had always felt very safe because of this. I was paid extra as well. 'Taking prisoners,' as FARC called it, i.e. blatant kidnapping, in the time I was there, was very popular and some 10,000 people had been taken and held to ransom. They tended to target lighter-skinned people deeming these to be richer than the average population and foreigners were particularly prized. Several had been taken and ransomed for many millions of dollars. FARC stated that this was a way of obtaining money to pay for hospitals, schools, etc. in the areas they controlled, but it was common knowledge that a lot went to individual commanders.

José resumed his talk.

'Any comments?'

Both of us shook our heads.

'There have been several attempts on disrupting our organisation under the new US funded 'Operation Condor' plan. It will be hard for you to understand the schemings that go on behind closed political doors, but they are particularly prevalent in all Latin American countries. Argentina, Chile, Brasil, Paraguay, Bolivia and Uruguay are the key countries concerned in the operation, right-wing dictatorships backed by the muscle of the USA, essentially the CIA. They call it a cooperative effort by the intelligence/security services of several South American countries to combat terrorism and subversion. In reality, the aim is to assassinate opponents of these right-wing governments. It is repression and rule by terror. Guerrilla organisations are used as their excuse to murder government opponents. They want to suppress, no eradicate any communist ideals from countries so that neoliberal economic policies can be maintained to the satisfaction of both parties.'

Again he glanced at us.

Not surprisingly neither of us had heard of such a plan. We smiled to encourage him to continue.

'El Comandante himself was targeted to be assassinated. It happened some two years ago. A team of US Special Forces under the command of Col. Bob Lear tracked him through the jungle to near where Camp Diamante exists today. Then there was little of note to be seen, just a few tents. Luckily we also have excellent soldiers and the Americans were spotted long before they approached the camp. We tracked them and caught most of the group when they set up a standby base near our camp. They confessed,' he grimaced at this point, 'that the aim was to capture him, but we knew exactly what capture meant.'

He spat on the ground at this point.

'I've just mentioned 'Plan Colombia,' and this worries FARC a lot. It is as stated, an organisation set up to eliminate left-wing Latin American movements. These people are concerned that FARC might take control of Colombia and moves are afoot to send troops from the US and no doubt other countries to fight against us. Politically, it will be sold as a war on drugs, but the reality is very different. If it happens, then we have some heavy battles ahead of us my friends. US technology of GPS and laser-controlled bombing could make life very difficult for us, as currently the government's 50 lb. bombs are dispersed very inaccurately. The US also has heat scanners, which means we would have to be scattered into groups of less than 25 people, as this is the minimum number they need to pick up body heat signals. However, this does not concern you two.'

Bowing his head at this point, he simply stared at the ground lost in his thoughts. I felt a wave of sympathy for him. He was a man on a mission.

'I think I've said too much, so I'll shut up.'

He reached over, poured out coffee from the jug and took a sip.

'Well, Sonnel, what's the decision?'

'I'm in,' was the reply followed by handshakes all round. 'What's next?'

We sat silently for a minute or two to let all he had said sink into our heads. Sonnel broke the silence.

'Ok. Now, how about getting packed, have an early siesta and then lunch? José, you've been driving for many hours and must be very tired.'

We duly trotted off to our respective rooms. I threw myself on the ubiquitous hammock that exists in every room and within seconds fell asleep.

I awoke to the sound of many people singing and shouting, 'Hola.'

Sonnel had roused the hotel staff to gather outside my room at 1 pm in an attempt to sing like a choir of Hebrew slaves from the opera Nabucco. I rose, showered, dressed and went downstairs.

The two of them were sitting at a table drinking beer and nibbling on cheese, *aborrajados, chicharroncitos, yuquitas* and chomping on fried chicken and bread washed down by a few Aguila brand beers.

As I entered, Sonnel looked up and asked the question we were both curious about.

'José, you've talked a lot about El Comandante. Who is he?'

He looked at us with a surprised look on his face.

'Who are your heroes?'

I replied, 'I have an eclectic mix, Fitzroy Maclean, Paddy Leigh Fermor…oh many.'

Sonnel stated, 'Gabriel Garcia Márquez, Pablo Neruda, Fidel Castro.'

He glanced up. His next comment startled both of us.

'My El Comandante is Rue Kosyan. When studying in Russia, he came across a Russian commander of that name who became his hero. We all have our heroes and Rue Kosyan was his. He is the man you call Rod.'

*   *   *   *

Pablo Escobar abruptly put down the phone and paced along the lounge floor, smacking his clenched right fist into his left-hand palm. Lucky, who was about to enter the lounge, observed the pacing and hitting and made an about-turn. When Escobar was in this mood, he knew from experience that the wise move was to back off. The last time he had seen Escobar so animated was when he was waiting to hear if his ordered assassination of Justice Minister Rodrigo Lara and Presidential candidate Luis Carlos Galán had succeeded. Standing as a member of the Liberal Renewal Movement who supported Galán, his attempt to become a member of the Chamber of Representatives of Colombia had been blocked by Galán himself and this made him a sworn enemy.

Left-wing guerrillas of the M-19 movement financed by Escobar had stormed the Supreme Court building because the Court was considering an extradition treaty with the US for *Los Extraditables*, i.e. the cocaine cartels. Hostages had been taken and a series of bombings in public places had been too much for Lara to accept, so he had made it his mission to prosecute Escobar. A wrong move as Lara and Galán paid for it with their lives and the treaty failed.

Ordering the deaths of people such as the Head of the Anti-Narcotics Unit of the Colombian Government, dozens of judges and more than 500 policemen meant nothing to Escobar, but Lara and Galán had got under his skin and he wanted both dead, very dead.

Moving to the large kitchen area, he poured out a cup of coffee and stood reflectively beside the large plate glass window and looked out over the immaculate lawn. The question running through his mind was who amongst his many enemies had ordered the hit on his sisters. It pushed the good thoughts of the imminent demise of Juan Bautista right to the back of his mind.

'Tienen que ser los hermanos Orejuela del cartel de Cali.' ('It must be the Orejuela brothers of the Cali syndicate.')

This was exclaimed through clenched teeth. 'It has to be the cartel.'

The Cali cartel's origins were in kidnapping. Herman Buff, a Swiss diplomat was one such person when the cartel were called *Las Chemas* and led by Luis Fernando Tamayo García. However, the lure of drugs proved to be irresistible and this meant not only a name change, but a whole new outlook on ways of generating vast amounts of money and laundering it. Gilbert Orejuela was Chairman of the Board of Banco de Trabajadores, as well as having set up the First InterAmerican Bank in Panama. This not only enabled deposits of vast cash payments to be made with no questions asked, but also the taking of loans with no repayments ever being recorded in the books.

Over several years Escobar had many confrontations with the Cali syndicate board, nicknamed the *Los Caballeros de Cali* (Gentlemen of Cali), which consisted of the Orejuela brothers, Gilbert ('El Ajedrecista,' The Chess Player) and Miguel ('El Señor,' The Lord) and their cartel partner 'Chepe' Santacruz ('El Estudiante,' the Student). They had even financed a clandestine operation to kill Escobar hiring ex-Special Forces soldier mercenaries to fly in via a Huey helicopter painted in police colours. The helicopter had crashed killing the pilot and the troops had to escape to safety through the dense mountainous rain forest of Colombia.

It was when Pancho Hélmer Herrera Buitrago, an ex-motor mechanic joined the cartel executive board that an escalation in violence occurred. Before his joining, the Cali cartel had preferred to trade mainly in marijuana and persuasion was via the simple threat of violence. Although shying from any act of violence himself, Herrera loved ordering it and his arrival had upped the ante. The Board were very happy with him and gave him control of the drug trade for the cities of Yumbo, Jamundi and Palmira.

Escobar mused for several moments. He could hit back at their offspring and one Jorge Alberto Rodriguez, the son of Gilberto Orejuela, sprang to mind. He knew that he and Herrera were in the US right now. Jorge was in charge of the numerous cocaine distribution cells that existed in many US cities, all acting independently of each other. Each city dealt solely with Jorge and he was the sole link back to Colombia.

'No', he jumped up, thumped his fists together and shouted out loud. 'It has to be that homosexual bastard Pancho Herrera.'

No love existed between these two men and Escobar loathed homosexuals. Herrera had been instrumental in a recent bomb blast that had demolished Escobar's new Monica apartment block in the El Poblado neighbourhood. He had also formed a group called *Los Pepes,* which along with the government had but one intention and that was the killing or capturing of Escobar. This was typical of the loose arrangement that existed between all groups in Colombia, factions changed sides with comparative ease. In return, Escobar had hired 20 assassins clothed in Police and Army uniforms to attend a football game at Candelaria where Herrera was going to be present. They shot 19 people but missed Herrera.

Escobar's uneasy relationship with the Cali cartel was currently relatively peaceful even though recently he had financed the M-19 group to kidnap Marta Ochoa, the sister of the Orejuela brothers, asking for a $20 million ransom. This had been rejected and as a result many M-19 members had been abducted, tortured and killed. Escobar found himself in a difficult situation but eventually decided that his best strategy was to ally himself with the Cali cartel and after three days she was released unharmed. His decision came after a prolonged meeting when the Medellin and Cali cartels joined forces, somewhat ironically as kidnapping was typical of both parties, to form the *Muerte a Los Secuestradores* (Death to Kidnappers or MAS).

Escobar's mind could multi-task efficiently. He would deal with Herrera on his return, so his thoughts now switched to Bautista. He would be in Colombia within the next week and later would be time enough to think of him. Adriana and María were his main concern. He had made the decision almost as soon as he had received Adriana's phone call.

Picking up the phone, the Verona number was dialled.

*   *   *   *

The next morning, Sir George relaxed in the old vintage style bath complete with brass pipes and faucets. It reminded him of the bathroom at the Pen Y Gwyrd hotel at the foot of Snowdon, known to mountaineers everywhere. Whenever he was there, he used to vigorously soap himself and reminisce on the fact that Ed Hilary and Sherpa Tensing Norgay had lain in that very same bathtub.

He rose and dried himself, again grateful that the air conditioning was still running. His dress was shorts, a cotton shirt plus cotton jacket that had numerous baggy pockets and large buttons, socks, a pair of stout boots and a Panama hat.

'I look like Jungle Jim in this outfit. If only Johnny Weissmuller could see me now.' He realised that this reference to THE Tarzan in his eyes would only be understood by a greying, ageing, western population, but so what!

He continued looking at his reflection and tried to visualise the same man over 30 years previously. He sadly shook his head. 'Did I once wear the winged dagger beret,' were the softly spoken words? 'I have gone to seed.'

Exiting his room, he made his way to the small dining room.

'Nine o clock prompt,' exclaimed the Rector. 'Bravo, as today we are only going to Cartagena. You look set for the jungle. I've asked Prof Juan Gallego to join us. He should be here any moment.'

As he spoke the door opened and in walked the Professor.

'Hola. Buenos dias.' The Rector and Sir George both rose from the table and shook hands.

'I don't think an introduction is necessary. After all, Juan Gallego was at your lecture last night.'

Sir George grinned. 'And what did an archaeologist think of a chemistry lecture albeit one geared to a generally well-educated audience?'

'Stunning is the only word that I can come up with and as a lefthander myself, a 'coochy paw' is I believe an expression that you use. I associate left-handedness with intelligence, out-of-the-box thinking and artistic talent. God must be a leftie.'

A big grin crossed the face of Sir George.

'In that case, let's eat this stunning breakfast.'

Coffee was poured and plates of eggs – a choice of fried, poached or boiled and toast was divided up.

Gallego picked up two boiled eggs.

'These have a very high ooporphyrin content,' was the remark.

'What?' exclaimed Sir George.

The Rector smiled. 'It refers to the pale brown pigments in eggshells of, for example, a hen. He had me on it last week that is why I know. Juan has an extraordinary way of learning English. Each day he opens a dictionary and learns a new word. Every two weeks he gets tested on them to see if he can remember what they mean. He is excellent and has even taught me what mellifluous and eleemosynary mean.'

'Let's get on with breakfast, as this highly educated conversation is a bit beyond my pay grade,' smiled Sir George. 'I'm a good trencherman.'

Both Colombians looked at him.

'That's the new word for today.'

They all laughed and continued a light conversation while they ate breakfast. Afterwards, seated around a low table in comfortable chairs near to the massive window through which purple blossomed bougainvillaea gently wafting in the morning's light breeze, almost touched the glass. Gallego produced a sheaf of papers.

'Our itinerary. Today we drive down to Cartagena and stay the night at the Las Américas Casa de Playa hotel right on the beach. You know that it is a World Heritage city and it is lovely. The drive down is mainly along the coast passing long linear sand beaches. I feel like a tour guide explaining all this to you, but it might help.' He smiled. 'Unfortunately, there is a large erosion issue with this coastline and one of the most famous hotspots during the last 20 years is the 18-21 km sector of the main road between Barranquilla and Santa Marta where massive erosion rates of as much as 20 metres per year have been recorded. Erosion is largely human-induced. Damming of rivers, for example, has stopped coarse-grained sediments from reaching the coast to form our beaches; fine-grained ones do and these badly affect our coral reefs. Our government's coastal hard protection measures to combat erosion, using breakwaters, groins and gabions have been in reality a disaster. You will see all these at Cartagena, a colonial city of about a million people.'

He paused and drank some coffee.

'Its founding was in 1533 by 200 sailors from Cartagena, Spain, who called it Cartagena de Indias, but the city was built on an older village called Calamari.' He smiled. 'You might know this delicious dish. We'll have some tonight at a little place I know called Calamar Cevicheria. After 20 years a fire destroyed all wooden buildings and this was the start of the stone buildings in what we call the Old Town, as distinct from the modern skyscraper one. So you have two adjacent towns. You have castles, a cathedral and gold museums, you name it and it's here.'

He put the papers down.

'Next day, we go to Bucaramanga, a city set deep between mountain ranges with snow-capped peaks and this is my favourite place. En route, I'll take you to Morrorico where there is a superb view of the city plus a statue of the Sacred Heart. We will stay at the Hotel Plazuela where the university has a favourable discount from the management. The city is in the northeast part of the Andes mountain range, located on the La Ribera del Oro and is justly called the City of Parks (*La Ciudad de Los Parques*). We will pass plantations of pineapple, tobacco, corn and some coca. I'm sure you will want to see the latter, it is the basis of cocaine.'

He beamed. 'I want to show you Giron an old colonial gold mining village with historic architecture where we have unearthed some interesting findings from that era. Knowing of your varied interests,' he turned to Sir George, 'I hope you will enjoy this part of your Colombian itinerary?'

'I'm looking forward to it immensely,' was the prompt reply, but his thoughts were elsewhere.

'We could, of course, fly to Palonegro International Airport, but alas we will travel in my old Jeep and I must warn you that Jeep travel is not deluxe, but you'll see much of our country.'

'A minor point,' was the reply and as he uttered these words, his mind focused on the future. He knew that the present was going to be by far the best part of his visit. What was going to happen post the trip was in the lap of the gods. With that, he made his excuses and left the room after agreeing that a 10 am departure was in order.

Arriving at his room, he made a quick phone call.

4.

Paddy and Zafar sat outside the small courthouse. Bleary-eyed and with a splitting headache, Paddy eyed his cellmate of the previous night. The high morning temperature and humidity were making him sweat profusely and dehydrated as he was, this did not help with his headache or temper. The only thing he was grateful for was that English was widely spoken in this, the North Caribbean Coast Autonomous Region (Región Autónoma de la Costa Caribe Norte; commonly called RACCN) part of Nicaragua, one of the two autonomous regions in the country.

'Well thank god that's over, as I wouldn't want to spend another night in that rat hole of a jail.'

He tried to spit on the ground but had no saliva to do so.

'So Zafar my lad, they decided that we are partners and have taken my truck as payment for the fines plus expenses involved and ordered us to leave the country within 24 hours. We are deemed to be undesirable characters. Bloody hell, before jail last night I'd never met you in my life. Talking of jail, I now know why they call the local tribe Moskito and this place the Mosquito Coast. Last night I was eaten alive.'

He looked at the red blotches on his arms and glanced at Zafar.

'I've seen your face. If mine's anything like yours, god help us.'

He suddenly bent forward and retched. Nothing came up.

Zafar looked at his companion.

'Look, there's a fountain across the street. Let's freshen up there.'

They got up and walked across the dusty road to sit on the fountain's rim. Splashing water over their bodies and faces helped a lot and Paddy drank greedily. Zafar looked longingly at the water.

'If we jumped in now, it'd be straight back to jail,' was the comment.

'No way to that and my head is splitting,' groaned Paddy. 'All I recall was dancing last night to that erotic Palo de Maya music.' He guffawed. 'Ok trying to dance, when this bloke came up and hit me. I didn't start the fight, so why was I slung in jail? It's bloody unfair.'

'You weren't trying to dance,' was the reply, 'you were trying to undress her in the middle of the dance floor and she didn't like it and slapped your face. The bouncer came over, tried to reason with you and you hit him. A bad move that, as you would agree if you could see your face. Shall I say that irrespective of mosquitoes, it's rather bruised? That's what happened. All hell was let loose during your fight. You are a big strong man and the bouncer was laid out, but not before you had taken many punches. Others joined in, the place was smashed; chairs were flung around, the bar was wrecked and bottles were flying everywhere. It was absolute mayhem. Police came in and we got arrested. I was the innocent bystander who ended up in jail because of you. We were the only foreigners in the club and funnily enough the only two people arrested. That's why they took your truck as payment.'

Nothing much was said for a minute or two.

Zafar continued. 'I must thank you though, as in our cell were two others and they attacked me, held me down and had taken my trousers off ready to rape me. The noise woke you up; you saw what was happening and laid into them. I was so glad that you were there and can't thank you enough.'

'My god, did I? All this is a blur. I remember nothing.'

'There's a street food vendor over there,' Zafar pointed to the left, 'let's get some *Gallo pinto* (beans, rice and grated coconut) then we can have the national dish of *quesillo* (tortilla and soft cheese) with *tajadas* (deep-fried plantain). We'll feel better with food in our bellies.'

Paddy reached under his shirt and found his money belt, which included his passport. I found out later that this was invariably almost glued to his waist. I think he even slept with it.

'Thank god I still have this.'

The two walked across the dusty street, bought the food and lemonade and sat down under the shade of a jacaranda tree.

'Well Zafar my boyo, we have to leave this place or else....' He grinned. 'I for one won't be sorry to get out of this damn country. The gold panning was pretty hopeless and it certainly wasn't a bonanza for me. I think we head for San Pedro airport and out. You game for it?'

'Of course, but where to? I have a proposition to put to you.'

'Carry on. I'm all ears.'

'In the courthouse, I heard that you were a mining prospector looking for gold. Is that right?'

'I guess so and a pretty useless one. I've been looking for minerals all my life. I made it big once at the La Libertad mine, but screwed it up though I still have hope.'

'Excuse me a minute, I won't be long,' said Zafar and walked across to a café two doors away.

Several minutes later he returned with his right hand behind his back.

'Open your hand.'

Paddy did as requested and Zafar placed his right hand over that large horny hand. Into it was dropped a green object.

'What do you think of that?'

Paddy squinted and held it up to his eye.

'Bloody hell, It's a fine dark green emerald. I can just envisage the hot mix of the scarce elements of beryllium, vanadium and chromium turning it into this beauty. If I recall rightly, Periodic Table numbers 4, 23 and 24, respectively. I just love those numbers and this stone. Absolutely beautiful. I can picture these elements oozing through rock cracks and crystallising out to form gorgeous emerald crystals. It's a lovely stone with a great hue, deep tonal colour, eye clean, strong saturation. I'd say investment grade. It's damn good. Where did you get it?'

Zafar grinned. 'Those two men would have had a shock if they had sexually assaulted me last night, as to answer your question this is where it has just come from.' He laughed and patted his butt. 'I keep it there in a charger. But to answer your question, I found it by pure accident in a stream about 100 km southeast of Boyacá, near Chivor in the Colombian eastern Andean ranges. Unfortunately, I did not find any others. I went there on a long holiday after recently coming into some unexpected money. I always had an interest in geology so went to do a little prospecting expecting to find absolutely nothing. I found this. Then I came to Nicaragua, as I was told there were better prospects. Alas, I found nothing here. This is my nest egg for when things get hazy.'

Paddy drew a deep breath. 'You were given bad advice my friend. There is gold here but emeralds are not very much in evidence. You should have stayed in Colombia or gone to Brasil. These are the main countries in the world for emeralds. However, finding high grade emeralds in streams is like playing for high stakes at a Las Vegas casino. One lucky roll and you can be very rich indeed, though usually one does not get that luck.'

Zafar took back the stone. 'I realise that now. My idea was when back in Europe I'd sell it. But you, with your experience, if you would just agree, we could go to where I found this and maybe get more. You would know where to look for the mother lode. I believe it's termed that. This could provide our stake money.'

'Zafar, it looks like we're partners. Bogotá, here we come.'

*   *   *   *

The next morning, the august academic trio assembled for an 8.30 am breakfast. Sir George was the last to enter the dining room. The other two were drinking coffee, their breakfast plates shoved to one side.

Prof Juan Gallego motioned Sir George to the seat next to him.

'Before you sit down, the Rector has to leave now, so say your adios,' he smiled. 'Me, I'm going to have another coffee, it's so good,' as he sipped another mouthful. 'It's the best in the world.'

'I have a bus to catch back to the University,' was the cheerful comment by the Rector, 'and I can see by the expression on your face that this is something Vice-Chancellors of Oxbridge would not do. We are much more egalitarian out here plus the journey is pleasant and I can do some reading of reports, usually asking for more Departmental money. I enjoy the ride. It relaxes me.'

He held out his hand. 'Anyway George, I hope you enjoy your stay in Bucaramanga. I've enjoyed meeting you again. As always it is a pleasure to host you. I look forward to seeing you again on your return from the 600 km journey.'

Sir George took his hand and said similar things, although, in his heart, he knew he probably would not be seeing this good man again. As the Rector left, into his mind occurred a phrase made famous by George Orwell, 'in times of universal deceit, telling the truth is a revolutionary act.' I am in a country where revolution seemingly is the norm and telling the truth cannot be said, flashed through his mind.

Gallego and Sir George finished breakfast and spent a leisurely time packing their respective cases. As they set off in the old battered Jeep, after travelling a short distance Sir George happened to mention that the going was slightly bumpy.

'You wait,' said a grinning Juan, 'then you'll feel the bumps. This is nothing.'

The start of the drive was again along the coast and soon the high-rise buildings became scarcer, as did roundabouts and the further they went, the more scattered became villages and houses until a rural landscape became the norm. After stopping at km 18-21, they passed a large sculpture of a whale.

'Juan, please stop. What's that?' His fingers pointed at the whale. 'Why here?'

'Whale fishing was once popular around here, but now is no more. It's just a sentimental structure for a bye-gone age.'

Sir George's thoughts roamed back to recordings he had heard of the low vibrations produced by whales. The mammals live their entire lives surrounded by water that supports their vast bulk. The noise they emit can travel hundreds of miles underwater and be heard and recognised by other whales. Moving slowly and with refined grace, they can dive to depths of over one km pre surfacing where they blow out a spout of foul-smelling breath and take in a lung full of air. In all his travels, he had never seen a whale and made a mental note to rectify this matter. 'If I come out of this alive,' was his added thought.

Arriving at Cartagena, Sir George loved the beach side hotel and the meal at the Calamar Cevicheria lived up to expectations. He slept in the big double bed and dreamed of Glenys, his fiancée.

The next morning, they had a leisurely breakfast and swinging inland, the journey alternating between scrub jungle and savanna and the bumps became bigger. Juan had to slow down many times as Sir George was unused to Jeep riding. Too much time spent in laboratories and meeting room chairs had softened him up. However, nature's scenery never ceased to please him and he remarked to Juan.

'Nature is exhausting my dear chap because it has a raw beauty that keeps changing its face throughout day and night and yet it keeps smashing you in the face with that beauty. I love nature in the raw.'

Juan did not even think of replying, he just concentrated on the road that was becoming more rutted by the hour. It was late afternoon when they reached Bucaramanga. Before going to the Hotel Plazuela, Juan insisted on taking Sir George to look at the Giron excavations they had made in the old gold mining settlement.

'We can do Morrorico in the morning so let me show you this?'

They spent a half-hour looking at the ruins and Sir George was moved but made no comment. 'You could turn this into an old western town and sub-let it to the movie makers. If Spain can make spaghetti westerns, then so can Colombia.'

Juan chortled. 'Ah but this is just the *hors d'oeuvre*,' was the reply, 'because tomorrow we will go some 100 km to see the real excavation that we have been keeping under wraps. It's a rare example of the 200 BCE-400 CE Calima culture. This is very new and exciting, as it was a highly stratified culture. I am tremendously enthusiastic about this dig. We have obtained many red and black ceramics signifying a religious context, as well as some gold brooches and necklaces. It has the potential to become one of the most important sites in Colombia.'

He paused.

'Now for the hotel and dinner. I especially want to treat you to a meal of *Santander-mute, Hormiga Culona* and *fricassee.*'

'And what culinary delights might these be?'

'Well I believe in English, the former is a soup made up of grains and different meats; followed by what is colloquially called Big Ass Ants, which are rich in protein while the last one is made up of viscera and goat's blood to be served with white rice. It all dates from the pre-Hispanic era.'

'Charming, I can't wait,' was the dubious retort.

With that, they jumped back into the Jeep, or in Sir George's case, sat down in the seat very gingerly. At the hotel, he pleaded tiredness and wanted a rest pre-dinner, so went to his room and had a long soaking bath. Post this he laid on the bed and thankfully skipped the planned dinner. He slept the night through just like a newly born baby and was very glad that he had missed dinner.

Waking up in the early morning, he glanced out of the window and saw the majestic peaks of the Oriental Mountain range rising from the plateau. The air was clear and he breathed in deeply. After showering and dressing, going down the ornate staircase he saw

Juan munching on what he later discovered was a type of fudge made from puréed fruit or pressed caramel, termed *bocadillo veleño*.

'Just the job before coffee and breakfast.'

'I apologise for missing the meal last night,' said Sir George. 'I was shattered and my old bones felt as if they were disjointed.'

'No problem, they can warm the meal up for you if you wish?'

'That will not be necessary,' came the prompt reply. 'Coffee, eggs and toast will be fine. I don't eat much for breakfast and anyway, at this altitude, I'm not very hungry.'

Breakfast was ordered and served. Juan produced a map on which he had plotted their movements with a red pencil. Pointing to the map, he added. 'Morrorico and then we head west and can swing round to look at the Oro River canyon, that's if you want to. There's a spectacular overview of it at this tourist spot.' His finger pointed this out on the map.

'From here we go some 10 km southwards and turn off here onto an old mule trail.' Another point was indicated. 'Then we travel to the dig, which is not marked on the map, but it's about here.' The finger rested on a blank spot on the map adjacent to the mule track.

Sir George paid particular attention to these details and asked a few pertinent questions. He decided that after all he was hungry. An extra plate of eggs and toast was ordered all washed down with that great coffee.

'Right, leave in about 30 minutes,' said Juan. 'I'll go to get some provisions for the journey. I suppose you'd like some beer?' was said with a grin.

'Absolutely.'

Going up to his room, Sir George made a quick phone call; the gist of it referred to a mule track junction some 10 km south of the scenic overlook. He packed, went downstairs to wait and ordered another coffee.

*   *   *   *

Daler Hanoz paused on the top step of the Lear jet that had flown him, Adriana and María to the small airport at Medellin. Two days had passed since the phone call had been received to come to Colombia. However, he did manage to see Aida. They had gone to the airport, checked in and en route to the private lounge, Hanoz accidentally bumped into a couple who were exiting. A briefcase had fallen spilling its contents to the floor and a takeaway coffee he had been carrying splashed coffee on the woman's dress. Apologies, cash for dry cleaning and business cards were exchanged. Much later, I had a letter from Hanoz, in which he stated that the person was called Markham and their paths had recently crossed in Ireland, an amazing coincidence.

The sun blazed down from the morning's cloudless sky and he quickly put on his new sunglasses. As he did so, Kate's image came flooding into his mind. The airstrip was small and only one other small plane could be seen. A makeshift shed constituted the arrival area and baggage personnel were already unloading the voluminous amount of luggage that Adriana and María had accumulated. All he carried was hand luggage, which included a copy of Vasari's classic book, 'Lives of the Artists'.

Below him was Adriana and at the foot of the steps, María was ensconced in the arms of a stubby, black-haired, moustached man. Hanoz knew that this must be the infamous Pablo Escobar. He also noticed a nearby carload of hard, mean-looking men who he guessed were Escobar's security squad. They tried to stay quietly in the background, although there was no background. It was simply a large field and three Mercedes cars were grouped around the plane and the five black-suited men rather stood out. No one else was within 100 m of the plane.

The phone call from Escobar to Adriana had been brief. Come back to Colombia immediately and bring Mr Hanoz with you if possible because he wanted to thank him in person. Hanoz liked the idea of going to Latin America, as he had never been there. Apart from seeing some old friends in Italy, he had nothing planned for the near future and was glad to accept the invite. He was also curious to meet Escobar because he had heard and read a lot about the drug king.

He went down the steps slowly. Escobar saw him coming and immediately swept María aside, give a quick kiss to Adriana and gave him a big bear hug followed by two pecks on each cheek.

'No tengo palabras para darte las gracias,' ('I cannot find enough words to thank you.')

Hanoz grinned. 'I do not speak Spanish, but can guess what you are saying.' he stopped and added, 'What I did was something that any red-blooded man would do, or I hope he would.'

Escobar nodded and turned to hug Adriana simultaneously gesturing to one of the large Mercedes cars. It slowly rolled towards them.

'Where are the Immigration and Customs?' asked Hanoz. Everyone standing around the car grinned.

'You're looking at them,' remarked a smiling Escobar in English while pulling out a cigar case from his inner pocket. 'Welcome to Colombia Mr Hanoz and in particular to Medellin. Please,' he gestured, 'let's get into the car and we can all go home. I'm sure that all of you are tired after a long journey, although the plane is very comfortable, but nothing beats arriving at Hacienda Nápoles and having a welcome drink.'

With that, they all scrambled into the luxurious black sedan and conversation was stilled until they arrived at the mansion. Hanoz was amazed at the lush rolling lawns, the river, ponds and vistas of the rolling verdant hills covered in tropical vegetation. In the early morning with the sun casting shadows over the whole scene, it did look like a magical Hollywood setting. His eyes narrowed.

'There's something in that river that looks like a hippo, but it can't be, so what's it?' he asked.

'Hippopotami,' squealed Adriana rocking back and fore in delight. 'There are four hippopotami there. I love them all as they are so ugly, huge with stubby little legs and yet so beautiful. Did you know that they can stay underwater for about 5 minutes?' She clapped her hands in pure delight.

'I bought them in New Orleans,' said Escobar. 'I just liked the look of them.'

The car drew up at the main door, which opened suddenly.

'Ah Lucky, please help us with the luggage?'

'Certainly *El Padri*,' said Lucky.

'Welcome back Adriana and you too María.' Lucky helped them out of the car and turned to face Hanoz.

'I'm Lucky.' He held out his hand.

Hanoz shook it.

'Hopefully, by name and nature. I'm Daler Hanoz, from Turkey.'

Lucky smiled. 'I know all about you. Pablo told me all about what happened in Verona.'

'Grab the luggage and let's get inside after which Lucky will get you a drink, as you all must be thirsty,' came from Escobar and he led the way indoors.

'No we'll just go up to our rooms,' came from Adriana. 'We'll see you both later in the afternoon.' They left.

'I'd love a beer,' said Hanoz.

Hanoz paused at the entrance and gazed around the large hall from which open doors allowed glimpses of a dining room, study, lounge and conservatory. All were large and furnished with exquisite taste. The front door itself was a work of art, a heavy oak frame into which a large stained glass window had been inserted. The glass was all squares and rectangles, composed of many shades of red, yellow and blue, arranged as if in a Mondrian painting. It was a sunburst of colour and Hanoz could not wait to close the door to see how sunlight brought out the beauty of the glass.

Many paintings covered the walls and he recognised several, but one, in particular, took his eye. He gave a start when he saw the, 'Nativity with St Francis and St Lawrence,' painted by Caravaggio.

He crossed the room and stood to gaze in awe at the painting.

Escobar joined him.

'You like it?'

'It's breath taking. The Bethlehem stable, the brown background enhancing the central figures of a naked Christ, the ox, a straw bed, the dress falling from the shoulder of the exhausted virgin, shepherds, an angel flying in with one arm holding a scroll with Gloria written on it, the other arm pointing to heaven. All this and the two saints, absolutely magnificent. The pure image clarity is amazing and the underpainting that breaks the line edges giving a definitive texture to the work. Marvellous. I love it. In fact, many years ago I made a private vow to see all of Caravaggio's paintings, as I am besotted by his work. Seeing all of course is impossible, as many are in very private collections,' he smiled, 'just like this one. I never thought I'd see this painting. I'll not ask how you obtained it.'

He grinned again flashing those white teeth that made him almost irresistible to women.

'I'm not one that is really interested in paintings,' said Escobar, 'but it has a certain degree of charm.'

Hanoz laughed.

'A certain degree of charm! Caravaggio is a most unusual and magnificent painter. I came across him when I first visited Rome,' he flashed a smile, 'I had a job to do.' He did not elaborate on the job but did on the visit.

'I was staying in a small guest house near the Piazza del Popolo besides the Porta Flaminia. One day I was sitting in the square drinking a cappuccino and noticed a stream of people going into a small dusky basilica called Santa María del Popolo sited at the edge of the Piazza. I followed them and saw that they all headed for an alcove at the far end of the nave. What I saw blew my mind and literally, the hairs rose at the back of my head. Two huge paintings extended almost from ceiling to floor. They bowled me over. Their titles were, 'The conversion of St Paul,' and 'The crucifixion of St Peter.'

He paused. 'The first painting has a big tan coloured horse, a palomino probably that dominates the scene. St Paul lies on the ground with outstretched arms encapsulating the animal's profile. The horse according to Caravaggio stood in God's light, while in the background an ostler gently holds its shaded head. The animal looked as if it had been returned to its stall dead tired after a hard day of toil. Caravaggio often depicts a violent scene with muscular executioners ripping open someone's body, but not in this painting. Here, Paul has an expression on his face of complete acceptance of God's will. The use of light, striking against dark corners is incredible. It is a masterpiece of darkness and light, incidentally this term is called *chiaroscuro,* giving a strong, bold contrast between light and dark colours, almost akin to 3D. His backgrounds are inevitably dark with a shaft of light coming from a corner like a theatre spotlight that illuminates the bodies he has painted.'

He paused again and took a sip of the beer that Lucky had brought him.

'The second again has a large yellow-tinged backside this time a man's, which almost hits you in the face. Incidentally, the material on his backside has the same colour, brushstrokes and lighting on it, as has St Lawrence's robe, who stands on the left-hand side of the painting in your, 'Nativity with St Francis and St Lawrence.' Three executioners lash to the cross, an already nailed, but a calm, introspective, serene-looking, upside down St Peter. To me, Peter embodied pure and utter desolation, the colours are even muted and it had intricately drawn dirty feet, fingernails bitten to the quick. Gestures are shown in the four arms of the people, especially the executioner hauling the cross upright from a rope stretched across

St Peter's back. No landscape is shown and blood does not gush forth from open wounds, only appearing in small streaks.'

He stopped for another second or two.

'This man was a genius even though he was in life a murderer. He killed Ranuccio Tomassoni in a duel in Rome and was an extremely troublesome person, one you stayed clear of. He had a foul temper and was always involved in brawls in the streets and taverns mainly in Rome, Naples and Malta. But what a painter.'

'Bored?'

'No, I'm not bored but fascinated. No one has explained paintings to me before.'

Hanoz continued.

'I then went to the Piazza Navona to the San Luigi dei Francesi church and saw a few more paintings such as, 'The calling of St Mathew.' Caravaggio had that rare ability to depict humble careworn street people coming out of the darkness and into light. He could put expressions on faces like no other painter. In the Uffizi gallery, Florence, is a painting called, Judith and Holofernes. It represents a scene from the Apocrypha, where Judith posed in sculptured serenity is cutting off the head of the Assyrian captain Holofernes, who had raped her. The model for Judith was Filide Melandroni and she appears in many of his paintings, as do many onlookers. They must have been close friends of his and therefore cheap models. Ready to catch the severed head is an old servant and she has a very superbly painted cruel look on her face. The red tent is a gushing torrent of red blood. It is simply magnificent.

He paused.

'The same scene has also been portrayed by a brilliant contemporary female artist, Artemisia Gentileschi, who lived in Rome, Florence and Naples and it is equally as powerful. When she was 12 years of age her mother died and she had to look after her three siblings. She married and had five children by her husband, but only one survived. She was in love not with her husband, but a noble Florentine citizen. In this painting Judith is not serene. Judith grips Holofernes by the hair and just saws away. It depicts two muscular women holding down the immense brutal Holofernes. One sees his raised fist as he attempts to hit her servant's head and the hand is almost as big as her face, a disturbing disproportion that hammers home the sheer physical power of the painting. Anguished faces, large eyes, strong noses, flushed cheeks, huge hands, bodies that rush at you out of the canvas, explosions of gushing arterial blood flood the sheet and spatters upwards. Yet Judith's stance appears as if she is giving birth to Holofernes. You'd love her work. Gentileschi had been raped by another artist, Agostino Tassi and was tortured during a public trial in order to verify the truth. What an appalling thing to have to undergo. Tassi was found guilty but escaped punishment because the Pope liked his paintings. What an injustice.'

He stopped. 'You've heard enough of my talking about two of my favourite painters. They are people I could talk about for hours on end.'

'On the contrary, there are one or two Picasso's, a couple of van Gogh's, a Goya and a Salvador Dali hanging in the lounge. Let's go in and in due course, please could you explain those to me? I've no idea as to what they represent.'

At that moment, Lucky approached pushing a trolley. He had noticed how Hanoz's effortless charisma had been absorbed by Escobar and immediately a stab of jealousy shot through his body. He felt threatened by this man. Much later Hanoz told me that he sensed that there was something strange concerning Lucky's behaviour to him. Envy, jealousy, he did not know what, but something bothered him about the man.

'Further drinks,' was said and two large bottles of Poker beer and two of Costeñita were offered along with small plates of *Tajadas, Yuquitas, Empanadas* and *Chicharroncito*s. The ubiquitous coffee was also present.

'I have also asked cook to serve you later with some *Bandeja paisa* and *Mote de queso*.'

'Lucky that's fine. I have some talking to do with Mr Hanoz and I think we might be some time.'

Turning to Hanoz, he said, 'after what you have done, may I call you Daler?'

'Of course, Pablo.'

Both grinned.

Escobar turned to Lucky, 'That will be all then Lucky. We'll see you later, as I want Daler to know how appreciative I am for what he has done for me.'

Lucky smiled, nodded and left the room.

Escobar gestured towards the open lounge door. 'Let's sit down. I want to talk with you. I only wish my family were here to meet you, but they are in Florida at the moment on holiday. Adriana and María were going to join them from Verona.'

They entered the lounge with Hanoz pushing the trolley and sank into two of the luxurious cane chairs that were dotted around the room. It had a magnificent vista of the grounds and Hanoz could not help but ask a question.

'Are my eyes deceiving me?' and he pointed to a rounded structure to the right of the lawn.

'Yes,' was the reply? 'It's indeed a bullring and we have occasional tournaments there. No bulls are here. I might think about it for the future, but, No. In reality, it would be very impractical. Bulls need space to roam and if you came across them on foot, you would be gored to death. I like to wander around my grounds. With them, one would always have to be on horseback.'

No comment came from Hanoz, but there was a quizzical look on his face and one raised eyebrow.

'I am amazed, hippos in the river and ponds and I believe we passed a zoo on the way in. I saw a giraffe's head sticking out over the stockade and I did see an elephant. Now I find a bullring. This is simply unbelievable.'

'You've not seen anything,' Escobar grinned. 'If you like to ice skate there is a rink here. My security people call me Frost because of that.'

The grin became even bigger. 'Remind me to show you the stables. We'll go for a walk there in a minute or two.'

Hanoz just looked at Escobar and changed the conversation saying, 'Tell me, who and what is Lucky? He sounds English.'

'He's a fascinating chap. He's been working here with me for a few years and is a useful chap to have around. He prefers to be known by that name, but we recently had a few drinks and he became maudlin. He told me that his real name is Richard John Bingham. He is Anglo-Irish and a British Lord, who was partial to gambling. He left Britain rather hurriedly in 1974 after some nasty business with a nanny for which he is suspected of murder. He is the 7th Earl of Lucan. He told me all this a few months ago.'

Escobar smiled. 'But I already knew all about that. You must realise Daler that knowledge is power these days. Just as I know you served with a Parachute battalion and then became a mercenary before joining MIT. But since then you have been a bit of a mystery.'

He took a sip of beer and looked expectantly at Hanoz.

The reply that came did not unsettle him in the least.

'I agree and that is why in my case I have a very small file on Pablo Escobar, courtesy of the internet in Verona. A Member of Parliament in 1982, the cocaine king of Medellin. It's probably not as detailed as yours. I do think having two submarines is rather over the top.'

He raised his glass. Escobar did the same and both men laughed.

5.

Colombia.

The trip down to Camp Diamante was hot, bumpy and dusty and we spent a night at each of the two subsidiary camps visited. On the drive not much talking was done and José seemed preoccupied with his thoughts. Most of the time Sonnel and I dozed or talked about FARC. We were in an area that changed at will from savanna to tropical rain forest. We would suddenly turn off the road and follow a rutted track until we reached a clearing. There, with a mass of tangled trees surrounding an open area could be found some two to four dozen men and women some lying in hammocks, others sitting around playing cards at homemade tables. The air was hot, humid and sultry, but I noticed that weapons were invariably close to hand. I hoped Camp Diamante would be better than this one. I shuddered at the thought of sleeping in these surroundings even with a mosquito net around me. The air throbbed with the latent promise of night time visitors buzzing in one's eardrums. Introductions about us were made to the soldiers and then they would loosely gather around José. He would give what I found out later to be the standard speech.

'Comrades in Arms, the Government of our country is extremely corrupt and we have to erase the current system whereby some 1% of the people enjoy an extremely rich life while 99% simply exist. We exist to overthrow this system. We tried to form a political party with the Union Patriótica, but this was wiped out by our Government's right-wing death squads, so we have no choice but to be guerrillas. The army has been carrying out *falsos positivos* where innocent people have been extra judicially killed by offering money, medals and even holidays for military units achieving high body counts. We have been told that soldiers killing six 'enemies' are eligible for bonuses of up to 20 million pesos. We are the largest and best guerrilla force in our beloved country and operate a parallel state which extends over more than a third of the country. You are well aware that Alvaro Uribe, ex-Mayor of Medellin and now a Senator has long had an all-out offensive against FARC and is angling for more aid from the US. To this end, there have been several attempts on disrupting our organisation, all underwritten by the US. The latest is their 'Operation Condor' plan, but we shall overcome these obstacles.'

He went on to explain the Condor plan and spoke passionately for another half an hour. In the end, he would be loudly cheered. At this first camp, eight diesel drums were unloaded from the trailer followed by arms and ammunition, followed by a meal and sleep in a hammock slung between two trees. The remaining arms were for the second camp, which was reached the next day after a drive of about six hours. At the camp we again had a simple meal; bread, beans and plantain washed down with water. The soldiers, this time about 60 in number and of both sexes, were all lean, mean and hungry-looking. All had that 1000 metre stare in their eyes that dedicated soldiers everywhere have. I knew several men who had served in the UK Parachute Regiment that had the same mean look.

I asked José as to what happened if pregnancy occurred in the love stakes. He replied that abortions were the order of the day, as the camps were no place for children. Contraception was mentioned at all camp meetings. His comment was that children would appear when the class struggle was won. As a doctor, he had carried out many abortions. He grinned as he remarked, 'Latin Americans and romance do go hand in hand. This class struggle had now been going on for many years and in my mind would go on for many more, so for some soldiers, children would indeed be a luxury.'

The next day we departed for Camp Diamante and passed through similar terrain as had been seen previously, i.e. rain forest and savanna. Arriving at the main camp, I was disappointed. In my mind's eye, I had envisaged a large area that resembled a parade ground, together with an imposing main tent for large meetings, latrines sited downwind, kitchen facilities upwind, perimeter guards etc. It was more like a scene from the film Fitzcarraldo and located in a much larger clearing with secondary jungle marking the camp perimeter. My impression was of a disparate collection of tattered tents and huts, soldiers still lolling around the base, but always with weapons kept close at hand. There were only about two dozen soldiers milling around. José enquired about Carlos Antonio Lozada, but as well as Rod, he had been called to western Catatumbo, along with most of the soldiers. They had finished dinner, which was *carimañolas, tripitas* and *pescado frito y arroz de coco* (basically tripe, fish and rice). Sonnel and I did not fancy any of it.

The organisation appeared to be very lax and it was noticeable that the soldiers had a sullen look on their faces, unlike their contemporaries at the other two camps. I sensed an uncertain atmosphere here and was not wrong.

After introducing us to the gathering, José disappeared to the kitchen area to talk with two other soldiers that I gathered were the senior officers left behind at the camp. Some dozen soldiers then gathered around Sonnel and me. Most had the typical Colombian build, slim and wiry and as tough as teak. One person stood out from the crowd. He was very tall, taller than me, heavily built, unruly bearded with deep inlaid and what looked like encrusted piglet eyes. His badly tattooed forearms bulged with muscle. Lunging towards me, he deliberately brushed heavily against my shoulder. I staggered backwards as a result of the unexpected lunge.

'Yo odio a los europeos y a los amerianos,' ('I hate Europeans and Americans,') was snorted from his thick-lipped mouth that exposed some missing teeth.

Sonnel turned towards him and interjected. 'Hey, I'm a Colombian. Why did you make that remark to my friend?'

The Brute, as that is what I'd mentally called him, swung round to face him.

'Shut your mouth, I'm talking to this dude,' was said in English and he pointed at me. I was intrigued by his usage of the term dude. I did note that there was a small TV screen in the camp. I had glimpsed it in a wooden hut that I was later told was the recreation area. He must have been an avid watcher of US films.

Sonnel was roused.

'Don't talk like that to me, especially using that tone of voice.'

With that, the Brute turned quickly and threw a punch at Sonnel that caught him plumb on the jaw. I swear his feet were lifted from the ground due to the force of the blow and he slumped to the floor with what looked like a broken jaw bone. He was unlucky in that the earth was uneven and many stones littered the area. His head hit one with a deafening thwack. This was followed by another, as a boot smashed into Sonnel's head, just above the ear the place that has the thinnest bone covering in the head. Blood spurted from his ear and mouth. I knelt, cradled his head in my arms and felt for a pulse. Nothing. I could not believe it, Sonnel, my old mate from university days was dead, just like that. Dead in an instant. It was then that the early red mist of anger came over me once again.

The red mist of rage that I had first encountered as a teenager. I had suffered from being picked upon and bullied by boys invariably older than me. I always fought back but usually was beaten. Occasionally, when I had been sufficiently pushed and prodded, I had felt the sudden urge to hurt my tormentors and had surprised everyone, myself included by how vicious I had then become. I termed this the red mist phenomenon and found out later that this was a common enough name for it. It was like looking through a dim red haze. Losing your cool is probably the term I should use.

My parents had tried to channel this explosiveness in my character by sending me to a local gym for boxing lessons. I took to the sport and loved punching the heavy and speed bags, sparring and became quite good. Only on five occasions and not once in the boxing ring did that red mist come over me and after each episode, I was ashamed of myself, as I easily beat up the people concerned. Most gym members enjoyed the camaraderie, but there were a couple who enjoyed having Saturday night punch ups where they used their newfound skills to perfection. I was one of those.

At university, I continued boxing but soon realised that the sport was not for me, it was at a different level and I found that my compatriots were much more skilful. I was not as good as I thought I was and too many left jabs kept hitting my nose. One day a poster appeared in the university gym advertising a new club for the martial art of *KI* Aikido and I took to this sport in the manner born, a duck to water. I gave up boxing and became proficient at Aikido achieving 1st Dan status by the end of my undergraduate studies. It was drummed into me that one walked away from confrontation and one was only allowed to use the learned techniques if a life-threatening situation occurred. This was only lightly referred to at the boxing club. In the past, outside of the dojo, I only ever had one occasion to use my Aikido skills, but that is another story. I might add that my background also contained blue belt status in *Kyokushinka* Karate, a sport that I took up during my post graduate years. For a short while I also dabbled in Bruce Lee's *jeet kune do*, but could not stomach the vegetable-heavy, dairy-free diet that was a dictum of the philosophy. I guess I was a martial art nut case. All I can recall now is a comment made by Bruce Lee, 'if you love life, don't waste time, for time is what life is made of.' A very apt comment in my current circumstances. I must admit that these skills came in very handy when living in out of the way places, but that, as the saying goes, is water under the bridge. They are no use to me right now, but I did find that these skills did cut down my red mist episodes.

But not this time. Slowly rising from the ground, I felt anger rising, coursing through my body. The Brute was facing me front on, one foot forward, one back and his hands hung loosely by his side. I noticed that they were slightly curled, as he was awaiting my response. A big grin occupied his jeering face and he was jabbering away to his mates, all the while keeping his eyes fixed on mine.

Facing him, I automatically went into the stationary on-guard position, raising my hands, left outstretched, index finger raised and right close to my body. I was obsessed with rage and was completely enveloped in the red mist. I loved the feeling, as along with the adrenaline rush, it swept through every part of me. I wanted to obliterate this person. I wanted revenge and let the mist envelop me. My mouth felt dry, a vein in my temple throbbed, muscles twitched and my heart rate increased at the thought of the imminent fight. It felt so good. I was ready.

*   *   *   *

Copje and Vilas stood outside King's Cross station and hailed a taxi. The morning's work had been relatively easy and not too stressful. They had the task of filling the vacant position of a corner street drug dealer who had been arrested. This was a common occurrence within the drug trade. In this case, the dealer had been undercutting rival sellers in the hope of increasing profits. He ran the risk that his rivals would either beat him up, or report him to the Police, who would arrest him and stasis would once again occur. These matters did not unduly trouble the Albanians. They would pass the word around that a vacancy had arisen and many of the 'light druggies' would be chasing for the post. The central aspect for Copje was picking the right person, one who used drugs solely for recreational purposes rather than as a means of existing. They had chosen a suitable person and now wanted some lunch.

Both loved Asian food. Yesterday's lunch had been in the Hong Kong restaurant, in Soho's Chinatown, where they had feasted on *Dim sum* the round wicker bowls of delicious dishes, which were brought around the room by young, smiling, attractive Chinese girls. Their favourite was *bao*, a steamed ball of dough with the centre filled with meat or vegetables. Their preferred dish was pork. This had been followed with fried beef *Ho fun* all washed down with Tsingtao beer, brewed in the clear waters of the Shandong peninsula.

'Bugis Street Brasserie, Cromwell road, please.'

'Right away, sir.'

They got out on arrival at the Brasserie, located on the corner of the Millennium Gloucester hotel. Copje could never get over the brutal pre-stressed grey concrete monolith that was the hotel building. It reminded him of a Stalinist interrogation centre that would probably be found in any sizeable Russian town. He half expected to see KGB agents swarming around the place. The Brasserie was completely different. The beige interior complete with ceiling fans and slatted screens on several windows gave it a tropical feel, but it was the food that they craved.

Seated at an empty table, there were very few to be seen, the waitress arrived fairly quickly so they were able to order almost immediately.

'Two dishes of chicken *satay*.' As Vilas said this, his mind leapt to the heavily spiced rubbed chicken thigh smeared with an occasional piece of skin fired to a crisp on the grill. His mouth salivated.

'And for me,' interjected Copje, 'I want a bowl of *laksa.*' His mind brought up the image of that coconut milk thickened broth, filled with noodles, chilli, seafood, chicken and for all he cared, Uncle Tom Cobley and all, 'and he,' pointing at Vilas, 'I know will have your classic *nasi goreng*. We'll also have some cucumber *raita* and to finish we will have banana fritters. But first, please bring us two bottles of Tiger beer.'

The beers came quickly and they sat back in anticipation of the meal when Copje's phone rang. The conversation, in Albanian, lasted several minutes while Vilas looked questionably at him; no doubt thinking if he was about to miss lunch?

Copje said. 'After lunch, I've got to get back, as something has come up. I have exactly one and a half hours to get there, so call the girl and tell her we're in a hurry.'

It would not be a very good idea to be late for a high-power emergency meeting.

One hour later, Copje hailed another taxi and left for Rookwood House, the notional headquarters of the Hellbanianz leaving Vilas to sort out the bill. Vilas was pleased to do this, as it meant that he had a free afternoon and these did not come round very often. When this occurred he invariably did the same thing; he went to a strip club in Great Compton Street, Soho. A dingy entrance led down a flight of stairs to a darkened auditorium where usually a dozen or so men gazed wistfully at the strippers and waited their turn to move into the front seats. He was let in for free and nodded to the heavy who was sipping a cup of coffee whilst sitting at the back of the entrance desk.

Some months previously he had helped out at the club. It was wintertime and four strapping rugby players had turned up, all the worse for wear by drink. They had caused a commotion and one had tried to clamber on the stage. The heavy had collared him when the other three decided to join in the melee. There were too many for him to handle, so Vilas, who had been sitting quietly in the second row, stepped up. He dispatched the three within seconds, while the Club heavy concentrated upon the first one. They ruffled them up a bit before throwing them out of the club. The management was very grateful to Vilas, so was the heavy and ever since then he was treated as an honoured guest.

This was fine by Vilas, as he had been enamoured by one stripper Leah by name. She was a dazzling brunette who danced to a popular song at the time sung by Al Martino, called 'Blue Spanish Eyes.' She came on stage in a beautiful electric blue dress set off by two white bows on the shoulders and for the record, she had sparkling blue eyes. For some reason, he was aroused when she undid these bows and he was in a state of heightened expectation until she stood naked on the stage. The final unclasping of her G string and throwing it forwards... he imagined that it was for him alone. It seemed that her blue eyes and smile that drilled into his eyes were also meant solely for him. He was the only person in the Club who ever applauded her. The hunched figures of the male clientele had other matters to attend to. He had never met her, as immediately she performed she took off for another club and did the same routine. He knew that soon he would make an effort to meet her. She enchanted him and he knew the management would help out, they'd even told him her real name, Ann Harriet Jenks. Meanwhile, his excited imagination was on fire.

At Rookwood House, Copje took the lift and on exiting knocked on flat door number 21, pushed it open and entered the sparsely furnished room. It contained a long table with eight chairs, a sideboard on which bottles of water, beer, wine and spirits were placed, as well as jugs of coffee, plates of nuts and crisps. No comfortable chairs were in evidence. There were four people seated and he was gestured to a chair.

The chairman Ferdi X, as he preferred to be called started talking as soon as Copje was seated.

'*Përshëndetje*, I have some news for you all relating to our friends in Colombia. You are aware that talks have been held between the Orejuela brothers and us. In essence that means me and Gilberto. As you know recently I went out there to meet him. Now very early this morning, Pablo Escobar in Medellin phoned me and wants a meeting with us immediately. All here know that there is little love lost between the Cali and Medellin people, but these two cartels virtually control the cocaine trade in Colombia. They have a little help from FARC who rely on the cartels for distribution of the drug around the globe. However, FARC is too busy fighting the government to get involved in distribution. They control vast areas of coca-growing, but it ends there.'

He looked around at the four people sitting around the table. No one spoke.

'Escobar is anxious to expand more into the European market, especially the UK and is aware of our contacts with the Ndrangheta, one of the richest criminal groups in the world. Incidentally, this is one smart man, as I do not know how he achieved that knowledge. Anyway, to continue, he wants an emissary to come to Colombia to look around and have talks to see what can be done for importing more cocaine to the UK. He wants a deal that will be advantageous to both parties. If possible, he wants a meeting immediately as he has to depart for the US very soon. Apparently he has some urgent business that needs his attention.'

Pausing, he took a sip of coffee.

'As a result of this, I have come to a decision and would like, you,' he pointed at Copje, 'to go to meet Escobar. Details will be made available after this meeting. Any questions?'

There were none. No one dared question Ferdi after he had made a decision. He would be happy to discuss any matters, would listen to coherent arguments and his mind was open to change, but when a decision was made by him, that was final. Several people had found this out at the cost of their lives.

'Thank you, gentlemen. The meeting is now closed. Anton, I want to talk with you.'

The other men rose, shook hands and left. Ferdi pushed a sheaf of papers towards Copje who picked them up and idly scanned through a few of the sheets.

He looked up.

'I'll go through them later. When do I leave?'

Tomorrow afternoon,' was the reply. 'Escobar wanted this meeting as quickly as we could make it due to his US trip. Now take off and carefully read those papers. You will be away for over a week. Cash and tickets are in that file. The return ticket is open, as I do not want you to be bound by time. The stay length is up to you, but I have provisionally arranged for a two or three-night stay to be spent in Bogotá so that you will be fresh when you meet up with Escobar. Just call him to tell your arrival date and approximate time. All you need is your passport and for emergencies, your credit card.'

He stood up.

'Report back to me daily if possible and I hope that you will be successful. Be careful as Escobar has a vicious reputation. I know you are quite capable of taking care of yourself, but you will be in his domain. Tread carefully and keep alert at all times, as the man's a born killer.'

They stood up and Copje left the room. Entering the hallway, he nodded to the dark-haired man sitting in the far corner and heard Ferdi say, 'Ah Mr Matteo Messina Denaro, the Cosa Nostra and I meet again. Please come in.'

The next day, Copje found himself on flight KLM 1000 en route to Bogotá and Medellin; Business class of course. He settled back in the seat, sipped his champagne, nibbled on hot, salted peanuts and glanced at the menu. He had never been on a long haul flight before and was determined to enjoy it, but was slightly bemused to be given a present of gin in a small bottle shaped like a toy Amsterdam house. He asked for more champagne and tilted the seat. This was the life he was meant to lead, but Sally was not with him. As this thought crossed his mind, the fingers automatically tightened their grip on the champagne glass and it almost snapped. However, the charming air hostess who smiled and fussed over him was, well, charming to say the least. He discovered that he liked the jet style life and her. On the flight, there were only four other passengers, one a young Maltese woman, Wendy by name slept the whole trip and three Colombian businessmen who read spread sheets for the whole flight. Therefore he chatted with the flight attendant whose name was Erika. He found that he was strangely attracted to her. She had travelled around Colombia by bus. In her view that way one saw parts of the country that a typical tourist would never see. This had appealed to him and he idly wondered how it would be if they could have met and done that together. He dismissed the thought.

*   *   *   *

Juan turned up an hour and a half later and Sir George mentally muttered to himself, 'Oh for German punctuality,' and shrugged his shoulders.

'Ah Sir George,' was the greeting. 'I got waylaid by some colleagues and they insisted upon a coffee. You know how it is.'

'Maniaña time is the motto out here. No problem, but as I have also been drinking coffee all morning, I have to visit the toilet pre-departure. Incidentally, when will that be?'

Juan looked at his watch. 'Well, I think we might as well have an early lunch before we go. What do you think?'

An inaudible groan came from Sir George. 'Why not?' was the response. 'If you can't beat them, join them.'

'Pardon?'

'Nothing, simply an old English expression.'

They trooped back into the hotel and had lunch.

The thought came into Sir George's mind that Juan would now suggest a siesta, but that was dismissed when he said;

'Right we'd better be off. I think Morrorico can wait until tomorrow. We are a bit late. So let's go.' With that, he picked up his satchel of provisions, stood up and stretched.

'I hope those joints of yours have recovered, as this track is rough. We have a team of six people on the dig, so I bought some fresh doughnuts and bread for them, as well as stocks of beer. Come on, let's depart.'

Exiting the hotel, they got into the Jeep and took off. Forgetting that he had just stated that they would miss Morrorico, a slight detour took them to the panoramic view of the city, so it was well past noon before they started the journey.

Their drive was along the flat inter-montane basin between the Central and Eastern Ranges of the Andes, which stretches over a large area of north-central Colombia. Juan pointed out that the basin's edges were marked by the Palestrina Fault to the west and the Bucaramanga Fault to the east, the basin having a width of 80 km and length of 450 km terminating to the north in the Santander massif itself. Sir George only had the vaguest idea what this meant but nodded sagaciously. He simply gazed around as the flat plateau stretched all around them as they made their way to the famed Oro

River canyon. Even the road was fine and Sir George did not complain.

'I hope you have your camera with you,' was Juan's comment, 'as the views of the Canyon are truly spectacular. It never ceases to amaze me and I'd put it on par with the US Grand Canyon.'

When they arrived at the scenic overlook his companion had to agree. Both again marvelled as to how water could carve through apparently solid rock to create such a spectacle.

'We are here at a bad time for photos,' said Juan. 'Early morning or late evening is the best as you then get the contrasts. We might try for the evening shot on the way back.'

Sir George did not comment, as his back had started hurting and he knew there would be no evening shot. They left and continued down the road to the mule track turn off.

'Fasten seat belts now,' said Juan. 'That is, if I had any on this old Jeep,' and he slowed down to turn into the track. It was quite noticeable how the vegetation changed, now it became thicker; more shrubs appeared as well as the odd tree.

Some 5 km down the road it happened.

Rounding a sharp bend, a truck was parked squarely across the track. Standing beside it were six soldiers and one flagged them down. Juan slowed to a stop. One of the soldiers sauntered forward.

'Get out and keep your hands away from your pockets.'

'FARC,' whispered Juan, 'do as they say.'

Sir George said nothing.

They climbed out of the Jeep and the officer, Sir George presumed he was one, gestured to him to get into the front seat of the truck.

'We're FARC,' was called out, 'and we seem to have a nice hostage here. 'You,' and he gestured to Juan, 'are free to go. I'm requisitioning the Jeep and you can walk back to the overlook. We will take care of your passenger. We will take very good care of him, as I think he means much money.'

With that, he ordered one man to drive the Jeep then followed Sir George into the truck.

As the truck rumbled forward Juan's eyed locked with Sir George's. A wry smile crossed Sir George's lips and he shrugged his shoulders helplessly. He was on his way, but what the future held for him was still a big unknown.

A bottle of beer was passed to Sir George by the smiling officer.

The long drive covered many different scenic and vegetation types, as they descended from the basin. Oil fields were seen in abundance as the area is one of the leading oil producers in Colombia and they came close to a few of these. He noticed the signs of Casabe, La Cira-Infantas, Palagua, all edging closer to jungle territory. At Lisama the last signposted oilfield, the officer shouted out. 'Soon we will arrive,' and banged on the side of the truck. About an hour later, the driver started punching the horn and shots were heard, as soldiers in the back fired their rifles into the air. In a swirl of dust, the truck swerved into a jungle clearing and lurched to a stop.

6.

Colombia, Nicaragua.

I eyed my opponent and backed away from him. He simply grinned and did not move. Keeping my eyes on him all the time, I casually went through a minute of *Kata* or form exercises to focus my inner (thoughts and feelings in my mind) and outer (the external event that was about to happen in my fight with the brute) reality. I particularly wanted him to see how I did the fast/slow movements. The balance between these movements is the key to sound *Kata*. I did the 54 move *Kata* rather than my usual 108, finishing with a *Kimi-no-kata* from Judo that I sometimes used. I did not include CMX *Kata*. I had also spotted a small sand ridge a few steps from where we stood, so moving over to it and still keeping my eyes on my adversary, straightened the fingers of both hands and drove them into the sand as hard as I could. I did it six times whilst letting out a yell that would expel negativity from my body. All was done deliberately so that unease could creep into his mind. I knew from experience that well-done *Kata*, with its fast arm movements and leg kicks, does demoralise an opponent. If one can achieve this, then the battle is half won.

These movements also summon up the mysterious life force, vital energy or what is termed, *Ki*. I recall seeing an Aikido 6th dan arrange 6 people in a line in front of him. They were all told he was going to hit/push the frontman and they should resist the backward movement that would ensue. All took up their positions some with arms around the waist of the person in front of them, others had hands gripping shoulders and all had braced legs. A sprinkling of black belts was in that column. He summoned up *Ki* and struck. The whole line collapsed. The frontman told me afterwards that the initial push to the chest did not seem to be very hard, but the momentum wave that came after was incredible.

Straight after this demonstration the *sensei a*sked for a volunteer. I found myself pushed forward, my colleagues all saying, 'here he is.' I was bowed to and reciprocated and he brought a chair onto the tatami mat and gestured me to sit. I obliged. A fat cushion was produced and tied around my midriff.

'I am now going to demonstrate the one inch blow.'

A ruler was produced and his fist was measured so that it was one inch (2.5 cm) away from the taut pillow.

Turning to me, he spoke.

'I want you to tense your stomach muscles. I am going to hit the pillow hard. Are you alright with that?'

'Yes *sensei*,'

Be prepared.'

I tensed my muscles and my gaze centred on that fist, just one inch from the cushion. A split second later I found myself on the floor with the remains of a shattered chair around me and a slight ache in the abdomen. I shuddered to think of the damage that a one inch punch delivered by him could do to an unprotected abdomen.

I looked at *Ki* as a mastery of balance. This and the ability to generate the whole body force that ended in the finger tips/hand/leg as they hit an opponent is the key. I shouted out my intense *Kiai* or war cry. I stood up and once again took up my *Kamae* or basic stance. All the time I was doing this our eyes never wavered from each other, as I was half expecting him to attack me. I was prepared for this, but nothing happened. He simply watched and attempted a brief yawn. I was unsure if my drill had affected him.

I approached slowly keeping my body turned sideways, weight firmly on the front leg, back leg about a shoulder width apart, one arm outstretched loosely in front of me, the other below it as if holding a dagger. This is the basic movement called *Tai no henko*. We circled each other. He lunged forward quite fast, swinging a right-hand punch that if it had landed would have sent me reeling to the ground complete with a heaven of stars spinning around my head. It did not land.

Turning, I blocked it and unleashed a *Munasuki*, a front of body blow that landed squarely on him. He yelped and I could see that it had hurt. As he lurched past I swept his legs from under him and he fell to the floor. I could not help myself. I gave him a gentle kick in the ear saying, 'This first one is for my friend Sonnel.' I then backed off and casually gestured for him to get up and continue the fight.

As he rose, I sensed that he was becoming uneasy and this made me slightly careless, because he jumped and caught me with a pile driver blow right in my ribs. For an instant, I had forgotten my *Maai*, the knowledge as to how far one should be away from an attacker, the critical distance in any fight. As I covered up, he tried to get me in a bear hug and onto the floor. On the floor, I'd have had no chance, as he was much heavier than me. Turning inwards I kneed him hard in the groin and immediately head-butted him, splitting his nose that spurted a stream of blood. In the same movement with a *Teisho* (heel of my hand), I slashed the nose end upwards intending to drive his septum into his skull. The pain must have been massive. Backing off I finally delivered an *Ushiro geri* or backwards kick which made him fall to his knees. All this took place in one swift moment.

He got up and I lifted my right leg high, keeping the body upright, no leaning to the side and thought of hitting him with a *Yoko geri* sidekick. This is a very difficult technique to achieve from a standing position, so I used a *Mawashigeri jodan*, a roundhouse kick to the head, aiming for the temple where there is a large artery near the skin surface. He staggered backwards and I repeated the move several times. I did not want to rupture it, as if not treated immediately this can cause death. I wanted just to bruise it.

He was beaten. I changed tactics and went for his face because I wanted to make a complete mess of that ugly mug. I was starting to enjoy myself and became the boxing club youth who enjoyed street fights long ago where no mercy was showed. I was going to put him through hell and then kill him. I was invincible. The red mist still enveloped me, muscles tensed and relaxed and adrenaline pumped through my veins. It seemed like a drug was coursing through my veins. I used *Shuto*, the knife-edge of my hand to hit an exposed Adam's apple and he gasped. I did not deliver a full blow, as that would sever his windpipe and the fight would be over in a minute or two. I wanted him to suffer.

He staggered upright and I proceeded to turn his face into a doughy mass of cut flesh and blood and also took the opportunity to break his arms. I hit him with many different *Atemis,* the general term for strikes of any kind, all one after the other with no respite; *Hijiate kokyu nage,* where I used his extended arm as a lever and snapped the elbow joint; *Hijishima*, where I locked out his other elbow against the joint; *Kotegaeshi* where the wrist is twisted in its natural direction and snapped and *Nikajo* a key wrist lock whereby merely holding the opponent's palm and wrist out in front of you and applying a little downward strength, the opponent's knees buckle and give way. I always motioned him to get up and to my surprise, he usually did. These attacks made it now impossible for him to hit me with his hands. I was enjoying the thrill of battle and the feeling of *Zanshin* or awareness started to flow through my body. I was bringing into play all the *Gooshin waza* self-defence techniques that I knew and all the *Kangeiko* or winter training that I had done in my early years was paying off.

One eye was closed and the other, well he must have been blinded by the blood when I hit it with my two fingers in the snake position. I was trying to rip the eye out. I missed and the flesh around it was swelling fast. I swung my leg and the hard toe of my working boot hit his shinbone. A crack was heard as the bone splintered. As he lurched downwards I booted him very hard in the head, just as he done to Sonnel and he fell to the ground. I did not want this. I wanted him back upright so that I could inflict maximum punishment. On the ground, I could only kick and then choke him. I decided to do both when I felt arms grasp me from both sides.

'Enough Adam. That's enough, stop it now.'

This came through the mist. I struggled, but three people were holding me; two holding an arm each and the third had me around the neck. I stopped struggling.

'All right, it's ok.'

I was slowly released.

The Brute was comatose on the ground and badly in need of medical attention.

'We heard the shouting, abandoned our meeting and came to see what was happening. One of the soldiers told us the cause of this. It's all so needless,' said José.

He knelt and placed two fingers to the neck feeling for a pulse.

'He's dead Adam,' was voiced very quietly. 'They don't know it yet,' he gestured to the soldiers, 'we'll keep it that way, as there is something I must do.'

With that, he turned and uttered something to his fellow officer who ordered the soldiers to fall in. They lined up opposite him. There was an apprehensive look on their faces. They knew what was about to happen. I did not and just felt sick at what I had done. What happened next took place very rapidly.

'You all know as to why I am here. I have come on an extremely grave matter. You will be aware that we recently received ransom money for a French national Alex Mooser. Some of that money was stolen from our safekeeping. All monies received are for the cause, which is to overthrow this corrupt government. You all know who the culprit is and now we know. You also know that the penalty for this matter is death.'

He stopped and looked around. 'No comments?'

'All right,' and with that, he drew his Makarov pistol, walked over to the brute and with a double-tap put two shots into his forehead. A dribble of blood oozed from the wound. No one said a word apart from José.

'He has now paid the penalty. Freud once stated that the aim of all life is death. Here is proof of it.'

He holstered the revolver. 'All right. Dismissed.'

Stopping four men, he ordered them to bury the soldier outside the camp perimeter. They saluted and obeyed.

José turned to me, 'My meeting with my fellow officers was to discuss this case. Ransom money was dropped by parachute recently at a destination about 60 km from this camp. It was brought here and then stolen. We knew it must be here somewhere. We suspected him and the men knew it was him. Idiot that he was he boasted about it to a few, but the final proof was when the stack of money was found buried near his hammock. He had no opportunity of getting away with it from here, but my guess is he would have deserted very soon after leaving camp. I was told that there has been surliness in the camp for the past two weeks due to this matter. As usual, the men did not want to inform on a fellow combatant. This misplaced loyalty caused some issues. Now it is ended and we can get back to normal.'

He placed a hand on my shoulder.

'I'm very sorry to hear about Sonnel. It was all so unnecessary, but that I am afraid is the tragedy of war. Innocents frequently die. What shall we do with his body? Do you want him returned to his parents?'

I was in a daze and barely heard him. I had killed a man.

With that, a truck enveloped in a cloud of dust rolled into the camp with its horn blaring and rifle shots fired into the air. Stopping just in front of us, several soldiers jumped down from the tailgate and two grime-covered figures clambered down from the front. One had a smile on his face as he saluted José; the other had an even bigger smile as he said, 'Hullo José, it's lovely to see you again.'

José replied. 'Que tal hace mucho tiempo que no te veo, amigo,' ('It's been a long time since I saw you, my friend,') and they warmly embraced each other.

Turning to me, José said, 'Sir George is a very old friend of mine. He taught me chemistry at Oxford, before relocating to London and the good life, I might add, as well as winning a Nobel.'

Sir George turned to me. 'And who might you be?

'I'm George Fusano from the UK.'

He then winked at me and with a broad grin on his face added, 'I've just been kidnapped by FARC. Surprise, surprise. Now I'd like some food and my bed.'

*   *   *   *

One advantage, possibly the only one according to Paddy, of the small San Pedro airport was that there were daily flights to Miami where the pair had decided to sell the stone. The arrangement made was that Zafar would keep half of the agreed price; the other half would sponsor their search for emeralds in Colombia. From many encounters over the years, Paddy had dealt with a Miami South Beach fence named Frank Dervan. As much as he trusted anyone in the game who dealt with non-provenanced precious stones, Dervan was acceptable to Paddy. The man had an office at Espanola Way located a few blocks from the famed one-mile strip of Ocean Drive, South Beach. The area had some of the best street food to be found in the city and as he thought about it, Paddy realised that he was hungry for western food and culture. He had been away in the backwoods for far too long.

The packing of possessions was swift. Both travelled light and the cab ride to the airport was short, but they found that the next flight necessitated a five-hour wait. That was fine for Paddy - there was a convenient bar to be sampled, but before settling in a comfortable cane chair and starting on his first beer, he first sent an email to Dervan.

'You know Zafar,' he said. 'I am an inveterate accumulator of trivia. Look at this,' and he inserted the @ symbol into the email. 'This was invented in 1971 by Ray Tomlinson and was the start of all electronic mail. Don't you find that amazing?'

'Not really,' was the laconic reply. 'But I'd still like a drink, even though I've taken the Arab way of life, I draw a line on this point. So let's have one.'

'Why stop at one,' was the reply. 'Now you mentioned the Arab way of life and I'm curious, so tell me, how did the Italian Rio Alebar become Zafar the Arab?'

'All right, as we are going to be partners, I guess you need to know. I'll try to make it as concise as I can, but first, let's get the beers in.'

The following is the gist of that conversation told me in the jungle by Paddy on the morning when Hanoz departed to look for Zafar.

'My parents owned a large rice farm in a town called Vercelli located on the edge of the Po River flood plain. That was where I was born at 6 pm to the music of Dean Martin singing, 'Little old wine drinker me.' Dad wanted to name me Deano; my mother was a Beatles fan and wanted John, Paul, George and Ringo, but thankfully sanity prevailed in the form of my grandparents who insisted on the family name of Vittorio for the firstborn male. Later on, a sister Gianna and brother Paulo turned up. Gianna is now married and lives on the farm. My parents are now dead and my brother worked in the Tourist Office at Santa María Novella in Florence, but is now in the Head Office in Roma. I loved that farm, especially working in the fields with immigrant labour during harvest time. If you ever see the film Bitter Rice with Sylvana Mangano, well it was just like that. I eventually left to do a degree in biochemistry at Milan University followed by a Master's at Bristol University, UK. On moving to London for about a year, I rented a room with kitchen/bathroom access in Vine Street, London. I was employed as a chemist by ICI and became heavily involved in research within the fertiliser industry. It was a well-paid job and I was looking around intending to buy a flat.'

According to Paddy, Zafar had to stop for many seconds before announcing, 'my social life was not very good and I might as well tell you right now that I'm gay.'

When Paddy heard this, he jerked upright spilling some beer before taking a large swallow of what was left. I could just about imagine that scene as Paddy was a heterosexual man to his core.

'Bejesus. Gay. I've never met a gay person in my life. By god, you look and seem a normal type bloke to me even though you've a funny name.'

'Not all gays mince around the place and act high camp. Most of us are what you term, normal-looking people. We keep ourselves to ourselves and don't go looking for trouble. Unfortunately, trouble comes looking for us, as you'll know in a minute or two. We have to put up with a lot of abuse and often violence. I know a few men who have been killed because they were gay and also several females who have been gang-raped for being lesbians.'

He downed his beer and called a waiter over.

'Another two large beers please and keep them coming when you see we're empty.'

Paddy nodded agreement and when they turned up, Zafar continued.

'I was a frequent visitor to London gay clubs such as Bang, Napoleon, Boots, Kinky Gerlinky, Scandals and of course the Joiners Arms in Tower Hamlets where Dave Pollard welcomed 'joyful sinners.' Many clubs were located in pub cellars. The scene shifted in 1978 when the Embassy Club in Old Bond Street opened. The atmosphere there was likened to that of Club 54 in New York. One year later, Heaven opened at the Arches in Villiers Street, near Charing Cross Station and it was, well, just heaven for us. It was the biggest venue of its kind in Europe. I well remember the first DJ there a man called Ian Levine, but it was a DJ called Tasty Tim that we all lusted after. He had the pick of our crop.'

He stopped to take a large gulp of beer.

'This is where I really met similar minded people and could stop putting on a presence and just...., well I could be myself. In Italy, we have a saying, '*mal commune, mezzo gaudio,*' which means a trouble shared is a trouble halved and it was a joy to share things at these clubs. I went there one weekend and met up with a nice young Dutchman and we enjoyed ourselves. About three in the morning we decided to go home and I was invited back to his flat in Kilburn. That's when it all went haywire.'

Pausing for a moment to collect his thoughts, he continued.

'The flat was reached via a cul de sac and getting there meant using an underpass. On entering the underpass two burly men suddenly appeared from nowhere and jumped us. They were brazen and took delight in giving us a savage beating all the while telling us why. They had been watching Philip van Martin that was my friend's name, for some time and had decided to go in for what they termed queer-bashing. After a minute or so, one hit with a cosh knocked Philip out cold, but I tried to fight back. I managed to knee one of them in the groin and a lucky blow hit the other on the nose. This incensed both of them. The bigger man crashed me to the ground and he was much too strong and big for me. I ended up curled in the foetal position receiving a savage kicking by both men. To cut a long story short, my cheekbone was fractured, two teeth were knocked out, plus my nose and four ribs were broken and an eye socket badly damaged. I had a punctured lung, kidney damage and my thigh had somehow been deeply cut. I was spilling blood and I had bruises all over my body, especially my testicles. I was spitting blood from my mouth.'

He stopped there for a moment.

'I don't know how long I was unconscious. I came round to find an elderly man with a white goatee beard gently holding my head.'

I recall him slowly saying, 'Hullo, can you hear me? You're in bad shape. I'm getting you to hospital.'

'I came round in hospital a day later and remained there for 10 days.'

Zafar paused and finished off his glass of beer. Paddy did the same and within seconds new beers appeared.

'Thank you,' was said to the waiter who replied with a nod and smile.

'Did you find out who the person was that helped you?' enquired Paddy, adding, 'and who did it?'

'Yes, but it was much more than that. My saviour came to the hospital every day to see me. His name was Saleh Omar Zafar al Harbi from Iraq, an architect by profession who had escaped from the brutality of the Saddam Hussein regime and was now a low-grade employee with one of the London international architectural firms. At least he'd obtained a position in his professional field unlike many of his compatriots who had to take menial jobs to survive.'

'He was a real intellectual and if I close my eyes I can hear him speaking the words now.' He paused and shut his eyes.

'I will teach you the five pillars of the Faith; Shahada, Salat, Zakat, Sawm and the Hajj. I have studied at Baghdad's House of Wisdom where they translated Greek texts into Arabic, as well as the impressive scientific and philosophical works of al-Kwãrizimi and al-Kindi. I am especially fond of Ahmed ibn Hanbal one of the founders of one of the four schools of Sunni thought. He was a man flogged by caliph al-Ma'mum in the 9th century *mihna* or Inquisition, which delighted in persecuting traditionalists. I have written a book about him and am currently researching another book on probably the greatest Islamic philosopher who ever lived, namely Abu al-Husayn ibn Sina, born in Bukhara in the 10th century AD and known to the western world as Avicenna.'

Zafar opened his eyes and was silent for a while.

'I owe him my life, as I was losing a great deal of blood and would soon have bled out to death. With his belt, he had even applied a tourniquet to my thigh to stop blood loss. I asked about Philip, but he must have scarpered when he regained consciousness because I was the only one that Saleh found and I never saw Philip again. When it came to discharge from the hospital Saleh even offered to put me up at his place, but I felt that was too much and anyway, while in bed I had developed some other plans. I wanted revenge. After discharge, I went almost daily to his home to see him. He was a lonely, kind, old man and it was he who introduced me to Arab culture. I moved into his flat for the last six months of his life to nurse him when he was incapable of looking after himself. I grew to love that gentleman and was extremely fond of him, so much so that I subsequently took his name and culture. I especially liked their idea of *xenodochy*, the hospitality offered to strangers. To me, he was the ultimate gentleman. Sadly he died of prostate cancer. I was the sole beneficiary in his will and that's why I was able to come to Latin America and try some prospecting.'

Zafar laughed.

'And now my friend, we come to the interesting part. When we were fighting on the ground, a wallet must have fallen from a pocket. When Saleh found me, I was lying on it. He had picked it up and put it in my bedside cabinet at the hospital thinking it was mine. When eventually I opened it, I knew the identity and address of one of the men. There was also £40 in it that was quite useful.'

Paddy became quite interested. 'What did you do?'

'In bed I decided to maim the bastards, but waited until I had fully recovered. I told you that I was a chemist and making a bomb is an easy task for someone like me. I worked with fertilisers and had access to centrifuges so a large IRA fertiliser bomb would have been easy to construct. It would have blown a house up, but I did not want to kill them. I could have put a small amount of PE4 plastic explosive into their phone if I could have obtained it and rigged it so that when I dialled their number it would have obliterated anyone within a few metres radius. It detonates at a speed of 8,000 metres/second. I just wanted to disfigure them for life, so I made two small bombs.'

'A what?' came from a horrified Paddy.

'A generic one made from petrol and potassium permanganate, and a red match head one. A regular fuse, e.g., M-80, but a firework will do, to set this one-off. One packs them with nails, screws, glass shards etc. The result is a big bang.

He paused and had another drink of beer.

'When all was ready, I used to go to their address, watch and wait. One summer evening I found them at home with the front door unlocked. They were watching TV. I opened the door. 'Good evening, gentlemen. Do you remember me? I can still recall the look of utter astonishment on their faces.'

'Bejesus I'd hate to get on the wrong side of you,' was the comment.

Zafar finished. 'The rest, as the saying goes, is history. Just to make sure, ten seconds after the initial blast, I opened the door and threw in two Molotov cocktails. Their faces were disfigured for life and one became blind.' When Paddy later told me this story in the jungle, he said that it took about an hour for Zafar to finish it.

At the end of the story, boarding was announced and they flew to Miami. Frank Dervan was a wizened old man who had a bad bent back due to arthritis, as well as a limp due to a botched knee operation. He had a thatch of thick, dyed, jet black hair and an old wrinkled neck that would not have been out of place on a vulture, but within that skull was a sharp business brain. It was hard to think of him as a person who as a young man had run away from home due to a doomed love affair and served five years in the French Foreign Legion. On examining the stone, he agreed that it had excellent colour quality, high tone and saturation. This together with the deep vanadium and chromium inclusions, he called them by their technical name of 'jardins,' made it a valuable stone, but he detected a slight feathering. Therefore it did not bring as much money as Paddy had hoped, but it was enough to set them up to go looking for the mother lode.

From Miami, they flew to Bogotá.

*   *   *   *

Santa Fe de Bogotá is over 2,600 m above sea level and is the capital, political, economic, administrative and industrial centre of Colombia. It is a chilly, cloudy city and the eastwards drive from El Dorado International Airport was short, as was Copje's breath; he did feel the effect of altitude. When he arrived at the GHL hotel in the Calle district, he carefully stepped out of the cab and was even grateful that his carry-on luggage was taken from him by the hotel porter.

It was midday and he had two choices, carry on until dusk or go straight to bed. The inflight magazine and air hostess had made the point that the better option was to carry on until bedtime, so that is what he decided to do even though he felt like death.

'Funny phrase that,' he said to himself, 'what does death feel like?' He had met men who had welcomed a quick death rather than one after prolonged torture periods. The thought of the Vilas killing in Lisbon immediately came into his mind. He was not in the least bit hungry, therefore restaurants were not on his agenda although he made a mental note to try *Tamale,* the traditional dish made from rice, pork/beef/chicken chickpeas carrots and various spices all wrapped in plantain leaves and steam cooked. At the moment, all he needed was liquids to counteract the dehydration effects of long-distance flying, which in his case had been augmented by too much alcohol brought by the extremely charming air hostess.

The thought of visiting the Planetarium was immediately dismissed. Lying in a reclining chair looking at the stars would soon induce sleep and he wanted to keep that at bay. It had to be a museum and the three choices were the National, Botero, or Gold. He had read about all three again in the in-flight magazine. Deciding on the latter, he hailed a taxi and set off to the Parque Santander determined to view its treasures and was amazed at what was there. He was fascinated by the various cultural epochs, the Llama, Yotaco, Sonso and Malagana and wandered around the second and third floors in a daze, looking intently at the intricately designed gold ornaments. He especially liked the Muisca golden raft that allegedly was the origin of the El Dorado myth.

Several hours were spent there and as dusk approached, he decided to call it a day, headed back to the hotel, had some drinks and then blessed bed. He slept like a baby and woke up the next morning feeling a different man. After a breakfast of hot, burnt, Colombian coffee, figs, yoghurt and toast, he was ready to face the day. The image of Erika came into his mind and he wished he had found out which hotel the crew would be staying.

He dismissed the thought instantly. He had a job to do. Consequently, his first stop, following Erika's comments, was to the Expreso Bolivariano bus company to book a seat on the 10-hour journey to Medellin for the next day. He made a mental note to phone Escobar from the hotel to inform him of his estimated arrival time.

Stepping out from the bus station and wary of the altitude, he decided to have a stroll around the place and sauntered up and down the hilly streets of the city. The high-rise skyscraper buildings poised against a background of even higher verdant clad mountains buoyed his spirits. He eventually found himself at the foot of Monserrate, a hill that dominates the city and reaches more than 3,000 m in height. A cable car was one route choice to the top, or one could walk. Copje decided he was in no fit state to walk, so bought a ticket.

Waiting for the cable car, he went into the lounge area to have a beer and almost bumped into Erika who was going in the opposite direction. He felt his heart rhythm increase.

'I guess it must be Kismet, fate whatever you want to call it, but it's my lucky day,' smiled Copje. 'I was just thinking of you. It's a surprise to see you. After serving me all that champagne I never expected to meet up again, but simply hoped that I would, as I just loved it all.'

A smile broke out across her face. 'Mr Copje, I presume. Two strangers meeting not on the shore, but at a funicular in Bogotá could be a clip from a Hollywood film. But we are not strangers. Are you going to the top?'

'I am and if you are as well, let's go together.'

That smile again broke over her face and laughingly she accepted and casually linked her arm in his. He felt great.

At the mountain top, the panoramic view of the city was superb. They walked around the platform together and the conversation was nonstop including many jokes. He found that she had a three night stopover in Bogotá and cursed the fact that he had just bought a ticket to Medellin for the next day then realised that he had not yet phoned Escobar. At that moment he realised that he simply had to postpone his visit. Erika was a bubbly, charming companion, with a lean body, a great sense of humour and a mass of flowing golden curly hair. The attraction he felt for her on the plane was the first time he had experienced that feeling for a member of the opposite sex since Sally had been murdered all those years ago. He wondered if she felt the same.

He was going to enjoy Bogotá.

They had lunch together at the La Macarena, where both tried the *Tamale* and deemed it excellent. A visit to the Botanical Gardens followed and acting on an impulse, he plucked a bougainvillaea flower from a shrub, placing it in her hair.

She giggled. 'You can be put in jail for that. I mean picking a flower from the Botanical garden, not putting it in my hair.'

'I don't mind. It was worth it just to smooth and touch that glorious head of hair.'

'Whoa, a flower to touch my hair, what would you give to touch my cheek?' she whispered coquettishly.

At that, he stopped, faced her and taking her face in both hands looked straight into her eyes and spoke.

'The world,' and kissed her.

Breaking apart she looked directly back into those slate-grey eyes just centimetres from hers. 'Life should be lived in moments and not units of time,' was murmured before putting both hands around his neck and feverishly kissing him back. Moving away, she took his hand and walked towards the cable car and on an impulse again turned towards him.

'There's a poet that I like. His name is Tennyson and he wrote a famous line in a poem about Ulysses. It goes, 'To strive, to seek, to find and not to yield.' She looked away before turning once again to face him, 'But I find I'm yielding 100%, as even on the plane I felt a particular attraction for you. I might add that this is very rare for me, but you didn't seem interested.'

Copje groaned as he heard those words. 'I felt the same but felt powerless to do anything.' He told her about Sally.

Later he made his phone call to Escobar, re-booked his ticket and had the best two days and nights of life since five years ago.

7.

London.

Near Milton Keynes, UK is a place called Hanslope Park, commonly termed HSP and in the grounds can be found many Governmental buildings such as Her Majesty's Government Communications Centre (HMGCC). The Technical Security Department of the UK Secret Intelligence Service (MI6) houses the building that is of interest to this story. In a secure first-floor room were gathered five people. The person chairing the meeting was Sir Nels Clifford. His rank was one below the Permanent Under-Secretary of State for Foreign Affairs. The person in this latter position advises the Minister of State for Europe and the Americas; heads Her Majesty's Diplomatic Service and is the second most senior-ranking Foreign Office Minister behind the Foreign Secretary, currently the Right Honourable Christopher Houseman.

The Minister and Permanent Under-Secretary could not come to clandestine meetings such as these, as they had to be above any action undertaken by these people. Clifford had come directly from Lancaster House, St James's, London, which the Foreign Office leases from the Crown and was a place from which he rarely moved. This was a very serious meeting.

The others were represented by Colonel Glyn Williamson from the SAS Regiment, Dr Mike Williams, the Deputy of the Colombian sector of the Overseas Trade and Development Department (OTDD) and two senior officials from MI6, Arthur Maxwell and Ron Southall. The men all knew each other very well, as they met once a month, usually at Lancaster House. They wondered why this one was at HSP. They were not told.

The Agenda, marked TOP SECRET FOR YOUR EYES ONLY, was brief and included six Agenda points for discussion. The last point was:

6. Policy goals, as previously enumerated:

a. Countering terrorism and weapons proliferation and their causes.

b. Preventing and resolving conflict.

c. The Current situation in:

> Iraq.
>
> Lebanon.
>
> Cambodia.
>
> Israel.
>
> Vietnam.
>
> Colombia.

Three hours were spent in discussions of the Agenda items. When it came to the last item of Point 6, Colombia, Sir Nels called a halt and asked for a further person to join them. In walked Major John Davidson, the Military Attaché from the British Embassy, Bogotá. He had been flown in specifically for this meeting and been busy drinking coffee and chatting to a pretty secretary while waiting in an adjacent room. Before the meeting, the chair had had a long conversation with him.

Introductions were made and a brief synopsis was given by Sir Nels about Sir George Fusano's visit followed by John Davidson regarding the state of play in Colombia, with special reference to the drug trade that was causing concern in Europe. FARC and Escobar's names were prominent in the talk. Davidson finished by informing them that a gun had been given to Sir George stressing that this was purely a precaution, as no situation was foreseen where it would be needed. It was more of a crutch than anything else. The Major stressed that Sir George had been in good spirits. Several specific questions were answered in non-diplomatic language. Towards the end, Sir Nels rapped the table.

'Just prior to this meeting, we had confirmation that Sir George Fusano has been safely delivered to FARC and is now at a place called Camp Diamante. Now you all know why he is out there. Phase I of Operation Albatross has been accomplished. Let us hope that Phase II can now be implemented.'

'How did you get this information?' queried the OTDD man.

'For that, you'll have to ask Major Davidson or Colonel Williamson,' was the laughing reply. 'But I'm sure if you have to ask Colonel Williamson, he'd have to kill you after answering the question.'

Colonel Williamson smiled. 'That will not be necessary, as I can confirm for all sitting around this table and I emphasise to no one else, that we have a troop keeping an eye on the camp. They have been there for two weeks waiting for him to turn up. He is quite safe, as any potential for trouble will occur when he moves away to, for example, Bogotá.'

These words came back later to haunt him.

The meeting came to an end and on exiting the room Williamson held back until the last person came out. It was Major Davidson. They clasped hands and hugged each other. They had been friends since Sandhurst days when they had been in the same cohort of cadets. Their career paths had then diverged, as Davidson had entered the intelligence Corps, Williamson the Parachute Regiment then SAS, meeting up again when Davidson had been posted to Hereford as part of what troopers called, the 'Green Slime' (slang for the Intelligence Corps and called due to the colour of their berets). Williamson, now a Major, had been invited back to command a squadron. He had remained there ever since. After a year, Davidson had moved sideways into the new Joint Service Interrogation Wing, which was an extension of the Intelligence Corps. There, dressed in Soviet uniforms, his team had enjoyed employing counter-terrorism techniques in very real and sometimes brutal interrogation sessions with camp personnel. His team 'broke' Williamson after 38 hours and this number of hours before cracking was a record that stood for several years. Afterwards, Williamson had collapsed onto his bed and slept the sleep of the just. The following day, in the time-honoured tradition of the British Army, he and Davidson had caroused the Hereford bars and rolled back into Bradbury Lines, both blind drunk and extremely happy.

'Great to see you again John,' said a smiling Glyn Williamson.

'Ditto.'

'Any hidden agenda that I should know about?'

'Nothing so far. It's gone like clockwork. Let's hope it stays that way.'

They chatted amiably for many minutes.

'Did you know that I spent some time in the Colombian jungle?' asked Williamson.

'No, I thought you did your jungle training in Belize.'

'I did, but being the cocky young Captain doing my first three-year tour in The Regiment, I wrote a letter to the Head Shed. In it, I stated that I'd enjoyed the jungle course, a bit of a misnomer that, as I lost some 7 kg in weight on that month out there. The gist of it was that I suggested it would be appropriate if instead of being pitchforked into a military jungle set up, might it not be better if personnel could be placed with jungle tribes for a period of several months to assimilate jungle lore and develop a feel for the jungle, to imbue one with the spirit of the jungle, to listen with your ears, enhance your sense of smell and see with your eyes? The latter is a bit of a misnomer, as in jungle your eyes are not that big a deal. Sometimes all you can see is a few metres in front of you. A sawn-off shotgun makes a very handy weapon in those circumstances. The other senses are much more important. The Head Shed liked it and put a pilot scheme in place AFTER initial jungle training. They did this due to cost, as usually a high percentage of any intake fail the training course.'

He paused. 'One of the things about the Kremlin Head Shed is that they move fast. A call was put out for volunteers for this new course and about two-thirds of the Camp applied. It was very noticeable that the Ice Cream Boys, as we called the Air troop crowd, weren't too keen to volunteer. They preferred swanning around the blue skies of California with Ray-Bann sunglasses, topping up their suntans and practising HALO and HAHA parachute drops. They trained a lot out there, as wind speed is vitally important for a drop and having aircraft hanging around waiting for a wind to drop is an expensive business, hence sunny, balmy skies are needed. I was in Mountain troop. Anyway, within a month I and a dozen others were picked for the scheme and I was posted to Colombia. In Bogotá I was introduced to a Lt. Gonzalo Alves who is now the head of the Colombian Army. He was my guide and within days we were ensconced in the Colombian Amazon jungle.'

He looked at Davidson.

'How about we finish this over a beer and a meal?'

'Ok, but I'll have to leave in 1-2 hours as I want to get to Cheltenham tonight, as Gold Cup day is tomorrow,' said Davidson. He ran his hand through his long, thick greying hair. 'I also need to have a haircut. I have an uncle, Tudor David, who is a bookmaker and was at university with Ian LeHur who runs a stable at Newmarket. Ian is an ex-jockey and it is ironic that now he could no longer ride. Swimming on a holiday in the Bahamas, he had been attacked by a Tiger shark and had part of his left buttock ripped away. Between them, I hope to have a few tips so that I can win some money.'

'Ok, let's go,' and they left for a nearby pub.

At the Red Lion, they sat in the beer garden. Ordering two plates of scampi and chips and taking a large gulp of bitter beer, Williamson continued his story.

'After driving on rutted roads and paddling along a wide river we ended up with a tribe called the Cohuano. Incidentally, they call the river the anaconda's son, but I never saw the father or the son, thank god. There I truly learned what plants to eat, what to avoid and how to respect the jungle. The instructors on our jungle course all had that respect and know how, but this was something new to me. I learned about the *yakruna* and *chircaspi* plants and how religious the people were, in a completely different way to what we conceive religion to be. I guess you'd say they were animists. I took a photo of one with a Polaroid camera. On showing him the resulting photo, when I started to take it back he brushed my arm aside and clutched it to his chest. The photo was his *chullachaqui*, his spirit which was a hollow version of him and I could not have it. Living with these people I actually put on some weight and then suddenly lost it.'

A swallow of beer followed. Wiping the foam from his mouth with a silk handkerchief, he continued.

'I didn't stay the whole of my expected time, as I went down with the flesh-eating parasite *Leishmania,* caught from a sand fly bite.'

He stopped and grinned at the baffled look on the Major's face.

'It's a big word for your little brain,' he smiled, 'but it is what is called an aprotozoa parasitic disease spread by the bite of infected female phlebotomine sand flies, although I can't tell their sexes apart. I usually swatted any that I could see. They feed on blood that they need for their damn eggs. In my case, sand fly proliferation was due to deforestation in the area, as rubber barons had started to move in and a new irrigation project had started up nearby. Rubber can equate to death for these villages, as in addition to sand flies, when trees are cleared away the bright, metallic blue coloured, day flying *Haemagoous capricorni* mosquitoes that live in the upper forest canopy, are brought down in swarms to ground level and when they bite, one can get yellow fever. The sand fly that bit me carried the *Cutaneous Leishmaniasis* (CL), the commonest variety that causes skin lesions, bloody big ulcers on exposed body parts. I was bitten on my legs and two weeks later abscesses developed and kept on growing.'

He stopped talking and rolled up his trouser legs.

'You can see that I still have scars after some 15 years. I was very lucky that I didn't have the *kala-azar* form or the even worse *mucocutaneous* variety of the disease. That is deadly. If untreated the death rate from that one is 95%. I found that I was losing weight rapidly, had a decreased appetite, prolonged fever, diarrhoea and abdominal distension. I tell you, it wasn't a very pleasurable experience.'

'What precautions can you take and what's the treatment?'

'Litres of DEET insecticide. Nothing is 100% effective, but we used the strongest we could find and that was Bushman Heavy Duty, with an 80% active ingredient of N, N-Diethyl-meta-toluamide. Then we slept as high up as possible 'cos those damn flies prefer to stay close to the ground. The trouble is that the flies are so small they can get through the nets that we slept under. We sprayed insecticide everywhere. Treatment has to include an immune competent system as medicine alone cannot rid the body of the parasite. If you do not get this a relapse of immune suppression will inevitably happen. Anyway, the villagers treated me with the *yakruma* plant, which helped, but Gonzales dosed me up with meglumine antimoniate and miltefosine then had me choppered out of the village and into the nearest local hospital and then back to UK. It took a long time for me to recover and treatment included chemotherapy.'

'Was your suggestion ever implemented into the training scheme?'

'Nah. They read our reports and deemed it a holiday and no good for real soldiers. However, it did confirm the thinking that winning over hearts and minds of the indigenous people was the way forward in any future campaign.'

They talked some more, ate, drank more beer, stood up, shook hands and departed. As he drove away, Davidson wondered again about his friend. He knew that he had been involved in many campaigns such as Brunei, Aden and Jebel Ashqab, followed by Operation Storm in Dhofar. The ferocity of the Dhofar campaign can be gleaned from the fact that it used up all the front-line reserves of ammunition of the entire British Army. He had emerged from these conflicts without any injuries apart from cracking several ribs, a result of a fall from a rock face during Operation Storm in an attack on the Sherishitti Caves. The caves were where Yemeni rebel forces had stored, amongst other armaments, well over 300,000 rounds of ammunition. He had also led a patrol to silence the ferocious Soviet-made 122 mm Katyusha artillery weapon where he had twisted an ankle, but had 'beaten the clock,' the Regiment's euphemism for conflict survival. The clock was a moveable clock tower at Bradbury Lines that had inscribed on it the names of every soldier who had died in training or on operations. It commemorated Corporal Keith Norry, one of the successful team who had established a new high altitude free fall record of 30,000 feet. He was killed when his parachute failed to open.

Turning on the car radio and as classical music flooded the car, his thoughts drifted to the next day and horse racing. He couldn't wait.

8.

Colombia.

Hanoz and Escobar spent more than a few minutes together, it was more than two hours, talking and drinking coffee that first morning. They got on like a house on fire and were at ease in each other's company finding it very comfortable to discuss any matters that interested them. Conversation ranged over many topics but always seemed to veer back to drugs and Hanoz's career. As Escobar freely admitted, his career was an open book!

'Daler, you are well aware that I have certain criminal tendencies,' he laughed at this point, 'but all I do is to supply a need, mainly to the US market and now more and more the European one, for a product that gives happiness to many people.' He noticed that Hanoz was about to chip in so added, 'of course it does cause a bit of unhappiness to a few, but in general it's a sound recreational drug and if the US and UK governments want to call it illegal, well that's nothing to do with me.'

Hanoz interrupted him.

'My background means that I have no qualms with that. It brings in money and that is what interests me. But I have read that there has been a lot of extreme violence, people being murdered in pursuit of market controls?'

'You cannot make an omelette without breaking eggs,' was the reply. 'The key to human relations is either domination or subjugation. Which do you prefer?'

'Touché.'

Escobar then changed the topic to Turkey, as he was keen to learn about drug movement there. This was an area where he had no control or current interest, but it might be of interest to him later and opposite him was a man who seemed to know a lot about the black arts of drug smuggling in Europe. He broached the topic by first talking about the Latin America position, giving a potted history of the Cali and Medellin cartels, followed by Hildebrando Pascoal of Brasil, a man who he greatly admired and who controlled Acre state on the borders of Peru and Bolivia. Hanoz later found out that Pascoal had arranged for a doctor to be killed, as he had failed to save his mother's life. He was as brutal as Escobar. The Mexican cartels of Tijuana run by Felix Gallardo and the Sinola run by 'El Chapo' Guzmán also came in for special treatment.

'So what's the situation with Turkey? I believe that there, it is south-east Asian/Afghanistan heroin that is important rather than cocaine?'

'True. Turkey is a big player and involved in that trade although the capacity is infinitely less than other countries. You obviously know that morphine was first extracted from the *papaver somniferum* poppy in 1803 and subsequently heroin from morphine in 1898. The Golden Throat area near the Burma, Laos and Thai borders is where the main crop is grown and is brought out by mule via the landlocked Shan states to Thailand. From there it is transhipped all over the globe. My guess is that about half the heroin that floods into the USA comes from this region. Laws for laundering drug money, or for confiscating drug assets are non-existent. I can name two Thai MPs who are allegedly involved in the drug trade, namely Mongkhol Chongsutanamanee and Nakorn Phanon and an indictment has been issued in California for the latter. Occasionally arrests by the police are made of low-level couriers, but the big boys are not touched. The Shan states annual production capacity is probably around 900-1,000 tonnes. The area 1,000 m above sea level and composed of rolling cloud-covered hillside, is ideal for poppy growing. Control is by the anti-communist Kuomintang who unofficially are backed by the CIA. Field laboratories, just as you have in Colombia, refine the heroin. Money obtained is used for buying guns and ammunition. As regards pricing, well ten kilos of heroin will cost about $150 in Hong Kong and fetch up to $600,000 in New York. Profit margins are massive.'

Hanoz paused for a moment. Taking a large mouthful of coffee, he looked at Escobar.

'Pablo, this is some of the best coffee I have ever drunk. My compliments. To continue, the routes into Europe are three in number. There is the northern one via Tajikistan and Kazakhstan, to Russia, Poland and either London or Amsterdam. The middle one is Afghanistan, Georgia, Turkey, Bulgaria and the Netherlands. The southern one is Afghanistan, Uzbekistan, Georgia, Ukraine and the Netherlands. This is the main UK supply route and if needed, extra heroin can be picked up from Chotto in Helmand Province, Afghanistan. The drugs cross the Yugoslavia/Bulgarian border at Kalotina and over 1000 trucks cross daily.'

'What you are telling me, correct me if I'm wrong, is that the Netherlands seems to be an important nodal point.'

'They are. It's Amsterdam, Antwerp or Rotterdam.'

'That's extremely interesting, as we have a lot of potential contacts over there. In fact, tonight we are expecting another guest, a Mr Anton Copje, who is coming here to discuss a few matters of mutual benefit to many people. I believe he has a lot of influence with the Italian Ndrangheta, which is probably the main mafia clan in Italy. He recently spent time in meetings with them in Italy. Mr Daler Hanoz,' he paused. 'I think you and I can make a great deal of money in the near future. I have taken to you and have been very happy with what I've seen, heard and researched about you. We seem to get on very well. We're on the same wavelength. Now I have to go to our capital in a few days' time and you should come with me. Are you interested in all this?'

'That depends upon what you'd like me to do.'

'At the moment, nothing. We'll await Mr Copje and take it from there. Apparently he and his organisation have connections with the Italian Mafia which I believe are second to none. I can assure you that the prospects, as far as I can judge are very favourable. Now let me take you outside to see the grounds and then we'll eat.'

They strolled through the large French windows and out onto the patio where Greek and Roman statues stood side by side with Inca relics and amazing exquisitely coloured very large, banded boulders from China. Masses of flowering shrubs covered the whole colour spectrum with a riot of colour forming an aesthetic background to the statues. One ancient stone wall was a mass of old bougainvillaea purple flowers, the colour of Imperial Rome. Fountains spurted jets of water high into the air. Escobar moved to one side and flicked a switch hidden behind a statue. Music flowed out of concealed speakers and water jets moved to the music.

'You like?'

'Yes, but Vivaldi always reminds me of a dental appointment.'

They both laughed and Escobar pointed at a nearby space.

'I'm hoping to put an Easter Island statue there.'

'I'm surprised that the Rialto Bridge, Venice, isn't there.'

'I did try to buy it but failed. Likewise London Bridge. Come on. Let me show you the stables.'

He led the way to the back of the house where a contemporary array of stables with horse boxes, feedlots, tack rooms were all conveniently integrated into a neat complex of buildings. Leading the way to an unobtrusive doorway, he unlocked it and stood aside allowing Hanoz to enter.

'Be my guest.'

Hanoz gasped once again at the Hacienda's array of novelty, richness and good taste. He was standing at the entrance to a very large lounge, which had a stage at one end with a small dance floor in front. The rest of the room was filled with expensive furnishings, comfortable chairs, sofas, low tables and along one wall was fitted an extensive well-stocked bar. At the far end, a circular staircase led to the first floor. Walking up it behind Escobar, he was shown several en suite bedrooms, ten in total, all complete with ceiling mirrors, well-stocked bars and amazing views over the grounds.

'This is where I can hold very intimate parties.' Escobar looked Hanoz in the eye. 'You should have been here last week. For the weekend I flew in some girls from the Follies Bergere show, Paris. Amongst other matters, they put on a super show.' He smiled expansively. 'Last month, we had a similar party with girls from the Crazy Horse saloon.'

A broad grin crept over Hanoz's face.

'Pablo, I think I'm going to enjoy my stay with you. Also, I'd fancy a trip with you to Bogotá,' was the only immediate comment that he could think of. A pause was followed by, 'when is the next party?'

'Just you wait. I have some business to take care of first. Then we'll see. My friend, work comes before pleasure. It's best that way.'

Unfortunately, Hanoz never made that party.

*   *   *   *

Copje departed from Erika at dawn, leaving her asleep on the King size bed. They had said goodbye to each other before going to sleep and both had felt that sadness that hinges on finding a strong mutual attraction between both parties and having to cut it short. They had agreed to meet up when Copje's business was finished. The effect this had on him was to make him take a long hard look at his current lifestyle. Was what he did worth it? His mind was troubled by this thought, as the answer that he kept arriving at was negative. He took one more look at her sleeping form, gently kissed her forehead and was still brooding upon that thought when he climbed into a taxi to take him to the bus station. Entering the Medellin bus and settling into a rear seat, he closed his eyes. He'd had little sleep during the night and now was a chance to catch up. To hell with the scenery was his last thought as he drifted off, this even before the driver had started the engine.

He was awakened four hours later by the bus stopping at a roadside service station. Everyone piled out and headed for the toilet and he saw that he was the sole non-Latin American passenger. Copje debated whether to have a coffee or not and deciding that he felt refreshed enough to not need any more sleep, ordered a strong Americano plus two croissants. As he looked at the latter he once again marvelled on the fact that it took 12 distinct laminations of kneaded dough and butter to create the perfect croissant. After eating two he decided that these had at the most two laminations and merited a score of 1 out of 10. Piling more jam on his last one, he ordered another Americano, which was rated 10 out of 10, visited the toilet and felt much better.

When he saw the driver leave, he got up, browsed through the small shop buying a couple of packets of mints before climbing aboard. The bus was reasonably full, but the empty seat next to him enabled him to sprawl out a bit further than usual. The legroom was still rather cramped.

In spite of the coffee, he slept. Waking up, he became more aware of the passing scenery. It varied between thick heavily foliaged mountains, broad meandering river valleys fed by thrusting vigorous streams over which the bus crawled over what appeared to him to be unsound small bridges. The bus stopped several times at villages that seemed more and more beaten up than the previous ones. Then the pattern reversed itself, so he presumed they had passed the halfway stage. People left, got on and all seemed to possess mounds of luggage. He dozed a bit and came awake with the tooting of the horn when the bus entered the Medellin bus station. He had arrived.

Descending, he collected his bag and looked around. Amidst the apparent chaos, he noticed a fellow European who nodded to him and he walked over.

'Mr Copje, I presume,' was said with an exaggerated drawl, as if he was Stanley and Copje was Livingstone.

'Correct.' A brief handshake took place.

'I'm Lucky. Mr Escobar asked me to meet you. Did you have a pleasant journey?'

'To be frank, I slept and dozed most of the way.'

'If I may say so, I've found that this is the best way to survive the journey, as the route is not what I'd call scenic. Anyway, let me have your case and we can get going. As soon as we get to the house, I'm sure you'd like a drink and some food? I know I always feel like that after a long journey.'

'Sounds delightful to me. I'm a bit thirsty. Let's go.'

'The Hacienda Nápoles lies outside Medellin.' Lucky smiled, 'However, I have taken the precaution of bringing three large bottles of cold beer for you to drink while we drive there. I know that I always need some liquid after such a journey. Not that I travel by bus very often.'

'Lucky, you're a true mate. Thanks and pass them over.' Lucky passed over a cooler bag and by the time they had reached the Hacienda, he'd drunk the three and was looking forward to the next.

They passed through the main gate and Copje noticed two guards at the gatehouse, both with Uzi submachine guns slung around their necks. They nodded to Lucky as the gate swung open. Drawing up at the house, the main door was open, courtesy of the guards ringing through to the house and he saw two persons standing there waiting to greet them.

'Mr Copje, can I say welcome to the Hacienda Nápole,' said one coming forward with his hand held out. 'I'm Pablo Escobar and this,' turning to the person beside him, 'is my house guest Daler Hanoz from Turkey. It's a pleasure to meet you as I'm sure we have a lot to discuss over the next few days; however, your late arrival has caused me a slight problem, as I have to go to Bogotá tomorrow for a meeting with the Government at the Capitolio Nacional. You can either come along or stay here. Decide later.'

Handshakes were given and taken for all parties.

'Pleased to meet you, Mr Escobar. I've heard a lot about you and look forward to our talks.'

'I hope that what you've heard has been positive,' was said with a slight smile. 'Now please come inside, as I'm sure you need a drink after that long drive. You must be thirsty.'

Copje exchanged a grin with Lucky.

'I'd love one even though Lucky helped out in that department.'

They entered the main hall and moved into the lounge. Copje was amazed at the luxurious tone of the place. He realised that a professional decorator must have been employed as the furnishings had that unobtrusive air of exquisite, subtle, no expense spared taste.

'We've just finished eating,' carried on Escobar, 'but if you are hungry, I can have some food put out for you?'

'A sandwich is all I need, as my throat is more in need of liquid than my stomach.'

'Lucky, could you please see to the sandwich request?'

'Certainly, and I'll get some drinks at the same time. Beers, G and T, champagne?'

'Capital,' was the non-commitment reply.

They sat down on the various comfortable chairs. Escobar sprawled on the sofa and a natural conversation ensued covering many topics. Lucky joined them and was motioned to a chair. As to the drinks, all had turned down beer and G and T opting to drink champagne and glasses were refilled several times, a servant appearing with a bottle of Krug whenever Escobar clapped his hands – and this gesture was done fairly often. After a while during a still in the conversation, Escobar remarked.

'I'm enjoying this conversation. It seems as if I'm amongst old friends, namely a Turk, a Colombian, an Albanian and an Anglo'-Irishman. It sounds like the start of a joke.'

He smiled.

'Not only that but Lucky here, our sole 'Englishman' is not just that, but he's a bona fide Lord. He's a cut above the rest of us in this room. May I introduce you to Lord Lucan? What a name.'

It felt like an explosion of chilled air had blasted across Copje's body. His face remained emotionless, but the fist clenched involuntary and glass shards, blood and champagne spilt on the polished wooden floor, as his hand exerted massive pressure on the thin stem of the champagne flute. He could not believe it. The man who had bludgeoned Sally to death was smiling at him from one metre away, poised in the act of pouring champagne.

'Mr Escobar, apologies,' was said whilst he tried to mop up the liquid.

Escobar stopped him as servants rushed to clear up the debris and mop the carpet.

A clean handkerchief was passed him to tie around his hand.

'Bring the first aid kit,' ordered Escobar and one servant immediately left.

The rest of the evening at the Hacienda Nápoles was spent in mapping out meetings to be held over the coming days. Lucky noticed that Escobar had arranged for private talks with Hanoz, as much as those with Copje plus a few other cartel members. Copje was surprisingly quiet during the discussions and eventually stated that he was tired and going to bed.

'If you don't mind, I think I'll miss out on the Bogotá visit and stay here tomorrow. I'm a bit tired and there is something I have to do.'

In his bedroom and with hot, angry tears running from his eyes, Copje repeatedly punched the bed pillow so much that he eventually ripped it. Sitting on the bed, holding his head in his hands, he rocked back and fore and an angry vein throbbed in his forehead.

'Lord Lucan,' he kept murmuring, 'at last he's going to pay for Sally's death.'

He lay down on the bed and concentrated on how to kill Lucky. The death had to appear accidental. Copje realised that he was in Escobar's territory and did not want any suspicion fostered onto him. He knew how brutal the cartel king could be and he wanted to leave Colombia in one piece. Lucky was going to die slowly that was for sure and Copje was going to keep saying Sally's name to him so that he knew why this was happening. The kill had to be tomorrow as Escobar and many security staff would be away in Bogotá. His blood felt as if it was pulsating through his arteries and he sensed that old thrill of combat. Undressing and snuggling under the thin coverlet, he let his imagination reign over the many possibilities.

Downstairs the others decided to follow his example as an early start was expected in the morning for the Bogotá flight. As they had eaten, some more sandwiches were sent to Copje and all left for their respective rooms.

At breakfast the next morning it took a great effort by Copje to not show his hatred of Lucky. He tried his best to appear jovial.

'Lucky will show you around the place,' said Escobar, 'so make yourself at home. 'We might be back tonight or tomorrow night. It all depends upon circumstances.'

With that, he and the others left the breakfast table and Copje and Lucky were alone.

Escobar, Hanoz and six security staff arrived at the airport to find that a slight mechanical fault with the Lear jet meant that they were grounded for a few hours and it was past 11 o clock when eventual take off took place. The jet went all out to get them to Bogotá. Escobar had radioed the meeting chair stating that they had been delayed but they would try to get to the Capitolio Nacional as soon as possible.

On the flight Escobar again briefed his security men stressing that violence for this meeting must be kept to zero if possible, emphasising that vigilance of the highest order had to be maintained at all times. Turning to Hanoz he offered him a gun stating that, if he agreed, he was being co-opted into the security team for this mission. Hanoz accepted it. The meeting was between Government representatives and Escobar. I later found out from Hanoz that Escobar was putting forward the option of personally paying off Colombia's national debt, which I must admit I found pretty amazing. One person paying off the national debt of a country was simply unbelievable; it belonged in the realm of fairy tales.

Landing at the airport, two black Mercedes cars were waiting and Hanoz and Escobar selected the rear vehicle in which to travel. They set off with a police escort, police cars in front and rear with several motorcyclists acting as outriders, horns blaring and blue lights flashing. Police at traffic lights blocked off traffic at all main intersections so no obstructions held them up. Hanoz told me that he had enjoyed the ride. It was the first time he had been in a convoy that made him feel as if he was a head of state.

This all ended when nearing the Capitolio Nacional, they saw a hotel window smashed because a chair had been thrown through it. Shards of glass splintered on the roadway directly in front of the two Mercedes and the chair hit the windscreen of the first car. The driver froze and braked to a stop. Any regular security driver would have driven away from the scene like a bat out of hell. The second car crumpled into its back and also stopped. Almost on auto pilot, Hanoz was first out. 'Get him away now,' was shouted, as he raced into the hotel followed by a security person and Escobar's favourite hitman, Jhon Jairo Velásquez, nicknamed Popeye. The others surrounded Escobar by jumping into his car getting the driver to reverse and drive quickly away. Tyres smoking, the car accelerated and screeched away taking Escobar to safety.

9.

Bogotá

Paddy and Zafar in the early morning and flush with money, duly arrived in Bogotá, courtesy of United Airlines. Paddy automatically took a taxi from the airport and booked a second floor suite at the Hotel de la Opera, central Bogotá. This overlooked and was adjacent to the Thomas Read designed neo-classical Capitolio Nacional of Colombia, the meeting place of both houses of Congress. The first thing they did was to luxuriate in the ornate bathtubs to try to eradicate the grime from their jail stay, which tended to persist despite numerous baths in Miami. As usual, this was accompanied by much drinking of Long John whisky by Paddy, a brand for which he had developed quite an attachment.

'This is the life me boy,' was uttered at periodic intervals between swigs of neat whisky. 'I was born to live like this, but somehow things went a bit astray.'

Zafar merely nodded an acknowledgement He had never been in a hotel that boasted two baths in the same room. His one beer was all he needed as he sank even lower in the foam speckled bathtub.

'What we need now is for a couple of girls to join us. Damn it, I was too impatient. Never mind when we go out later we can remedy that omission. It's still very early, so perhaps it'd be good to have a little rest before we roar into action.'

He threw a bar of soap at Zafar.

'How about it? You up for it?' He laughed and splashed away contentedly.

After soaking for over half an hour, they rose and dressed. Zafar gazed out of the window and remarked at the grand view of the Parliament buildings.

'When I think of the rice farm and the rural idyll I grew up in, this urban scene is something special and takes some beating. You know, I loved it when we planted rice. Many females from Bulgaria and Romania used to come to the farm to work in the fields. We used to house them in a big old barn, they ate and slept there and my brother Paulo, remember I told you about him? He worked in the Firenze Tourist office, Bigallo, Piazza S Giovanni 1. It's ingrained in my memory. Now he's in Roma's Tourism Office. He used to pick out the attractive ones and had a great time. He could give presents and more importantly, easier jobs. They didn't call him the Italian Stallion for nothing. I had to go along with the charade of pretending to want to sleep with the girls. I never followed him even then I knew I was gay, but just could not come out. I kept my feelings hidden and wrestled with that dilemma for several years, but family and the Italian macho culture stopped me. Apart from one summer, I led a miserable existence until I moved away to London.'

'I'm sorry that I made that remark about girls, but there's no way we can have an orgy in the same room,' came from Paddy. 'You and a bloke, no, no, no, Argh. Let's go down to the bar and have some food and a drink or two and experience some bloody good *craic*. Also, it might be a better idea to have separate rooms. I'll think about it.'

They left and went downstairs to the bar, little realising that things were about to change drastically when next they went upstairs. Looking out over the room as they slowly came down the staircase Paddy spied a couple of well-dressed, good looking females who were sitting at the bar casually sipping some kind of cocktail. They smiled at him when he entered and raised their glasses. That was all the invitation he needed. His Irish blood was up and raring for it - he was ready for whatever it was.

'I've been away from civilised society for far too long, so bye-bye Zafar,' was his comment as he shunted him to one side and headed towards them. He sauntered over.

'Good afternoon ladies would you care for a drink? If so come and join me and we will have a grand old time. My name is Paddy,

130

I'm from Ireland and I've just arrived in this charming city. What are your names?'

As he was mouthing these words, the only thought that came into his mind was that he wished Zafar was not gay and he had a true blue heterosexual partner with him so that they could pair off. This was followed by which of the pair to ditch, with the corollary of how to do it with panache? He smiled, as it was a lovely problem to have. He did think of suggesting a threesome, but told himself to concentrate on the priority of getting one of them to the upstairs suite.

Zafar smiled, shrugged, bought himself a beer and sat outside in the warm sunlit garden and thought about the emeralds he was going to find.

*   *   *   *

José and I slipped Sonnel into a body bag and I slowly zipped it up and we placed it in the truck. I mentally said my goodbyes to my dear friend. Sir George stood silently by my side with his Panama hat clutched in his hands. We had filled him in as to what had happened.

I asked. 'His parents live in Bogotá, so we must get him back there soon. Is today possible?'

'I don't know about today, it's far too late, but I'll make it possible,' replied José. 'There's a small airfield about an hour's drive from here that is used by the oil companies and they have several planes. Tomorrow, we should be able to charter one.' He grinned. 'Out here if FARC makes a request it's granted. We'll take him there and you can fly to Bogotá with him. Once there you will have to contact the police and tell them that he died accidentally when his head hit a rock. Your cover story is that you and Sonnel were holidaying when this happened and luckily you were near to oil company personnel. You chartered the plane and came to Bogotá where his parents live and you wanted the body to be in a morgue before informing the parents. Let's keep the story as near to the truth as possible.'

I nodded. I certainly wanted Sonnel to be in a morgue rather than in the hot, humid jungle atmosphere where decay accelerates with lightning speed.

I looked at Sir George and José. 'I'm a bit unsure as to what this kidnapping is all about as you two seem pretty friendly. It's almost as if the Stockholm syndrome has occurred immediately rather than over time. Has Sir George really been kidnapped or is he free to come with me?'

The two of them locked eyes. Sir George was the first to speak.

'This is rather difficult for me to explain but to answer your second point. No, I'm not coming with you. I'll stay here as there is a job to be done. I cannot go into details, but you mustn't talk with anyone about my being here. You are quite right in that this is not a so-called normal kidnapping. It's all been pre-arranged. That's all I have to say at this point. Like you, I have several friends in FARC who will look after me rather well. So good luck for your journey and let me repeat myself in saying how sorry I am that you have lost a good friend.'

I stood up and shook his hand.

He added, 'If all goes well, please look me up in London.' He passed me his business card on which he wrote his private phone number. Alas, I never had the opportunity of meeting him in London.

I slept poorly that night, so did José. The only person who slept and snored his way through the night was Sir George. In the early morning, José and I plus four soldiers drove the truck out of the camp to the Lisama oil field. On the perimeter was parked four small planes. We drove up to the main building and I stayed behind as José and his men entered. Some 15 minutes later a car pulled up, two men climbed out and entered the building. Five minutes later a group came out including José and his men and all walked over to the truck.

José introduced the group. 'Adam, this is Griff Vivian, the manager of the field and this is Keith Abbott the company pilot. The company has stated that they are only too happy to help with what has been an unfortunate accident. They have agreed to take you and Sonnel to Bogotá.'

'There'll be no charge,' said Vivian. 'We realise that accidents do occur and may I express my sympathies to you and your colleague's family.'

I thanked him and just wished that I had been a fly on the wall inside that building. I could just visualise José saying. 'I'd like to borrow your plane to transport two people, one alive, one dead to Bogotá.'

José was dead right. In this area, FARC was the undisputed king.

We moved Sonnel's body out of the truck and strapped him across the back seats. Rigour mortise had set in. I shook hands with José and the soldiers and wished them well thinking that was the last I'd see of them and we took off.

The flight was uneventful, we passed from dense jungle to savanna grasslands pre starting to climb as we approached the mountainous central spine of Colombia. The oil company had radioed ahead so when we landed at Bogotá, an ambulance and police cars were waiting. Sonnel's body was taken to a mortuary and I went to a police station where I answered a lot of questions and filled in countless forms. I was there all morning. I had to give an address, so asked for a good hotel and was informed that the Hotel de la Opera was a good one. On leaving, I took a taxi and it was only when we had arrived at the hotel that I realised it was one of the major hotels in the whole of the country.

I needed some time on my own, as I dreaded going to see his parents. The thought of informing them that their only child was dead shook me and I made up my mind to see them the following day. On entering the hotel and registering, my eyes and ears could not help but notice a large, boisterous, bearded man belting out an

Irish ballad, 'When Irish eyes are smiling,' to two very attractive women. He had a surprisingly good, light tenor voice. When he finished, I politely clapped.

Looking over towards me, he grinned and with a big smile on his face waved his arm beckoning me to join him.

'Why not,' I thought to myself so went over. That's how I met Paddy Mahoney.

Introductions were made and Paddy poured out a glass of wine for me and refilled the glasses of the others. 'You don't need cocktails when wine is as good as this,' was his comment.

The usual small talk ensued and Paddy was struck by the fact that I was a geologist.

'We'll have to have a serious talk later on, but not now, as this is party time,' was said with him thumping his fist on the table. He then started winking at me and inclining his head to one of the females trying to surreptitiously tell me that she was for me.

He stood up. 'This bar is far too noisy for me.' I looked around. It was relatively empty and the only noise came from him.

'Why don't we go upstairs and continue the party? Come along ladies don't be shy, as I can assure you that you'll not regret it. My pockets are deep.'

Smiles all round and with that a man entered from the hotel's garden.

'Zafar my buddy come here and meet Adam and some of my new friends. We are going upstairs for some *craic* so do come and join us,' adding sotto voice, 'only for an hour or so.'

I shook hands with Zafar and Paddy filled me in on their respective backgrounds as we talked, walked and waited for the ancient lift. We got off on the third floor, the wrong one, as I later found out. Flinging open what Paddy thought was the door to his suite, we all piled in and for a nanosecond paused. The two crouching figures by the window turned towards us; after that everything seemed to take place in slow motion, a blur, but in reality, it all happened very fast.

The two men who had been seated by the windows facing the square had quickly swivelled round to meet us, simultaneously dropping the large weapons they had been holding, hands snaking to their waist-belts. I was told later by Hanoz that one weapon was an RPG7 Soviet-made rocket launcher, while the other was the FIM-92A1 Stinger, which was a considerable improvement on the old Redeye shoulder-launched SAM missile. It had a passive infrared homing system and the 3 kg warhead was proximity fused for blast fragmentation. It would have made mincemeat of any car and its occupants. How two such bulky weapons and two rockets had been smuggled into the room was something that later on puzzled everyone.

They were in the process of drawing revolvers thrust into their belts when Paddy exploded. Picking up the nearest chair he had hurled it at one of the men who swayed out of its path and it smashed through the window. Paddy had followed up the chair's path and was onto the man before he could draw his revolver. I woke up at that point and charged the other. He had drawn his pistol and got off two shots. One gave me an upper arm flesh wound, the bullet entering and exiting leaving a neat hole through my arm; the other hit Zafar. I noticed the pain, but it did not stop my body charge and within seconds of cannoning into him we were on the floor. Luckily my good hand was clasped around the man's gun hand, but my punches with the injured arm lacked any force. I tried to smother him as best I could, kneeing him in the genitals whenever the occasion presented itself. Scrabbling on the floor with a man, who I realised was much bulkier than me, is not recommended, especially if one has a dud arm.

As we fought we occasionally bumped into the other two who were upright but they careered all-round the room swopping punches. They were evenly matched as both were big men. I took in this information even though I was scrapping and knew that we were fighting for our lives. Fighting seemingly went on for ages, but

I guess it was less than a minute when through the door came three men all with guns in their hands. One fired his gun before it was swept from him.

'No,' came a scream. 'It's too dangerous. Grab them.'

With that, he dived at Paddy's opponent and grasping an arm hit him on the temple, as hard as he could with the gun held in his other hand. The man slumped and head first hit the ground. Thump. Thankfully one of the others came to my aid stamping on the assassin's gun hand and incidentally mine, before kicking him in the head. His boot missed my head by a minimal margin, but it did the trick. The gun was dropped and he was out for the count.

We slowly got to our feet. Paddy had blood streaming down his face where he had been head-butted and one ear looked as if it had been chewed. Gazing around the room, I saw two females huddled in the corner clutching each other. One had been knocked down in Paddy's fight, but she appeared to be all right. Zafar was comatose and going to him, I realised that the other shot had grazed his skull and he was out cold. Feeling for a pulse I was relieved to find one.

The hotel security staff then appeared, followed by a manager peeping round the door. He stated that the police had been called. Our police escort had somehow disappeared. We introduced ourselves and milled around until a carload of new policeman turned up and took us down to headquarters, where people who had interviewed me some two hours earlier were amazed to see me back. It took some time to complete formalities, but the mere whisper of Escobar's name commanded instant respect.

Popeye then made contact with Escobar and heard that the security detail had taken him to the Bogotá house. Eventually, we were released and told not to leave the country. The police doctor dressed my arm and gave me a tetanus shot and antibiotics. As the bullet had gone straight through I was splashed with iodine, which stung like a wasp sting. Arrangements had been made for us all to regroup at Escobar's house outside Bogotá and that is where we all went apart from poor Zafar who had been hospitalised with suspected concussion.

The Escobar mansion, note not house, was located just outside the city. High walls surrounded it and it was luxuriously furnished, although according to Hanoz, not quite at the standard of the Hacienda Nápoles. It was in the hallway that I met Pablo Escobar. Although I had lived in Medellin for about two years, I had never seen the man but had heard all about him, as he owned the place. A stocky black-haired man with a big moustache, he stood in the middle of a large lounge that had a roaring fire going in a massive stone-built fireplace. Hanoz made the introductions. Paddy and I had our hands shaken and were given hugs.

'To say that I'm grateful to you both,' and turning to Paddy, 'your hospitalised friend, is an understatement. You foiled an attempted assassination today and I cannot say thank you enough. You must receive some of my Colombian hospitality for this, so I would like to invite you all to come to Medellin tomorrow and be my guests for as long as you want. The meeting here has been cancelled and we will continue with it another day. I have arranged with the hospital that your friend will join us here tomorrow around lunchtime; his concussion tests were negative, so they were happy for him to leave tomorrow morning. He is being kept in tonight more as a precaution.'

I eyed Paddy who grinned at me.

'Sure Mr Escobar, that's an excellent offer and on behalf of us all, I can say that we'll gladly accept it.' He added, 'I've always wanted to go to Medellin and now is the time.'

He certainly must have kissed the Blarney stone. Zafar later told me he had never mentioned going there and had apparently never heard of the town.

I said, 'I think a lot of credit must go to Mr Hanoz. Without his help we would have been in great difficulty.'

'Ah Daler. Yes, he appears to be a good man to have around when circumstances like this occur.' He smiled. 'I'm sure if his modesty allows, he'll tell you about some of his exploits.'

His grin became even broader. 'If he doesn't, I can fill you in. Now gentlemen, drinks and food are on the table over there. Help yourself.'

Hanoz injected. 'We must not forget your security staff Pablo. They also contributed to the success. They got you away as they should. We had some help from Popeye, but the car drivers need some rigorous evasive driving practice.'

'Of course. I gather one of the security staff tried to shoot a killer, or should I say a failed killer. The shot could have been fatal for anyone. Your shout stopped indiscriminate shootings and for that, I am grateful. Two men are now in police custody and we might get some information as to who is behind this. I just wish they were here in my custody.'

So for the next two hours, the four of us sat in the comfortable chairs and ate, drank and talked. Escobar was particularly intrigued with Paddy and Zafar's quest for emeralds and with my contacts with FARC. He kept bringing the conversation back to these points. Paddy was uproarious and made full use of the bar. I noticed that Escobar and Hanoz drank little.

I was intrigued by Hanoz, as he had appeared to be as cool as a cucumber during the fight and he certainly knew his way around a rough house, yet he was as sophisticated as they come and his conversation eloquently displayed a deep knowledge of the Arts. Escobar stated that he had to do some work and left us. I listened to some music and picked up a book to take to bed; Hanoz and Paddy seemed deep in conversation and I heard Zafar's name mentioned a lot.

As we left for bed, Hanoz leaned over to me and whispered. 'In essence, the men arrested are in his custody, as he bankrolls half the senior police force here. I think they are in for a tough time and don't think much for their survival chances.'

He winked. With that, we all departed to our separate rooms.

10.

Medellin, Bogotá.

Copje slept well that night and awoke in the early morning with a smile on his face. Retribution and destiny beckoned and he was eager for it. Bring it on. Rising and going downstairs, he decided to go for a run around the extensive estate. In London he usually tried for a 10 km jog each day. The morning air was fresh and standing outside the sizeable ornate doorway, he took deep breaths. He noticed a security man plus dog in the far distance, strolling and possibly checking potential hide spots in the many trees that dotted the grounds. He made a mental note to check this person's whereabouts for later in the day and the run took him past the drive entrance with its guards.

Looking in at the zoo he saw the carnivores being fed raw meat. He had thought of killing Lucky and doing just that with his body. This was soon discarded. It would arouse suspicion if a house guest of several years just suddenly disappeared. The body had to be found and a verdict of accidental death recorded. The run took him down to the small river and it was when he saw the hippos cavorting around that the idea came. Hippos are said to be the biggest animal killer of humans in Africa even though they are vegetarian. I do not believe this, as in my book crocodiles take that title. People simply disappear with crocodiles and are never seen again; victims of hippos invariably are left consistently badly mangled after being trodden by many feet. They are funny animals since they must live in water yet cannot swim. They just trudge and rumble on their short, stubby legs along the bottom of ponds, rivers and can stay underwater for some time. The four he was looking at were large, well over 1,000 kg (2,200 lb). He did not get too close, as he had been told they can run at 30 km/hr (19 mph) for short distances. In daylight he felt safe, as they usually came out of the water at dusk to feed on grass.

The jog back was very enjoyable. Now all he had to do was entice Lucky to come for a walk.

Back at the Hacienda he showered, changed and went downstairs for the early breakfast. Everyone was there and goodbyes were exchanged as the main party left for the airfield, leaving behind Adriana, María and Lucky and the house servants.

'I hope you slept well,' said Adriana.

'I had a great sleep and feel well-rested, how about you two?'

'Not that great, but it was okay,' was the reply from María. So María did understand a little English. They all laughed.

'What are you going to do today, do you have anything planned?' said Lucky.

'Oh, I have some paperwork to finish up this morning and then I think a stroll around the grounds to see the magnificent gardens of this place plus the zoo of course. I have heard many good things about it and am curious to see it.'

'If you like, I can accompany you after lunch and show you around,' said Lucky. 'Do you want to come along?' This was addressed to Adriana.

'No thanks. We're both still a bit tired and walking around the grounds just to see trees, lawns and the zoo is not my idea of fun. I would rather finish my book if you don't mind.'

Copje drew a deep breath. Fortune was favouring him.

'Fine that's decided then. I'll see you both for lunch, if you'll excuse me, I'll go to my room now and sort out all the paperwork, then I'll take a little walk. I think that Mr Escobar will want everything neat and tidy on his return.'

They both laughed at that remark.

'You bet,' said Lucky, 'he's a tarter for thoroughness and wants all the i's dotted and t's crossed. If you've never seen him in action, you're going to have a big surprise.'

'Well, as you have never seen me in action, you're also going to have a big surprise.' This remark was addressed to Lucky and under his breath was added, 'and it will be the last surprise of your life.'

Leaving the dining room he went upstairs to his room. Lying on the bed he went through what he had planned for Lucky. Copje was a big believer in going over everything in his mind pre any job, trying to find flaws in any plan and counteracting them. Then practice, practice and more practice until whatever was being done became second nature. He did not believe in luck. What was it that the golfer Gary Player had once said? 'The more I practice, the luckier I get.' He could not practice what he was going to do later in the day with Lucky, but he could run through it again and again in his mind. This was done for an hour and he dozed until 12.30 pm when the alarm went off. He padded to the workshop, picked up a few items and went down to the river. Returning, he went straight to the dining room for lunch.

Lunch was a pleasant affair with Lucky in sparkling form switching from English to Spanish to accommodate María in the conversation. Copje found that María really did know more English than she let on. The wines were first class and Copje made sure that Lucky's glass was kept full while he drank sparingly. He wanted a clear mind for the afternoon.

Sometime after 2.30 pm, they all retired to the lounge.

'I thought you two were going for a stroll?' inquired Adriana.

'Damn, I forgot all about that,' was Copje's reply. 'I must be getting old as my memory is not as sharp as it used to be.' He hoped that Adriana would remember this conversation. 'Come on,' this to Lucky, 'get your walking boots on and let's go.'

The men almost reluctantly rose from the luxurious easy chairs. Adriana and María remained seated. They said their goodbyes and five minutes later left the house.

Copje uttered a sigh of satisfaction. This was going to turn out just fine.

Strolling round the grounds meant a visit to the zoo, stables and then Copje steered the walk towards the river and the hippo area. On arrival, the hippos snorted and let out ferocious roars as they splashed and thundered around. When opened, their immense jaws displayed large yellowed teeth, whilst shaking their massive heads and wiggling their ears. He loved watching the ear wiggle. The four hippos submerged and their eyes followed the path of the two men.

At the bank was a large wooden seat and the men sat down to observe the curious animals. Copje had seen that the bench was on top of a steep slope that ended in shallow water. It had been deliberately sited there for safety purposes, as hippos cannot easily climb very steeply sloping riverbanks.

'You are looking at two tonnes of pork per animal,' said Lucky and that was the last words he ever uttered. Copje tapped him on the side of the head with a wooden mallet that had been hidden under a bush next to the seat. The measured blow knocked Lucky out for a few minutes and when he come round, duct tape had been stretched over his mouth and his wrists tied behind his back with the same tape. Copje had moved the unconscious Lucky to a small hollow on the river bluff made by the hippos and out of sight of the house.

Regaining consciousness, Lucky struggled.

'It's pointless old boy.' The words were uttered in a perfect parody of the drawl of an upper-class Englishman. 'You must try to relax, but I know it's hard especially when I tell you that Sally Rivett was my fiancée.'

Lucky suddenly stopped struggling and lay motionless. A tear started to moisten his left eye and slowly coalesced into a ball that rolled down his cheek.

'Yes, I thought that would startle you, you bastard,' and with that kicked him in the face; twice.

'I've dreamt of this moment for many years and in my dreams.' He aimed another kick at Lucky's face that smashed his nose from which blood spurted. A muffled groan came from the bound man. 'If I had you all to myself in a locked room there would be an array of instruments for me to use on you, for example, a blow torch with which I would dance the flame along your body, especially your genitals. I'd like to see your pubic hairs burn. Then I'd have a pair of pliers with which to rip off your finger and toenails. I can assure you this hurts. I've done it several times in the past. But I couldn't find any pliers. It's your lucky day, matey.'

He paused. 'I'd then string you up in the *strappado* or *corda* position.'

'Do you know what this is? No? Let me enlighten you. It's an old-fashioned torture technique thought up by the Medieval Inquisition, where your hands are tied behind you. I tie a rope to your wrists and haul you up by a pulley. Your shoulder joints get dislocated or torn out of their sockets. I'd leave you there for about half an hour as if I left you for an hour you'd probably die on me. I would not want that to happen. In that position, you could ponder on the political situation of the world or whatever it is you fancied.'

He gazed around. 'What a pleasant view it is here and such a lovely day, a super vista of trees, lawns and alongside a gentle river. All that's needed is a gin and tonic, or a whisky to make a charming scene. Lovely spot in which to die.' This was followed by another vicious kick to the face.

'That reminds me.' He left and went back to the bush by the seat, bringing back a bottle and a glass.

'I took the liberty of bringing some whisky here on an earlier walk.' Pouring out a generous three fingers, he continued, 'I hope you are taking all this in because I cannot do any of this to you. You see, when I kill you.' Copje looked at his watch.

'I'd say you have about an hour or two of life left before you meet your maker, or rather before you start stoking in hell.'

This was followed by two kicks, this time directly into the groin.

'Yes, I cannot do any of the many variations on a theme I had planned. One of the others was to gouge out one of your eyes with a spoon. I've just remembered that one, my, my. My memory of things I was going to do to you must be failing, as I forgot to bring a spoon. Guess it's the onset of old age. All I had planned was theoretical, as I never expected to find you. Therefore, I'm just going to amuse myself in what is left of your allotted time on earth. This will be followed by,' he paused at that statement. 'Would you like me to tell you? Of course you would, as you are enjoying our little conversation, aren't you?'

This time it was a hard smash of the mallet against a shin bone. The bone broke with a loud crack. Lucky fainted.

Copje simply sipped his whisky and waited for him to regain consciousness. When he saw the eyes fluttering, he continued.

'I'm going to crush a few fingers with this mallet.'

He searched around for a suitably sized stone. 'This one will do. I'll put your hand on this stone and wham.' He brought the mallet down onto the stone. 'Smash, bang, wallop and a few fingers are squashed.'

Lucky lay as still as a dormouse. All the fight had seemingly gone out of him.

'It's a pity I could not blow torch you because you must be feeling chilly just thinking of what's going to happen and that would have warmed you up a bit. But then, where you're headed, I'm told it's very warm.'

Another kick in the groin followed and this time Copje grabbed a hand placed it on the stone and swinging the mallet aimed a massive blow to the fingers. An anguished, muted scream came from Lucky.

'Oops, I only meant to smash two. Sorry. Now, where was I?'

This was followed by another sip of whisky.

'Ah, yes. I'm going to play some games with you and then guess what? You have nothing to say? Oh, dear me.'

He reached under the seat and produced a real of wire.

'I'm going to tie this to your ankles. Then I'm going to throw stones at the hippos to annoy them. They become rather angry when this happens. As we are on the river bluff, I'm going to toss you into the shallow part below me and goad them further. They will charge around and unfortunately you will be in their way so …phut. You will become a Lucky pancake and I hope it will be a slow cooking. I spent some time earlier today chucking stones at them and it really does rile them. This will not be the Charge of the Light Brigade, but the heavier brigade and boy are they big, heavy and cumbersome.'

Another gulp of whisky. 'Of course, if you think of Archimedes Principle they will not be that heavy due to being semi-immersed in water. Let that be some consolation to you.'

Another gulp. 'After a while, I'm going to haul your body in just to make sure that you are deader than a piece of mutton. If not, I'll finish you off before removing the wire and tape prior to throwing you back.'

He prodded Lucky with his toe. 'I hope you are taking all this in old man? Must say, I'm not looking forward to dragging you back here. I hope your leg will be still attached to the wire. It will be rather messy and I do not want to get blood and body parts on my clothes. Think I'll strip naked for that part.'

As he did so, he chanted,

> 'There was a young man called Lucky
>
> Who used to swim with the duckies.
>
> One day he went for a dip
>
> But unfortunately slipped.
>
> Hippos trampled and made him very mucky.'

He smiled. 'Ok, I know it's corny, but that is what's going to happen to you very soon.'

He just hit and kicked Lucky, waiting for him to regain consciousness before hitting and taunting him again, repeatedly saying, 'This one is for Sally,' interspersed with his poem. Then he threw him off the bluff ledge and started throwing stones.

Later, he returned the mallet, wire and duct tape to the workshop; the glass and half full bottle to the bar.

*   *   *   *

Breakfast at the Bogotá mansion was a sombre affair. Small talk was the order of the day after which Hanoz and I played a few games of snooker on the superb table located in, where else but the Billiard room. I soon realised that he was an extremely good player.

Escobar did not make an appearance until around 11 am.

'I've been on the phone most of the morning,' was his opening line. 'Apparently, the two men arrested yesterday committed suicide in their cells. This is most annoying as I wanted to know who put them up to it. I suspect whoever it is also arranged for the suicides.'

He grimaced and I noticed a smile breaking out on Hanoz's face.

Taking a drink of coffee and nibbling on a croissant, he continued. 'Never mind, I'll find out soon enough. Anyway, the good news is that I've been told that Zafar has just been discharged and will be here soon.'

'Ah, great news,' said Paddy who now had a plaster on his bitten ear, which Hanoz remarked made him resemble van Gogh, so kept referring to him as Vincent. This for some reason pleased the man; a man who had tucked into a massive breakfast of eggs, bacon, fried bread, tomatoes, mushrooms, beans and sausages, mentioning that he needed lots of food as, 'one did not run a Sherman tank on lighter fuel.' This was a common enough remark from him. I was surprised that he did not wash it all down with a swig of neat alcohol.

I arranged to meet up with them at the airport, as I had to visit Sonnel's parents and Escobar laid a car and driver at my disposal. They lived just outside Bogotá in a small town called El Salitre near to Lake Repressa San Rafael. I found the house very quickly. They were disconsolate with grief when I told them the news, as Sonnel had been their only child. I stayed for about two hours, shed tears with them and when I left, assured them that I would keep in touch.

Zafar turned up at the Escobar mansion around 1 pm and seemingly was in good spirits. Introduced to Escobar, hands were shaken and the standard bear hug was given. Paddy told me that Hanoz grinned at this show of friendship because the thought had gone through his mind that if Escobar had known he was bear hugging a homosexual, he'd have killed Zafar on the spot. They had a spot of lunch and then got into the Mercedes cars and departed for the airport, where I met up with them. The airport was busy that afternoon and we had to hang around for a few hours much to the displeasure of Escobar. Even he could not change flight patterns around although if he had been given access to the flight tower, I'm sure he could have. He had other matters on his mind and was always on the phone. Paddy, as usual, did not mind and was soon ensconced on a bar stool, one hand leaning on the counter, the other clasped around a drink. I have never known a man who drank so much.

The day was sparkling and visibility was excellent. The pilot asked if we would like the scenic flight. Escobar did not object, so we deviated quite a bit and he flew us around the mountains and plateaus of the central cordillera. Snow packed peaks, glacial streams snaking through the plateau, all in all, a winter wonderland. We then swept down to lower altitudes towards savanna and eventually the tropical rain forests. I knew that Camp Diamante was down there somewhere, but it all resembled a mass of tightly packed green vegetation in which thin streams of smoke hanging just above the tree line indicated an Indian settlement. This quantity of vegetation was only broken by the meandering paths of rivers, which are the primary means of getting around.

Eventually, we headed for Medellin and soon were debarking at the airport.

Adriana and María, were waiting for us. Escobar led the way out of the plane and stopped at the bottom of the steps to make the introductions.

'What, no Lucky?' was asked.

One of the security staff mentioned that he had not been seen since lunch.

'Very strange,' was Escobar's comment 'I wonder what's stopped him coming to greet us?'

We all piled into the cars and drove off. At the Hacienda the gate guards told us that Lucky had not left the grounds. Copje greeted us at the doorway and was introduced to Paddy, Zafar and me. He said that just after lunch he had gone for a walk with Lucky and had come back for a siesta before going out for a run. No one had seen Lucky since.

Escobar thought for a moment and turning to his security detail said, 'All right, he might have had a heart attack or fallen. Start a sweep of the grounds right away.'

'Yes, *patron.*'

With that, we all entered the main lounge and drinks were made available. Escobar excused himself saying, 'I have several things to do, but dinner will be available in a couple of hours.'

We all sat down before a uniformed servant appeared to show us to our rooms. I had a back room that overlooked the river in the distance. It was next to that of Hanoz. Paddy and Zafar's were in the front of the house. I placed my small bag on the bed, had a shower, change of clothes and wandered downstairs. Hanoz was practising trick shots on the billiard table.

I gave a resounding clap when he pulled off a most audacious shot. A weak smile appeared.

'Fancy a game of snooker?'

'Only if you give me a 50 points start. Playing you in Bogotá made me very wary.'

'Done, set them up, please. I'm going to the John to pump some ballast.' With that and with drink in hand he ambled off to the toilet. I reset the 15 snooker balls and was waiting for Hanoz to return when the door opened and Escobar came in. Seconds later a security guard followed.

'Hemos encontrado Lucky.' ('We have found Lucky,') was the comment. 'Está mureto.' ('He's dead.')

The news that Lucky was dead was a shock, especially to Escobar. The men had brought Lucky back in a body bag. I never thought of asking Escobar why he kept a stock of body bags in the cellar. Ordinary people do not maintain such things in their household. I did not see the body but gather it was in a terrible state, as the bloat of hippos had trampled over him many times. I could imagine what that does to a body. One of the guards told me that his face was unrecognisable and probably every bone in his body had been broken and a leg had been virtually detached being connected to the body only by a thin strip of flesh. Think of a pancake was one comment and apparently two of the guards had thrown up on seeing Lucky's body.

The atmosphere in the house was sombre and even Escobar, who from what I knew of his record had seen many deaths – and also carried out killings himself – was almost silent. It had hit him hard, as he had genuinely liked Lucky. I thought that this was an unfortunate name for a man who had been trampled to death by four hippos.

'We'll bury him at the end of the eastern field,' was spoken by Escobar. 'He loved sitting out there by the tree just looking out at the vista. See to it.' This was addressed to one of his guards.

'Yes, *patron*,' and he scurried away.

'A drink to Lucky.' Walking to the bar he opened two bottles of Krug before filling tulip glasses for us all. We picked them up, raised them to our lips. 'To Lucky,' said Escobar. All downed our glasses in one mouthful. They were refilled.

'Sit down,' was uttered and we obeyed.

'I cannot deny that this has upset me, but life must go on. I intend to have meetings with Mr Copje over the next three days,' and he looked at Hanoz, 'with Daler as well. So you three,' his gaze took in us newcomers, 'can simply be my guests. Enjoy the place. It is a lovely mansion and there's plenty to do, although I'd give the hippos a wide berth if I were you. I think Lucky must have slipped and fallen into the ponded area. It was most unfortunate and the hippos reacted naturally. However, I shall not kill them. Any queries?'

Paddy started to say something, but an upraised palm stopped him.

'To continue. After our discussions, I will go to Florida to see my family and there are one or two matters that I have to discuss with members of the cartel, especially with a certain Mr Bautista who likes it so much in the US that apparently he refuses to come back to Colombia. I would also like to see the White House, as I have heard much about it, but, I repeat, you all are invited to stay here.'

He stopped to drain his glass before refilling it. 'You have only seen glimpses of my secretary, Helena,' he smiled at this comment, 'as she has been very busy, but I am sure that she will look after you in my absence.'

'I'll stop here as I want to talk with Daler, Paddy, Adam and Zafar,' this was said to Copje,' so if you'll excuse us, we will meet up later. I see that you Daler, enjoy snooker, so Mr Copje, would you like to take on the Turkish champion after the meeting?'

With that, he took another two bottles of Krug from the bar and motioned us to follow him into another spacious ground floor room that was his library. Browsing, I saw the title of one book, 'A complete guide to playing 3Nc3 against the French defence,' an entire chess book devoted to the permutations of a single move! I quickly moved on. Books completely covered two walls and a big partner's writing desk occupied one corner, while a conference table and chairs stood in the centre. He sat behind the desk and we gathered around him.

'Gentlemen. To say once again that I'm grateful is an understatement. I have thought about what I can do to show my appreciation. The decision I made is simple. I gather that you two,' he gestured at Paddy and Zafar, 'intend to go looking for emeralds. Is that right?'

Both nodded. Paddy, at last had realised that when Escobar was talking, it was best to shut up.

'And you?' was addressed to me.

'I don't have much to do and emerald prospecting has been a dream of mine since a child. I've been talking with them and was thinking of joining them. Now count me in. After all both Paddy and I have a lot of experience in this field and it could be a very worthwhile venture.'

'You Daler?'

'At the moment, I'm undecided.'

He nodded and was silent for a while. 'I know zero about emeralds and quite frankly do not care much for them. But I am willing to fund your fieldwork for one year. Buy all you want, trucks, boats, guns, provisions, camping gear. Think big, money is no object. Just let me know the figure and I'll bankroll you. Would that be that ok with you?'

All of us looked at each other. Paddy had a broad grin on his face, Zafar's was inscrutable. I have no idea as to what my expression was like.

'Bejesus, that's a magnificent offer, so it is.'

He held out his hand. 'Shake sir.' Escobar shook it.

'By the way, I have also obtained official permission from the government for you to look for emeralds. You will have it before you leave here. I would hate to think that you would be arrested as illegal miners.' His eyes twinkled. 'I guessed that this was going to happen and this morning set the wheels in motion. I know some important government people.'

With that he grinned and passed some papers over to Paddy and left the room. We looked at each other.

'What an offer,' came from Zafar. 'It's everything I dreamed of. Now we can concentrate on finding emeralds at no cost to us.'

'Right,' said Paddy. 'Get a paper and pen and let's start writing a list. We've only a couple of days to do this as he's off soon.'

So we started on the list which grew and grew and took up most of the rest of our stay at the Hacienda.

Meanwhile, Copje and Hanoz appeared to be sounding each other out and I had the feeling that they were very much at ease in each other's company. That was not surprising as they were both cut from the same bolt of cloth. Intelligent, fit people who frequently worked on the other side of the tracks. Over the next few days, it was noticeable that they were growing closer and closer together. I realised very early on in the various conversations I'd had with both, that they were hard men who had killed in their different nefarious careers. Later in the jungle, Hanoz opened up to me confirming what I had thought.

Most days Escobar was closeted with Copje and occasionally Hanoz would be called in. Paddy, Zafar and I just wrote down the quantities of material we would need for a year in the field. Knowing what I know now, we should have just taken the money and ran. We were curious about Helena, as we never saw her except for odd glimpses. I think Escobar kept her away from us. Perhaps he saw in Copje and Hanoz certain traits that he also possessed and they were much more attractive looking people.

Paddy was becoming a bit of a pain with his drinking and lapsing into wild Irish songs. I was considering my offer of help and decided that I could not stand a year of Paddy even though drink would have been curtailed. I'd do it for a month or two was my final decision. In reality, it did not last two weeks.

On Escobar's last evening, we gathered in the lounge post-dinner and this time even Helena made an appearance. She was indeed a stunning woman and I did not blame Escobar for keeping her out of sight. While most eyes were on her, Paddy was oblivious to her charm and gave Escobar the list of things we reckoned we needed. Ignoring the list, he simply looked at the total. Going to a wall safe, he came back with a stack of money all made up into sums of $1,000 anchored by tight elastic bands.

'Paddy, I think this will cover it all. I've added a few more in case of emergencies.' He smiled and reaching under the table brought out an old leather satchel and thrust the money inside.

'Take care you do not lose this. There are many bad people in Medellin,' was said with a broad grin on his face that crinkled up his moustache. Nodding to Copje, Hanoz, Zafar and me, he added, 'and obviously I do not include you four or the lovely Helena.'

With that, we all sat down and general chit chat took place. The talks with Copje had gone well and he was going to leave in the morning along with Escobar. Helena was also leaving. In our discussions, Hanoz had expressed an interest in joining us for about two weeks plus and we were only too happy to have him and possibly Helena's leaving made up his mind. We had decided to stay at the Hacienda until we had bought all that was required and our plans were to leave within the next three or four days. Escobar had no objection to it. As he and Copje had an early start, we left for bed at about 10 pm. Just as we were on the stairs, Escobar called out.

'As you are going off to the jungle, why don't you leave your passports here? It's much safer than risking losing them out in the field.'

Three of us passed them over. This was one of the best decisions I made as it saved one heap of later trouble. Paddy refrained and patted his money belt that seemed to be a permanent fixture around his waist.

'Mine stays right here, all the time.'

Escobar and Copje left at dawn waved off from the front of the Hacienda. Paddy went back to bed. Hanoz went for a run and on his return, sat in a chair and looked intently at the Caravaggio and Rembrandt paintings. He would do this several times a day sometimes walking and gently touching some area or minutely inspecting another part of the picture via a magnifying glass. Escobar had an extensive record collection and Hanoz used to listen to Glen Gould playing the 'Goldberg variations' (he preferred the second recording made some three decades after the first, as it to him seemed more reflective, seasoned and wintery); or Albert Schweitzer playing, Bach's 'Tocata and Fugue.' He and I used to try to get in an hour's exercise each day when we sparred with each other, drilling various moves until they became second nature. We started cross-checking our expedition lists again and again and each day post breakfast went to town on a buying spree. The expedition was gearing up. Three days after Escobar's departure our trucks were loaded and ready to leave. So were we. We left on the morning of the fourth.

11.

Jungle.

N
ow that we had financing and it was proper financing, Paddy had put on his list many items for which we had no real use, all done because money was no barrier. The original idea was to go to Zafar's location, then the Itoco River in the Muzo valley, a well-known emerald area was proposed by Paddy. I gave a veto to that area because I knew it was crawling with *quaqueros*.

I explained to the three that I had heard many tales when working at the Frontino mine about the activities in this area of the *quaqueros* and did not fancy going there one little bit. They were made up of large bands of rough men, who poached not only on the mines by salvaging waste tips looking for overlooked emeralds, but also scoured the riverbeds. Additionally, surveyed claim boundaries in the area were not always clearly marked and were a constant zone of dissent. It was night time that worried me most, as these people frequently robbed the safe houses that were used to store emeralds before they were transported out of the area. They also fought with other bands of *quaqueros*, of which there were many. Coming across four *gringoes* in the bush they would have no qualms about killing them and taking any emeralds they could find plus equipment.

Ostensibly the National Police patrolled the area and monitored all activities, but arrests could be counted on the fingers of one hand and in any case, jail sentences were laughable and invariably short. Corruption was far too easy and in the case of emeralds, one or two slipped to the arresting officers were usually enough for them to turn a blind eye.

Eventually and mainly because of me, we decided to go south east towards the almost 900 hectares of the Serranía La Lindosa, which was located between the Meta and Guaviare Departments and is the gateway to the largest national park in Colombia, the 6 million hectares Chiribiquete National Park. The Guaviare River marks the transition between the Amazon and Orinoco regions, two large areas with a high diversity of natural habitats. The main town – in all ways a frontier town, was San Jose del Guaviare, about an eleven hour bus journey from Bogotá and for us a hard two to three day drive and we camped en route. I told them that I had been there previously with Sonnel, on a short investigative gold project for Frontino, who wanted a geological report on the area. It was hopeless for gold mining, but we had found promising indications in the local streams that it was a worthwhile bet for emeralds because it was on the fringes of the Furatena emerald belt. There were also many high cliff rock outcrops in the region, which we had explored and we had come across some interesting extensive and spectacular rock pictographs that adorned the walls of rock shelters. We were not interested in these as the stunning limestone tabletop outcrops were our main interest, rising sheer out of the Amazon jungle. They are locally called *tepuis* and to the eye appear to be straight out of Conan Doyle's book, 'The Lost World,' with the Dr Challenger expedition finding dinosaurs on the mountain top. They are a spectacular sight and for us, they could be the key to a potential mother lode.

The area was in FARC territory, but my companions who knew my history reckoned that my contacts with them were good enough to take the risk. I was not so sure, but accepted their reasoning. If José was around, I thought it a good bet we would not be kidnapped and his base at Camp Diamante was within this region. I wrote Rod and him a note stating our aim and gave it to a local FARC contact that I knew. I wanted to go badly, as the idea of going emerald prospecting thrilled me, my boyhood dream coming true at last. The thought of Sir George entered my head and I wondered how he was faring, as the whole story of his being kidnapped was strange to me. I found out sooner than expected.

Paddy and Zafar drove one truck, Hanoz and me the other and we travelled all day steadily crossing several vegetation zones. As we did so, the air became more humid and sultry as we approached jungle vegetation. The roads also became narrower and more and more laterite ones appeared until eventually, it was four-wheel drive time. I was glad that our truck was towing a bowser full of diesel fuel, as we were going to need it. We had kept the vehicles topped at regular intervals, i.e. virtually whenever we saw a petrol station.

The map we were following was pretty basic, as were most maps of the rain forest area. I had a good idea of the geology of the country and was quite confident as to where we were headed. The plan, as stated, was to spend half the time here and the other half at Zafar's place. We never got the chance to do the latter.

At last, we arrived at a place where we made camp and a decision was made to leave the trucks and take to the kayaks that had been brought along. We unloaded sleeping gear, sturdy A-frame cots, mosquito netting and made a fire to cook some of the fresh meat we had brought. This, together with some vegetables and bread all washed down with beer put us all in a contented mood for the night's sleep. Paddy spoiled it all, as he went to the pile of provisions, browsed around inside and brought out a case of whisky.

'Secret supplies that I sneaked in,' was the comment as he took off the cap. 'Anyone for a nightcap?'

Hanoz was somewhat taken aback as he had vehemently argued that only beer should be taken on the trip. In his opinion, hard spirits had no place when one was working. He was visibly annoyed.

'Bah,' was the reply. 'You're only here for a couple of weeks and you don't know anything about life in the jungle, especially hellish places like we're going into.'

'That's where you are wrong, my friend.' The last word was virtually spat at him. 'Please don't try to tell me that I'm a novice. I've done and also taught the six-week jungle survival course in the Turkish Army and spent years in the Congo and most of that was jungle fighting.'

He glared at Paddy.

'To a person who has grown up in the luxury of the western world, the jungle is a deeply inhospitable environment. In daylight, the air is alive with the cries of birds, monkeys, but nighttime, my friend,' the last two words were again almost spat out, 'is a disaster. All is quiet except the buzzing of insects and the occasional roar of a nocturnal animal. You do not move around at night. To survive here is easy if you know what to do. I do.'

This was news to me and I looked at him in a new light. People who teach jungle survival courses tend to be attached to military Special Forces. Hanoz was becoming more and more a colourful character, but I sensed an atmosphere between him and Paddy. He did not seem to like the belligerent, loud-mouthed tone of Paddy's speech. In essence, he was a cultured man of violence, Paddy was more of the rough and tumble violent type.

I defused the situation. 'Oh, come on let's have a drink as we're all tired and I'm sure that Paddy here is only going to have the odd drink or two.' I crossed my fingers at that point, as I had seen where Paddy had hidden the whisky crate. There were at least eight crates hidden under the tarpaulin sheet.

With that, we all turned in. I noticed Paddy went to his cot clutching the bottle. Not an auspicious start was my thinking.

*   *   *   *

Sir George was a bit miffed. He had been kept in this camp for over a week and nothing was happening. He had expected to be kidnapped by FARC and then have meetings with the Secretariat. That was the plan, but most of the soldiers, including the best cook and the bulk of the officers, had been called away so that only about 20 people now remained. Whenever he asked the person in charge what was happening he received meaningless replies. He was tired of the oppressive heat and humidity, poor diet, fruit was just bananas galore with the occasional mango. All he had to drink was water, coffee, which was excellent and local beer. He missed his gin and tonic and the occasional glass of whisky. Occasionally a jungle animal, such as a spider monkey was shot and fresh meat made available, but in general, the food was humdrum.

He also missed the company of people with whom he could carry on an intelligent conversation, José had been called away and his Spanish was poor, so he had to mime simple tasks. The only good thing was that he was losing weight and excess fat was dripping away from his body. He was happy about that.

'I want my old lean, hard, body back,' he used to murmur to himself as he trudged around the camp perimeter. He did these laps four times a day and had upped the walks so that sometimes he was even jogging around the camp circuit. He also joined in daily callisthenics exercises carried out by the remaining soldiers. He was pleased that physically he was getting better but mentally was very bored.

He was sorry that he had not brought some books along to pass the time. All he had were his lecture notes and he knew them off by heart. Card games were the mainstay of camp life, but he had never been one to play cards. He sat out and just watched them.

One morning when he was jogging by himself around the perimeter, he thought he heard a voice calling his name. He shook his head and carried on. On the next round and at the same spot he thought he heard it again, but carried on. 'Am I hallucinating now?' was the first thought that came into his mind. On the third lap, he slowed down when approaching the spot and distinctly heard, 'Sir George.' He stopped.

'Put your hands on your knees and head down as if you're having a rest.'

He obeyed and looked around for the source. All he could see was jungle litter in front of him and the litter seemed to be talking to him. A part of the litter moved slightly.

'Sergeant Jon Rambert, sir. We are the troop that's looking after you, if you get my meaning, but I'm told you're safe here with FARC.'

Sir George stifled a smile. He had been told that British soldiers would be close at hand to help out if anything out of the ordinary happened. Now he was happy to see it confirmed.

'We have a sixteen-man troop here and one team is constantly on stag duty looking after you all the time. Our base is about two clicks away and we are in communication with Hereford. How are you, sir?'

'Bloody awful if you must know. I'm waiting to meet up with the FARC Secretariat to discuss some matters. I agree with you that I am under no duress with FARC, they asked for this to happen. I just have to wait until things develop. I must say that the damn diet here is so monotonous that it's killing me.'

'I sympathise sir, but if you pass by this spot tomorrow you might find a chocolate bar on the spot. Take the wrapper off and leave it here and eat the bar as you jog around. Be careful. I gather that once you were one of us?'

'One of the Hereford Light Infantry? Yes, but aeons ago.'

The litter mound stopped moving. Sir George straightened and started jogging. He was rolling his lips already in anticipation of a chocolate bar. He even had a second helping of monkey stew that evening and that night dreamt of nothing but chocolate.

On his run, the next morning, he stopped, put his hands on his knees and a different voice came from the litter.

'Two metres to the right, sir.'

He obeyed.

Passed through the litter mound were two chocolate bars. He could not believe that a soldier was just about a metre away. The camouflage was that good. He unwrapped them quickly, placed the wrappers on the ground and watched as litter seemingly rumbled slowly to it. He was relieved to see two fingers appear to grasp and withdraw it before continuing his run, albeit at a much slower pace. This again was more like a walking pace and every 10 metres, or so he yawned bringing his hand up to cover his mouth, as he had been taught at Eton. He mused that it did not take much to bring contentment to a person. He wondered what else he could persuade them to bring him, a tin of bully beef perhaps. He quickly dismissed this idea and told himself to be grateful for a few slabs of chocolate. Little did he know that this was the last time he would experience chocolate bars.

The day passed, as did the other ones. It was towards the evening when the meal was being prepared that all hell broke loose. Suddenly into the camp came trucks carrying many soldiers. Many shots were fired and Sir George, lying on his hammock, saw FARC people mown down. He did not know what to do but sat up. His white skin probably saved his life.

Three soldiers roughly turfed him out of the hammock and dragged him before a tall, thin man who was in charge. He looked sneeringly at Sir George.

'And who might you be?' was the comment.

Thinking quickly, Sir George replied, 'My name is Sir George Fusano and I have been captured by these rebels and I thank you for rescuing me. I'm sure her Majesty the Queen will be grateful for this act.'

'Her Majesty the Queen.' The tall, thin man roared with laughter and slapped his knee. 'Her Majesty the Queen. Is that our gracious Queen? God bless her.' This was followed by more slapping, but this time it was on Sir George's face. An extra hard punch, not slap, knocked Sir George to the ground.

'Do you know who I am?' he demanded of Sir George, who was lying prone on the ground. 'I'm Colonel Drew Ortsh in command of these men. Look around and see what we do to rebels.'

Sir George's face paled as he slowly rose and looked. The soldiers were in the process of de-capitating all the FARC soldiers and placing their heads on poles.

'Your skin colour has just saved you from a similar fate. I think that I'll get a pretty penny from your government, especially as you are a Sir.'

He laughed and Sir George bit his lip at having given his title to this man, but it had been an automatic response. He knew the name Ortsh full well. In briefings from London, it had been stated that his was the most brutal of the many small armies who roamed western Colombia. Nels Clifford had stressed that he should stay clear of this man. Even at that time, Sir George wondered how he could do this, but did not ask.

'Tie him to that tree.' He ordered one man and pointed to a nearby tree. 'We must celebrate our little victory today, but first let's have a ration of good Colombian rum and then get the hell out of here. We'll take him,' pointing at Sir George, 'with us. I think we can make a good deal of money out of this man. We leave in one hour.'

A roar came from his troops and Sir George's heart sank. A quick glance had showed well over 100 troops and he realised that with this many soldiers,16 troopers stood no chance unless they could bring in reinforcements and within an hour time slot that was going to be extremely unlikely. He thought that the British troopers probably did not have motorised transport so wondered how they could follow Ortsh's trucks. He was wrong; they had transport and could follow albeit at a slower pace.

12.

London.

The atmosphere in the room at Hanslope Park was sombre. As previously, the representatives of the Colombian sector of the OTDD, MI6 and the SAS Colonel had been summoned by Sir Nels Clifford for an urgent meeting.

Sir Nels dispensed with the usual formalities and did not even produce an agenda, for which he made an abrupt apology.

'I have called this meeting, as we have just had some bad news from Major John Davidson in Colombia regarding Sir George Fusano. He has been captured by one of the most unsavoury characters who are fighting in that country, a man called Ortsh. For further information, I call upon Colonel Williamson to brief you.'

Glyn Williamson stood up.

'I deeply regret having to announce this news. You are all well aware that we had a troop based outside FARC headquarters at Camp Diamante with orders to look after him. We had reason to believe that he was very safe there, as FARC had asked both British and Colombian Governments to put in motion an operation to sue for peace that we called Operation Albatross. FARC ostensibly kidnapped a world-renowned scientist and held him hostage in order to set up peace talks with their government. Both parties are tired of fighting and it was to be hoped that negotiating by this means would save face for both parties.'

He stopped and looked around. No one had anything to say.

'To this end and unbeknown to the Colombian Government, we infiltrated a troop of soldiers to the Camp Diamante area, before Sir George was taken to the area. His kidnapping was carried out extremely successfully, as all the people he met officially out there had no idea of the real purpose of his visit. We were careful that he knew his so-called kidnappers. Unfortunately, trouble in the east of the region meant that people he was supposed to meet were called away and he was left languishing in the camp for over a week awaiting their return.'

He stopped again. 'Any questions?' No one said anything.

'Our people made contact with him and even had time to pass him some chocolate bars.'

There was a burst of muffled laughter from the group.

'Then the unknown happened, something that was thought of as having a very low probability. We had always counted on there being many FARC fighters in the camp. However, numbers had been decimated by the eastern troubles and only some 20 or so were left behind when this rebel band of fighters hit them. The rebels were controlled by Ortsh.'

He paused and thought through his next words.

'Ortsh is like the curate's egg, good in parts, although the good is tarnished by the innumerable items of evil, as he is an utterly brutal monster, but a damn good leader of men. The latter exhausts his good qualities. His background is a Cuban mother and Australian/Russian father and he was brought up in Sydney. At the age of seven he was taken to Russia by his parents. In time, he joined their Army and was eventually sent to Angola as part of the Cuban assistance to the communist People's Movement for the Liberation of Angola (MPLA), to help in their fight for independence. He loved the fighting, blood, killing and brutality. His activities rivalled the atrocities carried out between 1885 and 1908 in the Leopold II private fiefdom of the Congo Free State, where over 10 million people died as a result of violence and brutality. He blotted his copybook whilst in Angola and was summoned back to Cuba, as his exploits had annoyed Castro intensely. He was admonished by Castro, demoted and put in charge of basic training for junior soldiers. This was his apparent punishment. After two years of this duty, he was sent to Colombia as part of their teaching team to help in training FARC soldiers to further the revolution. His Russian background made him an easy choice for this post. He soon got tired of that and formed his own group, it was then that he morphed into what I can only describe, as his Colonel Kurtz syndrome. I presume you have all read Conrad's, 'Heart of Darkness?'

Nods all around confirmed the statement.

'Soon his band of renegades, government troops etc. who joined him, revelled in the mayhem they could cause. What made them distinct to other groups was their discipline. He inherited a ragtag body of men, men who did not take too kindly to army discipline. Being a superb leader he installed in the men a mind-set that did not exist in other troops in the region. They are damn good at what they do and now they have captured Sir George.'

Another pause.

'Our people are in Colombia unofficially. They are there ostensibly, as the Kempley Fishing Club whose members are touring around fishing various rivers and streams. They are armed only because we have training teams in the country and they have had all materials they need from these teams. Our military teams attached to the regular Army are there to train Colombian soldiers to hunt down drug factories in the jungle and the nearest team is some 600 km. away. If the Colombian government knew that we had illicit troops in the country, diplomatically all hell could break loose.'

'Questions?'

Sir Nels looked around, 'None that I can see. Carry on.'

'Ortsh captured Sir George yesterday. Since then he has moved on and our troops are following his path. They cannot go too fast as Ortsh is a cunning rascal and frequently leaves a platoon behind to see if anyone is trailing him. He is a consummate professional soldier and we do not underestimate him one bit. We do not know what he intends to do with Sir George, but my guess is he will send a ransom note to the British Embassy. I pray to God that this is his intention. The fact that Ortsh killed all remaining FARC soldiers, but spared Sir George is a sign that this is probably what he intends doing.'

'What can we do?' came from Ron Southall, the MI6 man.

'Currently very little. Our men have yet to find out where Ortsh is located. Their estimate is that he is some six hours ahead of them. They cannot attack. He has too many soldiers and our troop is on a clandestine mission. Frankly, gentlemen, we have little choice but to hang on in there and hope for the best. Our other Colombian training teams have been put on red alert, but this is a delicate situation, one in which we have to tread carefully. As I said, we have some officers and NCOs from the Grenadier Guards, who are out there as part of a British Army Training Team (BATT) to Colombian troops. Unfortunately, they are over 600 km away. They have been authorised if possible to try to steer training to this region, but it depends upon their Colombian counterparts to listen and act on their suggestions.'

'Now do you gentlemen have not only questions, but suggestions?'

There was silence in the room. Arthur Maxwell the MI6 representative spoke up.

'Could we not own up to the Colombian government about this plan? Apologise profusely and promise a massive aid package. There have been several instances in the past when we have had to do this scenario.'

'No. Not in this case. Many hardliners in the Colombian cabinet would have a field day over this. If the moderates were in the majority, I would certainly think that we would have a chance. Unfortunately, they're not.'

'If we attacked them, what would be the likely scenario for Sir George?' asked Ron Southall.

'Unknown. He could easily be killed in the crossfire of so many bullets flying around. Anyway, I would not authorise such a mission as it would be suicidal for the troop. We have only 16 men out there. The estimate is they have 100 to 150 and as stated they are well trained.'

'What then do you suggest?' said Sir Nels.

'As stated, wait and see. It's a do-nothing answer I know, but that is all we can expect at this moment. Sir George knew the risk he was taking, but I must say none of us expected this to happen. It didn't come into our planning at all. As Rabbie Burns would have said, 'the best-laid plans of mice and men aft go astray.'

Several more comments were made until eventually the room fell silent.

Sir Nels stood up.

'I think I can call this emergency meeting over and I will keep all informed as matters develop. Colonel Williamson will be in constant touch with his men in the field. He will keep me posted and I will ensure that all of you are kept in the loop. All that is left for me to say is a heartfelt personal thank you for attending this meeting at such short notice.'

The atmosphere became even more sombre when all bar Clifford and Williamson had left the room. They sat down and faced each other across a table.

'I don't like this one bit,' came from Sir Nels. 'Sir George is really in a bad set up there, as the file on Ortsh is horrific. Some of the atrocities committed by him are unbelievable. He seems to be the devil incarnate.'

Colonel Williamson grimaced. 'Your file states horrific atrocities, but if I showed you our top-secret reports on him, gleaned by our Intelligence Corps and allies, your face would be going even paler than it is right now. Ortsh is a brutal sadist par excellence. It's a pity that our beloved Government and political masters do not like giving out information to other departments. I just love their open and transparent policies.'

He threw a quizzical look at Sir Nels, who simply looked him in the eye and said nothing.

He grinned. 'Interagency collaboration, the sharing of information together with systems and connecting the dots. Still politically neutral Nels?'

There was no comment. He continued.

'I know that Sir George was once in the army, but that was a long time ago and any jungle training, escape and evasion techniques that he learned has probably been forgotten. He is over 55 year of age and has led a sedentary lifestyle for many years. Even if he manages to escape he is in great danger and I can only hope that he manages this and our men meet up with him. How this can happen is beyond me at this moment.'

He paused. 'I'll fill you in on a few matters, unofficially of course.'

'As I stated Ortsh first came to our attention in the Angolan war of the 60s and 70s. It's usually referred to as a proxy war, a surrogate battlefield for what we termed the 'Cold War' between the Soviets and the USA. The war officially started in November 1975, when the country achieved independence from Portugal who had ruled the country for some four centuries. Over half a million skilled Portuguese Angolans fled the country in 1974-5 and the country descended into chaos. Guerrilla warfare had existed since the 60s, mainly by the People's Movement for the Liberation of Angola (MPLA), which was basically an urban grouping of mainly Mbundu people led by Agostina Neto that followed a communist ideology. The opposition party was the anti-communist National Union for the Total Independence of Angola (UNITA), composed mainly of rural Bakongo people led by Jonas Savimbi. Both groups were initially based in neighbouring countries and incursions into Angola were frequent. Support for the MPLA was mainly by Russia and its satellite territories, for example, East Germany and Yugoslavia, together with Cuba. The big guns supporting UNITA were the USA and South Africa. There were two other very minor factions in the country, namely the Front for the Liberation of the Enclave of Cabinda (FLEC), who wanted a separate state of Cabinda; and the National Front for the Liberation of Angola (FNLA), both roles were insignificant. The FNLA had the backing of Mobuto Sese Seko's Congo government, who had renamed his country as Zaire. If you recall, Mobuto, backed by the US, Belgium and France seized power from Patrice Lumumba who was assassinated in 1961 by Congolese rebels aided by Belgian Army officers acting on the orders of the CIA. China originally backed the FNLA, but soon switched to UNITA, as they deemed the group to be very inactive.'

He reflected on what had just been said.

'Quite a lot to take in. All clear so far?'

'Carry on.'

'The first report we received on Ortsh was when a clash occurred between South African forces in what was termed Operation Savannah. They had been sent to protect construction workers at a hydroelectricity dam at Calueque. Thousands of South African Defence Force personnel were involved in battles with MPLA and Cuban forces. The South Africans retreated and unconfirmed reports came to us suggesting that summary executions, plus barbaric and degraded treatment of prisoners were being carried out by certain commanders of the 6,000 Cuban soldiers involved. I'll leave it to your imagination as to what happened to them, but Ortsh was suspected of being the leader in these deeds. I said he morphed into Kurtz in Colombia. That was not so. He became Kurtz in Angola. Like Querry in Graham Greene's, 'A Burnt-Out Case', I believe he lost the ability to feel and had to seek it in new experiences.

'Still ok?'

A nod.

'In Angola, events moved on at a very fast pace. The MPLA captured 11 provincial capitals, UNITA struck back and with the help of South African forces took back several and as a result, 18,000 further Cuban soldiers were sent to help the MPLA in Operation Carlotta. In the political arena, a person called Nito Alves and his followers called the Nitistas together with his Chief of Staff José Van-Dunem, had been plotting to take over control of the MPLA. The 8th Brigade of The People's Armed Forces for the Liberation of Angola (FAPLA), another loose organisation who supported Alves, freed prisoners from the notorious São Paulo prison and captured the radio station. Cuban troops with Ortsh prominent recaptured the radio station and barracks. Many thousands were killed. Van-Dunem, the head of the 8th Brigade Jacobo 'Immortal Monster' Caetano and the political commissar Eduardo Evaristo were among the many executed. The result was further chaos and 4,000 extra Cuban troops being sent to Angola. Eventually, there were over 36,000 Cuban troops and 400 tanks there. It's here that Ortsh hit our headlines big time.'

He picked up a carafe of water and filled two glasses.

'Ortsh was given carte blanche to go after any person who had supported the plotters and slaughtered thousands of innocent people. He took his Cubans and went on a mission that left villages burnt out, bodies left to bake in the sun and multiple rapes together with sadistic torture. His men would surround a village, have a short discussion with the elders and a decision would be made if they were for or against Alves. Inevitably they would be deemed to be pro Alves. He was judge, jury and executioner. Ortsh's men had been divided up into three groups, A, B and C specifically to destroy a village. Villagers would be separated into groups of men, women and children.'

He took another sip of water.

'Each of the three groups had a specific task and they were rotated village by village. At any particular village, one group would take the children, march them away and after a kilometre or so the children would be told to run and the Cubans used them for target practice. No one was left alive. If they were, they simply had a bullet through their brain. You can guess what happened to the women. After the group had finished with them, the other groups were allowed to take their turn. If any woman struggled, she was simply shot. The men meanwhile after torching the village huts were marched away, again a kilometre or so. They were lined up in several circles, given heavy pieces of wood or hammers and told to smash them on the heads of the person in front of them until they died. The 'winner's' life would be spared. People who refused to do this were bayoneted in the stomach and genitals several times before being pushed to one side to die a slow death. A winner eventually emerged who had the honour of first being castrated and then having his throat slashed open by Ortsh himself. Ortsh did this in many villages and his name struck terror in Angolans. He was a crazed monster.'

He cleared his throat and took a further sip of water.

'I said I'd leave things to your imagination, but I'll tell you two things that I think you should know. Ortsh was notorious for immensely enjoying those moments of savagery. We have several witnesses who managed to escape and saw the described incidents. Their testimonies are in our files. The troops used to carry around with them a large steel drum. If any villagers put up a fight in the initial stages and I might add that there usually were several, one or two would be clubbed and tied up. After the shootings and rape, liquor would be available for the troops. They would build a pyre and put the drum plus villager into it. Usually, the villager would be unconscious, so they would wait until he had regained consciousness, then fill the drum with water and light the fire. They would drink and cheer as the poor wretch was boiled alive. If he attempted to get out of the drum, he was lightly clubbed back in via rifles. Another example of the torture they loved to inflict was strapping a victim to any iron bedframe. They would then roast him over the same pyre used to kill the other villager, turning him over at set intervals as they lowered him towards the fire. The whole set-up would take about 30 minutes to kill the poor wretch. Shades of St. Laurence and his gridiron, or even King Lear's comment that he is, 'bound upon a wheel of fire.'

He grinned. 'I guess I'm going back through time to my undergraduate English studies with that quote.' He finished off the carafe of water.

'The raucous cheering and drinking that went on makes me feel quite sick whenever I think about it. However, I repeat what was said earlier, he had the absolute loyalty of his men. To them he was not simply a hard but just commander, but a born leader and winner. The troops worshipped him. That is the type of man, no monster that now holds Sir George hostage. Anger erupts inside me whenever I hear the name Ortsh. I would gladly kill him and have no qualms about it.'

He smashed a hand down onto the table and tears of anger welled up in his eyes. A long silence ensued. Sir Nels could not help but gaze at the large calloused hand that lay on the table and remembered where he had first met Williamson. It had been an Open Day at Hereford for selected government personnel and after a visit to Dore Abbey and Ewyas Harold to see one of their training fields, a show had been put on for the guests. Two things stood out in his memory of that day. One was a talk in a place close by the Close Quarter Battle house (the Killing house), when the speaker had turned off all lights and in the silence, you could have heard a pin drop. In pitch darkness, he had droned on about how men in The Regiment frequently had to operate in darkness. Thirty seconds later the lights were turned back on and six men, black-suited and gloved, all with black headgear with night scopes fitted around their heads, were pointing M16 rifles at the audience. One such person was a metre away from him and the rifle barrel was some 20 cm from his head. The holder of the rifle had been Williamson.

Later, Williamson was part of a team that put on a martial art exhibition. He had performed what was called the *Kanku Dai kata*. It took him two minutes to perform the 65 graceful movements. It started with him slowly lifting his hands up and touching the thumbs and forefingers to form a small window to gaze at what he called 'emptiness'; it ended with a spectacular flying double kick. He did three 'shouts' or *Kiais*. This was where occurred what he termed the 'coming together of mind,' a massive focusing of body and mind, awareness and action being as one. Three red building bricks were then smashed through with one blow of the edge of his hand.

In the bar at the end of the day, he had met up with Williamson and in chatting and drinking, had wormed out of him that he had taken an English degree from Birmingham university, then left for Japan to learn *Shotokan* karate in a two-year stay at the Yotsuya dojo, Tokyo, reaching second Dan status. On his return he had made the military his career. Sir Nels took his gaze from that large hand. In his imagination, he could visualise those hands and legs beating, kicking and eventually crushing Ortsh to death.

'What can we do,' a pause, 'let's say, unofficially?'

'I can arrange for half a squadron to be based nearby in Panama, it will be commanded by a colleague of mine, Major Pete Bodsworth, but for that I will have to call in a few debts. We have a few good contacts within Colombia. Their current Army chief is an old student who was in the same cohort at Sandhurst as John Davidson and myself. He is very pro-British. What good that will do though I'm not sure, as the last thing we want to do is enter Colombia with all guns blazing. At least it is something.'

'Well, I'll leave it up to you, as I would prefer not to know anything. Being economical with the truth is one thing, but this is a completely different kettle of fish.'

They shook hands and left. Exiting into the sunlit grounds, Williamson looked around at the few people lying on the well-kept lawns, eating sandwiches, throwing Frisbees to each other, chatting or simply sunbathing. His heart went out to Sir George, as his imagination went into overdrive at what he must be undergoing. He brushed this aside, as in his job any emotion must be kept at bay and the focus kept on the immediate task. How on earth could he rescue Sir George?

Sir Nels recalled that on returning to London after the Hereford visit and attending a debriefing session, over a coffee break he had listened to one of the other civil servants talking upon Williamson. Apparently, when a young captain serving in the Brunei-Borneo campaign in the 60s, Williamson had been part of The Regiment's standard four-man patrol in the Pensiagan region of North Borneo, a region of unpopulated dense jungle. They befriended the local Kelabit tribe's folk via pidgin Malay their only form of communication. Great stress was put on winning them over by the 'hearts and minds' approach in which they succeeded. Deep behind enemy lines and out on a 10-day patrol they had inadvertently run into an Indonesian Army patrol that was looking for them; both had simply stumbled upon each other. Hand to hand fighting had taken place and Williamson had apparently killed one opponent with his bare hands. Sir Nels had no difficulty in believing it. Those hands were massive.

13.

Jungle.

The next morning, we washed in the river and over breakfast prepared the kayaks. I'd had a good night's sleep, but Zafar had somehow been plagued by mosquitoes owing to holes in his netting. He had not checked the equipment, bad news when one travels in rough, insect rich country. He had a swim in the river in order to wake up and I recall Paddy shouting to him to beware of pink dolphins and that he should swim in the evening. Paddy was quite taken with this legend. When night-time drew near, these dolphins would turn into handsome men who loved partying. If they ever met Zafar they could carry him away to the underwater city of Encante and according to Paddy, Zafar would go willingly. Zafar only ever swam in the morning; it was a quick swill in the evening.

Our idea was to move along the many rivers, panning sediments to see what minerals could be found. Then by following a sound statistical sampling strategy, we could work backwards towards the source material. It was a laborious and mechanical job, but one that had to be done and for two weeks we paddled up and down rivers. We did not expect to shout 'Eureka' in the first week or even month, but painstaking work would hopefully narrow down the boundaries until we hit pay dirt.

The muddy river we followed invariably twisted and turned and at each meander, bank undercutting was seen. Many pools and riffles were encountered, but rapids were small and we were able to navigate through reasonably easily. It was as if the river, flowing strongly against the outer bend of any meander was trying to push back the jungle. It failed. Fringing the banks were many large trees mainly of the *Annonaceae* family that were seemingly laced together by ubiquitous woody vines called lianas. In fact there seemed to be more of these gothic like structures than anything else. I could imagine Tarzan swinging through them shouting for Jane. Branches frequently were seen over hanging into the water and often were inter-twined with boulders, some worn smooth with time, others newly jagged. The *tornillo* trees towered above the rest while great buttressed *mashonastes* trees were occasionally glimpsed. Man is out of scale here and in the almost perpetual silence and monotonous coloured world (shades of brown, grey or green) of the true rain forest, one needs the assurance of fellow man. It inspires awe and wonder. Jungle law, the struggle for existence reigns supreme. Find food, make sure you are not food for some other animal and reproduce. A very basic set of axioms.

One did not venture much inland because progress there was very hard owing to secondary vegetation growth that quickly fills any space left by a gap in the forest cover. 'Slash and burn' agricultural patterns made by local tribes were readily seen. It is much easier to move through primary, multi storied tropical rain forest where the floor is relatively smooth because sunlight never reaches that far, hence etiolated plants. Vegetation is less dense and there is no rich humus accumulation. Often one did not even have to use a machete. I was always petrified that I would encounter a big, venomous snake, especially the bushmaster and there are many more poisonous snakes in Colombia. In Latin America the pit viper alone is the cause of more than 2,000 deaths per year.

The evening meal was looked forward to immensely and surprisingly, Paddy offered to do the cooking and proved to be excellent at the task. We allocated up to 30 minutes for fishing time usually catching a few that barbequed well for the evening meal. Post the meal we just sat around the fire on which wet wood was placed. This made smoke and tended to cut down the insect swarm. We huddled around that fire. Hanoz and I also used the time to do some practising and showed each other moves and counterattacks. I learned a great deal from him, but think that my contribution to his armoury of moves was minimal. His movements were like greased lightning and I found that I was ill-prepared to counter his attacks. He knew much more than I did about fighting where the aim was to kill someone. My training had not prepared me for this.

His had. I knew that several of my blows could kill, I had proved it, but his knowledge of other types of lethal blows was amazing. He 'killed' me many times. I succeeded only on a few rare occasions.

One particular moment stands out in my mind. Breathing heavily after a particularly heavy session, he stood, hand on hips and looked at me.

'Adam, you know about jugular vein compression that increases venous pressure in the head and turns a victim blue due to the brain blood supply being cut off. BUT, did you know that strangling can also put pressure on the parasympathetic nervous system that controls bodily processes like digestion?'

I had never even heard of this system, so shook my head.

'A major nerve in this system is the vagal one and you can die instantly from neck pressure on this vein. It's a complicated mechanism but pressure instructs the nerve to simply stop the heart beating. A famous UK pathologist, Sir Keith Simpson once wrote about a soldier who at a dance had given an affectionate tweak to his partner's neck and killed her.'

He showed me the move. It was ridiculously easy

One night and under the light of a gibbous moon we sat around the blazing fire and swopped stories. We had decided that each of us would tell the others of the best and most satisfying job they had ever had. From what I recall, these were the tales told.

Daler Hanoz:

'Stories around the fireside reminds me of my boyhood, when the elders of my village would gather us young girls and boys and start to tell folk tales about the Anatolian plateau. Once upon a time in the old, old days, when the mouse was a barber and the tortoise baked the bread, there was a great mountain called Kaf Daği on the edge of the spirit world. This used to be the starting point of whatever tale they had decided to tell and we would be entranced. Kaf Doğu is somewhere in the Caucasus range between the Black and Caspian Seas and in Arabic is known as Jabal Qaf; in Persian, Kuh-e-Qaf. They would then take us on mythical journeys where princes are cursed by witches and turned into, for example, stags, everyone is at the mercy of *peri* (fairies) or *ifrit* (demons) that populate the Turkish fairyland. I think in the west it would be similar to the stories told by the Brothers Grimm or the Arabian Night tales with Scheherazade as the narrator. You must remember that stories such as these are part of mankind's most precious heritage.'

He stopped and picked up a beer can. Opening it, he continued.

'I am unsure as to what the word 'Best' indicates, but I will try to answer the question in a meaningful and non-fairy tale manner. I hope and trust that you will all accept this. It was best in that I really loved it and I was also helping my country. For me, this was the patriotic thing to do. I believe the best job happened after I had come back to Turkey and joined MIT, our Intelligence people. There I had a lot of jobs, but one was when I was selected for what we called Charm School, based in Trabzon.'

Here he grinned, looked around and continued.

'This was because of my outstanding lean, hard-muscled, chiselled physique, good looks, charm and language skills, or rather the ability to pick up a language quickly. It was not only a language that one could pick up there; the aim of the school in my case was teaching the ability to pick up women.'

I threw what remained of my beer at him, but he ducked and most of it missed him.

'As I was saying, Charm School. What a lovely name and Trabzon was a beautiful place in which to spend six months. There were about 40 of us split equally between males and females. We men were called ravens, the females were swallows and all worked to snare people in what is called 'a honeypot trap,' and/or to get them to fall in love with you. The methodology was to train people to seduce the opposite sex and we had a fantastic time... well, I did anyway. Some courses had the objective of same-sex seduction, but that was a course that I'd have refused to attend. I believe the Brits are the best in the world for that type of work.'

He ducked when I opened another can of beer, shook it and tried to spray him again. I missed. He continued.

'All 40 people were, how may I tactfully put it…. good lookers. It was heaven.'

He looked at me. 'I can see that you Adam, are already jealous of my good fortune, but I have no doubt that the Brits have a similar seduction school. Adam, you're not good looking enough. I don't think you'd get in.'

More beer was thrown. He did not move and beer splashed his shirt.

'Anyway, there we were taught good manners, etiquette and seduction skills. We, the men, had dossiers on the theory of how to approach women and what were the right things to say. Similarly the females were taught the correct replies, questions to ask and other skills. All involved a mixture of flattery, psychological manipulation and coercion. The theoretical work was based on the philosophy of a German called Immanuel Kant, whose idea was that the world as we experience it, is shaped by the forms of human thought and sensibility, arguing that philosophers should get out more to explore it in all directions, for example, art, music and love. I thought it rubbish and ignored it. This idea was picked up later in a 1970s book by Eric Weber called, 'How to pick up girls,' a process known as *sarging*, and we used this book. In essence, we had to make an assumption, before using a hook to draw her and then a challenge would be issued followed by a time constraint. Easy when you know how.'

He paused for a moment and looked around.

'Any questions? No, ok. We all had to practice on a person of the opposite sex. At the end of the course, each of us had to give an opinion of our various partners. It was a very comprehensive checklist. I slept with six candidates when there, including a compulsory night with the course leader, as I was rated the best student. You can say that I graduated with first-class honours.'

I threw yet again more beer at him, this time joined by Zafar.

'What a waste of good beer,' was our comment.

'I passed the course and was sent on intensive German and Spanish courses for six months each in Berlin and Madrid respectively.'

I interrupted him at that point. 'But you told Escobar and us that you didn't speak Spanish. We've never heard you utter a word.'

He looked pityingly at me. 'Adam, you should realise that one keeps cards close to the chest. Never divulge information that can be of use to any potential enemy.'

Later on, that remark saved our lives.

He continued. 'Needless to say, I practised what I had learned at Charm School in both cities. Now that I was ready to do the job I'd been groomed for, I was posted to our Embassy in Berlin, which as you're all well aware is a city surrounded by the German Democratic Republic, which everyone calls East Germany. Security is run by The State Security Service *(Staatssicherheitsdienst,* SSD), usually referred to as the Stasi. It is based in an old Wehrmacht's officer's mess at Berlin-Lichtenberg and has very close links with the Russian KGB. Its head is a man called Erich Mielke who fought in the Spanish civil war and remained an ardent communist all his life. Satellite headquarters included one at Leipzig, on am Dittrichring and incidentally, they had a very efficient execution site at Alfred-Kastner-Strasse. One of their aims was to infiltrate NATO, The North Atlantic Treaty Organisation, which Turkey joined in 1952 and this is where I come into the picture. There was a certain Colonel Seibold who was head of the Leipzig centre and was the man in command of NATO infiltration. He was also head of the *Zersetzung* (Undermining) section that used psychological warfare to break subjects.'

He stopped and looked at us. 'All clear so far?'

Nods all around.

'He had a very pretty Greek wife called Angela some 20 years his junior. My brief was the seduction of the wife to try to find out the names of their people who had been infiltrated into NATO. Our

Embassy people had been keeping an eye on her and reckoned that she was ripe for plucking by someone like me. The Seibold's had homes in East Berlin and Leipzig respectively. Naturally, I moved freely between the two cities. My cover was that I was a second attaché in the Turkish Embassy Culture section fostering more cooperation between our two countries. I did nothing regarding culture. My aim was focused on Angela. In my spare time I usually joined the Military attaché in driving through the Leuven triangle where Soviets and East Germans carried out a lot of armoured column movements. Turkey was particularly interested in the new Soviet T64 titanium armoured tank because we had very little information on it. The front plating armour was of particular interest since this is the thickest part of the tank. We also visited the Soviet firing range at Neustrelitz to try to pick up discarded shells. As soon as we had any information, which included photographs, we headed back to our Embassy in Berlin via the Glienicke Bridge.'

He stopped. 'I'm thirsty, so instead of wasting good beer by throwing it at me, I need a drink.'

I opened a can and passed it over. By this stage, Paddy had already had three beers and I could see him edging towards the spot where he kept the whisky.

'Where was I? Ah, the lovely Angela. It took me three months. We met at a reception arranged by the Italian Embassy and I put all my efforts into enchanting her. It worked a charm; incidentally, that was why the school's name was chosen. Our pillow talk generated a lot of good information and she fell deeply in love with me. She wanted out of East Germany and I had promised to take her to Turkey. I must admit I did feel rather badly about this, but a job is a job and my country came first. I did get a lot of useful information from her.'

He took another big gulp of beer.

'Anyway, to cut a long story short, one day, Colonel Seibold came home early and caught us in bed. He started to draw his Makarov pistol, but I had leapt out of bed and was on him before he could get an aim and threw him down the stairs. He landed at the bottom with one big,' a pregnant pause ensued followed by one word.

'Thud.'

'I hope you've killed the bastard,' came from Angela. 'So I went downstairs to make sure and broke his neck. I also wanted him dead, as he could have made big trouble for me. She looked down at me from the top of the stairs, naked as a new-born baby.

'Thank god. We can escape now my love,' she said.

My reply. 'But not just yet my love.'

I went quickly back up those stairs and we made love. I was excited as hell. I left about two hours later, but not before taking all the files from his briefcase.'

'Two hours?' came from Paddy.

Hanoz ignored him and took another swig of beer.

'I reported back to the Embassy and they put me on a flight home within three hours. Yes, I think I can say that as a job, it was great. I loved it.'

'What happened to Angela?' I asked.

'No idea. I am ashamed at my treatment of her, but it was a job. I told her to say a masked robber had turned up, killed Seibold and taken the briefcase and jewellery. I said I'd be in touch. Obviously that never happened.'

We all gave him a clap and more beers were passed around. I noticed Paddy now had a tumbler of whisky in one hand and a beer in the other.

'Anything important in the files?' asked Zafar.

'Yes, one in particular stood out. It concerned Ilich Ramirez Sanchez, otherwise known as the Venezuelan terrorist, Carlos the Jackal. He had been financed by the Stasi for many years. The file gave us information of the bombing campaign that he was going to unleash in France in the early 80s, with the aim of freeing his girlfriend Magdalena Kopp who had been jailed for possession of explosives. We passed the information on.'

There was a profound silence around that campfire, as we all remembered the recent bombings.

'Ok, who is next?' said Hanoz, clapping his hands and slowly enunciating each word.

I was surprised when Paddy stood up.

'I'll have a go if you don't mind.'

Beer in one hand, a whisky in the other, he walked into the centre of our cosy circle gathered around that blazing fire.

Paddy:

'Now no throwing beer, it's not allowed and that's an order. I'm not very good at this type of thing. I'm a practical man and do not have all this education stuff that you all seem to have in abundance. I have to tell you that I'm bi-polar, hence my mood swings. I'm essentially an efficient real-world man and proud of it. All my life has been geared to hands on issues and I'm good at this and guess I'm a loner. I find it difficult to get along with people, apart from my father and grandparents who I adored. I guess most of my affection for people relates only to those three and it has, I must admit, affected my behaviour to others throughout my life. It's something that I've missed out on. I've never really trusted other people and I include you lot in this. I think I'm rambling.'

'Yes you are. Get along with it, mush, mush,' came from Hanoz.

I tried singing, 'Why are we waiting,' but no one joined in, so shut up.

Paddy gazed around at the three of us and kept nodding his head.

'You might be surprised to hear that when I was a teenager, I was in the local church choir. This was on the insistence of my father, who loved his church. My mother had disappeared from my life when I was not even one year old. For some reason, I enjoyed the singing and rituals and was told that I had a good voice.'

I butted in at that point.

'Paddy, we've all heard you sing. All agree on that point.'

A grin spread across his face.

'Thank you and to continue. I've said I enjoyed singing, but one of the tasks of young choristers was to try to help others who were not as fortunate as we were. To me, this was an irksome task, as I was a believer in doing things and not relying on others for help. I was a very independent, probably troubled teenager, I might add that I was the only one who did not have a mother and this probably damaged me as a person and turned me into what I am now. Then one day, a Youth Worker called Bert turned up at the local Youth Club and boy, he was a breath of fresh air. Young and enthusiastic about turning a moribund group of,' he searched for a word, 'louts is the best description I can come up with. We were layabout, lager loving, louts. He turned most of us.'

He guffawed at this point.

'Louts, yes bloody louts, no good for anything or anyone. Anyway, by sheer dint of personality aided by a work ethic unlike anything I've seen, he turned us to his way of thinking and you know what? We enjoyed it immensely. Being with him became fun. He gave us all jobs to do, little jobs, but we all felt much better doing these things. One day he grabbed hold of me.'

Paddy took quick swig of beer.

'Paddy,' he said. 'I've a request for you. Will you help me on the weekend? I have to look after a group of young people who have Down's syndrome and have agreed to take them on an Adventure trail on the local mountain. Will you give me a hand?'

He paused.

'He was asking me for help. I did not have the guts to tell him that I had no idea what Down's syndrome was. I asked what we were supposed to do. His reply, in essence, was that about 10 youngsters aged from 11-16 would be bussed to our village along with their supervisor. We would take them on a walk of about 2-3 km, turning the walk into an adventure. For example, when we crossed over the local stream, we would imagine that it was a tropical river, just as we have here, full of crocodiles, electric eels, huge poisonous snakes and react accordingly.'

'Sounds ok for me, I look forward to it. What time do we start?' I said.

'They'll turn up about 10 am.'

'The weekend came around and sure enough at 10.15 am, a small bus drew up outside the Youth Club and out poured a motley selection of children, shouting and running all over the place. I thought we needed a sheepdog to herd them into place, sorry make that two. Eventually some semblance of order was obtained and off we went. I tell you, we did not even walk 3 km all day, but at the end of it, I was mentally and physically exhausted. They had a great time, climbing trees, swinging on precariously thin branches, splashing in the crocodile-infested stream and all the time I was running around trying to stop the most dangerous of their pursuits. You couldn't imagine some of the things they got up to.'

'Give us an example?' asked Zafar.

'Well, one child climbed a tree and then started crawling out on one of the branches. He was about 4 metres above the ground. If he'd fallen, he'd have been in big trouble and so would we. They had no idea of danger, but they loved the walk. They kept asking when they could come again. Bert replied that it was up to their supervisor. He was very non-committal and told us afterwards that it all boiled down to finance, as times were hard for generating cash. When we had them all back on the bus and waved them off, I was kaput, but you know what?'

He looked at us with an almost challenging air. No one answered.

'On reflection, I think I can honestly say that it was the best job I ever had.'

We were all amazed at the honesty that came from this little talk by a large, rowdy, crude, Irishman. We clapped him wholeheartedly.

'More,' cried Hanoz, 'we want more.'

'Well you're not getting anymore, 'cos that's all there is to tell.' With that, he took a large swig of whisky, gargled and downed it. It was followed immediately by the rest of the beer. He sat down.

Zafar got up and this is what he had to say.

Zafar:

'I suppose I had better add my penny's worth to the pot. While you two have been talking, I had to do some thinking, as in life a lot of intolerance has been directed at me and also some nasty violence. To answer the question, it has to be when I was working on a farm in the Po valley. I was 17 or 18 at the time when the annual rice planting was being carried out. For those of you who know nothing about rice, it is hard, monotonous work planting rice stalks into those paddy fields.'

He smiled at this and turned to Paddy.

'No disrespect to you Paddy,' emphasising his name. Paddy ignored the remark.

'I used to join in to help with it all. I loved it, but must state that like Paddy's answer, it was not a job, as I was not paid for my labour; you see my family owned the farm. We relied upon migrant workers, usually from Romania and Bulgaria who were housed in a few of our big barns, as well as locals who could work from their homes, The majority were peasant women, but there were always about 10% of men who came over with the intention of remaining in Italy and not returning to their countries. There were more chances of work here along with a better standard of living. One of these men was a youth called Franco. He was tall, thin and had long, wavy and tousled blond hair. The first time I saw him I was smitten. I happened to be riding one of our horses at the time, as I was on an errand to the village. I nearly fell from the saddle. He had on just a pair of shorts and was bending over planting a rice stalk; the sweat stood out on his bareback, his hair was being blown in all directions. It was a moment that I shall never forget.'

'What's his name again?' Paddy shouted out and I noticed that his face was even redder than usual.

'Franco,' came the reply. 'As you well know. Anyway, I continued to the village and came back as quickly as I could. I wanted desperately to stand next to this Greek god and plant rice with him. I got to our stables, unsaddled the horse, rubbed her down and put her into a stall. I was a lather of sweat and not all of it was due to riding. I had a quick shower before casually sauntering along to the fields to where Franco had been planting. He was not there. I was distraught. I asked about him and was told by the foreman that he had returned to the barn, as he was not feeling too well. I thanked him and hastened to the barn.'

'Bejesus, was he there waiting for you?'

'Not in the sense of your remark. He was there, but apparently, he'd been bitten by a snake.'

'Was it the pyjama python?' a guffaw came from Paddy who by now was drinking whisky straight from the bottle.

'I'll treat that remark with the disdain it merits. He'd been to see our first aid officer in a room we had put by for a medical centre. In reality it was an old tack room. The officer assured him that the snake was not poisonous, but just in case had given him a tetanus shot. I caught up with him as he exited and introduced myself. We shook hands. The touch of his hand sent an electric bolt through my body and we talked. It is easy to talk with Romanians; their language is similar to Italian. I have never understood this, as Bulgaria stands between our two countries and that has a South Slavic based language.'

'Bravo and get on with the juicy parts,' came from Paddy again.

'Why don't you shut up and leave him to tell the story his way,' interjected Hanoz.

'Because I don't feel like shutting up,' was the reply.

Hanoz just shrugged and smiled at Zafar.

'Anyway, within a short time, we had become lovers.'

'Whoopee, at last,' came from Paddy. No one took any notice of him.

'The workers were with us for a few weeks before moving to another farm and I can categorically say that this was my best job ever. I clandestinely visited the other farms during the nights. I felt so good during and after it.'

An even bigger round of applause came from us, as it must have been hard for Zafar to tell this tale to the bunch of heterosexuals grouped in front of him.

'Did you ever meet up again?' asked Hanoz.

'No, it was simply one summer of love and one that I'll never forget. It was a beautiful experience for me and as I said before, I'm not sure if you could call it a job, so perhaps I've stretched the definition rather loosely.'

'No, it was fine. Now then Adam, what have you in store for us?' asked Hanoz.

It's getting late,' was my reply. 'Why don't we postpone it until tomorrow night?'

'No way,' came from Paddy, 'we want to hear it now.'

The three of them clinked beer bottles and cheered.

'And now for the final performance is... Mr Adam Lathey,' clowned Hanoz.

So here is my tale:

'My story is similar to the ones told by Paddy and Zafar in that it was not a job I held and got paid for. The job I did for just one week stands out in my memory, as one of the most enjoyable that I've ever had. At that time I was a post-graduate in London and used to come home for a week or two in the vacations or for the odd weekend. This one happened to be the summer vacation. I had a close bond to one of my aunts and uncles who lived just three streets away from my parent's public house. One day my aunt Maisie, my mother's sister, came over to our pub.'

'Look here, Adam,' she started. 'Your parents and a few others from the pub are going to Blackpool sometime during November, for a weekend coach trip break to see the Illuminations. Cliff and I cannot go unless we have someone to look after our daughters. I might add that these were 6 and 8 years of age at the time. We have ALL decided that you are the perfect person to look after them.'

I took a swallow of beer.

'I liked the ALL had decided bit. No doubt this had been agreed over many gin and tonics in our pub bar. My mother added her weight to the request, followed by my father and I had no choice.'

Paddy guffawed. 'A babysitter, ha ha.'

I ignored him.

'But I've never looked after them before,' was my weak reply.

'Nonsense,' said Maisie. 'They know you very well and you know them. That's all you need to know.'

She turned to my mother. 'That's fixed then Loreen. Go ahead and book the trip to Blackpool.'

'But who is going to run the pub when you're away?' I asked my father.

'Don't worry about that,' was the reply, 'the brewery will send a relief manager for the weekend.'

My last card had been played, as I automatically thought that I would be running the pub. I left for London later that day with the weekend for Nov 14 firmly etched in my brain and entered in my diary. Come November, I decided to take 10 days off from my studies and as it happened that was a sagacious move.

I came back to Wales a few days before the Blackpool trip, as I wanted to meet up with a few friends, Pete Davies, David Keyes, as well as to see my nieces. I knew Tamsin Margaret and Isla Dorothy well; they had Scottish first names, because their father was a Scot,

Cliff McStott and had wanted Scottish names for his daughters. So I called in at their home.

'Uncle Adam,' they rushed into my arms when they saw me. 'You're looking after us this weekend. Hooray.'

I grinned. I liked the pair and we had had some good times in the past.

'I don't know what I have done to deserve this, but Yes, I'm in charge of you two and any misbehaviour will be dealt with by a good thrashing.' I banged my hands together.

They pretended to cower and then launched themselves back into my arms. I stayed talking with Maisie and Cliff and then went home. Over the next few days, I met up with my mates in the bar, had numerous games of darts and crib, but it left me plenty of time to think of what I was going to do with those two little girls.

We eventually waved everyone off to Blackpool and I was left to look after them. The first thing we did was to go to collect my suitcase, as I was going to stay at their home. They trouped after me to my room in the pub and looked around. Being a typical rock nut, I had rocks and minerals all over the place. Three pieces of rock caught their eyes.

'What are these?'

They pointed at three almost spherical pebbles brought from a local beach. They were that shape due to a combination of factors; jointing, fracture patterns and being adjacent to a Liassic cliff headland. Lias is a geological era when dinosaurs roamed that world. The almost cube-shaped lumps of rock that fell from the cliff face became very rounded as the sea rolled them about and due to the headland, they simply stayed in place becoming rounder and rounder eventually resembling various sized billiard balls.

'They are dinosaur eggs.'

'Dinosaur eggs,' was screamed in my ear. 'Can we touch them?'

That was the start of a week of permanent chatter about the eggs.

'Can we get baby dinosaurs?'

'Yes. I'm going to put them in the pub attic so that they can hatch. I even have one who has already hatched. His name is Dewi.'

Those were some of the worst words I've ever uttered. Immediately they wanted to see the baby dinosaur. I managed to calm them down and took them off for a snack and drink at the local Cavalli's Italian café. The next few days, all I heard was, Can we see Dewi?'

I had a variety of excuses.

'Oh, he has gone for a flight around the area, he is sleeping, eating, does not like to be disturbed.'

'I was bombarded with questions about him. I was glad I only had to undergo this for a weekend. On Sunday night, the bus arrived back and my parents told me that Cliff had had an asthma attack and was hospitalised in Blackpool. Maisie had stayed with him, so I had to look after the girls until their return. How I got through the next few days I do not know, as all they wanted to hear from me was more information about Dewi. They constantly pestered me to take them to my parent's pub to see Dewi in his attic room. It took all my imagination to placate two little girls, but you know what? I loved every minute of that job and was very sorry when five days later, Cliff and Maisie arrived home. I even went into the loft and made a little bed of twigs and grass and put a small amount of anthracite coal beside it, powdered obviously as baby dragons cannot eat large lumps of coal. I showed it to them once in daytime, telling them that he had gone for a flight. I emphasised he did not like to be disturbed at night when he was in his bed. When I moved out of their house, I told the girls that Dewi had grown his adult wings quicker than expected and had flown away. They were disappointed, but then Isla looked at me.'

'You have three more eggs that are about to hatch. Can we see these?'

I bid them a hasty goodbye.

14.

A few days later, the sun was in a sulk and the morning mist took ages to dissipate. I woke first and as usual, got the remnants of the fire alight and placed the coffee can on it. We had decided that today would be an early start because we were at the junction point of two large rivers. This meant an early breakfast after which we would separate into two parties. Paddy and Zafar would go along one tributary, Hanoz and I the other. We had agreed that the trips would last three or at the most four days and if nothing of note had been found, we would all return to the campsite where the trucks had been left.

Breakfast varied from beans and bacon, or beans alone if the bacon strips had gone unless we had some fish leftover from last night's dinner. The coffee smell roused the others and they tumbled from their beds. Zafar came blearily forward, as he was still being plagued by mosquitoes.

'I'm looking forward to another lovely day's work at the office,' came from Paddy, as bleary-eyed, he stepped forward to pour out some scalding hot coffee.

Little was said that morning, as we all knew what awaited us; dreary, back aching work that, according to Zafar, was worse than planting rice. Paddy used to moan that we should have brought along a few Romanian or Bulgarian females to do the work instead of us. They also had other uses, was his favoured remark.

Breakfast did not take long. A quick swill of plates and cups in the river was quickly carried out and Zafar had his swim. The rest of us were always careful with regards to the river, as the Colombian jungle not only had jaguars, beautiful and deadly, but unlikely to bother us, but also huge 9-10 metre long anacondas, piranha fish and a whole array of smaller but no less dangerous animals, like large electric eels. There was also an extremely poisonous frog called the golden poison arrow dart frog. The natives used to milk them and use the venom to coat blowpipe darts. The frogs come in a fantastic variety of colours, red, yellow, gold copper, green, black or blue, colours that warn off predators, an ability which I believe is called *aposematic coloratio*. As stated, none of us swam there, apart from Zafar. He never gave a reason, but I think it was some macho idea he had that made him want to impress us. I thought he was nuts.

We had three kayaks with us, two singles and a double. Zafar and Paddy took the double and Hanoz and I the singles. We shouted, 'Good luck' to each other and left on our separate journeys. On the tributary we had entered, we sampled rigorously but our luck seemed out. We found no traces of anything and at the end of the third day, Hanoz remarked,

'Sod this. This is terrible work for as far as I can see no rewards, I suggest we return.'

I tended to agree with him, so the next day we paddled hard and returned to base. Paddy and Zafar had not returned, so we built a fire, had a few beers, chatted about our past lives and Hanoz told me more about Copje with whom he seemed to have bonded. He was thoughtful when he remarked about Copje's newfound love of Erika and was silent for a while. His growing feelings for Kate were becoming more and more, evident as he then started talking about her. We finally called it a day around midnight and turned in for a sound sleep.

We both got up very late, had a brunch meal and it was in the afternoon when we noticed Paddy's double kayak coming downstream. He was alone. Walking to the edge of the water, we pulled the kayak ashore. Paddy seemed to be in a bad emotional state, his eyes were red and watery. He had a slight shaking of his arms and was mumbling to himself. We helped him out of the kayak.

'What's happened, where's Zafar?' I asked.

He slumped to the ground.

'I want out of this cursed country,' were his words. 'Zafar's dead. On our first day, we camped at the first tributary junction we saw. Getting out of the kayak, he somehow fell awkwardly and broke his leg very badly. The bone was sticking out into the air. I put him in his cot and gave him some morphine and that helped.'

He paused. 'I need a whisky.'

Hanoz looked quizzically at him and passed a glass and bottle. Paddy just took the bottle and drank a slug.

'Why didn't you return immediately?' I asked.

'I thought we could manage the situation,' was the reply, 'and Zafar did not complain. I left him there with food and water and went on upstream sampling as arranged.'

Hanoz interrupted. 'A bad break in conditions of high temperatures and humidity has to be treated seriously or blood poisoning and gangrene can set in very quickly. You were an idiot going on. You're a bloody fool. In the name of anything you hold dear, why didn't you return?'

'It's easy to be wise after the event,' was the sneered reply, 'but I thought it would be ok. On my return, I found that Zafar had died. The leg was in a terrible state. I left.'

'What do you mean you left,' exploded Hanoz. 'Didn't you have the decency to bury him? You could have brought him back in the kayak.'

I had never seen Hanoz so angry.

He continued. 'In my army days, if possible, we always brought back bodies to our base, even though it frequently put us in dangerous situations. You should never have left him.'

'Oh, Mr Wise Guy, Mr Know All,' he sneered. 'No, I left him in his cot as there was nothing I could do. I took the mosquito netting as mine was rather worn, as was his, but two are better than nothing. That's all. I'm fed up with this damn country and incidentally of you. I'm leaving now and will take one of the trucks.

I've had it up to my ears with filth, rivers and shovelling buckets of dirt. You can keep the kayak and what's in it.'

He got up and I stepped between Hanoz and him. I sensed that Hanoz was about to explode and knew that if he did, he could easily kill Paddy. What has happened since stopping him was one of the worst mistakes I have ever made. I should have let Hanoz kill him.

'Cool it,' I said and pushed Paddy to one side. I did not want to put a finger on Hanoz. He was so wound up.

'You bastard, I'm going upriver right now,' said Hanoz. 'If I stay here, blood will be shed and it won't be mine. First tributary junction?'

A nod came from Paddy. With that Hanoz put mosquito netting and provisions into the single kayak, jumped in and paddled off. Paddy said nothing and we watched until he disappeared around a bend in the river.

'Is that all you've got to tell me?'

I obtained no reply. He simply got up and started collecting his things.

'I've had it, Adam. I'm off and don't try to stop me. I'm leaving Colombia straight away. I reckon that half the equipment is Zafar's and mine, so if I take a truck, it's only fair. You can keep all the gear. Zafar was a sound bloke.'

With that, he paused before sitting down, opening a bottle of whisky and after taking a big gulp told me more about Zafar's earlier life. I was surprised.

I said nothing and simply listened, watched him get up, pack his personal gear and clamber into a truck. I noticed that two cases of whisky had been taken along with his gear. He had some drinking to do if he was going to leave Colombia immediately. Nothing more was said and with a slight wave of a hand he drove off. Unfortunately, the next time I met up with him was in Thailand.

I went fishing, ambled around the camp and did some serious thinking. I knew that Hanoz had intended staying for only about a couple of weeks. Being alone in a wilderness area let alone in a tropical jungle was not to be recommended for anyone and I had more or less decided that I'd also pack this venture in and leave with Hanoz. So I had a few beers, checked the small containers in the kayaks to see if the first aid kits, survival gear and fishing lines, etc. were ok and went to bed. On some whim, I added Paddy and Zafar's mosquito nets from the double kayak.

I drank many mugs of coffee and started cleaning up the camp ready for leaving after Hanoz got back. It was towards dusk on the third day that I saw the kayak coming downstream. This meant we would not be leaving that night. Hanoz paddled to the shore and jumped out looking tired, grey and gaunt.

'Let's get this beached first.'

Looking round he saw that a truck had gone.

'So the bastard has left.'

'Yes, he went almost straight after you.'

Hanoz snorted, 'If he'd been here now, he'd be a dead man. What's the term the Americans use? Terminate with extreme prejudice? I'd be very happy to terminate him with or without prejudice. He left Zafar to die up there all alone. I found his notebook and in it he'd written that Paddy had left him. He was in his cot, decomposing rather badly and gangrene had set in. I buried him as far away from the river as I could manage.'

He passed over the notebook. 'Have a read of this. I need a drink.'

With that he walked to one of the case of whisky that Paddy had left and lifted out a bottle and a couple of glasses.

'I cannot believe that he just let Zafar die, it's inhuman.'

He poured three fingers into each glass and handed one to me.

'Just read.'

I flicked through the pages. It was hard reading, especially as I had known the man. It started by asking whoever found it to send it to Paulo his brother and the address was given. The last page made shocking reading.

Paddy has left me here to die. He has not helped at all apart from placing food & water plus morphine by my bed.
He's always drunk & just gone down river.
I am helpless & my leg is black and swollen. It hurts. Thank god for morphine. I am going to take the lot — blessed oblivion.
I hope paddy burns in hell.

I closed the small notebook and placed it into a small plastic case before putting it in my shirt top pocket. Amazingly that shirt was never frisked in our subsequent adventures and survived all kinds of treatment.

'I'll see that it gets to his brother, but I'll take out that last page.'

'Thank you, Adam. If I ever meet up with the bastard, I'll kill him.'

He got up and put more wood on the fire until it was blazing merrily away.

'I leave in the morning. Are you coming?'

'Absolutely. I've also had enough of this place. Let's have a few beers to celebrate the end of this venture and also we can drink a toast to Zafar.'

That is what we did. We built up the fire, had several beers and turned in hoping for a sound night's sleep.

I awoke sometime in the early morning with the sun just about peeping out from the far riverbank, by the feel of two gun barrels crashing into my back.

'Levántate.' ('Get up').

'I don't speak Spanish,' I cried and saw that Hanoz had already been ousted from his cot and was standing quietly between two armed soldiers. They ignored my comment and another torrent of Spanish was said followed by several blows to my body. Two soldiers gathered up our kit and hauled me upright. Hanoz and I were marched towards the fire where stood a tall, rangy whipcord thin, lean man apparently warming his hands.

'It was rather nice of you to make up this fire. My men spotted it and we came to investigate. Who are you and what are you doing here?'

He turned and bright, intelligent inquiring eyes looked straight at us, but all I could notice was a broken nose and military crew cut. He had a pearl-handled Colt revolver strapped around his waist. Apparently, his hero was George Patten the US Army General of World War II fame. We stated our names and I volunteered the information that we were looking for minerals. He opened our bags and one item caught his eye. It was a pair of handcuffs. Hanoz had told us that whenever he was going off on an adventure, he always carried these with him. They were trick ones. His view was that if he was ever caught, the captor would almost always use the handcuffs to secure him. He was right.

'Who do these belong to?'

'Me,' said Hanoz.

'Not many people have had the pleasure of being cuffed by Colonel Ortsh,' was said, as he clasped the handcuffs around Hanoz's wrists.

Ortsh stepped back. Mine were tied with wire.

Nothing was mentioned for a minute, as everyone laughed at the scene. Then machine-gun Spanish came from Ortsh's mouth. We were grabbed, beaten; our boots taken away and we were pushed along the track until we came to one truck. The rear door was opened and we were thrown in. There was another figure hunkered down in the corner who furtively turned to see us.

'Well look who it is,' said an unkempt and bruised Sir George. 'Adam, welcome to my humble mansion. Introductions to this gentlemen,' and he turned to Hanoz, 'can come later. We do seem to have landed ourselves in rather a pickle with this chap Ortsh.'

15.

The door slammed shut and the light disappeared. The place smelled to high heaven, a fact that Sir George apologised for, as he had to use one corner as a lavatory. Neither of us replied to that statement. I introduced Hanoz.

I felt my way towards Sir George bumping into Hanoz who was doing the same and we all eventually met up. Hanoz had slipped out of his handcuffs and was busy undoing my bindings. Sir George had heard the clink made by the 'cuffs as they fell to the floor.

'What's that noise?'

'Handcuffs falling to the floor. Have you ever been cuffed?'

'For pleasure or crime?' retorted Sir George.

I could sense the grin that would be stretching across Hanoz's face.

'One point to you, Sir George,' was all he said as my hands were freed.

Sir George had been captured over a week ago and he filled us in on our captors. It was not a nice story. When he'd finished Hanoz remarked to me.

'And that's not all. I overheard them talking about tonight. They're going to have a rest day drinking our beer and whisky. At dusk, an impromptu event is due to start with you and me as the star performers. They intend to have some fun pre killing us. We've got to get out of here as soon as possible.'

Turning to Sir George, he questioned him about how he was fed and exercised.

'They bring me food and water in late morning and let me walk a bit and I try to do any ablutions then. I always have two soldiers with me. I get locked up until night when I am let out again. I think this is an old ammunition truck that is why it's not open like the others. It's solid and I have been unable to find any chink in the design.'

There was quiet for a while and I digested what had been said. It did not sound very hopeful.

'Right,' said Hanoz. 'We have to get any guard to open this door. It's the only way we are likely to get out of here alive.'

He paused for a moment.

'Adam, go and sit by the door and crouch in the corner. I'm going to hammer on it calling out that Sir George is very ill, possibly dying. If he looks in, he will see Sir George gasping on the floor and hopefully will enter. If he does, jump him and put your finger between the trigger of his rifle and the guard. He must not let off a shot before I deal with him. You might get a broken finger, but that's better than dying later on. If there is more than one guard, well we just deal with them and hope for the best. There will be at least two guards if Ortsh is as good as Sir Gorge says. We must pray for one only for this ploy. We'll give them an hour so they can drink up some of our booze and perhaps become careless. After all, as far as they are concerned this place is escape proof.'

He stopped. 'Comments?'

Sir George said, 'I'm all for it. They want to keep me alive for a ransom, but I'm with you.'

'Now, let's try to get out of this hell hole.'

I said nothing simply because this was all above my level of comprehension. I did know that we were in a massive mess and that Hanoz was the only person who could conceivably get us out of it. We waited for what we deemed to be about an hour. Hanoz worked his way to the door, hammered on it and started shouting out.

'Ayuda! El hombre que está aquí está muy enfermo. Necesita ayuda. Creo que se va a morir.' ('Help, the man in here is very ill. He needs help. I think he is dying.') He repeated these words over and over.

I felt despair creep over me because nothing happened for some time. Then I heard bolts being drawn back and tensed up. I concentrated on the one thing that I was to do - stopping a shot being fired.

The door opened and daylight pierced the truck's darkness. I saw a shadow appear on the truck floor.

'¿Cual es el problema?' ('What is the matter?')

I made myself as small as possible in the corner. Hanoz pointed to Sir George, who was rolling about at the back of the truck uttering loud moans and occasional screams.

'Se está volviendo loco por el dolor. Por favor, ayúdale.' ('He's going crazy with pain. Please help him.')

One foot appeared on the truck floor and the other soon followed. He was crouching and the rifle was pointing downwards. As the form materialised in front of me, I leapt forward jamming my finger into the trigger guard. I immediately felt the pressure on it as he tried to pull the trigger, but no gunshot occurred. Simultaneously Hanoz had crossed towards him and with his two arms around the guard's head, snapped his neck. He snatched at the rifle and in doing so the movement broke my finger. It throbbed like hell.

He tore off the guard's boots and searched him, coming up with a knife and a small box of ammunition. He glanced at the boots and tossed them to me.

'Not my size,' was uttered. 'Let's move.'

The boots fitted and cautiously the three of us clambered out of the truck. Hauling the guard out last, Hanoz closed and locked the doors before picking up the guard in a fireman's lift.

'We'll hopefully have a few hours start, as they will only open up the truck to let Sir George out for his stroll. I'll dump our friend in the jungle somewhere. Now let's make for the river, very, very carefully.'

Sir George added, 'Give me the rifle. Even though I am a possible bargaining chip, they still like their fun and I'm not going back.'

With that, he held out his right hand. Three fingers were very swollen and purple with the nails ripped off.

'I was tortured as they wanted to try to find out more about me. I used to be damn good with a rifle in my youthful Army days and my trigger finger still works.' He smiled, 'I'm left-handed.'

I was left with the knife.

We could hear chanting and singing from our camp and we slowly retreated towards the river with Hanoz making a slight detour and coming back minus the body.

'I stowed him up a tree, so perhaps he'll not be missed.'

We slowed as we approached the river and sure enough, a guard was sitting in one of our kayaks smoking and drinking from a tin cup, which we later found contained neat whisky. I know because I drained it.

Hanoz held up his hand palm outstretched and we stopped. He beckoned for the knife and I passed it over. The guard was some 50 metres from us and there was not much cover. Luckily he was facing downriver and away from us.

'I have to get him again without a shot being fired. If you have a god, start praying to him now.'

With that, he stood and took many controlled breaths. I was worried about the state of his feet, which had many scratches and blood streaks on them, however the ground in front was sandy, which would help. He stopped his breathing exercises and leapt forward. He ran fast making sure that his feet went into the sand and not the odd bit of scrub that was on the beach. He ran on the soles of his feet and I did not hear any sound. He moved towards his prey like the ultimate, merciless predator that he was. As he reached the guard, some instinct made the man turn. As he did so, Hanoz buried the knife in his neck, grabbed his head, pulled it backwards and sawed away almost severing the head. The knife emerged from the front of the neck in a gory mess and arterial blood spurted everywhere, but Hanoz paid little attention. He dropped the guard, frisked him while beckoning for us to join him. He took the boots off, tried them on and grinned.

'Good fit. Stick him in the kayak. Sir George, take the front seat of the double kayak. Adam, tie this kayak,' pointing to the one the guard was in, 'to yours and let's get the hell out of here.'

A quick look at the kayak's containers showed that all our items were still there and I thanked the gods for nudging me to put in those two mosquito nets. We kicked sand over the blood-stained beach and paddled downstream as fast as we could. When we had rounded a bend I started breathing easier.

'We must put as much distance between them and us as is possible. Therefore we are going to paddle through the night and next day. Be prepared for a hard slog. I don't like the idea of a night-time paddle, but we must take that chance. Follow me.'

I settled back and as I did so noticed how thin Sir George was. He had seriously deteriorated since last seen. His skin had a yellowish tinge; he had developed a hacking cough and was sweating profusely. Paddling wise he could not keep up with Hanoz and merely tried to paddle with sporadic strokes.

A few kilometres downriver we veered into the bank and Hanoz took the guard into the jungle, returning about five minutes later. We put everything from the towed kayak's containers into ours, filled it with dirt and stones and smashed it, before towing it into mid-river and letting it sink. That was the only stop we made in that part of the trip, a trip that ached muscles I never knew I had.

The next evening we stopped at a river bend and crawled out of the kayaks. I could hardly stand and my backside was raw and puffy due to chaffing. My arms were also dead. Even Hanoz stumbled when he got out of the kayak to help lift Sir George out.

We had not eaten for two days, but had rainwater to drink, which was plentiful and was collected in every utensil we had. At least we had regularly taken malaria tablets, unlike Sir George who we suspected had gone down with a bad case of malaria during his stay with Ortsh. I pulled the kayaks out of the water and into the tree line. We had not been dry for two days and our clothes stuck to us and ominous rashes had started to appear and itch.

Hanoz laid Sir George slowly on the ground then went to pick leaves and grass to make some sort of bed for him, He picked up a few saplings that had stranded on the beach and by sticking those into the sand made a frame over which he draped a mosquito net and *basha* sheet. Sir George was placed inside this. I meanwhile had drawn in the four fishing lines that we had trailed behind the kayaks. We were lucky as two large and three smaller fish had been hooked. I gutted them and went to gather grass, twigs and wood in which to make a fire. I snapped off the end twigs from trees as these are the driest part of a tree and therefore most likely to burn.

When we had finished these tasks, Hanoz remarked.

'Ok, Adam let's forage and see if we can come up with some vegetables and fruit.' He tried a grin which did not work. 'Cross your fingers.'

Within a half-hour to my astonishment, we had collected a variety of goods. When I say we, I mean Hanoz who had what seemed to be an encyclopaedic knowledge of what was good/bad to eat. The haul including *yams, yucca, kumba,* a purple fruit that is good when cooked and whose juice makes a decent fruit drink, together with some *jagua* which made another good fruit drink. A *buriti* fruit tree was also found which Hanoz said made an excellent ultraviolet screen when put on one's body, as well as tasting good. All in all it was a veritable feast. One day of feasting, because after that came many days of famine.

At the edge of the small beach, Hanoz made a Dakota oven so that no fire could be seen and I used the steel and flint from our survival box to get a spark and by judicious blowing managed to get a fire smouldering from the grass and twigs I had collected earlier.

Whoosh, it burst into life. We placed the fish which had been cut into chunks into a pan with the vegetables, added water and waited for it to cook. Under instructions, I then threw the *kumba* and *jagua* fruits into a saucepan pressing down hard to mash them. Juice poured forth and I drained this off into two sampling pans. I stepped over to see Sir George, helped him upright and offered him a pan. He took it and drank and drank and drained the pan.

'My, that was a good drink, one of the best I've ever had,' was stated before he sank back down.

'We don't have time to make A-frames before dark and anyway I don't want anyone to know we've been here,' said Hanoz, 'and as it's a night on the ground prepare for some creepy crawlies. How's the meal coming along?'

'I'm frequently stirring and another twenty minutes should see us chomping away.' As I said this, I felt my stomach cramping at the thought of food.

Twenty minutes later, we were wolfing it down taking turns to feed Sir George. All of us sat back, as dusk approaches fast and light fades quickly in these latitudes. That was the last of the good foraging because later on things became very much worse.

Sir George stood up. 'I have a present to give to you both.' This was said with a wry smile. He pulled one of the large buttons that were on his thin linen jacket and unpeeled the cloth. We gasped as he produced a compass.

'This might come in handy. Always be prepared. MI6 insisted I take this with me. I don't really know why.'

'Great news but now Sir George, we have to make our own beds. As we only have one netting, Adam and I are going to cosy up together,' said Hanoz looking at me with a smile. I knew what the smile was about. We had no need of a compass. Our intention was to paddle downstream until we hit a village.

We stuck fallen branches into the ground, tied a rope to the tops anchoring the ends in the ground; slung netting and a *basha* sheet over the rope, took off our wet clothes, rubbed ourselves dry with a piece of towelling and collapsed inside. We didn't even say 'good night' to each other. Dry at last and oblivion. Mosquitoes might have found the hole in the netting, but I did not know or care. The rain hissed down that night but we kept dry.

The next morning we finished off the stew and juices and packed everything away in the kayaks, after which we put back on our wet clothes. The night might have brought out the creepy crawlies, but if so they had not affected our sleep. My muscles ached, but mentally I felt better. Sir George however, although he had slept, seemed to be worse. He was still sweating profusely and now had a heavy fever and his skin seemed to have gone yellower. Hanoz thought he had yellow fever contacted from wild mosquitoes. Colombia has more than 150 varieties of mosquito including the yellow fever carriers, the *Aedes* and *Haemogogus* species. Both of us had had our jabs for this but we did not know about Sir George. We dosed him with tablets from the small first aid kit, but it was evident that he needed medical treatment, which we could not give. We started to be worried. He was placed in the front seat as before and we took off. Paddling alongside Hanoz, I noticed that Sir George alternated between sleeping and watchfulness. He could not paddle. At times he appeared to be writing into a notebook which was kept in a survival container.

I threw out our fishing lines and settled into the rhythm of paddling. I felt okay except for my broken finger and my bottom. Both pained me quite a bit and were still red, sore and very tender. I had smoothed them with cream last evening, alas to no avail.

We paddled, slept and paddled some more and it was on the sixth day that it happened. We had camped on a small river embayment and as per usual, placed a very weakened and emaciated Sir George on the ground and surrounded him with netting and a *basha* sheet. We had been unlucky in finding any vegetables or fruit and had caught only eight small fish in total. We draped mosquito netting and a *basha* sheet over our grass bed, collapsed and slept the sleep of the just. On awakening, I went to help Sir George out of the netting. He was not there. I immediately woke Hanoz.

'The bloody fool,' was his reaction.

Besides his bed were some papers held down by a stone. We sat down and read them. The first sheet stated that he had always enjoyed the exploits of Captain Robert Falcon Scott of the doomed Terra Nova Antarctic expedition, but had always been drawn to Captain Oates, who suffering from frostbite and gangrene had left the tent saying, 'I am just going outside and may be some time'. As food was very scarce, Oates had made this sacrifice with the thought of saving the lives of his companions.

The note ended with the comment that he was a burden to us and that our hopes of survival would be higher if we didn't have to care about him, so please, he pleaded, do not come looking for him. He estimated that he'd have at least a six hours start. He wished us all the luck in the world. He loved us and if we survived would we give the other sheets to a wonderful woman called Glenys from Connich, her home in Scotland, or her workplace at the Cavendish Laboratories, Oxford.

Hanoz swore viciously. 'The crazy bastard.' He went snooping around the perimeter.

'He's a crafty one. I can't see an exit point landwards, so he must have waded up or down the river. You go upstream, I'll go downstream. We cannot leave the bugger; it's against all my instincts to leave somebody behind.'

He passed me a rifle. 'One-shot if you find him and I'll come fast as I can. If I fire, come back immediately. I've not wanted to fire a gun as Ortsh could be anywhere and it'd give away our position, but let's chance it this one time. We have to find him and bring the delirious old bugger back before nightfall. Somewhere along the riverbank, he'll either have collapsed, or headed into the jungle. If the latter, we must find the exit point where he left the river and try to track him. Come on, let's go.'

With that, he headed off downstream. I walked upstream scanning the banks for footprints or broken reeds. It was nearly noon that I saw a slight trail and what looked like a boot print. If this was him, I was amazed that he had managed to walk so far. I slowly followed the very faint trail, as he must have tried not to disturb any of the vegetation. I found him slumped against a banyan tree in an appalling state, almost skeletal with his eyes rolling around so that all one saw were the whites. His mouth was foam-flecked and sweat was pouring off his skinny body. He blinked and recognised me.

'Adam, why oh, why did you follow me?'

'You know Hanoz. He never abandons anyone.'

'I'm dying Adam. I cannot take any more of this.'

I put my arm around his shoulder and held him close.

'It's ok, we'll take care of you.'

He nestled in my arms and closing his eyes started to sob quietly.

'Get to the Foreign Office, Nels Clifford, tell him all.'

This was a great effort for him. He clutched my hand hard, with a hand that was almost transparent. I could practically see the bones in it.

He was quiet for a moment or two before blurting out why he had come to Colombia to try to foster a peace treaty between the Colombian government and FARC, his meetings at the camp with his army protectors, the torturing by Ortsh. It all came out in a torrent of words. Then at last.

'My letter?'

'We have it.'

A smile parted his lips.

'Tell her I love her.' With that he died.

I debated whether to try to bury him at that spot or to take the body back, but decided on the former. I had no implement so broke off a tree branch and tried to mark out a shallow grave. It took me a long time, but eventually, I placed this brave man's body into it and covered him up. I said a silent prayer, decided not to fire the gun and left.

When I arrived back, it was dark and Hanoz was sitting on the kayak.

'Well?'

I told him what had happened.

'He was a brave old soul,' was all he said. A few moments later, he stood up.

'Let's turn in and Adam, I want your solemn word that you'll get those notes to, what was her name again, Glenys and Zafar's brother? You have the notes?'

'Do you even have to ask? They are in my shirt pocket alongside Zafar's. I've put both into a small plastic case and they reside here.'

I patted the shirt pocket.

16.

We set off early that morning with only an occasional word being exchanged. The decision was made to ditch the single and take the double kayak. Hanoz thought it a better bet as we were both not in good mental or physical shape and we piled everything we possessed into the double kayak. Hanoz had done virtually all the paddling when with Sir George and I was struck by how much harder it was to control the larger kayak. I had suffered but he must have had a much more difficult time. Things along the river journey did not change. We paddled, rested at night, caught a few fish and scoured the banks for any fruit and vegetables. We found no vegetables or fruit.

The only carbohydrates we ate were obtained from two small palm trees found perched precariously at the water's edge. Hanoz whooped with joy when he saw them. We stopped, cut down the trees and peeled off the bark exposing the palm's centre, which we crammed into our mouths.

'This is termed a millionaire's salad,' said Hanoz. He looked round, spied a liana hanging from a tree and reaching up, cut it with a blow from his machete and swiftly did the same at foot level. Levelling off the branch he lifted it to his lips and drank the water that gushed forth.

He smiled at me. 'A great source of water in the jungle and it tastes good.' He passed it over to me and I must say it was very refreshing, with a pleasant after taste quite distinct to rainwater.

As I was drinking I felt a sting in my leg and saw that an ant had bit me. Hanoz also saw it.

'Damn it, that's a bullet ant,' was the comment. He brushed it off and stood on it.

'Adam, I have to tell you that it's called that because the pain is deemed to be worse than a bullet hitting you. You are going to hurt for a day or two. Luckily it's your leg and not your arm, so you can still paddle.'

I did not reply as a burning sensation was taking place in my leg.

'I've been shot, so I'll let you know,' was my laconic reply. Neither of us mentioned it again, but I can tell you that at times I was in agony.

We now resembled two scarecrows due to the weight that we had lost and our clothes were in tatters. After five more days of this, we rounded a meander in the river and saw… huts and smoke. Civilisation!

Well not quite, as there were some 50 or so thatched huts and possibly a hundred plus people who lived there. Children were all over the place, as were small pigs grunting, snorting and rolling on the muddy banks.

We paddled slowly towards them and were slightly put off as we saw spears, blowpipes and bows and arrows aplenty. Beaching, I held my hand palm up showing the universal peace sign. Hanoz voiced some words in slow Spanish, but no one seemed to follow him. Eventually, an old wispy, bearded man emerged from one hut and a very halting Spanish conversation took place. We had arrived at a village and as far as we could make out, there was a larger village four days journey downstream and after that a much larger place, I guess a town of some sort. It was difficult making sense of what he was saying.

A crowd had now gathered and I was a bit uneasy so scrabbled around to see if there was anything I could give them as a present. We had very little of that ilk in the kayak. In doing so, I dislodged one of the rifles that had not been used on our journey. Immediately there was a babble of conversation. They knew what a rifle was. Hanoz took it from me and after removing the rounds passed it to the old man. He gingerly took it and squinted down the sight.

'Boom, boom, boom.' He grinned and I relaxed a little.

Hanoz put in a round, looked around and aimed at a *paw paw* tree some 60 metres away. He fired. One pod exploded and the orange juice splattered the ground. The crowd went crazy. He passed the rifle over and the old man did the same, but all that occurred was the click of the trigger. He was puzzled, so Hanoz showed him the cartridges. He nodded.

After that, it was plain sailing. Hanoz showed the old man how to load, aim and fire the gun. The man did not push the gun into his shoulder for his first shot and it jarred the shoulder so badly that the gun was thrown down. A younger man picked it up and Hanoz patiently taught him the correct procedure. To the delight of the old man, he made a show of handing over both guns as presents, but they were declined. After a few more shots, the crowd were whooping with delight. Hanoz stopped the lesson then as we only had left some 50 or so bullets. Seemingly without warning, food and a kind of cava drink was brought to us. We were welcomed and had a feast.

We decided to stay for about a week, resting as we were dog tired. Then we intended going further downstream to the bigger town in the hope that eventually we would find civilisation and home. Alas, that was not to be. Hanoz spent the time hunting with the villagers and shooting a few wild pigs. I also did a spot of sifting of the river sands and to my astonishment found several emeralds. I put all my findings into a bag and stowed them in the kayak. I told Hanoz about this, but he did not care much for the fact. He was not interested in emeralds being more interested with the culture of the village and by now was conversing haltingly with the old man and even some of the younger ones. He even tried his hand at playing the music of the Bojo Magdelana, - *cumbia* – music that is the heartbeat of Colombia; *vallenato*, the swirling accordion music. He had an uncanny ability to pick up languages and culture very easily. He thought we had landed at a *palenques* village, one that had been founded by runaway slaves, who had intermingled with the Andaquíes or Coreguajes tribes. These villages are frequently found on tributaries of the Magdalena, the great arterial river of Colombia and all the others. He could not be sure. One night he came back very late and in a very happy, relaxed mood that lasted most of the next day. Apparently he had taken part in a shamanistic ritual (I had not been invited) that involved a bitter drink called *ayahuasca*. On my return to the UK I looked it up. I found that it contained dimethyltriptamine, used to treat depression. It undoes what has caused stress in the brain and makes new connections. The psychedelic experience comes on faster and more intense than magic mushrooms. It certainly relaxed Hanoz.

I joined them one day on a hunting trip and was amused to see how they took a drink in deep jungle. A quick slash at a convenient bamboo tree segment and a cup placed beneath it caught the water that gushed forth. A cut at another segment and the cycle was repeated. On our sixth day at the village, we had been hunting in the jungle and on our return were surprised to see two motor launches berthed at the rickety old pier. The flags on them were that of Colombia and my heart jumped. Safety at last and I hastened to the village, Hanoz following behind me. There were about a dozen soldiers in the village all talking with various people. I strode towards one who had what seemed to be faded stripes on his sleeve.

'Hola,' I ventured in my best Spanish followed by, '¿Habla usted inglés?'

The man turned and said something in Spanish and immediately their rifles were raised and pointed at Hanoz and me. I stopped in bewilderment.

'What have you been doing here in Colombia?'

I explained that I had been employed as a geologist with the Frontino Company and had been looking for emeralds. He stopped me at that point.

'Where is your permit?'

As far as I knew all our permits were still in the camp where Ortsh had attacked us, so I tried explaining this to the man. All the time Hanoz had not said a word, he just stood there.

'Passports.'

'They've gone astray,' I lied, 'as we were lost in the jungle and have been trying to get out for some time.'

The soldier then rapped out a few words in Spanish and some men started searching the kayak eventually coming up with my little bag of emeralds and the two rifles.

'I believe you are illegal miners,' were the next words uttered. 'Arrest these men,' was suddenly shouted.' Turning to me, he said.

'You have no passports or permits. You have in your possession two Government Issue rifles. How did you acquire these, as they are issued only to our soldiers? I am taking you to my superiors for further questioning.'

With that, he rifle butted both of us and we were bundled into the launches and did not even have time to say goodbye to our new village friends. I was very apprehensive about his last remark. If the rifles were from soldiers they probably had been taken from government soldiers killed by Ortsh. If so we were seriously in big trouble.

The next few days were a horror story. We were handcuffed, bundled into a closed canvas sided vehicle, shipped like cattle across Colombia and my very red and sore backside and finger ached abominably. We were barely given food or water and stopped for two days at a military camp. There, we went informed that our status was such that we were going to be taken to a Bogotá prison due to having government arms in our possession, apparently a Federal offence. I was now very worried.

We were transhipped in what seemed to us to be a cattle truck and some two days later found ourselves bundled out in what I found later out was the notorious La Modela prison, Bogotá. Half of me rejoiced at the fact that we were in the capital city, where Embassies galore existed, but the other half sank as we were slung and kicked into a filthy cell where we were kept for I believe three days. It contained a pail in the corner for a toilet and two sagging cots over which two bug-infested dirty blankets were placed. Daily meals, if one could call them that consisted of a large jug of water and a bowl of some nameless stew. The walls had iron rings hammered into them where prisoners of old and I believe new, were chained. Luckily, this did not happen to us.

On the fourth day, our jailor a sallow-faced runt of a man who had two others to back him up, entered our cell and kicked us out. It was nearly dusk, but we still blinked at the light. We had been kept in semi-darkness for the whole time.

'I want to see someone from the British Embassy.' My shout was in vain.

The man leered at me.

'La Picota prison,' was uttered and my heart sank. This was the infamous prison in Bogotá that even I had heard about.

Conditions in this prison were no different to La Modela except that the cockroaches were bigger. Again no one came to see or charge us, but I was delighted that we had not been separated. I was also amazed that my shirt pocket still had in it the letters of Zafar and Sir George. I put this down to the fact we were wearing the same torn and tattered clothing that had served us for the past few months. Consequently, no detailed searches had been carried out.

We were there for two nights. In the morning of our third day, a jailor opened our cell door and we found ourselves presented with a large pepper steak, mushrooms with a heap of fried potatoes, all served with a flask of excellent coffee. We were bewildered but grateful and did not complain though the thought of the condemned man's last meal did pass through my mind. Betjeman's comment also raced through my mind. 'On our deathbeds, we're not going to regret all the work we didn't do. We're going to regret all the sex we didn't have.'

As it happened, it all worked out fine.

Around lunchtime, our jailor returned and beckoned us out. We cautiously followed him down corridors past cells crammed with prisoners who shouted when we passed by and eventually found ourselves in a large courtyard. We must have passed through a half a dozen locked corridor doors before being led to a small door in the high wall. He opened it and invited us to pass through. We did and found ourselves outside the prison gates. The door slammed shut behind us and we realised that we were free.

Two large Mercedes saloon cars moved slowly towards us and who should step out of the first one but Pablo Escobar and Popeye. His security team followed from the second and I waved cordially to two of them. They waved back. A feeling of relief spread over me and my legs turned to jelly. Hanoz told me later that he had felt the same.

'My friends, forgive me for not giving you a hug,' smiled Escobar, 'but you two do look slightly dishevelled. I've just returned from the US and heard that two *gringoes* had been arrested on serious charges. I found out it was you two, so I had you moved to this prison. It is,' he chuckled, 'far easier to arrange matters here as the governor is a friend of mine.'

I started to say something about being innocent, but he waved me to stop.

'Listen carefully, as time is of the essence. I have a few enemies around here that can still block your escape from Colombia. Here are your passports,' and he thrust them into my hand, 'and here are two single business class tickets to Naples. I choose this place because I know from talks with Daler that he was headed there after Verona. Unfortunately you have two stops, Madrid and Milan Linate so it is a long flight. Now get into the car, back seat please for obvious reasons and let's get going to the airport.'

He added with a smile. 'You don't by any chance have a nose peg on you?'

With that, we were bundled into the car and sped to the airport. On arrival, as we exited at the Departure stop, Escobar thrust into my hand an envelope containing $100,000 and this was, well... what would you say? For us, it was a tremendous and life-saving gesture.

17.

Italy

When we waved goodbye to Escobar, I was sad. I was well aware of the brutality associated with the drug Lord of Medellin, but he had been charming to us and could not do enough on the hospitality front to make our stay as comfortable as possible. To me, Pablo Escobar was a fascinating, ruthless man, but we never saw the callous side of him. I must admit that part of me was curious in wanting to know what had happened to Juan Bautista, but in the car could not get round to phrasing the question. Hanoz reckoned he would have been beaten to death with a baseball bat in some USA cellar, no doubt by our saviour, as he had been visiting the US.

Hanoz and I looked at each other. Our clothes were simply ripped rags that had not been washed for weeks. If they had I'm sure they would have disintegrated. We were unkempt, bearded and smelled to high heaven. When we smiled at each other, we burst out laughing.

'The business class people will all leave to go down to cattle class if we walked in,' I said.

'Even the cattle would walk out,' was the reply. 'We can't have that. Anyway, let's check-in.'

The girl at the check-in desk did not look at all happy to see us. She scanned our passports, rechecked our tickets and called her superior. We just stood there smiling at her. Eventually, her boss came over to us.

'Excuse me sirs, but there might be a slight problem. We do keep some spare clothes available for people who are in a rush to board a plane and do not have time to change their work clothes.'

I liked the use of the words work clothes. Ours were not worthy of the term, their only worth was being used as dust rags and that was optimistic.

'Perhaps you'd like to see them and make use of our bathroom, but I'm afraid we do not have a shower there.'

Hanoz replied. 'No thanks, we'll make use of the shower in the Alitalia lounge. Thank you.'

With that he breezed past her. I followed and from the corner of my eye could see her busily ringing someone. En route Hanoz said.

'Ok Adam, first stop a clothes outlet.' Hugo Boss was the first we saw. On entering a man sprang to his feet.

'Probablemente señor esta usted en la equivocado,' ('Perhaps you've come to the wrong store sirs,') drifted away into the ether when he saw the fistful of $100 bills in my hand.

'¿Señor, como podemos ser de ayuda?' ('How can we be of service sirs?') came fawningly from his lips.

Twenty minutes later I had bought a few pairs of trousers, several shirts and a tan jacket. Hanoz went for a Massimo Alba cotton-corduroy lightweight sloop suit plus four shirts and a ribbed N. Peal cashmere sweater. Underwear and socks completed the purchases. They were all packed up and we sauntered out, two hobos with $1,500 of clothing all packed up in two fancy boxes with the Boss label on. I did wonder if the police would stop us. We did not see any.

The same ritual was carried out at a shoe, watch and sunglasses shop, followed by some toiletries, then a luggage shop where we bought some carry on suitcases. We should have bought those first. We were now ready for the Alitalia lounge. At the desk, the standard female receptionists were there with two gentlemen. As soon as we appeared, the men made a beeline towards us. Obviously, they had been waiting for two unkempt *gringoes*.

'Would you care to follow me sirs,' said one, 'we'd like to have a word with you.'

We obliged and were escorted into a small private room.

'It's about personal hygiene,' said the other.

Hanoz was about to say something but collapsed in a fit of giggles.

'What do you mean?' I enquired. I walked closer to him and sniffed. 'No, there's nothing wrong with your hygiene. I wouldn't worry about it.'

He backed off, 'No. No, it's not my hygiene, but if I may say so sir, you do not appear to have washed for many weeks and your, how can I say it, clothes smell rather strongly. We think our other business-class passengers would not like it.'

Hanoz had now stopped giggling and butted in.

'Have you seen who bought these tickets?'

'No.'

'I suggest you check'.

The man left. Returning in a few minutes he whispered into his colleague's ear. The man paled. I felt sorry for him.

He looked at us carefully. 'There seems to have been a slight mistake. Welcome to Alitalia's flights to Madrid.'

They hurriedly left and Hanoz and I spent a full 30 minutes in the bathroom, exiting with long, clean hair, clean-shaven and with the stink of the jungle hopefully washed away. The clothes fitted beautifully. After taking the plastic container with the letters from my shirt pocket, we left the rags in the washroom bin. I wish we could have burned them, but time was pressing. We did make time to drink a bottle of champagne in the airlines' lounge before entering the plane and I purchased a D H Lawrence novel. I also bought some cream for my backside which was a real pain in the arse for me and that's speaking literally, figuratively and metaphorically. The champagne tasted like nectar though I'm not sure as to what nectar tastes like, not being a god.

The whole journey was a very long haul (36 hours), so we simply chatted, drank and dozed. It was there that I learned a bit more about his life and also more about what happened between Copje and Lucky. I knew that Hanoz had grown close to Copje, but did not realise how close. I guess it was because they were of a similar type, educated, but hard, ruthless men when the occasion demanded it. I could not believe what Copje had done, but Hanoz simply said that he would have done the same. He waxed on about how Copje's life had changed from that of a law student to one involved in the drug trade due to the killing of Sally. His next remark threw me.

'I envy him now, as he seems to be besotted by this Erika lady. You know, he told me that he's going to find her and then going back to university to finish his law studies. He's going to turn his life around. I'm thinking of doing the same with Kate. She's a wonderful woman and the life I lead only has one ending. I want to postpone that for as long as possible. I've been pretty lucky so far.' He smiled at the word lucky.

'I guess Lucky was not so lucky to meet up with Anton,' was added.

My own life seemed rather humdrum after his soliloquy. He wanted to know my plans. Plans? I had finished my contract with Frontino and in my room at Medellin, I had some clothes, books, audio player etc., which by now the hotel had probably confiscated and sold.

'I have no plans; I feel as if I'm on a bit of a holiday.'

'Fine then let me show you Sicily, one of my favourite islands, but first, we must pay a visit to my old pal Ricardo Manasho who owns a flower stall in Naples. He was with me in the Belgian Congo and is a much older man than me. He's one of the best.'

So we chatted, continued drinking and dozing until eventually we arrived at Naples.

*   *   *   *

Clearing Immigration and Customs we caught the airport shuttle bus to the main railway terminal (Rettifilo) at the Piazza Municipio. En route, as we were passing the cemetery, he warned me that the station area was the Napoli criminal hot spot so be careful. He pointed to a road sign indicating Pozzuoli.

'Birthplace of Sophia Loren,' was murmured.

'Who's that?'

A shake of the head was the only movement from Hanoz.

'Your education is sadly lacking. What have you been doing with your life? Wake up man and start living.'

An apt remark in the present circumstances. On arrival at the station, he grimaced.

'Take care here, but telling a martial arts expert to be careful! My... But seriously, there are some nasty people here. Over there,' he pointed to the opposite side of the square, 'is the Duchesca area where tourists can buy a Nikon camera and find only a big stone when they open the camera pack at their hotel. Let me show you something.'

We turned into the railway station concourse and he immediately pointed out two elderly people who were blatant tourists. He was black blazered, tan trousered, topped with a flat white cap, she in a floral crinoline dress. They were trailing two hand luggage cases and anxiously looking around. With one hand the lady was clutching a large raffia bag, the handle held tight to her breasts, the other holding a small hand bag.

'Look at those two. I feel sorry for them, as they must now be marked as a target by the criminal classes. Let's have some fun. I'm going to do my good deed for the day and help them.'

With that, he took off his jacket and gave it to me along with his case.

'Stay about five metres behind and look out for a heavy. Soon an innocent-looking cherubic bloke is going to approach these two and ask if he can help. Irrespective of what they say he will walk with them. Then soon one of two scenarios will play out. Either he will stage a halt and they will listen to him and there is a chance that the raffia bag will be placed on the floor and the hand bag simply held loosely. If so something will be pointed out, they'll look away and the raffia bag taken and handbag arm cut by a strong knife or gardeners' secateurs. They will not immediately notice this. Or the two bags will suddenly be snatched. They would prefer the former. In both scenarios, they will be passed to a third party, usually female, who happens be walking away from them. The raffia bag will go under her raincoat that is draped on her arm and she will act as though the handbag is hers. The people behind these crimes are dab hands at psychology and know that for elderly people, it is the female who carries passports, money etc., so they are the prime target. Interfere only if you see the heavy moving in. Then get involved. Understood?'

'Perfectly.'

With that, he set off after them keeping about three metres away and sure enough within 100 metres a cherubic looking man sidled up to the couple. I could not hear the talk as I was looking for the heavy. I had picked him out easily. He had joined the wave of people walking along the concourse. Short but heavily built, his head rested on his shoulders and he appeared to have no neck. He was wearing a Polo shirt that displayed heavily muscled and tattooed arms. The cropped hairline seemingly started about two centimetres above his eyebrows. His nose had a large slant indicating it had been broken many times and his gaze roamed over the people in front of him. I slowly made my way so that I was positioned behind him. From my peripheral vision I could see the couple and Hanoz.

I waited and then it happened, I think the total time must have been about two or three seconds. A halt occurred, the raffia bag placed on the floor and two men suddenly inserted themselves behind the woman. One picked up the bag. That was enough for Hanoz to explode into action. I have seen many *sensei* cover a few metres at an unbelievable speed, but for me Hanoz was number one. He took a few steps forward, jumped and his left foot rammed against the bagman's head with explosive force. The man must have been unconscious before he hit the ground. Twisting in mid-air the same leg retracted then shot out again and hit the other man in the kidneys. I heard the grunt escaping from his mouth as he dropped the bag. As Hanoz was landing, he grabbed a wrist, turned and straightened it in one movement before smashing his other upturned hand into the elbow joint. I heard the bone crack just before a squeal of pain came from the man. Kicking his legs from under him, he threw him hard to the ground so that his head hit the concrete.

The cherubic man had started to move and was able to grasp Hanoz's two wrists. No doubt he thought to incapacitate Hanoz and the heavy could move in. I smiled and all my attention was now focussed on the heavy. I knew what the next move would be.

'Me tienen hasta los buevos,' ('Bad move, buddy.') I heard Hanoz say those words, as he raised his right arm and brought it hard across to the left and smashed it down on the man's arm breaking the grip. His left fist than scorched to the nose but I am told he missed it and hit the mouth instead which produced a gash of blood and two teeth. It was a small respite, as in the classic manoeuvre, the right hand palm followed up and hit the nose striving to drive the septum upwards into the brain. The man collapsed.

The heavy had taken two strides forward and stopped. Then he took another stride.... but this time backwards. I think that seeing Hanoz dispatch three men so quickly made him think twice and he turned away. Picking up the bag, Hanoz said, 'Madam, I believe this is yours?'

They were all over Hanoz and the Carabinieri and Police soon arrived. The latter arrested the three prone men and dispersed the astonished onlookers. Hanoz signalled me to stay away and they all went to the station Police headquarters for about an hour where the necessary paperwork was carried out.

Eventually, he appeared and walked up to me.

'Adam, all in a good day's work,' and quoted from Nietzsche's book, Untimely Meditations. 'Any action requires oblivion, i.e. all human unhappiness is derived from a deficiency of forgetting,' a quote that was somewhat ambiguous to me. I never ceased to be amazed at the knowledge he had in that head of his. He put the jacket, on and retrieved the suitcase.

'Now we have to make a phone call to reserve our tickets for the overnight ferry to Palermo in Sicily. Thankfully, Italy is a country where a little extra cash goes a long way.' Finding a box, he phoned the company and after five minutes put the phone down.

'We're on the 8.15 pm ferry, docking at 7.30 am and it has cost us an extra $100, but we now have a cabin for the night. We meet a Tomaso James at the dock terminal at 6 pm. So let's find Ricardo, my old Belgian friend. He spent five years in the Second Parachute Regiment, the 2e REP of the French Foreign Legion. This consisted of 1000 men commanded by Hélie de Saint Marc and was the only Airborne Regiment in the Legion. However, the Colonel joined the General's coup and when the putsch to try to force President General de Gaulle not to abandon Algeria failed, all NCOs were kicked out. He was one of them and went to the Congo. On April 30, 1961, at Thiensville, the Regiment was dissolved.'

We eventually found the flower stall. Ricardo was a powerfully built man but one who was going to seed. His paunch was developing nicely and in another year he would have to buy another belt as the current one was on its last hole. A bulge of flesh was pouring over it. I often wondered why men went around like this, a tightly cinched belt with an overflow of fat. His shaven head gleamed in the sunlight and the crooked teeth were chewing heavily on a pencil. He was doing a crossword.

'I'd like some roses for my wife,' said Hanoz in a serious tone of voice.

Ricardo looked up and jumped into the air.

'Daler,' and the two embraced curiously. They clasped their left hands behind the head and kissed the neck rather than the cheek. I gather it was an offshoot embrace similar to the one used in the French Foreign Legion that had been adopted by Congo mercenaries.

There was much hugging and rolling around.

'Ok enough,' said Hanoz and they parted with broad smiles. He introduced me.

'This is my friend Adam. Meet Ricardo.'

A bear's paw of a hand swallowed up mine.

'Cualquier amigo de este hombre,' ('Any friend of this man,') and he inclined his head to Hanoz, 'es amigo mio. Un placer conocerle,' ('is a friend of mine. Pleased to meet you.')

I muttered the inane things one says in such circumstances.

Hanoz turned to me.

'Ricardo and I have a lot to talk about most of which would bore you silly. Can I suggest that you give us two hours and then we will go somewhere? I want to show you something pre leaving Naples.'

'Hakuna matata,' was my reply.

A mischievous grin crossed Hanoz's face. 'But be careful as this is a perilous place and there are many people out there who are extremely nasty. Remember, it's a criminal hotspot.'

I gently poked him in the ribs.

'If I get in any trouble I'll yell, 'Daler, Ricardo, help. I promise.'

He grinned. 'Ok, see you later.'

'Alligator,' I added and wandered off. I was in an area with shops galore and spent some time just meandering around looking for potential 'marks.' I saw many but did not try any of Hanoz's tactics, although I did walk alongside a similar British pair and just chatted to them until they caught a bus. I passed a barbershop and went in for a luxurious cut-throat shave and haircut. I love the ritual of a cutthroat shave. First, the steaming hot towels wrapped around the face, then the stiff brush sloshing on clouds of shaving soap, then the pièce de résistance, the barber wielding the razor with panache and scraping, scraping away until all is done and another hot towel is wrapped around the face. Bliss.

Coming out I felt really good for the first time in a long while. Finding a small café just outside the station, I bought an English newspaper for something to do and had a *baba*, a soft cake and espresso. This was a typical Italian breakfast I had been told by Hanoz. Ok, I was slightly late for breakfast but who cared!

I sat there for some time and drank two Americano coffees. I was happy and contented to just look at the world passing by, especially the women. What is it about them that excite men? They came in all shapes and sizes, but about 20% of them were lookers and they knew it. The way they walked, tossed their hair about in a very erotic manner, or simply just glanced at you.

I got up and walked around the neighbourhood. It was a typical Neapolitan one with flats everywhere, traffic with horns blaring, cars parked on zebra crossings and a hubbub of noise. I stopped for some street fried snacks, basically *pastacresciuta* and *panzerotti* and the two hours flew by. I made my way slowly back to Ricardo's flower stall.

They spotted me coming and both rose to greet me.

'No trouble then?' asked Hanoz.

'Oh, just five fights and an attempted stabbing, that's all.'

'Marvellous,' was said by both.

'We have to go now,' said Hanoz, 'but I'll stay in touch as always.'

They embraced and did the kissing act once more. I shook hands and again that bear paw made me wince. Hanoz picked up a huge mass of flowers and thrust them at me, picked up another lot and dropped a wad of cash at Ricardo.

'Ricardo, say nothing.'

Turning to me, he smiled.

'I bought these to give to the many women that we will see as we exit. Give some to them in the ratio 2:1, older to younger and just smile.'

'Arrivederci,' I said and with a wave, we left him. Ricardo walked a few steps with us and I saw that he limped.

'A gunshot wound from the old days. It gives me pain occasionally.'

As we left, Hanoz made a comment to me. 'Let me put you straight on one matter where this is some very wrong thinking. Contrary to popular belief most mercenaries have a strong ethical and moral code. When needed, they have the ability to switch immediately to that inner primordial urge of violence; and then are able to quickly switch it off. Ethical codes are associated with one's profession e.g., The Hippocratic Oath sworn by doctors, as distinct from moral ones that are individual. However, morality can be thought of as a function of behaviour with respect to the danger level. When in dangerous situations one frequently cannot adhere to the moral structures associated if one lives in safe areas. That is why atrocities occur in war zones.'

He stopped and shuffled the flowers.

'Ricardo got that limp in a fight with two Germans who were serving with us. Ricardo is a Jew and was unhappy in the company of ex SS soldiers, especially when he found out that these two had been members of the fanatical SS Das Reich division. They became infamous by killing 642 villagers in Oradour-sur-Glane, near Limoges where people were herded and locked into a barn and church and these places together with the whole town was set on fire. For obvious reasons our commando never really talked about

WWII, but those two were obnoxious, very loud mouthed and they loved killing. Morality was an unknown word to them. In their realm, in any given situation the only good native was a dead one.'

He paused for a moment and I could almost see him collecting his thoughts as he recalled those days.

'Everyone disliked them and Ricardo, Giorgio, you'll meet him tomorrow and me, stayed clear of them. Things came to a head one day when Ricardo was saying a prayer. He was doing this at the camp's perimeter and as they strolled by, the Germans taunted him saying he'd be a slab of soap if Adolph had his way. Luckily Mad Mike was nearby and saw and heard it all. In the ensuing fight Ricardo killed one man and left the other alive but badly beaten. As he was walking away, this man fired his revolver at Ricardo and the bullet caught him in the leg. Mad Mike shot and killed the man. Case closed.'

He looked straight at me. 'Ricardo was hospitalised for over two months and when he returned, we had a massive *braai* for him.'

I looked at him. 'Didn't you ever feel fear in such situations?'

'You can be afraid in a risk-free situation; you can feel no fear in a high risk situation.' He shrugged. 'It's all about training and probabilities. If you are well trained and the people around you are as well, you back yourself in any situation. The fear goes as soon as action starts. That's not to say one gets a few wobbles once it stops. You are trained to default to the familiar that is why one practises the same routine all the time. It's called the *Einstelling* effect. Anyway, I have no fear in giving flowers away to pretty women. So Adam, let's blaze a trail.'

I felt a bit conspicuous but soon got into the swing of things and enjoyed passing out bunches of flowers. Two females flashed knowing smiles at me and spoke rapid Italian at me. Hanoz happened to overhear one.

'You're on a winner there Adam. Pity we're not staying.'

I did not react, but one was an extremely vivacious woman.

'Forget about her, as now I'm going to show you something extraordinary,' was said and a taxi hailed. He asked the driver to stop at a shop to buy mouse traps.

'Mousetraps, what on earth for?'

He laughed. 'Whenever I'm in Naples, I do this. It's a favourite joke of mine. I try to snare as many pickpockets as possible. I prime the traps, put one in my back pocket, one in my coat pocket and walk around. If someone tries to pick my pocket, I will know about it. I then turn around and break a few fingers to teach them a lesson. Simple really.'

Five minutes later, he was primed for this action and told the driver to take us to Ciro's restaurant at Santa Brigida.

'Here my esteemed friend you will taste the ultimate pizza. It's a Neapolitan one that has been made to exact proportions. Only buffalo milk mozzarella made from certain nearby areas is used. The dough will have been kneaded for exactly 30 minutes and left to rise for four hours. There are only two types of pizza, margherita, basically tomato based and marinara, sea food based.'

At Ciro's, we ordered two margheritas and they were superb, as was the bottle of local wine. Leaving we took another taxi, which took us for a half an hour ride to the Museo Capodimonte, via Miano, a near classical Bourbon royal palace sited within the large Capodimonte park.

'I wish that we had time to go to the Museo Archeologico Nazionale, as my interest in this subject due to Kate has been increased, but we simply do not have the luxury. So let's go to the first floor where you'll see something stupendous.'

At the Museo Capodimonte, as if I did not know what was about to happen, we made straight to Caravaggio's, 'Flagellation of Christ.'

'Ok, how long do we stay?'

'Adam, this is a chance of a lifetime for you to see a masterpiece. Unfortunately, we only have 30 minutes, as I want to take you to the Pio Monte della Misericordia in the via del Tribunale to see, 'The Seven Acts of Mercy,' and then the Galleri Di Palazzos Stigliana, in via Toledo, to look at, The Martyrdom of Saint Ursula.'

He gazed intently at the painting.

'This is heaven,' was the comment.

We spent the rest of the time gazing at paintings. At least Hanoz did, as my art interests were more in the Jack Vettriano mould and as for music, give me Shirley Bassey any day. When she sings, Something, my heart just flips.

Leaving the Caravaggio we viewed the other paintings eventually arriving at the docks at 5.15 pm and went straight to the ticket office.

'I'd like to speak to Tomaso. My name is Hanoz.'

The clerk got up and called through to an open door leading to a back room.

'Hey Tomaso, Come here, please.'

A slight, balding man emerged; he had half-moon glasses perched on the tip of his nose and was sweating in the heat despite a large fan that was blowing warm air around the office. I was surprised they did not have any air conditioning and remarked upon it.

'It's Naploli,' he replied. 'Nothing works these days; however, one gets used to it though.'

He gestured to us to come into the backroom. Opening a desk drawer, he brought out an envelope and held it out.

'I believe you requested these?'

Hanoz brought out a wad of notes.

'And I believe you requested these?'

He paid out the ticket and bribe money and the transaction was rapidly over. We left without further words being spoken. There were no handshakes or petty talk. It was pure business and I was glad to get out of there.

We walked out of the office and into the Piazzo Municipio the site of the ancient harbour and in the evening glow the Castello dell' Ova in the nearby Palazzo Reale looked superb. We ambled to the Piazza del Plebiscito, a big square between Reale and the Basilica di San Francesco de Paola and had a drink at the Gran Café Gambrinus.

'Well, I guess we had better board the ship and see what our cabin looks like,' was the comment. That is precisely what we did after he had thrown the mousetraps into a waste bin. There was nothing exceptional about the cabin, just two bunks, a small wardrobe and a bathroom. We slung our cases down and I bagged the lower berth, sinking into the bed to test it.

'Not a bad berth,' was my comment.

'Tell me that after a night's rest,' came the reply.

We went out and entered the main lounge and the smell of overcooked cabbage brought us to the dining area.

I sniffed. 'I think we can forget about good Italian cooking on this trip.'

Hanoz nodded so we went on deck and stayed there until the ferry left port after which we went down to the bar. There were not many people there at this time and we sat at a table ordering two large beers. Sitting with her back to us was a slim, dark haired female, mid-forties who was wearing white trousers and a golden-hued blouse and we could see that she was wearing glasses. She seemed to epitomise what a lady librarian would look like before she discovered vodka. The back of the blouse was fastened at the neck and an oval slit extended beneath it for some 15 cm. At the base, the bra strap fasteners were just visible.

I could see Hanoz looking at this so jokingly said, 'I bet you're thinking of undoing that. Right?'

'Easy.'

'Ah, come on,' was my retort. 'You've not even seen her face to face.'

Hanoz thought for a minute.

'We have been gifted the sum of $50,000 each. Would you care to bet $1000 that I could not?'

A rush of blood to my head made me say, 'Yes.'

'I told you that I was once a raven. I'll demonstrate the art of being a star plus raven. Watch and learn.'

With that, he stood up and walked towards her. Something was said to which she replied with a flash of teeth and within a minute or two, he had pulled up a chair and sat down beside her.

The rest of the evening, I watched them dine, have drinks, all the while laughing and talking. Never once did Hanoz make eye contact with me. Eventually, I saw them leave. Finishing my beer I went to our cabin. Hanoz was not there, so I read my D H Lawrence novel until I turned in. At 4 am the opening of the door woke me up.

'Where's my cash?' was uttered, 'and boy I'm a bit tired.' He flung himself onto the upper bunk and stretched out, hands behind head, a broad grin on his face. I got up, silently opened my case and counted out $1000.

'You forgot to add the ticket cost,' he grinned.

I counted out the money. He accepted it. 'I'll tell you what Adam. All expenses on the Sicily trip are on me. I'll treat you,' he grinned, 'with your cash. You should have gone to the school as you'd have learned a trick or two that would have been useful. I can give you lessons if you like.'

I flung my pillow at him.

'We have about three hour's pre berthing. Get some sleep and I'll call you.'

With that, I got up, had a quick shower, dressed and left. Hanoz was asleep before I had finished showering. I picked up a coffee and went on deck to watch Palermo appearing in the distance. I knew that Hanoz liked Sicily a lot and had visited the island many times, so I was quite content to go with the flow over the next few weeks especially as all expenses were being paid by Hanoz!

I woke him about an hour pre docking and sat on the deck watching the backdrop of heaving mountains get bigger and bigger and eventually the ferry entered into the hustle and bustle that went on in any major port.

'Incidentally, Imogen, my friend from last night, is a librarian in Syracuse, but does not speak English,' was said out loud. Hanoz had silently sidled in beside me.

I cuffed him. 'I give up on you.'

With that, the lady in question appeared and Hanoz ever the gentlemen, jumped to his feet and kissed her hand and introduced me.

He spoke to her in Spanish and translated the reply. Spanish is a useful language as one can converse with Italians; Portuguese is even better as they can understand Spanish and Italian, but the reciprocal is not generally true.

In this way, a conversation was carried out with me, saying all the correct things. We eventually left the boat. I was trailing Hanoz's suitcase while he escorted Imogen to the central train station. I winced at their embrace and swear that I saw a tear in her eye as we waved goodbye. I had to turn away to stifle a laugh that was starting down near my ribs and storming up to my larynx.

'Mi armor, adoro tu ondulado y largo pelo,' ('My love, I adore your long wavy hair,') was said and with that her hand languidly ruffled it.

18.

Sicily

We left the ship and Hanoz remarked. 'I am now going to introduce you to *arancini*. This is the general term but I can assure you that many varieties exist.'

I blinked.

With that he hailed a taxi, saying, 'Bar Turistico, via Simone Guli.'

The taxi driver grinned at him replying that he obviously new Palermo well. Hanoz simply nodded. The three kilometre journey took us past the prison, port workshops and the Marina Villa Igiea, depositing us at the Bar Turistico, which was right on the main road and surrounded by apartment buildings. We entered and I saw that even at 8.15 am it was full of locals and tourists and the air was thick with the smell of coffee. The long glass counter was divided; one half with sweets and cakes of all sizes and descriptions along with deep fried pastries filled with ricotta or chocolate cream; the other half heaved with bread, cheese, hams and sausages. We sat down at one of the blue plastic tables.

'We are going to have *arancina,* which is the Palermo version. They are little oranges of round, fried, delicious rice balls, bought to Sicily in the 10th century when the Arabs introduced rice and saffron. There is a choice: the heart can be butter and cheese, or ragu and peas, all contained in a deep-fried sphere of rice. In Catania, because of the nearness of Etna they are conical in shape and called *arancino.* It's odd that here they have a feminine ending, but in Catania it is masculine. I'll never understand the language.'

He left and came back with a plate of *arancina* plus coffee. The breakfast was delicious. We left, hailed another taxi and ended up back at the railway station. In the taxi, he turned to me.

'Adam. It's rather early to get to our hotel, so let's have a little walk and get ourselves a coffee and brioche. Then we'll amble along the Via Roma and cut through some side streets until we reach the Teatro Massimo. We could walk up the parallel street via Maqueda, but I like these back streets. There we will go to number 36, Piazza Giovanni Verdi, to the bijou hotel, All 'ombre del Massimo.'

He looked at me and grinned. 'I own half of it.'

Exiting the taxi, we sat down at a nearby café and ordered more coffee this time with brioches. I just love the Italian way of having breakfast. In this case almost a double breakfast.

'I'll tell you how I happen to own half. The other half is owned by Giorgio Davide and his wife, Chary. Giorgio is of Belgian/Italian origin and like Ricardo was in the Foreign Legion, this time the Spanish one. Incidentally, both these men saved my life in the Congo and that is why I have a special regard for them. We became firm friends, a friendship that has lasted post that damn war.'

He paused, sipped some coffee and ate a piece of his brioche.

'We were in Mad Mike Hoare's 5 Commando and the second in command, our direct boss was, Alistair Wicks. Moise Tshombe, hired a mercenary force of about 300 men, to try to get mineral-rich Katanga province to break away from a newly formed Republic of the Congo. It was called the Simba rebellion and located in Eastern Congo and in 1964 he became Congolese Prime Minister. Later Mad Mike led 5 Commando, a part of the Armée National Congolese, which along with 320 Belgian paratroopers commanded by Colonel Charles Laurent and with the help of Cuban pilots, evacuated some 1,600 Europeans plus a few hundred Congolese in Stanleyville. They saved these people from communist Simba rebels in what was called Operation Dragon Rouge. The American CIA, especially the 322 Air Divisions' five C130 Hercules transport planes was in the background for this successful attempt. Total deaths were 185 foreign hostages and thousands of Congolese who had been executed by the Simba rebels. We were with Mad Mike for most of the time, usually, fighting '*in enfilade*' using natural obstacles like fallen trees to conceal ourselves, as the Soviet-backed Simba's made one hell of a noise as they travelled. They lacked discipline and their organisation was one of utter chaos. We were not concerned with them as such, but we did fear their bullets as some guerrilla weapons had chemicals mixed with faeces. This meant that wounds became infected very quickly.'

He paused.

'We were in a small village near Boende, the capital of Tshuapa Province when the ambush occurred. This was uncommon because we were a much-disciplined outfit even though we invariably came from many different walks of life and regiments. Moral was very high and I guess I was blessed to find myself with a band of brothers who by and large thought alike. There were one or two wasters, but they were in a very small minority. I've told you about two already. Giorgio, Ricardo and I struck it off immediately and we hunted together.'

He stopped for a while, sipped his coffee and gazed into the distance.

'Where was I? Ah, Giorgio and Ricardo. We were sleeping when they attacked. They came from the direction of two of the wasters who were supposedly on sentry duty. They were asleep. We found their bodies afterwards lying peacefully on the ground with their throats slit. We lost many men that night but slaughtered hundreds. The rebels came swarming at us chanting words, ululating ferociously and throwing burning torches at the thatched huts we were sleeping under. One torch hit our hut and unfortunately we had a gasoline can there that exploded and brought down a doorway support. The three of us grabbed our M16s instantly switching to automatic fire. Giorgio and Ricardo charged out, I brought up the rear and stumbled when the door lintel fell on me. I put my rifle down to try to free my legs when two rebels appeared. One had his carbine raised to fire; the other was armed only with a spear. This was raised above his head, arm bent backwards and it had started its forwards thrust towards my chest. They can't have been more than three metres away. I scrambled for my rifle, but knew it was useless. I was visualising the FU funeral rites.'

'A what?'

'It was a saying we had when you were killed for a ridiculous reason. A lintel fell on your leg. Stupid what? You had a fucked up funeral.'

Another sip of coffee.

'Then I was deafened by the roar of Giorgio and Ricardo's rifles. They sent almost 30 rounds into each of the two, nearly cutting them into halves. Their innards fell out almost into my face and I can still remember that smell mixed with cordite. Nothing was said as my comrades lifted the lintel. I must admit that I was shaken.'

'Close shave what? inquired Giorgio with a grin. 'Come on let's get the rest of them.' Which we did.

We lost some good mates in that fight, three ex US paratroopers, the brothers Doug and Karl Stroman and Steve Leather. Charlie Finkle an ex US marine was another. Charlie did not die by a bullet or spear, but as a result of diving behind a tree in order to return fire and unfortunately landed on a black mamba (Dendroaspis polylepis) snake. We knew the snake as he'd shot it. The fight lasted for a half hour or so and throughout that period we were all rather busy. During that time he died.

I did not say anything, as I was fascinated to hear about this aspect of his life. Apart from my martial arts interest, my own life had been fairly conventional, school, university and job. His on the other hand, had incorporated many different areas.

'Well, I stayed on for a few more years before leaving and returning to Turkey and the military. Ricardo left along with me, but Giorgio stayed on for another three years. I found out later that the big Brass in Turkey had been keeping an eye on me and one day, Senay Giner, the Head of MIT approached me to join them. I was classed as A1 material for the jobs they did.'

He grinned at that remark.

'As you know, I was there for many years and the Charm School ones at Trabzon were great. It was around that time that I met Chary Landsrow. Chary was her nom de plume. She was an extremely beautiful, petite, British woman who had trained as a nurse but wanted life to be an adventure. She therefore did dance lessons and ended up as part of a dance troop in Ankara. She wanted to experience life but became involved with an awful crowd and got hopelessly in debt, so much so that she had to turn to prostitution to clear her debts. When I say a prostitute, I should emphasise that she was top of the call girl chain. She was a stunner, but was under the control of some extremely brutal Ankara drug lords and soon wanted out.'

He stopped and finished his coffee. We ordered more, this time with grappa.

'I helped her, as we had become very, very, good friends,' he flashed me a grin and wink, 'yes, very, very, good friends. I recruited Giorgio and Ricardo to help get her away. It's immaterial as to how we did it, but we did it and I can assure you that it wasn't easy. Anyway, we all left Ankara and I resigned, as I think this would have been the end of my career at MIT. Giorgio and Chary fell in love, married and settled in Palermo. Giorgio had always wanted to open a bijou hotel, but could never get the sums of money needed to buy one. Together we could, so that's how I half own a hotel.'

He drank the grappa in one swallow.

'Giorgio knows all about the time I spent with Chary and he also knows that I would never ever attempt anything with her again, likewise she with me. Our bond is stronger than sex, as it is complete and utter trust in each other's actions.'

He looked at his newly airport bought Tag Heuer watch. 'They don't know we're going to arrive,' he paused, 'in about 20 minutes, so let's amble.'

We trundled our suitcases through the crowded, noisy streets until we hit the theatre, the largest opera house in Italy and the third largest in Europe. It was an imposing building. Hanoz strode purposely towards one corner of the large square until we were outside number 36.

'Here we go,' was said as we pushed open the heavy dark wooden door. Entering the classic antique lift which was filled with the two us and our suitcases, we clanged shut the iron doors and crept slowly to the second floor. The lift was like something out of a classic old French film.

The plaque on the wall stated, All 'ombre del Massimo hotel. He pressed the bell and the door opened.

An explosion of sound filled the air, as a petite, vivacious person launched herself at Hanoz.

'Daler, Daler, I can't believe it, oh my, Daler, Daler,' was accompanied by some fierce hugging on both sides. After they had disentangled themselves, he managed to introduce me.

'Chary, this is another Brit who is a big mate of mine.'

I did not get the hugging treatment. Instead, a slim hand was extended for me to shake. I decided to do a Hanoz, so lifted it to my lips saying, 'Enchanted.'

Hanoz burst out laughing.

'I don't believe it. A Brit acting like this.'

'I had a good teacher,' was my reply.

She ushered both of us inside all the while clinging to Hanoz's arm.

'How long are you staying? Giorgio's away in Roma for the next two nights as he left early this morning, but you must stay to see him?' The questions came thick and fast.

When she had cooled down, she murmured.

'Ok, we now live in Mondello and you will stay with us. The house is not far from the La Torre hotel, where you once stayed. If I recall we had *Sfincione* there as well as *Pani ca meusa*. I am so excited to see you,' and she turned to me, 'and of course you Adam.'

Turning round she said, 'Oh excuse me, but this is Lynda Marsh. She's English, a cockney I'm told and is my right hand person for this hotel. She basically runs it as I pop in only now and again. You're lucky to catch me.'

We were each introduced to a tall, lean woman of about 50 years of age, with a close-cropped blond hairdo who spoke first in Italian and then English that had no trace of a cockney accent.

'Would you Adam and Eve it,' was my comment. 'May I use the dog and bone?'

'I've no idea as to what you're talking about. I left London, aged two when we moved to Worthing. I was 13 when my father died and my mother, who is Italian, came back to Italy and I've remained here ever since.'

Pointing to the telephone, I explained about cockney rhyming slang, adding something about the sound of Bow bells.

'Unbelievable,' was the snort. One of the first things I did on returning to the UK was to send her a Chas and Dave record.

After that, Chary did not let anyone get a word in edgeways. It transpired the next night there was a concert at the church with the open roof, Chiesa di Santa María dello Spasmimo. It was in Italian, but I was assured that I would be able to follow it even with my bad Spanish and she was going to get us all tickets. They were performing the Aeneid.

Stephano Giovanni, Giorgio's driver turned up and we all piled out to the car, Chary leaving Lynda in charge. We were told that Stephano was at our disposal for the rest of our stay, which was a big bonus, as driving in Sicily is not for the faint-hearted.

'He's also a part time hairdresser,' remarked Chary glancing at Hanoz. There was no comment.

Mondello was a beautiful old seaside town with lots of summer houses. Their house, however, was a permanent abode and in a lovely position overlooking the sea. The first thing Chary did was to put Albert Schweitzer on the record player and the sounds of Bach's Prelude and Fugue in E minor filled the room.

'If I recall right this, along with Beethoven's 5th symphony in C minor, Opus 67, incidentally the recording we have is by the Pittsburgh Symphony Orchestra, together with his 9th, plus Bach's Goldberg variations, are some of your favourite records.'

'Ah, the little Prelude and Fugue. Beautiful. Now if only I had a glass of wine or even the bottle in my hands....'

'Point taken.' She disappeared and came back with a bottle of Nero d'Avola. This was carefully poured out into three glasses, which were then raised and Hanoz was toasted. As an afterthought, I was as well. We sat down on the comfortable chairs in the lounge and I was a third party to their chat for about an hour when Hanoz remarked, 'We're very selfish here. Why don't you two get to know each other whilst I listen to some great music?'

With that, he stood up, poured out more wine and settled himself in front to the two main speakers.

'I'm truly sorry,' said Chary, 'but seeing Daler after so long, it well...,' she stopped. 'Anyway, I am sure that Daler told you about us,' she smiled coquettishly. 'I grew up in the south of England and trained as a nurse at St Mary's hospital, London.'

'St Mary's,' I butted in. 'I know it well. I was at Imperial College and used to walk past it to Paddington Station to get a train to South Wales.'

She had an enchanting voice. Living in Italy for so long had even given her English a slight Italian accent. We found out that our London sojourns had overlapped by one year. We drank another bottle of wine, talked about plays we had seen, places visited and the usual memorabilia of people who had lived in the same area. 'Did you see this, were you there when etc.' and we chatted for about an hour. I felt myself relaxing all the time. She was an exceptionally vibrant and intelligent woman.

Eventually, she turned to Hanoz. 'Now it's time for dinner and I'm going to cook us some pasta. Will *vongole* be ok?'

Both of us agreed.

'But only on the condition that we help you,' I said.

'No way, you two sit down and have some more wine. It won't be long, let's say a half-hour?'

With that, she flounced out and I re-joined Hanoz to listen to Beethoven and the choral was splendid, as was indeed the eventual dinner. We all chatted until nearly midnight when reluctantly I excused myself and went up to my allocated room, as I did not wish to be a gooseberry. It was big and luxurious; the whole house was, obviously Giorgio had prospered.

The next morning Hanoz said to me. 'Adam, you don't have to leave us alone, as I repeat nothing is ever going to happen between us. She is Giorgio's wife, the wife of one of my best friends. Giorgio would kill me if it happened and believe you me, you do not want to cross Giorgio.'

These words came from a born killer, a man of action.

Breakfast was served by the maid, a Croatian called Marina and it was simple, coffee, yoghurt, fresh fruit followed by toast. Chary then excused herself, as she had to go to the hotel and we were told that Stephano was in the kitchen ready to take us around Palermo. When we had finished, we all trooped out to the car and she was dropped off at the hotel. Stephano did not speak any English, but had received instructions for a whirlwind tour of Palermo from Chary and off we went.

Before setting off though, Hanoz turned to me. 'The first step is to deposit most of our money in a bank and then we'll ship it out later.'

I passed a querulous look at him.

'Isn't it a bit suspicious depositing such a large sum of cash in a bank?'

He grinned. 'Adam, you have a lot to learn about life my friend. This is not only Italy, but it is Sicily, Cosa Nostra country and here $1 million is not a large sum. No questions will be asked as long as we have passports and an address. We have both as we will use Giorgio's address.'

With that, we went out and found the nearest bank and after some form filling, ended up with bank accounts. The manager did not even bat an eyelid and we put $40,000 each into our respective accounts. The rest we pocketed.

He saw my bewildered look. 'Adam, $40,000 is peanuts here. We have to leave it there for a few days, it's the law, while we enjoy the country, come back to Palermo and transfer it out to our own banks. Mine is Credit Suisse in Geneva, as I like their banking laws. I presume yours is in the UK?'

I nodded assent. 'Yes, I have a Lloyds account in my home town.' I pictured the wry look that Keith Young, my dark haired wiry, typical Welsh looking bank manager would give when he saw this amount added to my bank balance.

'Good. Let's re-join Stephano.'

Our first stop was the mountain that overlooked Palermo, Mount Pellegrino. The climb up was steep and I felt sorry for the few cyclists who were toiling up it and even more for the people who at some of the religious festivals crawled upon their knees to visit Saint Rosalie's cave. Her bones rest at the monastery. She died in 1166 and is the patron saint of the city. The story is that she lived in a cave on the mountain, the one that today is the pilgrimage site. In 1664 a plague hit the town and a hunter had a vision, which told him to take her bones and parade them around the town three times. He did this and the plague went.

A visit to the Duomo followed. It was an eclectic mix of Norman, Catalan and Baroque, whilst at the back could be found Moorish architecture. The Catacombe dei Cappuccini was next. Here mummified bodies filled the walls of the tunnels and it was quite ghoulish to see how well preserved some of them were, especially a little two-year-old whose parents had permission to place her there in 1920. Her golden curls particularly affected me. Next stop was the Pallazzo dei Normanni, the seat of Parliament for the island and built by Roger 11, a Norman knight. I never realised that the Normans had turned up in Sicily round about the time William the Conqueror had arrived in the UK. They ruled for about a century. The building and exhibition centre was fantastic, as was the jewel of the Cappella Palatina.

That was enough morning's culture for me, so I demanded lunch in the Capo open-air market district and we had a few beers and a *panini* at Dainotti's. Feeling much better and as a geologist, what I wanted to see was the *kanats*, the ancient underground canals that brought water to the city from the surrounding hills. Stephano took us to one of the entrance points, but we were told that one had to be a member of an organised group to enter these caverns, individuals were not allowed.

'Where's Escobar when we need him?' I said to Hanoz.

'Still in Colombia and we are in Sicily,' came the reply.

What Stephano was able to do though was to take us to a stick fighting school. Sticks of about six feet in length of stout ash wood were a standard weapon for the poorer class of people in medieval England. I seem to recall that this was the favourite weapon of Long John of Robin Hood fame. These Italians sticks were much longer than British ones, they were more like poles to me, but the principle was the same. Attack with a left swing, right swing, jab forwards, with parries being made to counter the attack. I had a go and enjoyed it immensely. Hanoz simply watched.

This was enough for me, so I politely asked, 'I've had enough for the day, so how about rest and a drink?"

This was acceded to basically because both Stephano and Hanoz had had enough of chasing around Palermo for *kanats*, so we spent the rest of the afternoon at a convenient bar.

The evening at the church with Chary sitting between us and stars above was fantastic. The acoustics were superb and the play full of action, some of which I understood, all aided by some sterling music. I enjoyed it immensely. The siege of Troy, Achilles, Agamemnon and his wife Clytemnestra, their daughter poor

Iphigenia sacrificed to Artemis so that Agamemnon's fleet had favourable winds to Troy. Helen, Paris, Hector, etc. were well portrayed. I particularly enjoyed seeing Agamemnon being dispatched when Clytemnestra and her lover Aegithus murdered him on his return to Greece; she, in turn, was killed by her children Orestes and Electra. Truly a mind-blowing bloodthirsty era. The drive home was lovely as the air was balmy, a light breeze was evident and we rolled into the house at midnight.

'The end of a lovely day,' said Hanoz. Chary and I agreed, so we decided to have a few drinks. These ended at about 3 am, when Chary glanced at a clock.

'My god, Giorgio will be here at 10 am. I'm off to bed and so should you two.'

We agreed and I slept the sleep of the just.

The next morning, breakfast was a bit late for me and when I went down Chary and Stephano had already left for the airport. Apparently, the arrival of Hanoz was to be kept secret. The maid served me the usual Americano. Hanoz preferred a morning cappuccino and we had scrambled eggs and toast. Like all good Italians he stopped drinking cappuccino at midday.

We sat and talked while waiting for Giorgio to arrive. I was dying to see what type of man he was, visualising a very large person, crew cut, muscular. I had a shock.

The door opened and in came Chary and her husband. I expected a bull of a man to come striding in. However, alongside her was a small, lean, bald type, with a very pronounced pointed skull and amazingly piercing blue eyes. He stood and stared.

'It can't be,' he uttered before rushing to Hanoz and clasping both arms around him gave that ritual kiss. 'Daler, oh my god,' was followed by more hugs.

I was eventually introduced.

'Any friend of Daler's, is my friend,' said Giorgio.

246

We all sat down, wine was poured and the usual reminisces took place.

Giorgio looked at Hanoz. 'There is a very old Italian saying, '*Non c'è due senza tre*,' which roughly translates as good (or bad) things comes in threes. I hope this is the start of the run.

Chary grabbed me.

'Let's leave them to talk for a while. Come on I'll walk you around town.'

With that, we made our excuses and left. The town was small, but we headed for the main square, walked around the port and generally chit-chatted about many matters. Chary especially wanted to know about the UK, as she had not been back for about 15 years. My knowledge was somewhat sketchy, as I had been away for many years myself and had only been back for short stays. We had a typical breakfast a *brioche* into which blobs of ice cream had been placed and we also ordered a *granita*. We walked around a bit then drank a few Apeiro spritzers at a bar followed by some *panelle*, not too much because lunch was being prepared by the maid. Chary was excellent company, bubbly and with a mischievous sense of humour and for her age had a fabulous figure. She was a lean, very attractive woman and told me that she worked out every day, as did Giorgio. He was lucky, she remarked, in that he couldn't put weight on. His metabolism was such that he could eat and drink to his heart's content.

After two hours away, we made our way back home to find both men arm wrestling on the dining room table.

'What's the score?' she asked.

No reply came from two intensely concentrating men. Then Hanoz's arm was slowly pushed to the table.

'Currently, it is 22 to me, 20 for Daler,' came from Giorgio.

I must admit that this shook me. This small, wiry man was beating Daler Hanoz. I looked at him with much more respect than previously.

'OK. Game over, let's eat,' said Chary. She led the way into the dining area, where a phalanx of food had been arranged by Marina plus several bottles of wine.

'I'm afraid a siesta will be needed after this,' said Hanoz.

Two hours later, we staggered off to the bedrooms.

That evening we went to dine late. I was still full after lunch so just had an appetiser and two cold Peroni beers. Hanoz and Chary were also abstemious, but Giorgio had first and second plates plus a dessert, all washed down with a white Malfa wine from the Aeolian Islands. Hanoz had insisted on this and I knew why. It reminded him of Kate. It was a pleasant evening and as it went on, I felt myself relaxing in their company. Giorgio, in particular, took great care in bringing me in on any conversation.

'We have discussed our past lives in detail,' he said turning towards me. 'Now it is the present and I am truly delighted to meet you. Daler tells me that you'll stay for one more day and then he is showing you around Sicily in our car driven by Stephano.'

'Yes, and I'm paying for it all.'

He roared with laughter. 'Yes, Daler told me all about that bet. You must never bet against a raven in matters of love.'

'I learned that much too late.'

'Chary used to tell me that the girls where she worked would be happy to do it for nothing if it was Daler. I don't know why he went there.'

'Boredom,' was Hanoz's reply. 'One wants to get away from the routine of writing or reading reports. Anyway, let's change the subject. What are we doing tomorrow?'

'I thought we could go to Ustica and do some SCUBA diving,' said Giorgio.

'Excellent idea.' Daler looked at me. 'How about you Adam? Giorgio and Chary are both instructors.'

'Never tried it and don't think I will, but I'm happy to come along and snorkel around.'

'Done. I'll drink to that,' said Chary producing another bottle of the excellent wine. 'We will leave early, so an early night is called for.' She looked pensively at Giorgio and Hanoz. 'Remember we're diving tomorrow, so don't drink too much.'

With that, she went off upstairs and I followed. I do not know how long the other two stayed downstairs, but I believe it was a long time.

The trip to the island, north of Palermo was great. They had a speed boat and a sailing boat in the marina and we took off in the former. The island of Ustica is rocky with numerous grottoes and the water was, as they say in the adverts, gin clear. In the morning the trio suited up and spent about an hour and a half visiting many caves and photographing the many varieties of fish to be found there. We had a picnic lunch washed down this time with *Fizzante* water before they hauled out more tanks and spent another hour or so underwater. I splashed around snorkelling on the surface glimpsing them now and again. They even surfaced occasionally to talk to me.

The afternoon came to a close and sun-kissed and with slightly reddened flesh for me; the others were nut-brown in colour, we headed back. Showers were called for and another sumptuous feast had been prepared for dinner. We had meat *falso magro,* (thin meat slices wrapped round onions, bacon bits, egg and cheese) followed by *pesce spada* (swordfish) and *spaghetti alla Norma* (tomato and eggplant). Rough bread was available to mop up the juices and this together with bottles of wine, made it a meal to remember.

Giorgio produced a box of cigars, but all of us declined. So he picked one and lit it with a joyous smile on his face.

'One of my few vices,' was the remark. 'I love one after a good meal.'

I must admit that even though I am a non-smoker, I find the smell of a good cigar rather nice, so sniffed away. Giorgio saw me sniffing and smiled.

'Breathe in more deeply,' was the comment and you might even get a taste for it.'

We chatted until midnight then unsurprisingly we all went to bed.

The next morning at breakfast, Chary said, 'Now I think your tour is going to take about three weeks plus according to Stephano. We will be without a car for all this time,' she pouted, 'that is how much we value your friendship.'

Hanoz gave her a quick hug. 'I know my darling, but I'll come back at the end to see you.'

Little did he know that this was not going to happen. With that, we all hugged, kissed and left.

*   *   *   *

The trip around Sicily left me in a whirl. Culture and the more the merrier was the order of the day. Hanoz was unstoppable, reading up on places we were going to visit until well into the night. As for me, culture had not been very high on the agenda when growing up in a small town based on the iron and steel industry. Someone once told me that Mussolini when he heard the culture word, 'reached for his revolver.' I felt the same. There was a big gap in my education about this word. All I knew was that there was a thing called a rugby culture in my childhood neighbourhood and that involved massive amounts of beer drinking.

Places and museums passed me by in a blur. I gather that we stopped off at the medieval mountain top town of Taormina and saw a performance at the Teatro Greco built in the 3rd century BC and rebuilt in the 2nd century AD. From there, we took a trip to smoking Mt Etna, which I enjoyed. At Segesta it was Greek Doric temples; Erice was a lovely mountain village dedicated to the fertility goddess Aphrodite or Venus, take your pick in Greek or Latin. The old monastery was now used as an International Conference Centre and on the walls were scribbled signatures of the people who had lectured there. Hanoz pointed out to me Richard Feynman's name and mentioned a few books that had been written about him.

'Feynman, a Nobel Laureate is one of my heroes,' he murmured. Feynman was one of my heroes also. I looked at him and yet again was impressed by the eclectic knowledge of the man.

He carried on. 'An amazing man not only of theoretical physics but a bongo drum player, a man who taught himself Portuguese for kicks, artist, safecracker, decipherer of Mayan hieroglyphics from first principles. What a magnificent man.'

Trapani saw us take a boat trip to Pantelleria, a stark volcanic island near to the African Tunisian coast where we sampled *Cous Cous*. Marsala saw us at the local archaeological museum looking at Punic warships. I tried the local wine, but for me, it was much too sweet. The seven temples of Selinunte were seen, Hercules, Juno, Castor and Pollux et al. Piazza Armerina was okay. I liked looking at the first-ever bikinis worn by girls exercising and imprinted into the superb mosaics at nearby Casale. There we lunched on *Boca di Lupo*, (literally wolf's mouth) consisting of veal stuffed with egg-plant, ham and parmesan cheese.

Syracuse was interesting and at the Parco Archeologico, I was impressed by the Ara di Lerone, especially the altar of Heron where huge sacrifices of animals were made by the Greeks to the gods. I loved the harbour designed by no less a person than Archimedes. We missed out of Messina and instead stayed at the summer house of Giovanna, Giorgio's mother who lived in Ragusa some 30 km away.

The house was located on a dune remnant at Corso Oceano Atlantico, Caucana. On opening the back gate, a walkway took one 20 metres to the sea. There we stayed simply swimming and fishing, drinking and talking for about a week. I was very glad of the rest, as my brain was flayed by the places and things we had seen. It was all a mishmash in my mind, yet Hanoz had a clear vision of all sites. Mind you, he had kept a notebook of where we had been, what had been seen followed by much scribbling in the book, then reading up about the next stop. We only made two trips from Caucana and they were to the nearby lighthouse where there was a first-class restaurant, Il Barocco. At Modica we bought the famous chocolate all made according to a secret Aztec recipe. It was okay for me, but I found the texture a bit granular. Stephano told us about a super small trattoria called, Sale e Pepe in the new town where we had a local delicacy *Lolli che Favi*. It was delicious and we had two helpings each.

Evenings were spent sitting on the terrace drinking wine or beer and merely talking, amongst other matters, about our Colombian experiences. I felt a bit uneasy in these talks, as I was ignorant about life in general and had no knowledge of the Arts. Time after time he kept referring to the magnificent Caravaggio and Rembrandt paintings that Escobar had on his walls. I suggested that he had got Escobar interested in art. All I had back was a big grin and a shake of the head.

'No way,' was the comment. 'He has some great paintings hanging on the walls, but to him, they could have been views of Blackpool beach by Joe Bloggs. He just isn't interested in art.'

My life had been geology and martial arts; Hanoz had the lot, yet he patiently listened to me. Time and time again, he talked a lot about his admiration for Copje. He would then go silent and talk about his growing feelings for Kate. I could see that he was distinctly smitten with her.

After a week of relaxation, he turned up at breakfast one morning and before even sitting down said,

'Adam, I've made a key decision. There is an old Japanese saying, *'ichi-go ichi-e,'* meaning remember the unrepeatable nature of moments. Those moments I spent with Kate left an indelible mark on me. I have to see her again. I am leaving here and going to Los Angeles because I cannot stand not seeing her. This has been gnawing at my heart for some time now. Anton is going to turn his life around and get out of crime all because of his feelings for Erika. I am going to do the same.'

He passed a book to me picked out from Giorgio's library pointing out two lines of a Browning poem.

'These lines epitomise my feelings.'

I read them.

'Grow old along with me/the best is yet to be.'

I did not comment and he continued.

'I have enough money to last for a very long time, but I have always wanted more and this has been my Achilles heel. So I am going to Ragusa this morning to see if I can get a flight out from Catania to the USA for tomorrow night.'

The news did not stun me, as after our many conversations I was half expecting it.

'If that's what you want, go for it,' was my reply and I rose and shook his hand.

I also gave him the Lawrence novel. 'Please read it on the plane. There's a line in it that reads, 'I am he who aches for amorous love.' I grinned. 'You fit that bill 100%.'

'Ok, I promise. Now I'll tell Stephano,' was said with wry smile and off he went in search of him.

This left me with a slight dilemma. I could stay as long as I wanted, but with only Stephano for company, I did not fancy that. After some thinking I decided also to leave and return to the UK. I had more money than I ever had in my life, so a month or so in the UK, thinking about my next move might not be a bad idea.

On the return of Hanoz, I told him this.

'Capital, let's get the ball rolling and go to Ragusa and see a travel agent. But first, let's open another bottle of Giorgio's wine to celebrate the occasion.'

This we did and another Nero d'Avola bottle was consumed. Some breakfast that was. At Catania, he was able to get a next day flight to Rome and a night-time connecting flight to New York. I was not so lucky and had to wait another day before a London flight had an available seat, so booked a room at the Airport hotel. Stephano could drop us both off there and head back to Palermo.

Hanoz felt somewhat bad that he was not going back to see Chary and Giorgio, but later that evening telephoned stating his reason and both wished him all the best. Back at the summer house, it was a sombre evening, as we both felt that we were off to new adventures. He passed me a card with an address on it in Istanbul.

'If you ever want to get in touch with me, this address is a shop run by Atila and Ozlem Asur. They are very close friends of mine and any mail to me is sent to them.' He gave that old familiar smile of flashing white teeth. 'Any contracts I get go there. I phone them, they send it me wherever I am in the world.'

I gave him the address of the house in Wales that my parents had retired to and I had kept on as a base since their death. Houses were hard to sell in Wales at that time, especially in small villages. I had several relatives who were happy to look after the terraced house, airing the place, making sure the heating was on in winter, so that it was always in a reasonable condition. I rarely used it, but it was a pleasant sensation having a permanent bolt hole.

We sat on that veranda until very late in the evening and ended up drinking another bottle of Nero d'Avola finishing off the bottle on top of the drinks we'd had previously. The silences were comfortable and the talk was, as one would expect of Paddy, Sir George, Zafar, his close comrades from Congo days, the fate of Juan Bautista. When Escobar and Lucky was mentioned, the pause in his speech was noticeable. He reflected for a moment and then came out with a bombshell of a statement.

'You know Adam; to me there was something that didn't quite fit with Lucky. He didn't have that cut-glass accent the Brit aristocracy have. Didn't you notice that he had a lilt in his accent that didn't sound Irish to me?' He smiled. 'He might perhaps have even come from Wales. I think he was a person who perhaps had a very vivid imagination. If true, I guess he liked the idea of being

Lucan, as it gave him a feeling of someone who was in the public eye. It gave his self-esteem a big kick, rather like Thurber's Walter Mitty character. If so, then he died a horrible death for nothing.'

I was speechless.

'The life you've led is incredible. You should write your autobiography,' was my comment.

He snorted. 'You are not the first person to make that remark. One of our mates in the Congo was the brother of the novelist A J Quinnell. I stayed with A J when I was last in Malta, where we drank most nights at the Gleneagles bar. As your religion is rugby, you'd have liked him. He was a rugby flanker who had played for Hong Kong and he made that same remark. My comment was that it would be a novel about Caravaggio and probably Artemisia Gentileschi, with food occasionally thrown in, crime and drugs would be subsidiary. There is an Italian word *gazofilacio*,' he smiled, 'I know it sounds like a Kama Sutra position in a petrol station, but it means a treasure chamber of the mind. These paintings are my treasures. Do you know what A J said?'

'No, but I'm sure you're going to tell me.'

'He had a great novel published called Man on Fire, which was also made into a film with Denzil Washington as the lead. Some critics savaged the book, calling it a gourmet and geographical tour guide around Italy rather than a thriller. His comment was that if I wrote the book, to ignore any criticism of Caravaggio and food and just do it. He made a fortune from the novel and subsequent film.'

'What more is there to say,' I muttered.

He rose. 'One last thing. The painter Lucian Freud once made a comment about Caravaggio. Know what it was?'

'No.'

'You feel as if he is telling lies. I would like to talk to Freud to find out what he meant by those words.'

'Come on; look at the time, 1 am. Let's get to bed.'

At the airport, we said our goodbyes and after the shaking of hands and hugs, I said.

'Daler, there is something that you could do for me.'

'Yes. Name it and if it's possible you know my answer.'

'When you get to New York, have a haircut.'

He gently punched me in the ribs, turned around and went through the Immigration gate. As I watched his plane's vapour trail dissipate in the sky, I fervently hoped to meet up with him again. I never saw him again; never will and incidentally, my backside still ached. I made a telephone call to Wales.

19.

USA.

Juan Bautista was sitting in a rattan chair outside a café on South Beach, Miami. On the small table in front of him was a cold bottle of water together with a plate of calamari and salad. He was slow eater, so between sips of water, nibbled at the food. He sat back gazing at the scene unfolding before him. People of all ages, sizes and sexes ambled along the boardwalk. Their choice of clothing was eclectic. Some were almost naked; others dressed in a variety of garments that ranged from the height of fashion to clothes that might have been brought out of a 1940s closet. Muscle men strutted about the beach opposite him, heaving weights around, posing on parallel bars and oiling their bronzed bodies. He never failed to appreciate them.

Juan himself was no muscle man and whilst he liked to look at the bulging biceps of these young men, he'd never wished to be one of them. His build was slight and wiry and for 43 years of age was quite fit. In his youth in Bogotá he had been a promising distance runner. Living at altitude had given him an advantage of people who lived on the Pacific or Atlantic coasts of Colombia and he had run a dozen marathons with times that ranged from two and a half hours to three.

He had just come from a gospel singing church. As a lapsed catholic, one of his odd hobbies, for want of a better word, was to attend diverse places of worship or various healing centres. He wanted to see and hear what they did and enjoyed making up stories as to why he had come there. He had attended many meetings of, for example, Alcohol and Gambling Anonymous, drug rehabilitation centres, mosques, synagogues, Buddhists retreats. At the latter, the Mount Baldy Monastery in California, he had been made very welcome and was mightily impressed by the set up. He had hoped to meet Leonard Cohen and was disappointed to hear that he was in a retreat phase.

His eyes took in the scene, but his thoughts were far away. He had been away from California now for about three weeks and was missing it. This morning he'd received a telephone call from his US boss Tony Moreno telling him to return at once to Los Angeles, as Escobar needed to see him back in Colombia. The voice tone had been abrupt and at the call's end he had felt distinctly uneasy. All through life his instinct had variably proved right and had never failed him. The thought crossed his mind as to whether he had been found out by Escobar and a sudden coldness enveloped him. A shudder ran through his body and he felt sweat coming out through his body pores and it was not due to the Miami heat.

He was part of the Pablo Escobar empire and had originally been sent to the USA to sort out a problem on the demand side of the Escobar's extremely lucrative drug trade. He had been picked for the job as his English was excellent, which it should be. He had attended the American College in Bogotá, where both parents were teachers. This middle-class background was not to his liking. Frequently he had misbehaved and proved to be a headache to his parents. He had discovered cannabis very early, but done enough at school to pass all exams. When he reached the age of 18 he left home to go to stay with a fellow close student friend who lived in Medellin. This boy, Camilo by name, had invited him to visit and he jumped at the opportunity. Medellin opened up another world, namely the world of drugs. It was here that he first met Pablo Escobar. Camilo's parents were also involved in his drug empire and soon he had been drawn into what to his eyes, was an exotic and wondrous world.

Escobar had spotted his intellect and energy and started moving him up in the hierarchy that surrounded the drug king. Escobar first put him in jungle laboratories where coca was turned into cocaine. He spent seven years moving around various laboratories interspersed with stints back at Medellin. It was in the Colombian jungles that he learned the chemistry involved in producing cocaine, being taught by chemists mainly from Europe. They worked for very large salaries.

The indigenous natives of the area tend to mix coca leaf with, for example, lime and water chewing it into a wad. There was no demand for this from Europe and the US, as it resembled chewing tobacco and involved spitting out residues. In the west cocaine had a certain high society status; it had class. The demand was for a more sophisticated recreational drug whose effect could last for up to 90 minutes.

He well remembered his introduction to the world of cocaine. Escobar used a fleet of chemists and helpers in his jungle laboratories, all headed by André von DeShire, ex Professor of Chemistry, Leipzig University. It was at a one-day meeting in Escobar's Monica apartment block in Medellin, attended by 20 people and in his mind he could still hear the Professor's voice and see his use of flip charts, showing what to him were very complicated diagrams of chemical reactions.

'Some 350 kg of dried leaves are needed to obtain 1 kg of cocaine and there are six harvests a year. In brief, the leaves are soaked in any dilute solution of a strong acid, for example, hydrochloric, or sulphuric (which is the same as battery acid, but much stronger). This aqueous solution is mixed with an organic solvent such as petrol, kerosene, ether or benzene, to remove unwanted organic chemicals. The mixture is stirred and steeped for several hours. Separation of the two solvents is easy because the organic solvent floats on top of the aqueous acidic layer and this is drained off. The aqueous layer is spread out in shallow bowls and evaporation by the sun does the rest, it is the same principle for obtaining salt from sea water in hot climates. One simply scrapes off the cocaine hydrochloride when it crystallises out of the solution. Sometimes additional substances are added to the product such as sugar, lactose or chalk in order to bulk it up a bit. This is done simply to widen the profit margin, as it lowers costs and the additives have no pharmacological value. However pharmaceutical products such as phenacetin (a common pain reliever) and levamisole (used as a deworming agent) are sometimes added to enhance the experience of taking cocaine. These two products now constitute 80% and 65% respectively of adulterants and tended to be added during drug production or just after importation. All ensure more dosages per batch of cocaine and can be purchased legally. Any questions?'

If memory served him, no one had anything to say. Most in the room only wanted instructions not theory, but he concentrated intently upon the talk, as he knew that later he would be tested by Escobar. Prof DeShire resumed his presentation.

'It is also possible to produce pure cocaine with a simple procedure on the aqueous layer that contains the cocaine hydrochloride. Before it crystallizes, a base such as caustic soda, bicarbonate of soda, or even a strong detergent can be added. This converts the cocaine hydrochloride to pure cocaine, sometimes known as 'free base', which can be crystallised from the solution. This is the purest form of cocaine and sold either as powder or in the form of small lumps (rocks) and is called 'crack' cocaine. Heating the latter makes a crackling sound, hence the name and it liberates this very potent pure cocaine. These are the easiest forms in which cocaine can be produced and sold. It can be smoked, snorted, or injected. Inhaling produces a euphoric state within seconds, but its effects last for a shorter period of time.'

He absorbed all this information easily. Cocaine is now the second most used illicit drug (after cannabis) in the world.

It was on his last tour of the jungle camps that the idea floated into his mind and was always brushed aside. Drugs have always been cut to give bigger profits the term used was the 'bash' and 'smash' trade and cutting purity to about 40% was the norm. The thought that played on his mind for a long time was if one was cut by an extra 1%, the profit of a dose would be very small but the enormous volume sold meant a massive return. The thought was immediately dismissed. It was only when he had left Colombia for the US to oversee drug distribution for Escobar that this idea came back with a vengeance and it happened when he was 35 years of age, after Escobar had seen his potential and groomed him to take over part of the US distribution centre for cocaine. Juan had jumped at the chance and now spent a lot of time on the US east and west coasts handling the drug shipments that kept flooding in from Medellin.

He had a ready army of recruited dealers via Tony Moreno and had quickly settled into the job. He enjoyed going to the many parties to which he was an honoured guest and relished seeing people insufflating cocaine by 'tooters,' i.e. hollowed out pens, long finger nails, banknotes and even tampon applicators. They would spill cocaine onto a flat surface, e.g., table, mirror, where it would be divided into bumps, lines or rails before being snorted. Sometimes people smoked freebase and crack cocaine, which involved having a small glass tube pipe, frequently called stems or basters, inhaling the vapour. As cocaine is fat soluble it is easily absorbed into the fatty tissue of cells and easily and quickly crosses the blood-brain barrier, until it reaches those all-important receptors that gives the 'buzz.' As cocaine hydrochloride is water soluble, more will be metabolised in the liver and excreted in degraded form via the kidneys and therefore is somewhat less potent than some other drugs. He enjoyed watching people make fools of themselves and enhancing his income.

The idea he'd had in Colombia now seemed very feasible. When in Colombia the force of Escobar's power made any attempt to tamper with drugs impossible. If found out it meant a very nasty death, usually being battered to death by a baseball bat, after first having legs and arms broken. Now he was in a position to dilute the cocaine by a simple 1% extra and had amassed a fortune within a few years. Life was good. He had considered increasing the dilution level by 2%, but that was adding to the risk of being found out and the thought of the retribution that Escobar would unleash if found out banished the idea immediately. He shuddered every time this occurred, coming out always in a cold sweat. He was scared stiff of Escobar. The best course was to take a very small and insignificant profit per dose.

Finishing his food and taking a last drink of water, he rose and stood by the kerbside light ready to cross the road to the beach. He heard sirens in the distance becoming louder via the Doppler Effect. At the green light he started across the road in the company of three others. With sirens screeching and blue lights flashing, a red Ford Mustang travelling at over 70 mph, closely followed by a police car careered around the corner and smashed into the four people who were halfway across the road.

Three months later, Joshu Sasaki, Abbot of the Japanese Rinzai Zen, Nyorai-nyokyo sect at the Mount Baldy Zen Centre in California, was looking out of the window at the lovely, haze rimmed San Gabriel Mountains when the post was brought in. Opening one letter he saw that it was from a firm of lawyers in San Francisco. The letter stated that the late Juan Bautista, had willed his entire estate of $58 million to the monastery. Bautista had escaped Escobar's famed baseball bat, but at what price?

20.

UK, Italy.

I flew to London and caught the train home from Paddington station. Entering the station, I passed St. Mary's hospital and my thoughts went back to Palermo and Chary. Our London sojourns had overlapped slightly and I would have loved to have met her in those days. To read on the train, I bought a newspaper, magazine and an Iain Banks book, 'The Wasp Factory'. I wanted the 'Tit-Bits' paper but found that it had closed down. Grhh. I tried to catch up on events of the UK and the world and found out that I was really out of touch. A full-on miner's strike had erupted, Nissan car manufacturers from Japan had started a factory in Sunderland and the long-awaited Thames barrier had at last been opened, which would alleviate possible flooding of London. One item struck a chord with me. Police had raided a schooner moored on the Dengie Essex peninsula and captured a multimillion-pound drug haul. Shades of Escobar.

I browsed through the paper and magazine and did not have a chance to open the book. A few hours later, I arrived home. The house was warm and snug as expected, so I unpacked and had a beer, there were always bottles in the larder. I was home, but what was I going to do? The thought of home had been a warm nugget in my brain for the past few days, but now that I was here, a vague feeling of anti-climax came over me. I shrugged and opened another beer. There is an ancient Italian saying, *'Chi beve solo si strozza,'* i.e. he who drinks alone will choke. For the next two weeks, I almost choked.

I kept putting off the call to London, as asked for by Sir George, or chasing up Zafar's brother. Instead I visited the few relatives I still had, including my two nieces who had grown rather alarmingly since last seen, as well as various friends. In the evenings I revisited the Harp Hotel the pub my parents had kept and had many drinks with locals and old mates like Derek Jackson, Ray Halls, Ted White, Rob Morgan and Andy Cooper. I even found time to go out for meals with two ex-girlfriends of mine, Julie Mathews and Rosemary Farmer and their husbands. I kept putting all thoughts about visiting Glenys in Scotland for Sir George and Zafar's brother in Italy to one side, as I did not relish meeting them. Similarly, I did not telephone Sir Nels Clifford, but I did send a Chas and Dave record to Lynda Marsh. I drank more beer and spirits at home and arranged for a hospital visit, as the cause of my aching backside was due to all the paddling I had been doing when sitting in puddles of water. This had been diagnosed as haemorrhoids (piles) and I had the operation privately. Interestingly, my surgeon, Sally Corbett and I, were in the same form at secondary school. It's a small world. A week after this, I received a letter from Hanoz. It contained terrible news.

He had flown to New York and on to Los Angeles where he went to the Goldman-Sachs office. There he was told the news that Kate had died in an automobile accident two weeks earlier. He was completely devastated, all his dreams shattered. He stated that he was going to Ireland on a job and thought I might like to join him, as it was an exciting opportunity for someone with my martial art skills. I could teach some of the people he was working with. He meant the IRA and I think he had some sort of death wish. Re-reading the letter showed the utter desolation he was feeling. Knowing what I now know, not going was about the worst decision I ever made in my life, as instead I went to Thailand… and met up again with Paddy.

There was a PS in the letter. He stated that as he was in Los Angeles he might visit Escobar for a week en-route to Ireland. Escobar had written telling him that if possible, he would like to see him again as he had a present for him and that he and I were no longer wanted by the Police or Immigration so could visit with no problem. He also mentioned that he had just met the man whom he had encountered whilst spilling coffee over his partner at Verona airport. Talk of coincidences.

The letter spurred me on. I phoned London and at the Foreign Office switchboard asked for Sir Nels Clifford. I was informed that he was a very busy man and could I please state my business and if necessary, he would get in touch with me. My reply was, 'I'm a friend of Sir George Fusano and have information about him.' My telephone rang minutes later with Sir Nels on the line.

I travelled to London and met up with him in Whitehall. I told him all that had taken place in Colombia. He did not interrupt me. When I had finished, he stood up.

'We did not know he was dead, as a ransom demand has been made to the Embassy.'

He excused himself saying that he had to make a few telephone calls. He came back over an hour later.

'I'd like to take you to lunch at my Club,' was his opening remark, 'as what you have told me has some important repercussions.' We left for White's Club, 37–38 St James's Street, where he ordered two glasses of dry sherry for both of us and with no consultation, pheasant for lunch. This was a pleasant affair and he talked with passion about many government policies, a subject that was of little interest to me. Post lunch over brandy and coffee, a waiter came over to inform him that a telephone call had come for him. He left and soon came back.

'What I have to say to you is for non-disclosure. Is that understood?'

I nodded.

'As you are aware, Sir George was working for us to bring peace to Colombia.'

He told me more about FARC and also the fishing party incorporating more detail than Sir George had told me. He ended by saying that the so-called fishing party had now left Colombia and were stationed in Panama where they have just been joined by another troop from D squadron. They had permission to enter Colombia at the request of the Colombian government and to liaise with the Colombian army. AH 64 Apache gunships and Chinook helicopters, were to hunt down irregular warlord armies rather than just drug smugglers. They had not entered Colombia yet, as the authorities were trying to find the whereabouts of Sir George and the initial SAS troop had lost contact with them.

I could not but help asking. 'Irregular warlords, does that include FARC?'

He smiled, 'No, not FARC, they want peace with them. It's specifically geared to Ortsh and others like him. They asked why we wanted to eliminate his outfit in particular, but were quite happy to accept any excuse. We have been looking for him, but knowing Sir George is dead, we can, how shall I put it, remove the kid gloves, come out into the open, produce the heavy fist and exact some kind of retribution.'

He smiled again. 'I think that Sir George would have appreciated that. I can assure you that The Regiment takes its tasks very seriously, especially when one of its ex-members has been involved.'

I nodded again and he continued.

'That call told me that as result of satellite surveillance by the US, Ortsh's group has been found and new orders have been given to, shall I say, seriously take them out. I expect confirmation of their demise to come soon.'

With that, he stood up and shook my hand.

'I'll keep you informed by telephone. I'll also let Gladys know.'

We left. He returned to the Foreign Office and as for me, I went for a coffee at Paddington station and took the train to Wales. I had two more trips to make.

Back home I loafed around for three days then phoned the Cavendish laboratories and was told that Glenys had taken some of her annual leave, as a result of hearing of the sudden death of her fiancée. She was now back in Scotland with her parents, Eddie and Jane Michael. I immediately set about booking a berth on the night train to Scotland. The next day, I returned to London and caught the train. I enjoyed the 'tadack tac, tadack tac' of the wheels on the track immortalised in Auden's poem of, The Night Mail. 'This is the Night Mail crossing the border/Bringing the cheque and the postal order'. He wrote this poem for the General Post Office and it was set to music by Benjamin Britten. I have always loved it and on the train slept like a newly born baby. At Edinburgh, I caught another train to Inverness and hired a car to take me to Connich some 40 km away, where the Michael's lived.

It was a raw, lovely morning to be in the far north, blue sky, sun shining, but with a hint of snow in the air and little traffic was encountered on those long winding roads. I felt alive for the first time in weeks. The hell of that Colombian prison was shed from my mind, as the John Milton phrase, 'the mind is its own place,' floated into my sub-consciousness thoughts. I drove slowly through villages of grey stone houses and wished I had purchased a geological map, as the varied rock outcrops interested me, but not enough to make me stop.

The drive alongside the Beauly Firth was enchanting, but was even better when I came to the River Glass. Carn Gorm peak looked lovely bathed in the morning light. The Michael place was in more of a hamlet than a village and I quickly found their house by going into the only small shop and asked for Eddie Michael's place. His house was built in the log cabin style, almost like a Swiss chalet. Knocking on the door, I was struck at how beautiful and peaceful were the surroundings.

The door was opened by a tall, balding, grey-bearded man wearing a Hawaiian style shirt and jeans.

'Yes.'

'Good morning. My name is Adam Lathey. I was a friend of Sir George Fusano. I was with him when he died.'

'Good god, you'd better come inside.'

He ushered me into the large open plan front room in the centre of which was a large wood stove, which was pumping out heat galore. Stretched out in front of it was a dog, who looked at me, wagged her tail and went back to sleep.

'Our guard dog Polly,' was said with a smile.

I took off my coat.

'You people know how to keep a house warm.'

'Laddie, you can never be too warm.'

He stretched out a hand. 'Eddie,' and turned as two females and a boy entered the room. This is my wife Jane, our daughters Gemma and Glenys and young son Kenzie.'

I shook hands with them all and turned to Glenys.

'I know that the government has informed you of the death of Sir George, but may I offer my condolences.'

She clasped both my hands and pecked my cheek. Glenys was very attractive, tall and slim with green-grey eyes and sharp cheekbones.

'Thank you, but did I hear you say that you were with him when he died? I gather he was killed in some kind of gun battle. The details given us were rather sparse as we could not understand why he was involved in a gun battle. He was out there simply to give a few lectures.'

We all sat down and Eddie produced a bottle.

'I think a dram or two of Ardberg would not be inappropriate?'

'Speaking for myself, I'd love one.'

The others nodded their assent. Sipping the whisky carefully, I told them the story. There was no doubt in my mind that the government had not told these lovely people the truth, but to hell with any consequences. I had decided to tell them all we had been through apart from the beatings. They listened in silence with Glenys clutching her parent's hands.

When I had finished, I passed over to Glenys the note Sir George had written.

'He asked me to give you this in case anything happened to him.'

She took it.

'I'll read it later when I'm alone,' was all she said.

I was with them for about two hours and left after drinking several drams of whisky. Gemma and Jane were teetotallers. I think Kenzie was allowed two drams and the three of us almost emptied the bottle. I returned to Inverness along the Milton road and stopped at Loch Ness and No, I did not see the monster, but parking helped sober me up. I left Inverness the next morning feeling somehow despondent, as my thoughts were with Glenys. I did not know what was in that note, but I did know that Sir George had been head over heels in love with her.

I stayed one night in London and before catching a flight to Rome bought an Italian phrasebook and pocket dictionary. In Rome, I checked into the Nuovo Hotel Quattro Fontane and made a quick phone call to Paulo Alebar making an appointment to see him the next day, as he was tied up for the rest of the day and evening. What can one do in Rome, the eternal city? What a question, so I set off to see the Colosseo where over 50,000 spectators could watch the games. I uttered the words, *morituri te salutant* (men about to die, salute thee), as I walked around the arena. My imagination ran riot as images kept tumbling into my brain. I had to go the Porta del Populo to see the Caravaggio's that had so entranced Hanoz. I must say that they were superb, so I hurried on to the Piazza Navona built on the site of the Domitian stadium in the 1st century AD and saw the other two paintings that he had raved about.

I sat on the surrounding wall of Bernini's Fontana dei Quattro Fiumi and was content. All that remained was to find an eatery, have a sleep and finish off my task in the morning. Rome is full of eating places, so I ambled off and to my surprise, I ended up at the Spanish Steps, or as the natives call it *Scalinata*. Writers galore, Stendhal, Byron and Thackeray had come to view these steps and now I was seeing it. I had dinner in a nearby restaurant; unfortunately it was a poor meal and I headed off back home to bed.

I was lonely and felt miserable as I turned towards the hotel area. En route back and on impulse, I bought two bottles of Nero d'Avola in memory of Hanoz. Entering the hotel and sitting down in my room, I suddenly realised that it felt cool. I decided that I was going to go to bed straight away and would need a blanket, so looking the word up in my dictionary, I phoned the night manager.

'Buena sera, Vorrei una coperta,' I asked in my best Italian.

'Certainly sir, would you want coperta grades A, B or C?,' came back the answer in impeccable English.

I blinked at this, as I had never heard of graded blankets. A must mean something like an alpaca filling, that's how my mind was working.

'Oh, ah, Grade A.'

'Certainly sir, I'll get one to you as fast as I can.'

I got up, switched on the TV and poured myself a large glass of wine; I sat down again and played around the channels but could not find anything in English, so after some 20 minutes or so switched to a soft music channel and relaxed in the chair. I had almost forgotten about my request when a knock came at the door.

'My blanket,' I exclaimed and stood up to open the door.

I did this and you can understand my surprise when in walked a gorgeous, beautiful, young woman.

'Ciao,' and she winked at me as she strode past. She was wearing a white trench coat a la Humphrey Bogart that ended at the knees; long suntanned bare legs exited the coat ending in a pair of white stiletto heels. She had a white cap on her head, which when taken off revealed a mass of auburn curls which she swished around her head. It was like watching a meteor shower.

She smiled again revealing a row of sparkling white teeth.

'Hi, I'm Gabby, can I have your name?'

'Adam.'

She saw the glass in my hand.

'I'd love a glass of wine,' and sat down on the bed. 'This is a nice room you have here, but it is a class hotel.'

She must have seen the puzzled look on my face.

'Oh, dear. Are we at cross purposes? I'm your *coperta*. In Italian, the word is slang for a girl.'

Now I realised what the grading was about.

'Anyway, let's have a glass of wine. Come and sit by me and we can at least talk whilst we drink it.'

I was mesmerised and looking at her brought back memories that had been dormant in my brain for far too long. I brought her a glass and sat down beside her.

'Adam, tell me about yourself?' She smiled. 'The night manager told me your name.'

She sipped her wine.

'I'm always curious about people and what they do.'

I started talking to her and the stresses of the past few months came tumbling out of my mouth. She had an amazing presence that relaxed one immediately, as well as being an out of this world beauty. What was Margaret Hungerford's famous line, 'Beauty lies in the eyes of the beholder?' Well, this beholder certainly rated her as, stunningly beautiful, the ultimate woman. As well as the Colombian story, I told her about my childhood, eventually explaining why I was in Rome.

'You've had an awful time,' she said quietly before getting up and filling both our glasses.

The room somehow did not seem cool at all. It wasn't and I learnt afterwards that it was an old trick played on selected male customers by night managers. They simply turned the heating off. It was turned on again when the customer returned to his room in the evening, after he had made a phone call like mine.

'I'm feeling warm,' said Gabby standing up and taking off her coat. She had on a black svelte dress that reached mid thighs and those long, brown, shapely bare legs were shown to perfection. She refilled our glasses yet again and sat down beside me on the bed. Leaning back, she turned sideways and pumped a pillow into place, which pulled her dress further up one thigh. Putting a hand up to her head and her elbow locked onto the pillow, she gazed at me.

'Do you like?'

What could I say? She would have graced the cover of any fashionable magazine. She smiled coquettishly at me. I could not utter a word. I was entranced by her.

She pulled me down beside her.

Thinking of anything to say, I asked. 'What about you? I've told you about my life. What's your story?'

She thought for a while and then told me. She had been born in the south, in Bari, to a poor farming couple. At school, she found the work easy and when she was 16 her parents had decided to get her out of school to work on the small farm. Her schoolteacher had tried to stop this, as he had realised her potential. The matter had been resolved when a wealthy nearby landowner had offered to pay for her education, which her parents had accepted. He had noticed the blossoming natural beauty. On completing high school, he had suggested to her that she should go to university in Rome, where he would provide her with a flat in a choice area and a generous allowance. He would visit occasionally – in fact about once a month for a long weekend. He had been a kind gentleman who had treated her like a Queen. The arrangement had continued for two years after university when she had obtained a teaching post in the area. Then he died.

She found that he had willed the flat over to her, but the flat expenses took most of her teaching salary and by now she had become used to the good life, the *dolce vita*. She realised that she was a naturally beautiful woman, one who could turn the head of any man and had signed on with a top model agency. After one year she had made herself known to night watch personnel of the top Roman hotels, quit the agency and now did this job for about one night a fortnight. It had proved to be very lucrative and gave her the time to attend university courses, where she had signed on for a higher degree.

As she talked, her fingers had opened a button of my shirt and her nails were making circular patterns around my chest. I stayed mute and another button was popped open, followed by another.

'You like it?' she purred.

'Who would not?'

'Adam. Close your eyes.'

Soon my shirt was unbuttoned and her hands roamed over my stomach. I felt them reach behind me and a pulling movement indicated that I should lift my bottom from the bed. I obliged and my trousers were slowly moved to my knees and then taken off my feet. I felt the bed move as she stood up.

'Adam, open your eyes?'

I looked up and as I did so her arms reached behind her back and the dress slowly unzipped and sank to her feet. She stepped out of it.

'Adam, do you still like?'

I gulped. Her slim, tanned, toned body was terrific and the tan lines stood out from the white flesh.

Her low-cut black bra was slowly unhooked and her small, beautiful, pert breasts thrust upwards freed from the restraint. She would have passed the pencil test 100 times out of 100. She was stunning. I reached up to try to cup them.

'Not yet Adam,' and she hooked her arms into her briefs and they slowly floated to the floor. I gazed mesmerically at her naked body. She was shaved and a goddess.

Dropping to her knees, her arms continued with their smoothing circular movements on my body. She knelt towards me so that her nipples just touched my chest and she moved them slowly and erotically around.

Smiling she murmured, 'I can see that you really, really like me.'

I groaned and reaching up my arms clasped around her back bringing her body to mine. Our bodies pulsed with the same rhythm as our hearts and I was lost.

She left at 8 am as she had a 10.00 am class. I will never forget that night or her. It was worth the dent it made in Escobar's money.

Post breakfast I walked to the Tourist Bureau and at 11 am entered and asked for Mr Alebar. I was politely shown a seat and rose, as a small, bald Italian bounded in. He had a slight paunch that indicated many lunches/dinners and one that was going to get bigger as he aged.

'Adam Lathey?'

'That's me.'

We shook hands and I found myself being hustled outside.

'Why don't we go to a nearby restaurant that I know and we can talk about Rio.'

Rio. It was strange to get my head around that name when to me he was Zafar and I guess always would be. We strolled along some side streets when suddenly he stopped and sniffed the air.

'There was an Air Cavalry Colonel in the film Apocalypse Now, who played Wagner's, Ride of the Valkyries full blast when his napalm-spewing gunships attacked a Vietnamese village. It reminded us of the opera's screaming female warriors out to scavenge battlefield corpses. His remark was that he loved the smell of napalm in the morning.' He gave the air another sniff. 'A cigar store perfumed the desert like a rose,' Jorge Luis Borges wrote that line in a poem. I love it and prefer it to napalm.'

With that, he smiled, took another sniff and went into the nearby cigar store. Emerging a minute or two later I found a large cigar thrust into my hand and he lit his up. I thought of Giorgio, thanked him and put it in my pocket. Ten minutes later we were ushered into a small unpretentious restaurant.

'This is Luigi Cipriani, the chef and owner.' I was introduced and we took a window seat.

'First, a martini is called for,' resulted in two glasses appearing as if by magic.

Luigi winked at me.

'I know Paulo,' was all he said, followed by, 'the usual?'

A nod came from Paulo. We chatted for a bit and it was after the tripe soup dish that he asked me, 'and how is Rio?'

I was horrified, as I had been under the impression that he knew about Zafar's death. Thinking about it, how could he have known? I looked him squarely in the face.

'I'm afraid that I'm the bearer of sad news. Rio is dead. He recently died in Colombia. I was there with him and he asked me to give you these notes.'

I passed his notebook over minus the last page.

Paulo turned pale and a tear rolled from one eye. Nothing was said for a minute or two.

'Tell me what happened.'

I gave him a bowdlerised version of the story of mining, a broken leg, blood poisoning, gangrene.

'Was there nothing that could have been done?'

'I'm afraid not. We were too far away from any hospital and he died while we were en-route to the nearest,' I lied.

The *pasta carbonara* arrived just then, but he pushed it aside. I did the same and he poured out a big glass of white Orvieto wine,

'I cannot take this in right now. We were not close, he was closer to our sister, but this is still a big shock to me. Excuse me for a moment.'

He stood up and walked out, returning some five minutes later.

'Thank you for being so understanding.'

He picked at his pasta. I had eaten my dish. He asked many questions and when he had finally run out of things to ask, called out to Luigi.

'Grappa please, three glasses.'

When these arrived, he gave one to each of us, stood up and shouted.

'To my brother Rio.'

We drank, Luigi insisted on a photo, Paulo left his food. He said he could not eat and we left. It was a tranquil walk back to the office. When we reached it he shook my hand.

'Thank you for telling me about this. I shall read my brother's thoughts later today.'

He went inside and that was the last I saw of him. I felt extremely deflated and despondent about it all and ambled aimlessly around the city eventually finding myself at the Forum, the heart of old Imperial Rome. I climbed up the steps of the hill that lies at one end of it to the Colle Capitalina, walked past the giant sculpture of Marcus Aurelius and sat in the small garden that overlooked the Forum.

As well as Gabby, the thought of Hanoz and Copje and their hopes of finding love and happiness kept drifting into my mind. I was in my thirties and had never experienced such feelings. Was there something wrong with me? I sat there for an hour or so. I had Gabby's number but on numerous occasions when I called, I just had the answerphone. I left messages. I'm ashamed to say that for the rest of the day, I lurched from bar to bar until at the hotel in the early morning hours, I met the night manager who was a different young man and knew no one called Gabby. With no reply to my calls, blessed sleep came upon me at last.

The next morning I woke with a bit of a hangover and decided that Rome's pleasures could wait for another time. I had envisaged retracing the Italian footsteps of Hanoz and me, visiting Ricardo,

Chary and Giorgio once again, but suddenly that idea paled. I wanted to get back to my own little house and sulk, so made my way back to the airport and flew home. For a week or more, I hardly left the house and drink bottles piled up in the garage.

I was sinking into a sloth of depression, my dopamine and serotonin levels were falling rapidly and my mind was in a place all of its own. I only woke up from this depression when glancing at a newspaper while having lunch in a Swansea pub; a small column caught my eye. It stated that a Colombian Army Special Forces team and I did grin at this point, had obliterated a rebel group led by a Colonel Ortsh. No causalities of the team had been reported and all members of the rebel group had been killed in some severe fighting.

'I guess this is atonement for you Sir George,' I muttered, adding, 'rest in peace old man.'

This made me phone Sir Nels to find out what had happened and was invited to join him for lunch the next day at White's. He did not like to talk over a public telephone. I went to London and met up with him. What happened was that when the camp had been located, the Panama based SAS troopers had immediately helicoptered into Colombia to a forward base. One day later, as dawn broke, government jets had launched a blitz of bombs and napalm at the camp, followed by Apache helicopter gunships in an assault that lasted for half an hour. Chinook helicopters had then moved the troopers into the site. It was carnage with bodies and body parts strewn everywhere and there was little resistance. Positive body identification was difficult, but on one mutilated body they had found a pearl-handled revolver.

Hearing this acted as a kind of catharsis to me and spurred me to do something with my own life. So I stopped feeling sorry for myself, quit drinking, started going to the dojo again and generally got my life back into shape.

21.

Burma

One day, I was thumbing through some Geology and Mineralogy journals, when I saw an advert asking for geologists to work on a one year project in the Shan States of Burma. Now, this was a country run by a cabal of billionaire generals, called the Tatmadaw and large areas including the Shan States were forbidden to foreigners. I had heard Hanoz talking about this area and my curiosity was aroused. I applied and after an interview found myself in that country for a short stint. There I somehow got tangled up with General Lo (and his glamorous daughter)[1] who some of you might recall was the opium warlord of the Golden Triangle the area on the Burma, Thai and Laotian borders, which produces some 1,000 tonnes of raw opium a year. That is again another story one which I guess will never be told. I was virtually out in the field all the time except for two rest and recreation stays at the Sule Shangri-La Hotel, Sule Pagoda Road, Rangoon. The job was pretty boring. There were six of us in the field and god knows how many soldiers and we never mapped anything of note.

I left as soon as the contract was up and went off to neighbouring Thailand for some real rest and recreation. My worst mistake ever.

---

[1] See Ireland Nemesis

22.

Thailand, Malaya.

I travelled around Thailand and marvelled at how cheap living was in that country, eventually landing up at the Nuova City Hotel, Bangkok. I was in the bar having a drink when a hand clasped my shoulder. Turning around, to my amazement I saw a grinning Paddy Mahoney, there for as he put it, rest and recreation. I had given much thought to what I would do if I ever met up with him again and had come to no conclusion. What he had done was very wrong, but we all knew that Zafar would not have survived his injuries. Blood poisoning and gangrene are two evils that exist in tropical lands far away from modern medicine and it usually meant death. Hanoz would have tried to get Zafar back to camp, but even he would have failed to save his life. Noticeably neither of us mentioned Colombia.

I put those thoughts to the back of my mind when we caroused all night along the Bangkok strip, bar after bar, showgirl after showgirl until I virtually begged him to go back to the hotel.

'You wimp,' he snarled and tried forcibly to push me away. Wrong move. Even though I was filled with drink, one arm blocked his push and the other aimed an abridged *yokomen* strike taught me by Hanoz at his head. I pulled up just short.

'Never do that to me again,' was my snort, 'Remember, I've more tricks in my background than you've had hot dinners.'

He nodded and hailing a cab I returned to the hotel. Late the next morning, I was woken by a loud knocking at the bedroom door. I got out of bed and opened the door. It was Paddy and obviously he had just returned.

'Be Jesus, storming night old mate,' and a bleary, red-rimmed eye winked at me. He had forgotten what had happened and had had a perfect time with some escort. He jabbered a few sentences at me before lurching off to bed. I showered, went downstairs for brunch, the usual good old mutton curry and settled in an armchair to read The Malay Times. I almost dropped the paper, as it had a picture of Fidel Castro at a Cuban rally and by his side was Ortsh. He had not been killed. I put the paper down and for a while was undecided whether to phone Sir Nels or not, but reason told me that he was bound to know about this. I calmed down, had a couple of drinks and took a small walk before returning to the hotel. I had a few more drinks before sitting down to read the rest of the paper.

Paddy re-appeared in the late afternoon and sat down opposite me. I nodded.

'Whoa, Adam Lathey me boy, that was a night to remember.'

I folded the paper as I knew from experience that I was not going to read anymore.

'Well, I'm glad that you've sobered up, you old bastard,' was my opening remark.

He nodded and produced a sheaf of papers from his back pocket and started talking.

'We are in the Pacific Ring of Fire where tectonic plates have been colliding, separating and subjected to volcanic/earthquake activity. Resulting processes have forced a soup of chemical-rich material to the earth's surface for Millenniums. Now take tin, for example, the 49th most abundant element in the earth's crust and a part of that soup,' he winked at me. 'This is mined from Cassiterite (SnO_2 the tin oxide ore), usually, black and invariably associated with granite rocks that are plentiful here. Some 80% is mined from placer deposits, secondary deposits washed from the primary lode and found in river channels, as it is harder, denser and more chemically resistant than granite. Sources can contain as little as 0.015% tin, but still be a commercial economic figure.'

I interjected. 'Ok skip the geology lecture; I had enough of that at Imperial College. What are you driving at?'

'Adam, what if I told you that in Perak, Malaysia, I think I have hit upon a large deposit that could give 5% tin?'

I sat up in my armchair when he mentioned the figure of 5%. If the deposit was that large, when developed this could mean a colossal amount of money to its discoverers – and I might add, even more to the developers who would use either dredging, open pits or hydraulic action, all way beyond our means. A lone prospector can make a lot of money from items such as diamonds, rubies, sapphires, but when it comes to commercial ores, only big mining firms have the resources and infrastructure to develop the find. This did not bother me because if Paddy was correct and we played our cards right we were on the verge of a fortune. Finding the mother lode and recording a claim meant we could sell it on for megabucks.

The next couple of hours were spent pouring over the reams of papers that Paddy produced. He had identified an area in Perak, the fourth largest state of Malaysia, which stretches from Selangor to the Thai border. As Paddy had said it was located on the edge of the 'Ring of Fire,' which was a promising start. The geology of the area was sparsely mapped, as dense jungle-covered large tracts, but enough had been done to show the main rock divisions and there were abundant granite outcrops in the area. Paddy had spent two months in the selected area and had collected a small number of meticulously labelled samples, from both *in situ* rock and river sand/gravel deposits. These had been assayed in Kuala Lumpur and in my hand I held the laboratory reports. I was impressed.

'Why are you showing me these?' I asked.

'I need someone with your professional background to verify what I found and to do further work in the area so that we have a larger sample base. You have the necessary academic clout. If it is genuine, it could mean a fortune to both of us, split 60:40.' His eyes narrowed as he looked at me. 'I found the place, so it is only right that I take the larger share. If a partner dies, the claim goes to the remaining partner. I have the relevant papers with me.'

I looked at Paddy. He must have spent some time on getting these together. When though? He passed over several sheets of paper. I read them slowly for the next hour and scribbled a signature before giving them back to Paddy.

'Here is your contract, now you sign it. It's as you've stated and has my signature.' He signed.

'Let's go NOW,' was uttered by Paddy.

With that, we left the lobby, packed our bags, paid the bills and hailed a cab for the airport. Our destination via Kuala Lumpur, was Ipoh the capital of Perak state. Arriving there we booked in at the Merton Hotel and immediately set about renting a Land Rover safari, large trailer, a motorised longboat, camping gear, food and all the paraphernalia that modern-day prospectors needed. At night-time Paddy would disappear for a while, no doubt getting up to lord knows what mischief. Three days later we took off, heading northwards through the Belum-Temenggor Forest Reserve.

Maps of the region were pretty poor and I relied upon Paddy to get us to the area where he had prospected. When the road petered out due to dense jungle, we took to the boat and after a while arrived at one of his sample points. We set up camp and started to sift gravel from the many streams and rivers in the area. We sieved sediment using standard placer techniques and as I had an early GPS phone we were able to pinpoint all locations, something that Paddy could not do on his original surveys. His labelling of samples had been very good, but his location method was to write: the first tributary on the left, second on the right, put a mark on a convenient sample point tree, rock etc. and a cross on his 'map' - slapdash in the extreme. After a month of this, we had many specimen bags all correctly labelled as to Latitude/Longitude and I could see dark cassiterite ore in many samples. Indeed in many places, we had dark ore bands over 15 cm thick exposed on the river banks. I was extremely hopeful.

Work was a full day and as evenings drew near we cooked a meal and drank *ais lengkong kuning* (yellow jelly, lime, sugar and water) before the inevitable whisky and this was how it all started. I don't know about you, but enforced living with a partner who rarely washed, drank too much (he'd drink three-quarters of a bottle to my quarter) and was garrulous in the extreme, leads to one thing only. He had a one-way brain set up that meant he was right in all words uttered and could not countenance any alternative argument, which inevitably led to trouble and in my case, it was big trouble.

Paddy found out that we were down to our last few whisky bottles and went into a tantrum, stating that one of us had to get back to replenish supplies, as he quaintly put it. He kept saying that he didn't like cities and I should go to obtain new supplies and get the sample assays done. I always separate work and play and wanted to stay another few weeks to finish mapping the area thoroughly, so was in a bit of a quandary. He was in a foul mood that night and did not snap out of it ever afterwards. I think his bi-polarism was working overtime.

We continued work for the next few days, but Paddy did little except glare at me and kept swigging out of a whisky bottle. I thought over what had been said. We had enough dried food to last and there was a plentiful fish supply from the river. Getting the assays done appealed to me, as I believed that we were on to something big and my geological mapping made me think I could locate the primary lode. Also, a break from Paddy who was driving me mad was strongly tempting. I mulled over matters for a few days, concluding that I should take off for a couple of days and decided to tell Paddy that fateful night. I carefully finished labelled the samples, giving the Merton Hotel as my address and filled in the standard assay form putting both names on it and the hotel address.

Paddy entered the main tent with a half-full whisky bottle clutched in his hand. He was red-faced and as usual, in a bad mood. I looked up.

'Paddy, I've thought about what you said. I'll go to Kuala Lumpur tomorrow. Is that ok with you?'

He looked at me intently and put his arm around me.

'Begorrah, bloody marvellous idea Adam. I'm glad that you've seen sense on this point. When you get to Ipoh, can you pick up a bag for me that I left with a friend of mine? It has a few old samples that I collected some time ago and you could hand these into the assay office for me. I might have hit a small patch of gold, but never got round to assaying it.'

Typical of the man was my thought.

He poured out some more whisky, including one for me.

'Let's drink to the success of the Mahoney/Lathey partnership.' He slapped me on the chest. 'Drink.'

He chuckled and mumbled away to himself. Then his behaviour changed and he became more and more confrontational and his language deteriorated. I guess it was his bi-polar side kicking in. He became aggressive, challenging every sentence I uttered, all the while muttering under his breath, every other word being a curse. I took a large swig from the bottle.

'Why are you so damn stroppy and belligerent to me? I said I'd go to-morrow for assays and whisky purposes, not to mention your damn gold samples. Why not try to be a sane minded person instead of being a drunken liability to one and all?'

Those words made him blink. He gulped some whisky and got up slowly. He staggered around the table and the next second I felt a terrific blow to my right arm. He had picked up a shovel and smashed the edge into my right arm. I almost vomited as the pain was terrible. I rose to face him and he dropped the shovel looking at me with a horrified gaze. I lost control of myself at that point. A machete was on a nearby shelf and left-handed I picked it up, pivoted to the right and lashed out at his thigh. I cut deep into the flesh and he howled with the pain. My arm throbbed cruelly, but now his past behaviour induced again that blood lust frenzy, one that coursed through my veins and I attacked him again and again, a frenzied slashing at any part of his body and I did not let up. As I hit him, I remembered chanting, as if it was a mantra, 'and this is for Zafar and this is also for him.'

I came to my senses several minutes later and realised that he was dead. I had run amok, an apt word in this instance as it derives from the Malay word *amoq*. Half of me was glad, the other half ashamed at what I had done. We were alone in the jungle; no other person was anywhere near.

My arm ached terribly and bruises were coming out, but I did not think any bone had been broken. I poured myself a whisky, but threw the glass away. I had killed another man. Ok, he'd hit me but the realisation of what he had done made him drop the shovel and he seemingly was ashamed of his action. I on the other hand, as I was fed up with his antics, had allowed rage to take over my persona and had killed, no murdered him. I wept, collapsed and fell into an exhausted asleep.

The next morning, I thought long and hard as to what I had to do. I slipped off my clothes, took the blood-stained walls of the tent down and threw the lot on the fire. As an afterthought I added Paddy's clothes and boots. I then dragged his naked body some three kilometres along a faint track and left it off track. There are some 500 tigers in Malaysia and I hoped that one would find him. I did not hold out that much hope, as reported attacks by tigers were sparse. It was more likely that a Burmese python or the larger reticulated python could have a go at swallowing him whole. Anyway, in that climate, a body disintegrates fast and invertebrates exist by the billions. There was blood over the earthen floor, but river flooding would take care of that. I threw the machete into the river.

Before taking off for Ipoh, I packed the samples in the boat and placed all remaining provisions in one bundle, slinging them up a tree hoping they would still be there on my return. Was I going to return? I did not know. My mind was in a whirl. The Land Rover plus trailer was where we had left it and it started the first time. Arriving at the city, I made a detour to the house where I was to pick up Paddy's gold samples. A shabbily dressed native came to the door and when I mentioned who I was, he grinned and passed over a large briefcase. I opened it and saw that it was filled with sample bags.

'I've been expecting you,' he replied. 'Paddy said you could call anytime. He asked me to take good care of you and offer you all hospitality. *Carpe diem*, were his words.'

I was surprised at this, as Paddy was not in any way a scholar.

'Let me give you a drink and drink it as if it's the last you will receive.' He grinned mischievously.

I accepted it and made my goodbyes. I had felt uncomfortable because all the while he had kept grinning wolfishly at me. Setting off to the airport, I left the Land Rover and trailer at Hertz and arranged for storage of the boat before entering the main building. I had decided that on arrival at Kuala Lumpur to book in at the Merton, record the claim, make a UK phone call and state that I was needed urgently back in the UK, then leave the country for an extended period, probably a year. I wanted out badly. After a year I hoped that the body if not eaten, would have rotted and the bones would hopefully have been chewed by animals.

I went to the Malaysian Airlines desk, bought a ticket to Kuala Lumpur and deposited the assay bags at the baggage drop, keeping only my small rucksack and Paddy's briefcase. I had very high hopes that the samples would confirm that a large tin discovery had been made. News of the find would necessitate lots of people working in the area and I did not want them finding any trace of a body. I sauntered through the usual formalities and eventually got on the plane. Arriving at Kuala Lumpur, I collected the assay bags and made for the exit where several Police were stationed with their sniffer dogs. One officer came over to me and the dog stopped, sat down and wagged its tail. I bent down to rub his ears.

'Excuse me sir, but could you step this way?'

I grimaced but followed.

'Are these your bags, sir?'

'Yes.'

'Would you mind opening them, sir?'

I obliged.

The officer ran through my rucksack, feeling the whole fabric then doing the same to the briefcase. He stopped at one corner and with a slight smile, slit it open, pulling a slim sealed white packet from the lining.

'What is this, sir?'

'I have no idea, as it belongs to a friend.'

It went from bad to worse after that, as the package contained a 100 grams of heroin and that is how I ended up in Pudu prison, built ironically above a former Chinese burial ground. In the next cell is another inmate. His name is Derrick Gregory and we have become firm friends. Under Malaysian law, section 39B of the Dangerous Drugs Act, anyone in possession of more than 15 grams of heroin/morphine, 1000 grams of opium and 200 grams of cannabis or 40 grams of cocaine receives the mandatory death sentence.

Paddy had stitched me up. He had wanted me out of the way to collect all money from our discovery and had planned the scheme well in advance. On my non-return, he would have come down to Kuala Lumpur, expressed astonishment at my predicament, collected the assay reports and hey presto, real money galore. Now on June 2nd 1988, I find myself still typing to ease my conscience. At the beginning of these notes is a Shakespearean quote by Macbeth about nihilism - a sense of the meaninglessness, absurdity of life. It is true. I have only one other request...

Addendum, 1988.

I the Pudu prison Governor, two warders, the padre and executioner have just read this document and we feel that I should add the following.

The prisoner was typing when the executioner came into the cell and said, 'Mr Lathey, my name is Tin Mahoney. Please follow me as it will be easier for all if you do.' The prisoner collapsed and cried out loud when he heard the name. His hands were tied behind his back and he was helped to the execution chamber where his legs were bound. He was hooded and hanged. It took less than 30 seconds.

We have read this remarkable story, collated the notes and sent them to a UK publisher.

Publishers Epilogue

Some further asides that may be made are:

1. To date, the Dalradian Gold mining company has spent £130 million on exploratory diggings around the town of Greencastle in the Sperrin Mountains estimating that the unexcavated gold deposits are worth over £3 bn. Paddy Mahoney was right.

2. In 2019, An Italian court sentenced 24 people to life imprisonment. They were personnel associated with Operation Condor and included the former president of Peru, Francisco Carlos Bermûdez. The total number of killings is unknown; 100 in Argentina, 45 in Uruguay, 22 on Chile, 15 in Paraguay and 13 in Bolivia were named, but these figures are probably an understatement. Their victims were drugged, stomachs slit open and dropped from planes in the Atlantic Ocean, or alternatively cemented into barrels and disposed of in rivers.

3. Pablo Escobar was shot and killed, along with his bodyguard Álvaro de Jesús Agudelo, alias 'El Limón' on 2nd December 1993 at Los Olivios, a district in Medellin. They were trying to evade capture by the Search Bloc. This comprised three different special operations personnel of the Colombian National Police (Policía Nacional de Colombia) focused on capturing or killing highly dangerous individuals or groups of individuals. His funeral was attended by 25,000 people. The Hacienda Nápoles has been converted to a theme park with four luxury hotels overlooking the zoo and there are now over 60 hippos to be found in the Magdelena River.

4. In Mexico, 'El Chapo,' head of the Sinola cartel and the heir to Escobar's global drug mantle, was arrested and escaped twice, before being finally caught by 17 Mexican marines after a gun battle at Los Machos. In 2019, he was sentenced by a New York court to life plus 30 years and now is incarcerated in the Federal prison, Florence, Colorado. His drug empire has been taken over by the Los Zetas cartel.

5. In 2002, Alvaro Utribe became Colombia's president and deemed that the only way conflict could be solved was via 'the iron fist' and introduced 'democratic security.' This resulted in the largest urban military operation - Operation Orion - in Colombian history, when the army under Mario Montoya (in 2006 he became commander in chief), 'liberated' a shanty town in Medellin. This was a body blow to FARCs attempt to gain control of an urban area from which they never recovered. It was alleged that various paramilitary groups, similar to that run by Ortsh, had supplied intelligence to the army, i.e. the army had operated beyond the law in collaborating with them. This has been denied by the army.

6. In 2016, FARC after more than 800,000 deaths, made peace with the Colombian government and from being a key obstacle for effective action against drugs, is now a key ally of the government. As a result of the UNgass milestone summit in 2016, much work has been accomplished on matters such as human rights, autonomy and flexibility under the current conventions, a move from a repressive response towards a more comprehensive approach and finally, combating transnational organised crime. A controversial element of the peace deal was the creation of a war tribunal which would investigate crimes against humanity allegedly committed during the conflict. This is currently taking place with 2,744 military officials on trial, with General Montoya being the main figure involved. On the 18th February, 2021, the peace tribunal released

preliminary results of its investigation into the false positives scandal following exhumation of mass graves. They found that from 2002-2008, at least 6402 people were murdered by the army and falsely declared combat kills to boast statistics. To date, there are still illegal armed groups wreaking havoc within the country.

7. In 1961, the UN produced a single convention on narcotic drugs prohibiting the production and supply of a number of named substances. It was an unmitigated disaster. In 2018 the UN had another special session on drugs, but the reality is that the global market in 2021 has a turnover of more than $32 bn a year.

8. With regard to the Ndrangheta and Shqiptare Albanian syndicates, they thrive. However, in December, 2019, more than 350 people were arrested in raids covering 11 Italian regions, but focused on Vibo Valentia, the heartland of the Ndrangheta's Mancuso clan. An elite Carabinieri unit known as the Cacciatori (the hunters) carried out most of the arrests. Nicola Gratteri, an anti-mafia prosecutor who led the investigation remarked that it was the biggest operation against organised crime since the 1986-92 Palermo 'maxi trials' when 475 were arrested. More than 24,000 wiretaps and intercepted conversations back up the charges. The trial, with over 900 witnesses, is expected to take place in 2021 and high expectations exist that it will be a milestone moment in the struggle against the Ndrangheta.

9. Criminal drug empires have expanded in the UK since these notes was written (1988), even though occasionally some major players are caught, for example, in Liverpool, Ian and Jason Fitzgibbon (the businessman and the muscle), arch rivals of Curtis Warren. In 2013 the Fitzgibbon's were jailed for 16 and 17 years respectively, for a multimillion pound heroin deal with a Turkish syndicate. This involved 114 half kilo packs of 60% pure heroin that cost €300,000 wholesale

from Turkey. It would have generated almost £7m at UK street value.

10. About half of Europe's 15,000 crack related treatment demands have been in the UK. Of people aged 15-34, 5.3% took cocaine in 2018, the latest year for which records are available, as against 3.9% in Denmark and the Netherlands.

11. New and innovative techniques regarding drug smuggling have recently come to the fore. For example, in August 2020, at least 17 people (13 Colombians, 3 Dutch and a Turk) were arrested in the Netherlands on a raid at a riding stable transformed into an illicit drugs laundry. Chemicals and carrier material were found, i.e. clothing impregnated with cocaine before being exported. The uncut street value was estimated as 6 million Euros.

12. These days especially in the USA, another more powerful ultra-potent synthetic analgesic opioid called Fentanyl is fast displacing heroin. It is cheaper and ten times as potent. One pill is all that is needed and it creates dependence. Strict regulations imposed in 2017 stopped the import of the drug from China, but Mexico stepped into the breach, especially in the Sinola and Guerrero states where cartels in order to maximise profits turned from being vertically integrated groups to outsourcing to specialists, e.g., logistics and money laundering. Farmers in these particular states used to cultivate marijuana and opium poppies, now it is akin to Colombia's jungle laboratories; they churn out synthetic drugs.

13. Mr Tin Mahoney has retired and expressed great surprize when told that he had executed his father's murderer. He had never met Paddy and had no recollection of the execution. It was just one amongst many.

14. The paintings stolen from the Isabella and Stewart Gardiner Museum, Boston, have never been recovered. Their worth is now estimated at $500 million. When Police visited the Hacienda Nápoles after Escobar's death, no

trace was found of the Rembrandt and Caravaggio paintings. It is surmised that they were given to Hanoz, as Escobar was greatly smitten with him.

15. In June, 2021, three people were arrested in an industrial estate at Medina del Campo in the Castila y León region, Spain. They had been smuggling 30 sacks of Colombian cocaine - placed amongst 1,364 sacks of charcoal - from Portugal to Spain. A complex chemical process camouflaged the drugs as charcoal and their shape and colour were virtually identical to real charcoal. The characteristic smell of charcoal being eliminated, they were undetectable to sniffer dogs.

16. In July, 2021, a light, single prop plane dropped in a reinforced canvas bag with 500 grams of pure cocaine having a market value of 8 million Euros, in the Oristano area of Sardinia before flying away towards Cabras and the sea. The pilot misjudged the drop point as the bag fell on the roof of a house on the outskirts of Baratici San Pietro, a village of 1200 inhabitants. It was a narcos-style operation, the first of its type in Italy. After an investigation by the Oristano police, led by Commander Francesco Giola, a 28-year-old Roman pilot was arrested.

17. Most of the main personalities mentioned in this book are now dead. Two who seemingly have survived are Ortsh and Hanoz. The former was last seen in Cuba, but information recently received, indicates that he fell out yet again with Castro and returned to Australia where he lives in the outback. Hanoz was arrested in England and jailed for working with the IRA[2]. He was released by the 1998 Good Friday agreement of the Blair government. His whereabouts are unknown.

18. The question posed by Sir George in chapter 3 regarding protein folding (proteins are amino acids that can twist and

---

[2] See Ireland Nemesis

turn into 1 followed by 300 zeroes shapes), had a massive breakthrough in late 2020, by the artificial intelligence group Deep Mind with its Alpha-Fold programme. As stated, most biological processes revolve around proteins and their shape determines function. When researchers know how a protein folds they can start to uncover what it does. The programme's accuracy exceeded meticulous laboratory experiments that often take many years.

About the Author

Allan Williams, Ph.D. D.Sc. C. Eng. C. Sci. MIMMM was originally a geologist and now is an academic and internationally known expert on coastal issues. He has authored/co-authored over 400 papers/books on coastal issues, ranging from erosion/deposition processes on beaches, dunes and cliffs, to management especially with respect to litter. Professorships have been held in the USA, Canada, China, New Zealand, Iceland and the UK and he has also lectured extensively in Colombia, Poland, Russia, Turkey, Malta, Spain and Portugal.

He is a qualified coach in cricket, athletics, badminton and swimming; holds the Royal Life Saving Association Distinction Award; is a parachutist and Judo black belt. A SCUBA diver, marathon runner and survival skills instructor, his hobbies have included showing pedigree dogs (dachshunds), Gujarati cooking, love spoon wood-carving and the making of stained glass windows.

He has been a musician with the Cardiff School of Samba and currently plays in a Ukulele band. He lives in Wales, UK and has worked in all places mentioned in the book. He has meet people, as diverse as FARC guerrillas, CIA and undercover agents, drug dealers and mafia personnel.

BV - #0025 - 130921 - C0 - 210/148/16 - PB - 9781913839123 - Gloss Lamination

16. ANOM (AN0M) was a very particular smart phone that promised absolute security and was developed from a prototype made by Phantom Secure, a telecoms company founded by Vincent Ramos in 2008, whose phones were modified Blackberries with camera, GPS microphone removed and remote wipe features installed. They were ideal for the drug smuggling criminal world. An FBI sting in 2015 on a Californian drug dealer Owen Hanson enabled the FBI to obtain entry into this murky world, which culminated in many arrests before the phones were closed down. This give birth to the idea of using specially encrypted phones, so in collaboration with Australian federal police (AFP), devices were developed and 50 Anon phones passed to three trusted distributors in Australia. Two people in particular were targeted, 'Mafia Man and Hakan Ayik, the latter's cartel smuggled an estimated $1.5bn drugs each year into the country. The scheme was unbelievably successful as criminals on a global basis started using this phone and every message was recorded by police. This culminated in Operation Ironside in Australia (Trojan Shield in North America) and on 7th June, 2021 more than 800 global arrests were made. One was on a Brazilian tanker bound for Australia laden with fruit juice at the port of Ghent, Belgium. Divers found three sacks of cocaine bricks worth £34m concealed in the sea chest – an inlet that draws sea water into a ship to cool the engines. Because of AnOM the divers knew exactly where to look, but now AnOM has been revealed this sting will never be repeated. By 25th July, in Australia alone, 693 search warrants have been issues, 289 alleged offenders charged, 4,788kg of drugs and 138 firearms seized and more than 50 members of the notorious Comanchero motor cycle gang arrested.

17. On the 9th July, 2021, six people were arrested when authorities seized more than two tonnes of cocaine estimated to be worth more than £160 million, from a luxury yacht named Kahu some 80 miles off Plymouth, UK. The yacht had sailed from the Caribbean and was intercepted in international waters near Guernsey in an operation involving the National Crime Agency (NCA), the AFP and Border Force.

18. Matteo Messina Denar (Diabolik) the Sicilian mafia's boss of bosses and wanted for more than 50 murders, has still not been caught and was last seen in 1997. It is thought he is being shielded by powerful Freemasons in Trapani.

Etc.